Prai

'With plenty happening, Giarratano is cool and calm at the controls. In a word – suspenseful.' *Gold Coast Bullletin*

'Leah's writing remains tight and true and really quite exciting.' *Courier-Mail*

'This stands up against any bestseller of the genre, and then its local setting makes it better.' *West Australian*

'Definitely one for those who like their crime novels tough and demanding.' *Australian Bookseller and Publisher*

Praise for *Voodoo Doll*

'Clinical psychologist turned thriller writer Leah Giarratano brings a wealth of professional experience to her art . . . a page-turner, note-worthy for its expert characterisation and often chilling psychological veracity.' *The Age*

'*Voodoo Doll* is more chiller than thriller. It's cleverly plotted and crackles along at an electric pace. I'm sure Giarratano has a growing fan base and it's great to see local talent getting an outing.' *Good Reading*

'This is a seriously good read. Giarratano is taking on the big guns, and winning.' *MX Melbourne, Brisbane, Sydney*

'I suspect a series. Bring it on.' Sue Turnbull, *Sydney Morning Herald*

'Plumbing the depths of her experience . . . Giarratano's writing has an air of authenticity missing from the work of her peers. Creepy, nasty and oddly compelling, it's definitely not light reading.' *GQ Australia*

Also by Leah Giarratano

Vodka Doesn't Freeze
Voodoo Doll
Black Ice

leah giarratano
watch the world burn

BANTAM
SYDNEY AUCKLAND TORONTO NEW YORK LONDON

Watch the World Burn is a work of fiction. All the characters and scenes in this book are fictitious and any resemblance to any actual person, living or dead, or to any current or past event, is purely coincidental.

A Bantam book
Published by Random House Australia Pty Ltd
Level 3, 100 Pacific Highway, North Sydney NSW 2060
www.randomhouse.com.au

First published by Bantam in 2010

Copyright © Leah Giarratano 2010

The moral right of the author has been asserted.

All rights reserved. No part of this book may be reproduced or transmitted by any person or entity, including internet search engines or retailers, in any form or by any means, electronic or mechanical, including photocopying (except under the statutory exceptions provisions of the Australian *Copyright Act 1968*), recording, scanning or by any information storage and retrieval system without the prior written permission of Random House Australia.

Addresses for companies within the Random House Group can be found at www.randomhouse.com.au/offices

National Library of Australia
Cataloguing-in-Publication Entry

Giarratano, Leah.
Watch the world burn.

ISBN 978 1 74166 814 8 (pbk).

Policewomen New South Wales – Sydney – Fiction.
Detective and mystery stories, Australian.

A823.4

Cover illustration by SuperStock
Cover design by www.blacksheep-uk.com
Internal design and typeset by Midland Typesetters, Australia
Printed in Australia by Griffin Press, an accredited ISO AS/NZS 14001:2004 Environmental Management System printer

10 9 8 7 6 5 4 3 2 1

The paper this book is printed on is certified by the © 1996 Forest Stewardship Council A.C. (FSC). Griffin Press holds FSC chain of custody SGS-COC-005088. FSC promotes environmentally responsible, socially beneficial and economically viable management of the world's forests.

For Joshua George. Major Arcana 8

*This book is dedicated to
Zac, Alexandra, Dominique, Gabriella, Jake,
Kimberly, Kirra, Luke, Max,
Rebecca and Samantha*

Evil indeed is the man who has not one woman to mourn him.

The Hound of the Baskervilles, Sir Arthur Conan Doyle

1

Thursday, 25 November, 8 pm
At eight pm, Troy Berrigan knew everything was going perfectly.

And then the screaming began.

Although afterwards he'd cringe remembering it for days to come, Troy actually dropped to the ground. Right there in the restaurant. Fucking training. But he snapped to his feet almost immediately and spun around. Oh for fuck's sake, look at her! He lurched to his right and ripped off a tablecloth. Plates and glasses smashed through the air. More diners screamed. Troy crash-tackled the burning woman and, on the floor with her, held her writhing body close, smothering her moans and the flames with the cloth. The stench of smoke and burnt hair and flesh filled his lungs. 'You're all right,' he coughed. 'I've got you. You're going to be all right.'

He was lying, of course. Which is what you do at times like this.

Rolling with her on the hundred-dollar-a-metre carpet of his restaurant, Troy blinked away images of the old woman – her head on fire, her arms reaching out to him, her face pleading, melting. Even then he knew he'd be replaying that scene in his head for years.

'Get the ambos!' he bellowed. 'Has anyone called the ambulance?'

'They're on their way, boss, they're coming. Is she all right?'

Troy hadn't looked up, but he knew that James, his head waiter, stood above him. In fact, Troy could probably have described every person within a five-metre perimeter. His senses were electric, and the moments clicked by in scene-by-scene frames. The woman was out. Fire too. Her heartbeat was like a trapped bird beneath him. He blinked rapidly a few times to halt the images that threatened to return from the past, trying to stop Jonno's blood staining everything red. His well-worn distraction technique was successful until the screaming started up again. Suddenly he sat in the middle of a park and it was his sergeant bleeding out in his arms.

'Troy,' said James, squatting next to him. 'What can I do?'

Back on the carpet in the restaurant, Troy turned to his waiter. He realised the shouting came from a male diner on his knees next to him, who was reaching out to the woman wrapped in the tablecloth. 'Help her,' the man begged. 'Oh my God, please help her!'

Dominique, another staff member, bent to try to console the customer.

'Is everyone else okay?' Troy asked James.

'Well, no one else is hurt,' said James. 'But people are

pretty upset.' He moved closer to Troy. 'This gentleman here is her son.'

'Right.' Troy turned to the middle-aged man sobbing at his left. 'No, don't touch her, mate,' he said, blocking the man's clutching hands. 'Get everyone out, James. I want you to evacuate.'

'What about him?' James indicated towards the distressed man, who shrugged free of Dominique. Her face was white, mascara smeared across her cheeks and the backs of her hands. Troy's ordinarily poised, unflappable sommelier now resembled a frightened fourteen-year-old.

'Just leave him with me, James,' said Troy.

Troy turned to face the man, who was still grasping at the woman. 'Please,' he said, restraining the man's arm. 'Don't touch her. You'll hurt her. She's alive, but I'm pretty sure she's unconscious. The ambulance is coming.' He looked towards the dining room. 'Dominique,' he called to the waitress, who'd already moved to direct the shocked, whispering diners towards the door. She turned to face him, her blue eyes tight, wincing. 'Call the police,' he said. She put a hand to her throat, nodded once.

Troy tuned out the noise of the patrons leaving the restaurant and the man sobbing beside him. Leaning over the elderly woman on the floor, he held his breath and tested the tablecloth over her face, lifting it carefully, almost imperceptibly, willing his hands to stop shaking. The cloth stuck. He let go, knowing that to pull further would dislodge lumps of burned flesh and skin. Fortunately, the fabric was cotton; other materials had a tendency to melt right into a burn. Where was the fucking ambulance?

'How did this happen?' Troy asked the woman's son.

'I don't know. I was on my way back to the table and I just saw her in flames, and then you pushing her down. Oh my God . . . Is she going to be all right?'

No, they never are. 'She'll be okay. It'll be okay.' Troy rocked back into a squat and put a hand on the man's shoulder.

Managing Incendie had been Troy's big break. Even the name was his idea – *incendie*, French for 'fire'. Fucking perfect, Troy thought, pushing his hand into his dark hair. What the hell is Caesar going to say about this? He hoped that James had called their boss. Caesar O'Brien, owner of five world-class restaurants, had given Troy the chance to run his newest and biggest, and he'd fucked it up. If James had reached him, Caesar would already be on his way here. Troy's gut recoiled at the thought.

'Mum . . . it's going to be all right, Mum,' said the man at Troy's side. 'Help is coming.'

'I think she's still out,' said Troy. 'My name's Troy Berrigan. I used to be a police officer. Sometimes the body shuts itself down when it's had a shock this bad. It's for the best, Mr . . .'

'Caine,' said the man at his side. 'David Caine.'

'And your mum, David?' said Troy. 'What's her name?'

'Miriam.'

'How old is she?'

'Seventy. It's her birthday.' David began to cry again. 'I brought her here for her birthday.'

Troy's head whipped around at the sound of movement behind him. Thank Christ, the ambos. 'Over here!' He stood and waved the officers over, then reached down to help the man on the floor to his feet. 'Come on. Let's wait over there, David. We've got to get out of their way.' He turned back to the paramedics – a stolid, stone-faced young woman and an equally implacable, grey-faced man who appeared far too old for the job.

'This is Miriam Caine,' Troy said to them. 'Seventy. She was alight. On fire. We still don't know what happened. She's breathing, but I'm pretty sure she's unconscious. I haven't lifted the cloth to make sure – some of the fabric has adhered to her face.'

Troy leaned against the bar for support while the officers bent down to the woman. He clamped his teeth together when he realised he was shivering.

'What – what is this?' The grey paramedic was on his knees at the woman's side. 'This was an *accident?*' He stared up into Troy's face.

Troy looked into the grey man's eyes, then back at the covered shape on the ground. 'I don't know what the fuck this was,' he said to the floor.

'Stop. Gina, stop!' The male paramedic used his shoulder to block his colleague as she drew out the patient's arm, tapping for a vein. She turned to face him, her lips a hard line, a deep crease now visible between her eyes.

'Preserve evidence,' Troy just barely heard him say.

The female ambo took a breath. The crease vanished with the lift of her eyebrows, and her face became stone again. She bent back to her kit and removed a hypodermic syringe.

'You wanna wait for the cops?' the man quietly asked his colleague.

'She'll die,' his partner answered.

Troy turned just in time to grip the arm of the man next to him before he fell to the floor. He used his bad arm, and his thumb and forefinger slipped from the man's jacket. He steadied the woman's son with both hands.

'Help her, please,' David Caine managed to say, his eyes closed.

Troy led him to a bar stool. 'They'll take care of her, mate,' he said.

And then in walked the cavalry. Police. Troy didn't recognise either of them, thank Christ. He definitely would have remembered the dark-haired female, and the big blond bastard wasn't someone you'd forget either. He gave Caine's shoulder a squeeze and walked forward to meet them.

'My name's Troy Berrigan,' he said. 'I'm the manager here.' Troy kept his hands in his pockets.

'Sergeant Scott Hutchinson,' said the blond bloke. 'This is Senior Constable Emma Gibson. What happened here, Mr Berrigan?' Hutchinson talked as he walked towards the paramedics. 'What've we got?' he asked them before Troy could answer.

'A crime scene,' said the grey man, preparing to roll the burnt woman. 'Better rope it off.'

'Fuck,' said Hutchinson. 'Yeah, all right.' He nodded to his partner. 'Emma, could you get back down to the patrons? Who knows how long they'll wait at the evac point. Get all their names and addresses, enlist the staff to help. Find out whatever you can from anyone who wants to talk. We can follow the rest up later.'

Gibson nodded once, her back very straight. 'The vic's going to make it?' she asked the couple on the floor.

The paramedics lifted Miriam Caine to the stretcher.

'Unknown,' said the female ambo, her voice as emotionless as her face.

A faint moan from under the tablecloth rocketed David Caine from his bar stool, which crashed to the ground behind him.

'Hey, hang on a minute, mate,' said the cop, Hutchinson, blocking Caine's path.

'This is David Caine,' said Troy. 'The victim is his mother.'

'All right, Mr Caine, but you're going to have to stand back there while we get your mother to the hospital,' said Hutchinson. 'You too, Mr Berrigan. I'm going to have to get you gentlemen to wait back over at the bar area.'

'I'll call for some uniforms,' said Gibson, radio out, almost at the door.

'Yep. And Emma, send up that big bald waiter. We'll get him to guard the door until they arrive.'

'James Macklin,' said Troy, leading Caine back to the bar. 'The waiter – his name's James. But he's my head waiter. I need him with the guests.'

'Just send up any member of staff, Emma,' said Hutchinson. The big cop then leaned in towards the ambos. 'Retain all clothing for evidence,' Troy heard him say, 'and record any utterances.'

The ambos steered the stretcher out of the restaurant, following the female officer.

'It's okay, Mum, we're going to the hospital now. I'll be right there with you,' Caine called. He pulled away from Troy and glared at the big cop. 'I'm going with her.'

Hutchinson frowned, and Troy quickly put a hand on Caine's shoulder. 'David. Wait, I need to get your contact number.'

The shorter man peered up at him for a moment as though he had something to say. Without breaking eye contact, he pulled a wallet from his jacket, flipped it open and withdrew a card. Troy pocketed it. He watched the man shuffle after the ambos towards the front of the restaurant. Just before they reached the exit,

Caine stopped and jogged back towards him. Troy's jellied muscles tensed. Was he going to cop a punch in the mouth from this bloke?

Still a stride away, Caine reached out to shake his hand, staring as Troy offered his own in response. Then, almost overbalancing, Caine grasped what was left of Troy's hand with both of his own.

'Thank you,' David Caine said. 'Thank you for helping my mother.'

Troy felt like a piece of shit.

Snapping on all the overhead lights, Troy surveyed the interior of Incendie. Except for the god-awful stench, there was no obvious indication there'd even been a fire. He paced the dining room with the two cops, but he could see nothing. There wasn't even any damage where the Caines had been sitting. Nothing was scorched. What the fuck?

No time for this. From his workstation in the centre of the restaurant, he grabbed a notepad and pen. He ignored the foul taste in his mouth and jogged out through the glass doors, heading for the elevator. He had to get down to James and the rest of the staff, to help them deal with the customers.

He paced the cube of the lift, trying to smother his anxieties about what would happen next. Surely he could keep the restaurant going. He couldn't lose this job; everything depended on it. Finally, the elevator lights indicated he'd reached the lobby of the five-star hotel and he jabbed repeatedly at the button to open the door. He sprinted across the foyer, waving away the gestures of hotel staff trying to catch his eye. He had to get to his own people first.

And there they were. Twenty metres down the block, waiting at the evacuation point. Around fifty of his well-heeled customers huddled together. He knew most of them would never want to see him or the restaurant again. If he'd had his way, he'd have instructed James to seat them all in the comfortable lobby, but the rules were clear. Fire anywhere in the hotel, and everyone in the vicinity had to be ushered to the evacuation area for a headcount. He found James and Dominique.

'Is the lady okay?' asked Dominique.

Troy shrugged. 'I hope so,' he said.

'What's going on up there now?' asked James. 'People are starting to leave.'

'There'll be more police here soon,' said Troy. 'They want to talk to people about what happened tonight. So we need to let everyone know that they should cooperate with the cops.'

'A few people have asked when we can go back up,' said James.

'They won't be going back up,' said Troy. 'I'll arrange a meeting room on the ground floor. When everyone's spoken to the police, get them a seat in the lobby restaurant if they want one. On the house, of course. I'll square it with management. Otherwise, we'll take their names and addresses and let them know we'll mail out a voucher for a free night at Incendie. Let the other staff know, James, and start telling the guests. Give me five more minutes to get a room sorted. I'll call you.'

Troy dashed back up to the restaurant. Hutchinson looked up when he appeared in the doorway and nodded him in. Troy made his way over to his workstation and began making the arrangements with hotel management. The duty manager was pissed. He'd already been up to the restaurant to find Troy and had been sent away by the cops. He told Troy that Caesar had been briefed, but that he wouldn't be coming back to the hotel until tomorrow. Troy looked at his watch. It was time to dial home.

'Hey, Luce,' he said when the call connected. 'Homework done?' He leaned back and smiled tiredly at the ceiling when his fifteen-year-old sister snorted derisively. Of course Lucy had done her homework. Since her first day in kindy there had never been a single problem with her schoolwork. Her brother, on the other hand . . . 'Where's Chris?' Troy asked.

'Still at Makayla's, I think,' she said.

Shit. 'Did you eat the lobster?'

'Yuck,' she said. 'I had toast.'

'Lucy,' he said. 'Do you know how much that stuff costs? That's the most lavish main course here. My boss sent it home with me especially for you to try. You know my customers pay shitloads for that dish.'

'Take it back there then,' she said. 'Bring me home the cash.'

'Yeah, right,' he said. 'Listen, did Chris come home after school?' At sixteen, Christopher was still as angry as he'd been at five, when Troy was awarded legal custody of him, but he was a hell of a lot harder to control. Troy thought back to when, at the age of nineteen – just a little older than Chris was now – he'd been appointed legal guardian of his then four-year-old sister and five-year-old brother.

'I'm not sure,' said Lucy. 'He could have got here first and gone right out again.'

Is his bag there? Troy wanted to ask, but didn't. He knew it wouldn't have been and he didn't want his little sister to have to lie to cover for her brother. Again. 'Well, don't go anywhere, Luce, and don't open the door to anyone.'

10

'What am I, five?' she said.
'Your brother should be there with you.'
'Well, come home then,' she said.
'Ha, ha,' he said. 'You know I mean Chris. Anyway, I gotta go, Luce. I love you.'
'Mmm-hmm. Good luck tonight. Are things going okay?' she asked.
'Ah . . . I'll fill you in at breakfast.'

Troy rubbed his right hand with his left, trying to soothe the pain in the two fingers that no longer existed. Phantom limb pain, the doctors had told him. Probably never go away. Fucking ridiculous. His hand had a mind of its own? Sometimes when the burning woke him, moaning, he wanted to scream at it – they're gone, you fuckwit!

The shotgun blast had vaporised his fingers in an instant, and his hand couldn't get over it.

2

Thursday, 25 November, 8.12 pm
'You can't blame everything on a bad childhood,' Jill Jackson said, and wished she hadn't. Under the desk, she forced her fingernails into the soft pads of her sweaty palms. The pain registered, but didn't distract her from her anger. She felt heat at her throat and tried to take a deeper breath. She could sense the eyes of the other cops at the Australian Institute of Police Management.

'No, Detective Jackson, you cannot. But your statement puts you on one side of a very complicated and interesting debate.' Associate Professor Gamble made a sweeping gesture with his arm; his thinning grey curls fizzed about his head as he strode towards her seat. He seemed oblivious to her discomfort. 'Let's follow your line, then.'

No, please, let's not, thought Jill. She'd been surprised

to find herself looking forward to the psych lectures in her Master of Criminal Intelligence degree. Right now, though, she would rather stick her pen in her eye.

'Let's take one of our own, shall we?' said Gamble. 'Good old Aussie boy, Peter Dupas,' the professor went on. 'He first tried to murder his next-door neighbour at age fifteen. Over the next twenty years he raped at least six women and murdered at least four others, almost certainly more. Given that he was in gaol for twenty out of his forty years – until he was locked up for life, that is – that's pretty good going. Well, so to speak,' he said, when a female class member made a grunt of disapproval. 'And he liked to slice the bodies,' Gamble went on. 'Particularly the breasts. He'd cut them right off. He broke into the morgue and got to corpses that way too.'

A male snigger came from the back of the room. The sound did not help with Jill's efforts to keep her anger in check. Any other day she'd understand the laughter – all cops used black humour to cope with stuff civilians could afford to be squeamish about. But this lecture had already brought memories of her own rape to life – and with them, the urge to fight or run. Nine times out of ten, she chose the former.

'Now, we know that most serial killers like Dupas have a history of abuse in their childhoods,' Gamble went on. 'The thing here, though, is there's no real evidence of abuse in the Dupas case. So, how *did* Dupas become this creature? *Why* did he commit these crimes?' Gamble stared at Jill.

'Because he's a sick fuck,' she said.

More stifled laughter.

'Just because there's no evidence of childhood abuse doesn't mean it didn't happen,' Nicki Coors said; she sat just a desk away from Jill. Jill realised that Nicki had made the outraged snort she'd heard earlier.

Gamble smiled delightedly and clapped his hands once. Loud. Jill flinched. 'And now we have our opponents on either side of the debate,' he said. 'Detective Jackson here says that psychopaths are born that way, while Officer Coors contends they must be created.'

'Actually, I'd rather not –' Jill began.

'Let's consider your diagnosis, Jackson,' said Gamble. 'Sick fuck, is, I believe, the disorder you've assigned.' He made three leaps from her desk to reach the whiteboard, and wrote 'SICK FUCK'. People laughed openly now. Underneath, he wrote 'Nature'. Jill shrank in her seat.

Professor Gamble trailed his marker across to the other end of the board, creating a horizontal line that stretched its length. On the far right he wrote 'ABUSED AS A CHILD', and underneath it, 'Nurture'.

'Let the games begin,' said Gamble. 'Anyone want to take a stance, argue that one of these positions is correct over the other?'

On the other side of Jill, Michael Westlake stood. Why it was that Jill's classmates, Toni and Roseanna, continually told her where, when and how they wanted to do this guy was beyond her. Rat-faced and slimy is how she'd have described him, if asked. No one ever did. She just listened to the other girls at lunch and remembered something urgent she had to do whenever she saw him approach. Which was often.

'Yeah, I'm with Jill,' he said.

Jill kept her eyes on the lecturer. Not in this lifetime, she told him in her head.

Westlake had the floor. 'You work in this job a while, you get to see some of these fuckers grow up before your eyes,' he said. 'And you can pick 'em, you know? Like you go out to their shitholes in Campbelltown and you can pick the little bastards that you know you'll be locking up a couple of years later. But it's not always the whole family. Sometimes their brothers grow up okay.'

'So these kids are born bad?' said Professor Gamble.

'Yep. You can see it,' said Westlake. He remained standing, owning his opinion. 'You can see it happen. There's a hardness about them. You can't reach 'em, even when they're, like, five or six.'

Nicki Coors coughed then spoke, her voice flaky, as though it lacked moisture, might crumble at any moment. 'Or, Westlake,' she said, 'maybe the boys you're talking about were the prettiest in the house.' She looked to have as good a flush at her throat as Jill could feel at her own. 'Maybe that kid was specially *chosen* by one or two of his ten or so stepdads? You ever think of that when you're out there visiting their *shitholes*?'

The tension in the room ratcheted up another notch and Jill felt a blanket of calm settle over her. Numbness. About time, she thought. Since the police had brought her home at age twelve, the numbness had kicked in whenever any emotion tripped her threshold. And the threshold was set pretty low. Any really strong feeling, positive or negative, could trigger the anaesthesia. Like when she was a kid and her mum bought three-colour ice-cream. Trip. Numb, right there. Or when her little sister, Cassie, chewed the feet off all her Barbie dolls. Instant fury and then nothing. Jill had grown up that way – with this emotional regulator. But one of the biggest problems – and thrills – of her life had been that the sensor had been on the fritz the last couple of years. Since one of her rapists had been killed.

Well, actually, since she'd kicked him to death.

'In fact, you're both right,' said Professor Gamble, returning to the board and bringing Jill's awareness back to the room. He used his pen to point at the word 'Nature'. 'There's substantial evidence to show that some children are born with very low levels of emotional reactivity, what some of us might call empathy. And they also don't react to fear stimuli like they should, they become bored extremely easily, and they're highly impulsive. As they grow, they seek out experiences that gratify and arouse them, regardless of the cost to others and even to themselves, and punishment and disapproval don't affect them.'

Gamble put the lid on his whiteboard marker and twisted the pen up behind his back. Jill wondered what the hell he was doing. Was he making some kind of point with this gesture? But when the professor's arm moved up and down, she realised he was just scratching an itch. He then tapped the same side of the board again. 'But a child like this who is born into a *loving* home, with consistent discipline, has a better shot at fitting in,' he said. 'Maybe they'll get their thrills playing aggressive sports. Maybe they'll develop high-powered careers and channel their aggression into ruthless business transactions.'

Gamble stalked to the other end of the board and scribbled an asterix next to the words 'ABUSED AS A CHILD'. 'But let's put the kid from down this end into a house with a paedophile. Or maybe a neglectful, drug-addicted mother, and a violent father. This kid is going to absorb all of that pain. He or she is going to suffer like any other child would, but when they come out the other side they're going to transform all that into hate, and then find ways to visit that suffering on as many people as they can.'

Jill listened to the quiet repositioning of the class around her. She could sense her colleagues' absorption in the topic. But for her the lecture had lost its heat. The professor's comments registered only at a cognitive level; she allowed herself to be diverted by watching the way he moved. He appeared ungainly and strangely lithe all at once; it seemed he might spring across a desk or fall flat on his face at any moment.

'But these examples are the extremes, are they not?' Gamble continued. 'Can we have one without the other? Can a child born into a loving family with these biological deficits become a monster, a true psychopath? And can a child born with the full range of human feeling have that obliterated by abuse?'

Gamble tried to stretch around with his hand to scratch his back again, but failed to reach. He capped the marker and scratched. Woops. Jill noticed that he'd capped the wrong end. Sure enough, when he turned, Gamble's white shirt was scribbled with black ink. The class sniggered. He ploughed on regardless, and they stayed with him. 'Because if this is the case, how are we to judge such a child?' He pointed to 'Nature' again. 'Is this child *born* evil? If so, how are we to evaluate the crimes he later commits? Is he not born with a disability – so to speak – an illness for which he is not responsible? Does he not succumb to this illness just as a child born with an inherited predisposition to cancer?'

Jill tuned out. She didn't need this philosophical shit. As far as she was concerned, you judge a person by their acts. How and why they came to commit atrocities, she didn't care. The fact that they did was enough. Catch 'em and lock 'em up.

She turned her thoughts tiredly to her earlier overreaction. She'd been feeling so great lately. Best she'd felt in years. The undercover operation she'd completed three months ago had brought down a major meth production syndicate with international links. Thanks to Gabriel Delahunt, her federal cop former partner, she and her boss, Superintendent Lawrence Last, had been credited with the bust. Last had been very grateful. He'd even recommended she begin this master's degree as a fully paid study vacation.

Jill smiled as she recalled her reaction to Last's suggestion. 'Do you think I need retraining? Do you want me out of the way?'

'Do you think you need to work on your self-esteem?' he'd responded.

Well, duh.

But the idea had grown on her, and eventually she found herself thrilled with the idea of studying. School for her had been a nightmare. Well, high school was, at least. That ridiculously hot day of the swimming carnival had changed her life forever. Twelve. Truanting. Smoking. Wrong. Of course she'd known that at the time, but no one deserved the kind of punishment she got. Dragged screaming into a car, blindfolded, raped and tortured for three days.

She stabbed her pen into her notepad. Why do I always have to go through this event every time something changes in my life? she wondered. Will it never end? The one experience she ceaselessly tried to erase from her memory popped up every time she tried anything remotely different.

But that was it, you see: different equals dangerous. Jill realised she'd spent the next twenty-two years of her life so carefully planning and orchestrating everything she did that her career had thrived – total dedication to perfection – and her love-life had starved – who could control and predict a man, for God's sake?

Jill felt the heat at her throat again, but this time it came with a secret smile. She dropped her eyes and traced circles on the desk with her finger, her blonde hair falling forward and hiding her face. Things seemed to be changing in that department too. She gave in to the daydreaming and thought about the outfit she'd change into when the class finished tonight.

What hasn't Scotty seen me wearing? she wondered.

3

Friday, 26 November, 7.02 am
This is the reason I went into politics in the first place, thought Sheila McIntyre. Standards in Australia are slipping. These people are just plain rude.

Thirty or so early-morning train travellers shared the shelter of the awning with her, but only a couple had taken a flier. Most wouldn't even acknowledge she'd spoken to them.

'Now, all I'm asking you to do,' she tried again, 'is to fill in one of these forms and post it back to the address inside. We need to let the government know that security at train stations in the west must be upgraded.'

People stared at their shoes or away through the drizzle, searching for the train. A grey-haired woman in a good coat met her eyes.

'I'm not just a politician,' Sheila said to her. 'I'm a

mum too. And I just don't think it's right that the children catching the train at Riverstone Station aren't as well-protected as the kids at Strathfield or North Sydney.' She held out a flier and the woman took it.

'And what about you, sir?' she said to a man in labouring clothes nearby. 'Do you think it's good enough that there are virtually no security cameras at this station?' She pulled another flier from the stack. Her confidence boosted, she leaned a little closer. Ugh, his breath!

'What I don't think is good enough,' said the man, his eyes jaundiced, his nose bulbous and crimson, 'is that half my bloody wages every week go to pay for you bludgers to sit on your fat arses and fuck up this country.'

'Oh . . . Well!' she said.

Someone laughed, and from behind her she heard, 'Piss off!'

Sheila smoothed at her skirt and stood a little straighter. I got up at five o'clock this morning to come out to these ingrates, she thought. She pursed her lips, thinking about the group of concerned citizens she'd expected to find here waiting to meet her, to support her, having seen her ad last week in their local paper. Well, maybe it serves them right that they have no upgraded amenities out here. She swapped the umbrella in her handbag with the fliers then stepped forward from the awning. She cracked the umbrella and tossed her head a little. I'll wait for the train out here, she thought.

Standing a little behind her, Carmel Bussa secured the top button of her camel coat. Not so much because she felt cold, although it was chilly in this rain at seven am, even in November. No, Carmel buttoned symbolically – to shut these people out. When her husband had had his stroke, she hadn't minded that she'd had to go back to work. In fact, she really enjoyed working with the young people in the David Jones Food Hall. Half of them were travellers, backpackers, over here from Europe, working hard to support themselves on the trip of a lifetime. Now, these kids weren't angels – far from it. The stories they would tell! She could never repeat some of their jokes to her husband – he would have insisted she quit immediately – but sometimes she had to step into the cool-room to stop the laughter, take her glasses off and wipe her eyes. The two gay boys, Sasha and Ferdinand – that was another thing her husband wouldn't understand – found it hilarious to make her laugh until she cried. Well, she'd admit these kids were crude, but they certainly weren't rude, and that's the one thing that really wore Carmel down. The rude people who caught this train.

Every morning she shared the train with these people around her. She understood that people were sleepy and probably didn't feel up to talking so early in the morning. That was fine with her. She had a good book with her every day, maybe a magazine when her daughter had finished with it. But she could not understand the rudeness. The night before her first day at work, she'd been hardly able to sleep and had arrived so early for the 7.10 train that she'd watched three trains go by. Her daughter had warned her – whatever you do, Mum, don't catch the 6.50. It makes every stop to Town Hall. The next had been a flyer, the 7.04. Her eyes had blurred with tears in the draught created as it flew by. Finally, she'd spotted the 7.10 approaching. She'd felt a little thrill – her first day in a new job, and she hadn't been on a train for years. Smiling, she'd stepped forward as the train pulled in and had been pushed, elbowed and shoved out of the way by the very same people standing around her now. One woman in a tunic had stepped hard on Carmel's foot and charged straight past her. By the time she'd limped through the doors, breathless, every seat had been taken. She'd stood all the way to the city, listening to these people snoring and farting, and grunting into their mobiles.

So Carmel felt for the politician standing in the rain in front of her. She wasn't surprised to see that others had now joined her, unconcerned by the drizzle and the annoying woman with the fliers. With the 7.04 fast approaching, they all wanted pole-position to get a seat on the next train, the 7.10. Carmel had given up on hoping for a seat – although she was on her feet all day in the deli, she couldn't bring herself to battle this mob every morning. She watched them surging their way closer to the edge of the platform, the politician lady caught up in the wave.

And then a whir of fabric. A shriek. What? What just happened?

The 7.04 screamed past, leaving a pink-tinged mist in its wake. But the screaming didn't stop. Carmel moved through the people ahead of her, certain she needed to get to the edge of the platform, but with no idea why. She hunched up the collar on her camel coat, although she felt nothing at all right now, not the rain on her cheeks, not even her feet as they took her towards the edge.

Carmel didn't even feel herself sobbing as she stood at the edge of the platform, staring down at the wet-purple mince and creamy globs on the track. She didn't feel it when someone pulled her backwards. She'd been determined to try to get down there. Someone had to cover that up. Like a fresh Christmas ham in the deli, Sheila McIntyre's jointed groin and whole leg shined slickly in the gravel. Apart from a sensible walking shoe, which was still on her foot, nothing else in the mess resembled anything human.

With two people losing their breakfast over the edge, no one noticed a man in a khaki parka spit down onto what was left of Sheila McIntyre. No one paid any attention as he walked away from the scene, turning his face away from the sole CCTV camera as he exited Riverstone Station.

As he left, he raised his hand for the camera in a single-digit salute.

4

Friday, 26 November, 7.35 am
'What a waste of time,' said Scotty, leaning on an elbow, his face inches from Jill's in the sheets beneath him. His huge bronze shoulder was a boulder above her.

'What a . . . what did you just say?' Jill lurched up from under him, looking to crack his chin with her head, but he recoiled quickly, grinning.

'Whoa, Jackson, you're dangerous. Good move. Now come here.'

On her knees, naked, Jill was frozen, but only because she couldn't decide whether to punch him or to bolt from the bed. Scotty reached up, wrapped a handful of her blonde hair around his hand and pulled gently.

'What a waste of time,' he said again, no longer smiling. 'We could have been together like this for eighteen months, instead of just the last two weeks.'

He moved his hand further into her hair and cupped the base of her head. He drew her towards him.

Blue eyes locked with Scotty's, Jill melted down to meet his mouth.

'I missed you,' he breathed, their noses touching.

'So you wouldn't believe this case I copped.' Scotty's legs were stretched halfway across Jill's lounge room floor; his feet pointed towards Maroubra Beach, where the morning sunlight on the waves glinted like sparklers on a birthday cake. His back was supported by the base of her chocolate leather lounge. He used her coffee table as his own private dining nook. Shovelling in tabouli.

She sat with her knees drawn up in a corner of the matching lounge, watching him.

'You sure you haven't got anything else?' he said, raising another forkful to his mouth.

'You ate everything else.'

'Anyway, so there's this new restaurant in the city,' he said. 'Last night, I'm sent over there because someone was burned.'

'Like in a kitchen fire?'

'Nah. Get this – an old lady is there having dinner with her son, and she just bursts into flames. It'll be all over the TV right now. Want to see if we can catch the news?' He searched around for the remote.

Jill swung her feet onto the floor and bent to look under the table. Nothing was ever out of place unless she had house guests. And Scotty was especially good at messing everything up. Still, he had his good points. 'So what was it,' she said, standing. 'An accident? A waiter cooking at the table?'

'Nope,' said Scotty.
'Electrical fault? Candles?'
'Nope. Nope.'
'What?'
'Exactly.'
'Huh?'
'I know,' he said. 'So we've had brief interviews with all the diners, except the son. The doctors don't think she'll make it, and she's definitely not talking right now. Her face copped most of the burns.'
'What'd the fireys have to say?' she asked.
'That probably an accelerant was used.'
'Shit . . . Probably?'
'They couldn't smell anything. They're investigating.'
'What'd the other diners see?' she said.
'Not much. No one saw anything but her on fire, and then the manager tackling her, putting out the flames. Everyone who had anything to say pretty much told me that they'd seen her eating with her son and then she was on fire.'
'Has the son got a sheet?'
'Nothing. And he was across the room on the way back from the shitter when she started screaming.'
'She got a psych history?'
'You think she set herself on fire?'
Jill raised an eyebrow, lifted a shoulder.
'We couldn't find a lighter or matches around her. I'll look into any psych history today.'
'What about the staff, the diners?' she said. 'Any squirrels?'
'Not so far,' said Scotty. 'Nothing's come up immediately, anyway. We've got a lot to get through there.'
'Interesting,' Jill said, leaning back into the lounge.
'Yep,' he said. 'So's the manager. You remember

when Shane Johnson got shot on the job in Prince Alfred Park?'

'Of course I remember. Some nutjob with a shottie.'

'Well, you'll remember that his partner was a constable, an Aboriginal bloke – Troy Berrigan,' said Scotty. 'Berrigan's the manager of this restaurant.'

'No shit! He was hit too, wasn't he, when Johnson was shot? And Berrigan got the fucker?'

'Yep. He lost two fingers. Still managed to get off a head-shot. Killed the perp.'

'That's him? Troy Berrigan – he's this manager?'

'Yep. He got out of the job a few months after.'

'Wow. A fucken hero. I wondered what happened to him,' Jill said, and paused. 'You know, I'm kind of missing the job.'

'You still liking the course?'

'Yeah,' she said. 'Yeah, it's good, but you miss the action, you know?'

'I got some action for you over here.'

'Pass,' she said. 'You smell like garlic.'

5

Friday, 26 November, 11.10 am
Troy awoke smiling, to the sound of a motorboat. Sitting on his chest. He opened his eyes and the cat smiled back. Crescents of gold glowed; the cat's eyes squeezed mostly shut by his smile. The cat sighed deeply and Troy matched it.

Then last night returned. The woman's face on fire. Did she make it through the night? Troy manoeuvred his wrist between the cat's face and his own, checked his watch. Eleven! He shouldn't have gone back to bed after waking the first time this morning; now he'd overslept, and that never happened. Ordinarily, he'd be up with the nightmares and to help Lucy and Christopher get ready for school. They'd be long gone by now.

But someone was in the kitchen.

'Hey, sleepyhead,' said Lucy from the sink. No school uniform.

'What day is it?' he said.

'I'm not going to school today.'

'Who are you, and what have you done with Lucy?' he said.

'Very funny. You said something happened last night and you'd tell me at breakfast.'

'I didn't say anything happened.'

'I could tell. What happened?'

Lucy had always been this way. Since he'd won them back from foster care, he'd tried to protect his brother and sister from his struggles to keep them together, from his worries about money, from the drunken midnight calls from their mother every couple of months. But Lucy always sensed when he was upset. When she was five she used to shadow him when she saw he was stressed; he'd turn around and almost fall over her. Golden-haired and fine-featured – it was usually only other Kooris who recognised her Aboriginal heritage. She had their father's bronzed skin, but their white mother's aqua eyes. As she grew older, whenever Lucy saw Troy upset she'd try to do more around the house, try to calm Christopher when he was having an outburst. But for the last couple of years – well, since the shooting – she'd always wanted 'to talk'. And there was no point trying to bluff his way through. Troy knew she'd keep nagging until he told her what was going on, how he felt. She shouldn't have to worry about his problems, but he had to admit he didn't know how he could have made it through without her.

'There was an accident,' he said.

'You want toast?' she asked.

'Thanks.'

'Did someone get hurt?'

'A customer,' he said. 'She was burned.'

'Shit. Is she all right?'

'I don't know. I think so. I'm going to go see her in the hospital today.'

'Coffee?' she asked.

'Thanks.'

'I'm coming with you,' she said.

'Where? To the hospital? You don't need to do that, Lucy.'

'I want to. You always have to handle everything on your own.'

'Don't you have to study? You've got exams coming up.'

'I'll bring my notes,' she said. 'Besides, we both know I'm gonna blitz them.'

Troy took the plate of toast from his sister. 'So modest,' he said. 'Well, if you want to come, Luce, that'd be great. I'm not really looking forward to seeing this guy again.'

'What guy?'

'The lady's son. He was so . . . grateful to me. It made me really uncomfortable. The whole thing kinda reminded me of Jonno.'

Lucy took a sip of her coffee, watching him over the rim. When he didn't speak for a moment, she asked, 'Why was he grateful to you?'

'I should phone him,' Troy said, 'before we go over there. Make sure we can visit.' Make sure she's still alive. 'Chuck my wallet over, would ya, sis?'

Troy found Caine's card and made his way to the phone. He rubbed at his right hand while he waited for the call to connect. His missing fingers burned.

'Ah, Mr Caine, this is Troy Berrigan. From last night. I'm calling to ask how you and your mother are.'

'Please, call me David, Troy. And thanks for ringing. Mum's hanging in there. She's still in ICU. They've got her in an induced coma.'

'It's just so terrible. I'm so sorry this has happened,' said Troy. 'Would you mind if I came over to visit?'

'You won't be able to see her.'

'That's okay, David. I just feel like I should come. I want to make sure you're all right too.' *Find out if you've remembered how the hell your mother got burned.*

'Sure. You can come. That would be very good of you. Actually, I'd kind of like the support while the police are here.'

'Detective Hutchinson mentioned he'd be coming out to see you,' said Troy.

'What do they want?' asked David.

Troy paused, furrowed his brow. 'Well, they have to try to figure out what happened. How this happened.'

'Anyway, you can come,' said David. 'My daughter's here. She's pretty broken up about her grandmother.'

'I'll be there in about an hour, David,' said Troy, ringing off. He stood. 'I'm first in the bathroom, Luce.'

She bolted for the door. *Never fails*, he thought.

'Hi, Mona,' Lucy said to the skinny Goth girl perched on the arm of a chair next to David Caine.

'Lucy,' said the girl.

'You two know each other?' asked Troy.

'Mona's in the year above me at school,' said Lucy. 'Sorry to hear about your grandmother,' she said to Mona.

The girl pulled at a piercing on her lip. *Goth or Emo?* Troy wondered. Luce assured him there was a huge difference. But they both wear black, have piercings, hate the world and are permanently depressed, aren't they? he'd asked her once. Yep, she'd told him. And they write poetry, trowel on eyeliner and think about offing themselves all the time? Yep. And they're different? he'd said. They're nothing *like* each other, she'd snorted. You're so old.

Troy watched the girls draw together, speaking quietly. He turned to Caine. 'Any news on your mum?' he asked. Unsurprisingly, the man looked as though he hadn't slept at all. He's changed his clothes, at least, thought Troy. He would have struggled to recall this man if they hadn't met under such traumatic circumstances. Approximately one hundred and seventy centimetres tall, thirty-five to forty, greying brown hair, average build, Kmart jeans and dull green shirt. Most people could live next door to this bloke for years and not pick him down at the local shops.

'The surgeon's coming to see her today. He's the best, apparently.' Caine grunted. 'Every specialist is supposedly the best. You never hear anyone say "He's okay" or "He's crap".'

Troy gave a tight smile. What do you say to that? 'Have the police been in yet?' he asked.

'Good timing,' said Caine.

Troy turned and saw Scott Hutchinson striding down the hall. The detective towered over a blonde woman in cargo pants and white T-shirt. He watched her as the couple made their way towards him and Caine. Hot, was his first thought. Cop, his second. Almost unconsciously, he dropped his right hand below his chair to hide his missing fingers. Suddenly ashamed of himself, he raised it again, coughed, and deliberately covered his mouth so she'd see. If any girl didn't want to know him with a hand like this, he didn't want to know her.

Bad luck anyway, he thought. Just as the couple approached, his instincts told him they were together.

'Mr Berrigan,' said Hutchinson, holding his hand out to Troy. 'Mr Caine. The nurses pointed us over here. You remember me from last night – Scott Hutchinson? You can call me Scotty.' He shook hands with Caine. 'This is Detective Jill Jackson.'

Troy watched Caine shake hands with Detective Jackson. Then she turned to face him.

'It's good to meet you,' she said, and smiled.

They know, he thought, feeling sick. Of course they know. It's their job to know who you are. Still, it had been a couple of years since he'd met anyone who knew about the shooting. He avoided police at all costs.

'I came to see how Mrs Caine is doing,' Troy said.

'Us too,' said Hutchinson. 'How is she?'

David gave them an update on his mother's progress.

'It's just the most terrible thing,' said Scotty. 'I'm sorry you're going through this.'

Caine nodded.

'We need to get a statement from you, if that's okay,' said Scotty.

'Sure, it's okay,' said Caine. 'But I don't know what I can tell you.'

'Let's just sit over here, shall we?' said Scotty, pointing across the visitors' waiting room to a set of chairs and a plastic table. 'We don't need everyone listening.' He nodded in the direction of Mona and Lucy, heads together, still talking.

'I don't mind if Troy comes,' said Caine. 'He was so great last night. I'd kind of prefer it actually.'

'Sure,' said Scotty, raising an eyebrow, just for Troy to see.

'Can you just go through what happened last night for us, Mr Caine?' said Scotty when the four of them had taken a seat. He had his notepad ready. Troy noticed that Jill Jackson also had a pad and pen ready. Caine cleared his throat. 'Call me David,' he said.

'Ah, you might want to wait a minute, Scotty,' interrupted Jackson. Troy snapped his eyes towards her, frowning. He felt he couldn't wait much longer to hear Caine's version of last night's events. Her eyes did not meet his. He followed her gaze and saw the dark-haired cop from last night striding towards them. What was her name again? Emma something? Troy heard Hutchinson shift a little in his seat, and he flicked his eyes around the table. Jackson's top lip curled in what would maybe pass as a smile if you didn't notice her eyes. Scotty ran a hand through his hair. When the newest entrant had almost reached their table, Scotty scraped his chair back and stood to welcome her.

'Ah, Emma. Great. We were just getting started,' said Scotty.

'I can see,' said Emma. 'Thanks for waiting.'

'Um, Mr Caine – ah, David – you remember Detective Emma Gibson from last night?'

Caine nodded once.

'And Detective Gibson, you'll remember Troy Berrigan?' said Scotty.

'Of course.' Gibson's grey eyes met his, her eyebrows raised.

'And –' began Scotty.

'Jill,' said Gibson.

'Hello, Emma,' said Jackson.

'I'm a little surprised to see you here,' said Gibson.

'Yeah, well,' said Jackson. 'I was with Detective

Hutchinson this morning, so I thought I'd come along, see if there's anything I can do to help.'

Troy didn't need his police training to be able to sense the tension between these three. Even Caine stared from face to face, his expression intensely curious. Troy wondered at the collective rush of blood that was betraying the intense emotions around him. Jackson had a fist-sized crimson blush at her throat, an almost symmetrical circle. Hutchinson's whole face had taken the same hue, while Emma Gibson's jet-black hair almost glowed against the perfect pallor of her face. He briefly wondered who he'd have chosen for a partner, based on these physical reactions.

Troy coughed. Once. Whatever was going on here wasn't important; he just wanted to hear about what had happened in his restaurant last night.

Scotty jerked into movement. 'Hang on a sec, Detective Gibson,' he said. 'I'll grab you a chair.' The big cop reached over and hooked a finger under the back of a chair at the next table. He swung it through the air in a single movement, and set it at the table near where Emma Gibson was standing. She slipped into the seat.

'All right, David here was just about to tell us what he remembers about last night,' said Scotty, turning back to face Caine. 'If you want to begin, Mr Caine?'

The animation dulled in Caine's eyes. 'Like I said,' he began, 'there's not much more to tell than what you already know.' His voice was as lifeless as his eyes. 'Anyway, I took my mum to Incendie for a surprise. I booked a while ago. My mum liked the name.' He shook his head. 'Can you believe it? After what's happened, and all? Anyway, we'd ordered and I'd finished my entrée. She takes a lot longer to eat than me, you see, and

I thought I'd just have a stretch – you know, walk around a bit, check out the view, go to the toilet – before the mains came. Anyway, I'm on my way back to my seat and I see her . . . she's . . . my mum's on fire.' His voice trailed away.

'I'm just a bit confused,' said Scotty. 'You didn't see she was on fire until you were almost back at the table?'

'I came from behind her. I'd gone once around the restaurant. I heard her scream before I saw her.' Caine paused, his eyes scanning a memory. 'I'll never forget that sound.'

'What did you see, exactly, David?' said Hutchinson. 'It's really important that we try to understand absolutely everything that happened last night.'

'Like I said,' said Caine. 'I saw my mother burning. God! What do you want me to tell you? That she was screaming? That her hair was on fire and her face was melting? What do you want me to say?'

Caine breathed hard, his hands flat on the plastic table, his eyes again alive. Troy wanted to tell him to take a break, to reach out a hand, but he sat still. The questioning had to continue.

'You're doing great, Mr Caine,' said Jill Jackson, her level voice cutting through the pall of emotion that seemed to occupy the table they circled. 'You're taking us back to what happened. We weren't there, and you're helping us to be. You're our eyes in there. Did you notice anyone –'

'What do you think happened, Mr Caine?' Emma Gibson interrupted, her pen poised over her notepad. Troy noticed that Jackson had put hers away. Huh.

'I have no idea,' said Caine. 'I'm just completely shocked.'

'Do you think the restaurant's responsible?' asked Scotty.

Thanks a lot, Hutchinson, thought Troy. Still, it was a reasonable question. He was surprised this guy wasn't talking to them only through a lawyer.

'I don't see how,' said Caine. 'There was no one cooking around her. There were no flames anywhere near our table.'

'Do you think someone could have done this to your mother? Is there anyone who might want to hurt her?' asked Scotty.

'Who would set an old lady on fire? Who would do something like that?' David's voice carried, and Scotty reached his hand out to touch Caine's forearm.

'Sorry, mate, I gotta ask things like that,' said Scotty. 'And, look . . . while I'm asking you upsetting questions, there's another thing we need to know. Could you tell us how your mum was before this happened?'

'What do you mean, how she was?'

'Like, was she healthy, happy? Would you say she had any big problems? Was she depressed?'

Caine stood. 'My mother wouldn't try to kill herself,' he said.

'Okay, mate,' said Scotty. 'Look, right now this whole thing is very upsetting and confusing. We can talk more another time.'

'I'm going to go and check on her,' said Caine. 'The surgeon's supposed to be coming.'

'Of course. I'll call in again tonight to see how she is,' said Scotty. 'And in the meantime we'll be trying to find out what happened to your mum.'

Troy stood and eyed the exit. He didn't want to follow Caine into the ICU, but he'd prefer that to staying to chat with these cops. He just wanted to get out of here.

But where was Lucy? He whipped his eyes around the room and spotted her, with Mona, standing before a vending machine way down the end of the hall.

'So, what do you think of him?' came Scotty's voice, behind him.

He's probably speaking to his partners, Troy thought. He turned around anyway. Scotty was waiting for his reply.

'He's pretty upset about his mother,' he said.

'You think so?' said Scotty. 'If it was me this happened to, I'd be up in your face demanding you find out what the hell happened.'

'He's probably just focused right now on making sure she gets through this,' said Jackson.

Troy felt Scotty's focus on him, and wondered whether he should tell him that he'd just voiced some of Troy's own thoughts. But an urgent bustle of staff at the ICU doors stopped their speech. They watched as, further down the corridor, a matching set of swing doors burst open and a blue-gowned doctor skidded through, bolting into the ICU.

Troy dropped his eyes to the floor at the same time as the cops. There was no need to comment on what was going on now. They'd all been in wards like this enough times to allow the cases from the past to fill the silence. Troy felt ghosts writhing in the space between them.

The ICU doors smacked back again, and David Caine stumbled through.

This face I will remember, Troy couldn't help but think. Now Caine wasn't a man you could walk past at the shops. Lips drawn back in a silent scream, his eyes were portals to madness. He stared at something no one else could see. Troy wondered whether he was watching his mother's soul leave the earth.

Caine took another step forward and stumbled, dropped to his knees, slumped forward, his forehead pressed to the floor.

Troy took half a step forwards, towards this portrait of misery.

David Caine threw his head back, his eyes crazed.

'*Mama!*' he screamed.

6

Friday, 26 November, 3.24 pm
'So, what are you going to do now?' asked Jill. She was sitting on the grass on a slight hill in Centennial Park, facing the lake. With Scotty sitting behind, wrapping her in his huge arms and legs, she felt she had just a little more control than had she been facing him. Being touched, held, was still weird; every now and then her nervous system sent a brief but terrifying message – are you sure this is safe? She felt the question now; her gut clenched, her thighs stiffened and her toes gripped the ground, ready to spring away.

Scotty rested his chin on her head. 'It's okay, J,' he whispered. 'Check out the ducklings.'

Jill focused on the string of golden cotton balls stumbling after their mum at the edge of the lake. Her nervous system backed off – all right, if you think you know what you're doing.

She reclined back into Scotty's chest. They'd headed to the park for lunch after the hospital, but the afternoon was slipping away and they both had places to be.

'So?' she said. 'What's next for you this arvo?'

'I'm gonna catch up with the fireys. They've got the fire investigation unit on the job.'

'Where're you meeting?'

'Incendie. They want to see the scene again.'

'I have to admit, this case is fascinating. I kinda wish I could be there.'

'Well, you can't come,' he said. 'You've got a lecture.'

'Is Emma going to meet you there?' she asked. Emma Gibson, jet-haired fantasy for most of the male cops in Sydney; probably for a good few of the females, too. In love with Scotty.

Jill felt him sigh into her hair.

'Yeah, she's already over there,' he said.

'Great.'

'Well, she is my partner, J.'

'Oh, really? I'd completely forgotten about that,' said Jill, and she was suddenly propelled backwards. Scotty had scooped his hands under the arch of her legs and rolled with her. On her back, on his chest, she kicked in the air, trying to hurl herself upright, but Scotty held her. Swiftly, he swivelled her round, let her legs go and tugged at her hands until she sat, straddling his chest.

'I'm not a fucking turtle,' she said.

He grinned up at her. His blond hair was mussed with grass, his smile made faint crinkles around his eyes. Huh. When did they get there?

'Tactically, not a good move,' she told him. 'You know I can go forwards and crush your windpipe with my knee. Or go backwards and wipe out the Scott Hutchinson procreation line with my elbow.'

'Why do you go all schizo-borderline when Emma's name comes up?'

'Uh, maybe because I'm sleeping with you, and doing that has been her New Year's resolution for the past couple of years.'

'Yeah, well. No one ever keeps those resolutions.'

She slid off his chest but stayed close. The fight left her and she curled her knees up, leaning into his body.

'We should get going,' she said. She reached out and smoothed her hand down his face, over the stubble on his tanned skin, smudging her thumb across his lips. He closed his eyes. She did too. It was not a big thing, but it was the first time she'd done anything like it in her life.

'Jill, I gotta tell you –' said Scotty, his eyes now open and locked with hers.

She pressed two fingers against his mouth. 'No, you don't,' she said. 'The talking thing – you know it's not my thing. Let's do it when we've got more time.' Like, when I'm drunk.

'Well, yours or mine tonight?' he asked.

'As if I'd sleep in your apartment.'

'I'll clean it for you.'

'Yeah? Well, you work on that and I'll see you there in six months.'

'You gonna cook?' he smiled up at her.

'No, you're gonna shop. Could you pick up a Chinatown duck and steamed broccoli?'

'And fried rice?'

'Of course,' she said. 'Gotta keep those carbs up. You're such a weedy little thing.'

Scotty stood and gestured that he'd help her up. Jill noted him repositioning his right foot higher up the incline and caught the look in his eye. She held out her hand, listless. Aw, what do we have to get up for? Scotty grabbed her hand and then reached out with his other to grab her waist. Not this time, baby. As he leaned over her, Jill stretched up and clamped a hand around the back of his neck, placed her foot on his stomach and straightened her knee. His weight shifted forward and gravity did the rest. Scotty's two-metre body tumbled forward and she rolled out of the way, watching as he turned the fall into a lithe somersault.

She lay on her stomach in the grass, her chin resting on her hands, her knees bent and her feet up in the air, swinging. 'You're getting slow, Hutchinson,' she said.

'Next time,' he said.

She smiled sweetly.

7

Friday, 26 November, 3.46 pm
Troy stood with the cops and investigators at the table closest to the bar, one row removed from the table at which Miriam Caine had dined last night. David Caine and his mother had last night been shown to a third-tier setting, seven metres from the window with the gorgeous city view, and far from the entry, where they placed the beautiful people. Whoever was seated up front had to add to the decor for the entering diners, had to intimidate them into jumping into the next bracket with their choice of wine.

Edward Chin, an investigator with the Fire Investigation and Research Unit, took them through his findings. 'The thing is,' he said, 'the lack of physical evidence at the scene is almost as telling as if we'd found a gas can with prints.'

'Well, except that then we'd be closer to identifying the perp,' said Chin's female supervisor. What did she say her name was? Troy wondered. Carol? Corrine? The surname came to him – Vrisakis.

'What I mean,' Chin hurried on, 'is that although this scene was preserved as quickly as possible, we've found nothing useful, and that just doesn't happen when a fire's been deliberately lit. There's usually a lot of trace.'

'And you're certain now that's the case?' asked Troy. 'That it was deliberately lit?' He directed his question to Vrisakis.

Vrisakis raised an eyebrow at Scott Hutchinson.

'It's okay,' said Scotty. 'Troy's not just the manager here. He's also a decorated ex-cop. He's good people.'

Troy tensed. He knew that he really shouldn't be listening in on this conversation. He was a civilian now, and Hutchinson could catch shit for allowing him to hang around. Gibson seemed antsy too. The glamour girl with the grey eyes hadn't steered them in his direction since he'd joined the group.

Vrisakis paused for a moment, staring right at him. Finally, she shrugged and continued. 'Yes, we are certain that it was deliberately lit,' she said. 'We got nothing from the tablecloth, but the victim definitely had accelerant on her blouse.'

Vrisakis took a breath to continue, but Gibson spoke first.

'Actually,' she said. 'I'm afraid we are going to have to ask you to leave now, Mr Berrigan.'

Troy looked to Hutchinson. Not now – please! He was finally learning something about how this could have happened. Hutchinson raised a hand to the back of his neck, rubbed. He gave Troy a half-smile. Troy sighed.

'Sorry, buddy,' said Hutchinson. 'She's right. It's time to go. You understand.'

'I'll wait in the kitchen,' said Troy. He could use the time to freeze some of the perishables – he might be able to save at least some of the money this place was going to bleed for the next few days.

'Actually,' Gibson said, moving towards him, 'it might be better if we meet you in the lobby.'

'Say, in half an hour or so,' said Hutchinson.

Emma Gibson tried to keep the irritation from her eyes as she walked Berrigan to the door of his restaurant. It wasn't his fault her partner was so soft on protocol. And what the hell was he doing bringing Jackson to the hospital, for crissakes. Emma hated that Jackson had no operational responsibilities right now. It was heaven when Jackson had been undercover – she'd had no time for Scotty at all. Now she was back, and much too close to him. Emma wondered whether Jackson would ever succumb to Scotty's infatuation for her. On her way back to join the others at the table, she pictured them together at the hospital that day. She felt like hissing. Maybe Jackson already had.

Emma rejoined Scotty and the fire investigators at the table. Better get this meeting going properly, she thought, praying that Captain Andreessen didn't ever find out that they'd begun it with a civilian sitting in.

'So you know for a fact now that accelerants were used,' she said to Vrisakis. 'I was thinking that there had to have been some kind of fuel up around her face. I can't believe how badly burned it was.'

Vrisakis frowned. 'Yes, but there's something else,' she said, furrowing her brow and turning to face Gibson. 'It's about the face. The fire pattern indicates that some type of accelerant was used, but it's not the methyl alcohol we found on her clothing.'

'What?' said Scott Hutchinson, lifting his head from his police-issue notebook. 'There were two *different* accelerants? What else was used?'

'We don't know,' said Chin. 'We're still trying to find out, but I doubt we're going to.'

Scotty turned to Vrisakis, held his hand out, his whole face a question. Help me understand this, his gesture read.

'Hospital treatment of the victim confounded the chemical trace,' she said. 'And there was not a lot of material left to work with. Most of the skin on the victim's head was pretty much burned away.'

Gibson winced.

'So how can you be sure it *was* a different accelerant?' asked Scotty.

'Flame pattern, ignition temp, odour,' said Chin. He stood with his hands behind his back, a soldier at ease. Vrisakis had her hands in the pockets of her dark slacks.

'I really don't understand this,' said Gibson. 'How is someone supposed to have poured flammable liquid all over an old woman and no one sees anything? And *what* odour – I mean, I didn't smell anything but a burned body, and the fireys at the scene said the same thing.'

'Well, as to the odour of the accelerant on the blouse,' began Chin. He sat down stiffly, sitting on his hands. 'Methyl alcohol in its pure form has only a very slight scent, which is of alcohol. It would have been very difficult to detect in this environment.' He pulled his hands out from under him and studied them. Finally, he clasped them in his lap, like an altar boy.

He's got a lot more he wants to say, thought Emma,

watching Chin. His hands are like his thoughts – they want to break free. He knows more than he's saying.

'And we didn't say that the victim had accelerant *all* over her,' said Vrisakis.

'Because what we'd have then is a fire trail,' said Chin. 'The accelerant fluid would have flowed down her body, and we'd have run-down burn patterns. We'd also have a liquid burn pattern area on the floor or table here. And because the fire was extinguished so quickly,' he continued, 'we would have expected some ignitable liquid residue recovery on the floor around her.'

Emma noted that Chin's hands now rested, but his eyes glowed with more.

Vrisakis pulled a tissue from her pants pocket, removed her glasses and wiped them. 'And that's why Inspector Chin here made the comment about the lack of evidence telling us a lot about this offender.'

'Go on,' said Scotty. Without a table to lean on, he sprawled awkwardly on a spindly dining chair.

'Well, your perpetrator planned this act for some time,' said Chin. 'The methyl alcohol on the blouse was squirted from a small device with a narrow propulsion point.'

'Like a syringe?' asked Gibson.

'Exactly,' said Vrisakis, voice flat.

'But there was an insufficient amount of this accelerant to reliably cause death,' Chin went on.

'None of this makes sense,' said Scotty. 'Is there anything else you can tell us about who we're looking for?'

'Your perp is a cool, collected individual,' said Vrisakis. 'Almost all arson attacks have no witnesses. This person had potentially eighty. You're not looking for your typical crazy. Like Chin said, this crime was planned and meticulous.'

'He has detailed knowledge about fire behaviour,' said Chin. 'Which means he may have committed similar crimes in the past, or have a law-enforcement background.'

Gibson glared at Scotty. He kept his eyes on his notebook.

'And your offender, who may or may not be male,' said Vrisakis pointedly, giving Chin a school principal eye, 'was of course in this room and in the vicinity of the victim within moments of her being ignited.'

A moment passed, then an elevator's chime sounded faintly outside the restaurant.

'I gotta say, it seems most likely that Miriam Caine set herself on fire,' said Scotty.

'Well, to explain the sequence of events, that possibility may be the most plausible,' said Chin. 'Given what the evidence tells us, however, that possibility is less likely than the fire being caused by another person.'

'How so?' asked Gibson.

'Well, we're not ruling anything in or out,' said Vrisakis. 'We should make that clear first off. But there's the matter of how the accelerant was applied. No trace of it was found on her hands, and no device has been located that could have been used to apply it. More importantly, we found no incendiary device – the implement that ignited the fire. With suicides, the deceased has the lighter or matches on their person; there's no option to dispose of the incendiary device, nor any reason to.'

'Couldn't it have burned in the fire?' asked Gibson.

'Nothing like that could have been destroyed so completely in this fire,' said Chin. 'We would have found it, or whatever it had been reduced to.'

'So you believe someone ignited her and took whatever they lit her with?' said Scotty.

'We don't believe anything, Detective,' said Vrisakis.

'We're just pointing out the preliminary evidence.'

'I still don't get the two accelerants thing,' said Scotty. 'Why would the perp do that? I mean, that would take more time. It'd put this fucker at even more risk of being caught. Why wouldn't he just double the amount of shit he shot onto her blouse?'

'I agree,' said Vrisakis. 'That, we can't help you with. It doesn't make sense, and I've never seen anything like it before.'

'So you're positive that there were two accelerants?' said Gibson. 'I mean, she was an old lady. Maybe what was on her blouse *was* enough to kill her.'

'There were two accelerants,' said Chin. 'Methyl alcohol has a high vapour pressure, which will flash and scorch a surface, and that's why the fire flashed so quickly on the blouse. But whatever was on your victim's face had higher boiling components. These take longer to ignite, but when they do, they're going to wick, melt and burn, leaving stronger burn patterns.'

'How revolting,' said Gibson.

'Quite,' said Vrisakis.

8

Friday, 26 November, 6.14 pm

Troy kicked on the door to his apartment with his foot.

'We don't want any,' Lucy said from inside.

'Open up, smartarse,' he said. 'These bags are heavy.'

When she opened the door, he immediately scanned the floor for Chris's bag. Frowned.

Lucy caught his expression. 'Don't worry, Chris called. He's having dinner over at Makayla's.'

'Yeah, well, he knows he's not supposed to. He's supposed to be home with you after school.'

Lucy shrugged, then helped him with the groceries.

'Tim Tams!' she said. 'You're a good brother.' She ripped the packet open.

Troy took it from her hands. 'Dinner, remember?'

She snatched the packet back, grabbed a biscuit and ducked out of her brother's reach.

'What do you think of Makayla, Luce?' asked Troy.

'She's all right,' said Lucy.

'And what would you tell me if you weren't being loyal to Chris?'

'Oh, if that was the case, I'd tell you that I think she's a particularly unintelligent, disrespectful little street girl, who'll be locked up or knocked up, possibly both, within the next year.'

'Well, good thing you're loyal to Chris, then, and you didn't tell me that, or I'd have to stop him seeing her.' He met Lucy's raised eyebrows with his own arched look, and they both laughed. As if Chris would do what Troy told him, anyway.

Troy's neck ached. He stabbed a steak knife into the shrink-wrapped plastic around his six-pack of beer. He twisted a cap off and hooked it towards the bin. Half the bottle was gone by the time the cap hit the bottom of the bin.

'Don't you think you should just buy cartons?' said Lucy, watching him. 'They're more economical than buying a six-pack every day.'

'I don't drink a six-pack every day,' he said.

She gave him the eyebrows again. 'You know we've got the addictive gene from Mum. You'd better check yourself before you wreck yourself.'

Troy finished the bottle. What a frigging day. 'What a frigging day,' he said.

'Yeah?'

'The fire investigators came out to Incendie again. They're pretty sure Miriam Caine was murdered.'

'That's horrible,' Lucy said. 'I mean, it's horrible for the woman, but you were there. You could have been hurt.'

'It could have been me or anyone in the restaurant.' He explained further when he saw Lucy's expression.

'Oh, I don't mean that I could have been killed, it's just that anyone could have been the killer, even me.'

'Oh, that's much better,' said Lucy. 'I'm so relieved.'

'I'm just saying, you know, that the cops are now going to look at everyone as a suspect,' he said. 'But don't worry, sis, they're not going to think it was me.' I hope, he thought. 'But it is freaky that I was so close to a killer. Bloody hell. I might as well have stayed a copper. I thought I'd be safer in a restaurant.'

Lucy put the remaining five beers in the fridge. 'God. Poor Mona,' she said. 'She came over this arvo.'

'Yeah?' said Troy. 'Did you guys have much to do with each other before this?'

'No. She's in a completely different crowd. But I think us being at the hospital when her grandma died – I don't know, I think she feels connected to me now. Like, she doesn't have to explain how she's feeling because I know what happened.'

'You're a good kid, Luce,' said Troy. He leaned into the fridge. 'Steak all right with you?'

'I've got honey-soy-garlic chicken drumsticks in the oven,' she said. 'You should be smelling them soon.'

'You see, this is why I buy you Tim Tams,' he said.

Troy grabbed another beer from the fridge, left the kitchen and dropped onto the lounge. He'd missed the top of the news and wasn't sorry. He'd had enough real life the past couple of days.

He put his beer on the table just as the key turned in the door. Chris walked in, dumped his backpack on the floor and then held the door for two friends to come in behind him. One skinny white boy wore a plus-sized basketball singlet that fitted him like a prom dress. The other had been here once before – Jayden, a Koori kid. He had the hood up on his baggy black sweatshirt, his obsidian eyes and broken nose in shadow beneath the deep cowl. Chris wore a hoodie too – a new one. Troy hadn't seen it before. His little brother's skin was the darkest of the family, but his eyes, today almost hidden by his trucker cap, were amber. The boys wore matching baggy jeans and bad attitudes. Without speaking, they moved towards Chris's bedroom.

'You guys want some dinner?' Lucy called from the kitchen.

'Nah, we're going out,' said Chris, without turning around.

'Where?' asked Troy, standing. 'I thought you told your sister you were at Makayla's tonight.'

'We just left there,' said Chris, his hand on his bedroom door. He closed it. Hard.

Lucy had moved. She stood between Troy and the bedroom.

'What are you going to do?' she asked quietly.

'Talk to him.'

'You've been drinking.'

'Don't start, Luce.'

'Well, promise me you won't –'

'I'm just going to talk to him.' Troy stepped around his sister, knocked on his brother's door.

'What?' Chris opened the door.

'Where do you want to go?' said Troy.

'Just out, you know,' said Chris.

'Yeah, I know,' said Troy. 'You want to go out and fuck around. Get into trouble.'

'You don't even know my business,' said Chris. 'How would you know I'm gonna do anything wrong?'

'Because you're wearing shit I've never seen before, and you've got no money to buy it. I reckon you stole it. Because you're speaking and acting like some wannabe

American gangster, and because you're hanging out with these two –'

'These two what?'

Chris now stood as tall as Troy. He thrust his chest forward, ready to go. His boys behind him watched; the white boy's eyes afire; Jayden's dead. Troy moved away from the doorway. He hadn't hit Chris for years. Raised the way they were, it had been an automatic reaction to give his brother a backhander, or even a flogging, when he'd done something wrong. But one night, when Chris was twelve and had been suspended again, Troy had walked into their unit and been almost physically ill at the sight of his brother dropping to the ground, curling into a ball, ready to take a beating. He'd pulled Chris up and hugged him, promised to never hit him again.

'Yeah, you'd *better* step back, boy,' Chris said. The white boy behind him caught Chris's hand in a ghetto slap.

Oh, for God's sake. Troy took a deep breath. 'Chris, I'm going to ask you again not to go out,' he said. 'I really want you to stay home tonight. I know you're going to get hurt or get in trouble if you leave. And I'm not a cop anymore. I can't get you out of any shit you get yourself into.'

'We're not gonna get in trouble,' said Chris. 'We're not gonna get hurt, bro.' The threat had dropped from his voice. 'What are you doing home, anyway? Aren't you s'posed to be at work?'

'Someone got killed at the restaurant, Chris,' said Lucy. 'Troy's had a shit couple of days.'

'Damn,' said Chris. 'Unlucky.'

Jayden walked towards the front door, a bulging backpack over his shoulder.

'You want some chicken, Jayden?' asked Troy.

'No,' said Jayden.

'What's in the bag?'

'My dick,' said Jayden.

The white boy pissed himself laughing, and Chris failed to stop a snigger.

'So you wear a strap-on, then, Jayden?' asked Troy. 'What, you just got a pussy in those pants?'

Chris and the white boy both shouted with laughter. Jayden gave him a death stare, and Lucy spoke from the kitchen.

'Oh, yes,' she said. 'This is just the kind of inspiring conversation I look forward to each evening. Opinion on world affairs, discussions about literature.'

Chris grinned at her. 'Save me some chicken, sis,' he said. 'Later.'

9

Friday, 26 November, 7.30 pm
Jill paid for her salad roll and iced tea and walked quickly to the doors of the college cafeteria. Almost out, she heard Roseanna call out behind her.

'Jill, wait up.'

Jill turned, forcing a smile. Roseanna's cop-issue shirt strained at the bust; like most of Jill's classmates, she rushed to the Australian Graduate School of Policing straight after her shift.

'Toni's just talking to Gamble about the assignment,' continued Roseanna, in the queue to pay for her food. 'I told her we'd wait for her.' She curled behind her ear a ribbon of dark hair that had escaped its ponytail. Her tray held a meat pie with sauce and a bowl of chips with gravy.

You're gonna need to go up a size in uniform after that meal, thought Jill, and then mentally slapped herself for the bitchy thought. Michael Westlake didn't seem to mind the curves. Next in the queue behind Roseanna, he leaned forward over her shoulder and whispered something close to her neck. That's gotta be quite a view, Jill thought. Roseanna's quick giggle was music. Jill was pretty sure she'd never laughed like that.

'Yeah, and then you woke up, Westlake,' Roseanna threw back over her shoulder.

'I got some calls to make, Rosie,' Jill called over to her, another foot out the door. 'See you in the next class.'

Professor Gamble's psych class had tonight focused on non-verbal cues as indicators of stress. Gamble had emphasised to them that should they ever find themselves interviewing a psychopath, they had to assume that almost everything said would be a lie. What was his line again? She tried to remember. 'It's never a question of *if* they're lying, but why.' Gamble had listed some behavioural indicators of deception, and Jill had found herself feeling frustrated and then anxious. Frustrated because Gabriel had taught her far more about the principles of kinesic interrogation than Gamble seemed to know. And anxious because that's how she always felt lately when she thought about Gabriel.

Which was a lot.

She slipped quietly through the shadowy corridors of the college. With just the one class here tonight, most of the old weatherboard building slumbered. The scented Manly evening breathed in through the open front doors.

In front of the building, Jill stepped out of her thongs and gathered them up in her hand. The tarred pathway held stubbornly on to the heat of the day. She padded barefoot over to the frangipani tree, its blossoms just beginning to burst in the dark green foliage. She threw her hoodie down onto the grass underneath and sat upon it, cross-legged. Took out her phone. Stared at it. Put it down.

Gabriel.

Scotty.

For twenty-two years she'd tried everything to convince herself that not all men were dangerous, that some could be trusted. But although by adulthood she'd accepted this intellectually, her body had never agreed. Dating was worse than the dentist, and given the choice between eating offal and having sex, she'd quite happily have sat down to a plate of boiled brains.

But then a couple of years ago, Scotty had snuck halfway under the radar. Her sensors had finally detected the breach and automated lockdown, but something had changed. She realised now that all of their super-competitive workout sessions and playful wrestling had happened simply because they couldn't keep their hands off each other. And now . . .

A slow, delicious smile spread over Jill's face and she reclined back on her elbows, seeing, smelling Scotty in her bed this morning. With Scotty she felt known, safe, loved. It was as though he could read her, anticipate her moods and go with them, her fears extinguished before they had a chance to take off.

With Gabriel she felt she didn't know herself at all. She felt inexplicably capable of anything. And that something deep inside her, something she'd never known had existed, was asleep. And waiting.

Jill hadn't spoken to Gabe for two weeks. She'd been busy having sex with Scotty. Right now, she wished she had a clone. That was a first. Most of the time she had trouble dealing with the one Jill Jackson.

She dropped her phone into her handbag. Forget about

them for a while, she told herself. She unwrapped her salad roll, picked at the lettuce, then wished she'd bought a pie. She half-wrapped the roll again and reclined on the grass. Her T-shirt rode up at the waist and the grass was damp against her hot skin. She shivered, and laid right back into it. Stars. Huh. She'd grown used to empty black skies in the city. Street and building lights outshone the heavens in Sydney. But here, above a nook of Manly forgotten by progress, the stars cavorted and winked just as they did above Camden, her home town. The chill bit deeper into her spine and she shifted, preparing to sit up, but a warm sea-scented breeze played through her hair and tipped her sensory scales from almost painful to pleasurable.

She wondered whether pain and pleasure were so closely connected for everyone else.

10

Friday, 26 November, 8.06 pm
After he'd helped Lucy wash up, Troy went back to the lounge room with beer number four. He turned the TV volume down so he wouldn't distract Lucy from her homework. He pulled at his bottom lip. *Oh, Chris, what am I supposed to do with you now?* He didn't know how to stop his brother taking the slide he seemed determined to take. He couldn't physically control him anymore.

He wondered how much Chris still thought about what had happened before Troy got them out of foster care. Their father had been dead two years, and Chris and Lucy had had four 'uncles' by the time the state took them in. Chris's kindy teacher had called DoCS when Chris had showed up one morning filthy and nursing his right arm. DoCS had taken him to hospital, and his broken humerus bone was their least worrying finding.

Watch the World Burn

When the doctor told them that the injury was most likely caused by abuse, they'd done a full exam. Chris had extensive anal trauma. He was four years old. They'd sent a squad car with sirens to get Lucy.

It had taken Troy months to get custody. But by age nineteen he'd effectively become the father of a four- and a five-year-old. He knew they were far better off with him than with his mother, but he often wondered whether he should have let them stay in a foster home with two regular parents.

Chris never spoke of the years between when Troy left the house and DoCS rescued them. Privately, Troy was relieved – for a few reasons. Firstly, he had no idea what he'd say to make his little brother feel better about what had happened – he'd probably say something stupid and make it worse. He also felt like shit that he'd left the little kids there when he took off. Life was pretty fucked up for him from age fifteen to eighteen, living where he could, but he knew that if he'd stayed no one would have hurt Chris that way. But mostly Troy was glad that his little brother kept quiet about those years because he knew that if Chris told him who'd broken his arm and raped him, he couldn't have lived with himself until he'd found the cunt and killed him. And then he'd be in gaol and the kids would have no one again.

He'd been pretty lucky with Chris and Lucy for the first few years. His great-grandmother, his father's nan, was still alive then; she was an elder in her community in Far North Queensland. When he was five, Troy had had the best Christmas of his life when his father had taken him up to Nan's. Years later, hearing about what had happened to her grandson's kids, she'd contacted Troy, offering help. So when he'd got a week off at the service station he worked at, Troy took the kids up to meet her.

Nan was a mum for six children under twelve in her own home, kids whose parents were drugged up, locked up or bashed up too regularly. And every day and night, Nan fed and consoled many more from the community. Some of her former charges were now old enough to help out, and Nan's home was bursting with children, breast-feeding mothers, great cooking smells and gossip. For a week, Chris and Lucy swam, ate fish, laughed and tore about barefoot. For the whole of the next year, they'd begged to go back.

Troy remembered that life-changing year very well. His long-held fantasy of joining the police force looked like staying just that, until the servo got done over by two druggies with balaclavas and a shotgun. Suddenly, he decided he was going to go for it – he wanted something better for his life. He'd worried that Chris and Lucy would baulk at a three-month stay with Nan while he studied on campus, but they'd started packing that night.

Lucy and Chris had been inconsolable when he'd told them, years later, that Nan had died. Thinking back now, Troy figured that this was the year Chris had really begun acting up at school – and giving him hell at home.

Lucy's giant ginger cat, Shrek, now thumped about his ankles. Bigger than most designer dogs, Troy couldn't believe that they'd managed to smuggle him into this rental apartment and keep him here for the past eighteen months. Had to have something to do with his tiny voice. Despite the fact that his paws were the size of racquetballs, he had a little squeak of a mew. Troy knew that Shrek was not operating on all cylinders. His golden eyes were slightly crossed, and he stumbled and bumbled his way through the unit, leaping up to furniture and missing, having knock-down brawls with the cat in the mirror every time they forgot to cover it. Shrek always had a bruised or split lip.

Right now, Shrek trilled in his little-bird voice for food.

'Yeah, yeah, Dumb Dumb,' said Troy; Shrek answered to both names. 'I'll get you some chicken.' Shrek wove and warbled his way to the kitchen with him, almost tripping him up. Troy sat in the kitchen with a beer while Shrek, up on the table, chortled his way through his food. Cleaning, dreaming or eating, Shrek let everyone know he was having a good time.

'I'm pissed off they didn't let me sit in on the rest of that meeting today, Dumb Dumb,' Troy said. But if he was honest, though, he thought Hutchinson and Gibson had been pretty sloppy in letting him sit in on even part of the fireys' findings. Crime Scene 101 told you not to let any potential suspect back onto the scene. Otherwise, if it turned out this person was your squirrel, they'd have had plenty of time to cook up a story, make it plausible for a jury. But no one would seriously consider him a suspect. 'Would they, Dumb Dumb?' Shrek gave him cross eyes, and bent back to his bowl.

Troy took the last beer back to the lounge. 'Too smart for your own good, aren't you, Luce?' He saluted bottle number six at her bedroom door. He nudged the volume up a smidge and reclined back on the couch.

Troy woke to the phone ringing and a wet patch on the cushion under his mouth.

'What the fuck?' he said. 'Christopher.' He scrambled for the mobile on the table in front of him but dropped it. 'Fuck!' He fell to his knees and reached for it. Lucy snapped on a light, blinking, in her pyjamas.

'Hello,' he said into the phone. 'Is he all right? . . . I'll be there in fifteen. Thanks.'

'Is he okay?' Lucy's eyes were huge.

'The fucker's got himself charged,' said Troy, looking for his shoes. 'What did I say?'

'Where is he?' she said.

'Copshop, Redfern. I'm going to get him.'

'What did he do?' asked Lucy.

'Vandalism, graffiti. Little fuck,' he said.

'You can't drive. You've been drinking.'

'I'm all right.'

'I'll get dressed. I'll drive,' she said.

'I don't think so,' he said. 'At least I have a licence.'

'You've taught me. I can do it.'

'Forget it. Cops get schooled in how to drive pissed. It's part of the job.'

'You're an idiot. I'm coming.'

'Hurry up then,' he said.

Troy washed his face, brushed his teeth and gargled. He then went back to the kitchen and scoffed some more garlic chicken. Entering a copshop smelling of mouthwash or mint gum was as good as blowing beer fumes in their face. Every drunk prick had tried that one.

'Ready, Lucy?' he called.

As Troy and Lucy left their apartment in the middle of the night to pick up their brother from the police station, Troy had a feeling that this scene would soon become familiar.

Troy parked the car in a one-way street near Redfern Station, wondering if he'd ever see it again. Graffiti covered the surface of every wall on the street. He kept Lucy close, and encouraged her to jog with him across Regent Street to the TNT Plaza tower building, which housed Redfern Police Station. The sight of his former workplace soured the beer in his gut. He and Lucy entered the station.

It had been four years since Troy had last been in here. It had been a home, then he'd become a hero, and finally he was hated. Thank Christ he didn't know the Koori female customer-liaison officer behind the partition. He gave her Christopher's name and she told them to take a seat. Troy dropped into a bolted-down plastic chair on the wrong side of the glass and waited.

'So, I was, what, twelve, when you left here?' asked Lucy. She walked past the noticeboards, picked up a flier about domestic violence and flipped it open.

'Yeah, maybe eleven,' he said.

Lucy put the flier back, chose another. 'You never really told me and Chris why you left the job, you know.'

'Didn't I?' he said.

'We always guessed it was because of the shooting.'

Troy looked over towards the partition. The liaison officer was too far away to hear them.

'But I remember you went back to work after that,' said Lucy. 'You came back here. You brought me back here once when your hand was still bandaged up.'

'You were cute,' he said.

'I had the mumps.'

'You didn't act sick, walking around here, talking to everyone. You climbed up on Singo's desk and scribbled all over his whiteboard. He lost half a day's work with what you rubbed off.'

'I don't remember that,' she said. 'So, if it wasn't your hand, why did you leave, then?'

'Are you going to keep nagging me until I tell you?' he asked.

'You know it,' she said.

'I was assigned to a smash-and-grab in a leatherwear shop that was just across the road there. Maybe forty leather jackets got boosted. It happened around five o'clock one morning. So we get there, dust for prints, and – surprise, surprise – the prints are in the system. Couple of local hoppers, just kids, not much older than you and Chris. So that afternoon I go around to their aunt's house – where they live – and half the street's wearing leather jackets.' Troy laughed, rubbed at stubble on his cheek. Lucy came and perched next to him, knees bent, feet up on the chair.

'Anyway, I go in and the kids are in bed. The rest of the jackets are all over the floor in their room. I bring the hoppers back here, feed them McDonald's, and they tell me everything. Thing is, they swear they only got eighteen jackets.'

Lucy rested her chin on her knees, blinking slowly.

'Am I keeping you awake here?' he asked.

'Keep going,' she said.

'So I figure that the shop owner's just doing an insurance scam – as you do – but there was nothing I could've done about that. Couldn't prove either of them were lying.'

Lucy leaned her head against his arm.

'So,' he continued, 'the next thing I'm around at the workers' club, just behind this building, and Singo and Herd, two of the guys I worked with here, are bragging about how they got to the smash-and-grab before the responding car, loaded up with a rack of jackets and pissed off.'

'Damn,' said Lucy.

'Yep.'

'So what'd you do?'

'Nothing,' he said. 'You don't roll over on another cop.'

'What happened then?' she asked.

'Well, nothing should have happened then,' he said, and sighed. He lowered his voice. 'But the next day I'm walking past the interrogation room and I hear something.'

'What?' she whispered.

'It was someone getting flogged. I look in, and Herd and Singo are kicking the crap out of the two hoppers. I mean smashing them. One of the kids is screaming; the other was past that, eyes rolling back in his head.'

'Oh my God!' said Lucy, sitting up, hand over her mouth. 'What happened?'

'I busted in there and pulled the pricks off of them. There was blood fucking everywhere,' he said. 'Herd and Singo were laughing. Singo fucking *thanked* me. Said he'd been having too much fun and couldn't stop. I asked them what the fuck they were doing, and Herd said the kids had been telling anyone who'd listen that him and Singo had boosted half the jackets. "So?" I asked them. "Isn't that enough?" they wanted to know.'

'That's disgusting,' said Lucy. 'What happened to the kids?'

'I got them over to RPA and one of the boys was blinded in one eye. The doctor said he couldn't save it and wanted to know what had happened.' Troy leaned his head back in the seat. 'I gave him a full report.'

'Well, that's good, isn't it?' said Lucy.

'Well, it's good in that it was the right thing to do,' he said. 'But Herd and Singo were charged and kicked out, and I became known as a mongrel dog whistle-blower that no one wanted to work with.'

Lucy opened her mouth to speak, her eyes burning, but at that moment the latch of the heavy security door clicked. Chris walked through, head down. Lucy rushed over to him. 'Chris, are you all right?' she said.

'Let's just get out of here,' he said.

After completing the paperwork, Troy was happy to oblige.

11

Saturday, 27 November, 7.33 am
'So, what's up with the case?' asked Jill, perched on the edge of the bath, wrapped in a towel.

'Which one?' asked Scotty, trying to manoeuvre her showerhead so it didn't spray straight into his face. 'Fuck, why do they always make these things so low?'

'It's the perfect height for human beings,' she said. 'And what do you mean, which case? The mysterious case of the spontaneously combusting woman.'

'Do you believe in that shit?' asked Scotty, giving up on the showerhead and turning around.

'Do I believe that people can just burst into flames for no reason?' she asked.

'Yeah.'

'Well, everything I've read says spontaneous combustion is bullshit,' she said. 'But I don't know.'

'Hmm.'

'Anyway, this case won't be the one to prove the doubters wrong. You said she had accelerant on her.'

'Two types,' said Scotty.

'It's completely bizarre,' said Jill. 'Where are you going with it today?'

'I'm going to talk to Mrs Caine's granddaughter and then go out to a community group she was part of – apparently she used to go out with them once a week. We'll look into whether she'd been talking about being worried about anyone or anything.'

'And the suicide angle?'

'It's still a possibility,' said Scotty, 'but it's gotta be unlikely. If she did this to herself, how did she ignite the fire? Why is there no evidence of it?'

'Very strange. You want some breakfast?' Jill asked, standing, and walking towards the door.

'Yes, I'm starving,' said Scotty, opening the shower and pulling her in, towel and all.

12

Saturday, 27 November, 10.12 am
'Would you cut it out!' Troy heard Lucy yell from her bedroom.

He walked to her doorway. Laughed. A beach ball-sized lump rolled around under a half-tucked sheet on Lucy's bed.

'It takes me half a day to make my bed,' she complained.

'I keep my door closed when I'm making mine.'

'Shrek, get out of there, you idiot!' Lucy tried to push-roll the lump to the edge of the bed. A fat paw swiped from under the sheet and the lump contorted again. Shrek made his happy noise while at war with the sheet monster.

'I'm going for a run, Luce,' said Troy. 'I'll be back around lunchtime. Will you be here?'

'Yep.'

'Studying?'
'Yep.'
'I'll bring back some ham and rolls.'
'Shrek!'

The pavement on Botany Road was not the most picturesque place to jog, but Troy wasn't interested in scenery. He had so much shit going through his head that he wouldn't have noticed if he was running through the Botanical Gardens. He couldn't sit still while his thoughts were churning. He kept replaying the scene at Incendie. Moving through the restaurant as he always did, watching customers, directing staff to a table when a diner was trying to signal for attention. He'd been right next to Miriam Caine when she screamed, but he'd been facing the view rather than her table. The customers closest to the windows were usually regulars, VIPs or groups, all of whom were worth more money than the customers closest to the centre of the restaurant.

Miriam Caine. Standing, arms flailing. Face and chest on fire. Troy drove his legs harder, trying to outrun the image. He could still feel her body writhing underneath him as he smothered the flames. For the last two days the sensation had plagued him periodically, usually morphing into Jonno's body in his lap, Jonno's warm blood saturating his crotch, his pulverised hand a useless lump impeding his attempts to stop the blood draining from the exit wound in Jonno's gut.

Troy's missing fingers burned and ached as he ran.

He understood what had happened that day with Jonno. He didn't like it, he didn't know why it had to happen that way, he wished it all could have run differently. But it made sense – from start to finish, what had happened was explainable. It could be told as a series of events, spoken as a story, written out.

But what had happened to the Caine woman at Incendie – that didn't make a story. There was no introduction, no main body, just a horrible conclusion.

The video replay about the day Jonno died kicked in, and he knew better by now than to try to stop it. Fucking thing would play, no matter what he did. He and Jonno responding to a mid-morning call about someone talking to himself in Prince Alfred Park. If you got all the poor bastards together who talked to themselves in Prince Alfred Park, he knew there'd have been enough for a good-sized party, especially if all the hallucinated friends and foes were also invited. So the call-out had been standard, and they probably wouldn't have responded at all, except that the caller had said that the language being used was particularly profane.

They'd pulled up in a bus zone and a white-faced woman near the kiosk had pointed them towards the toilet block. Troy had wondered ever since that day whether she'd seen the gun – and if she had, why she hadn't warned them. He saw her face again now – she'd disappeared after the shooting, but he'd never forget her. Why hadn't they asked her what she'd seen? Why hadn't they paid more attention to how pale and frightened she was? Instead, he and Jonno hadn't even stopped their detailed analysis of the last Rabbitohs game; they'd just wandered over to the brick toilet block and circled the small building, announcing that they were police.

Troy stumbled, negotiating a gutter crossing McEvoy Street. He righted himself, kept running, still trapped in his memories. What had emerged from that dark, dank doorway was a slow-motion nightmare he'd had most nights since. But back then it was real.

A two-metre monster in a full-length duffle coat stepped out, the parts of his face not hidden by a wild beard distorted by insanity. But the shotgun he held seemed the biggest thing in the space, and the only thing Troy wanted to do was to get the fuck away from there. Spinning simultaneously with Jonno, left hand scrabbling for his firearm, the other in the middle of Jonno's back, pushing him faster, Troy and his partner had gone flying with the force of the blast. The blast that ripped right through two fingers of his hand, and then through Jonno's thoracic spine.

Troy gripped his right hand with his left as he ran, flat-out now, trying to stop the burning. He didn't notice a woman yank her son off the pavement and out of his path when she saw him coming.

He remembered rolling on the grass in the park, coming up with his gun. The monster in black standing over them. Firing madly, single-handed, into its face, knowing he'd miss, knowing he was dead. And then the monster's hair had flown off, and it had swayed, crashed to the ground.

This part of the tape usually stopped here, thank Christ. Troy thought of that section as the horror movie. Later, he'd get the sob story show, followed by the bitter and twisted drama. The screening order was never predictable, but the basic program and session times remained the same.

But now he had a new addition to the library. Miriam Caine. His memories of her death were more frustrating than frightening. As Troy wound his way up Wyndham Street, he slowed to a jog, his breathing ragged. Why was she killed? How was she killed? He knew what had killed her, but he had no fucking clue how it was done. He tried again to remember the couple as they entered the restaurant. Dominique must have seated them. When was accelerant put onto her clothing? Who lit her up?

How on earth did this happen? And why?

13

Saturday, 27 November, 12.03 pm
'Good girl, back you go. I'll see you tomorrow.' Jill hefted her favourite new thing – her shiny blue Dyson vacuum cleaner – into the cupboard in the hall. 'Well, maybe not tomorrow,' she muttered, padding back to the kitchen. She told herself she'd been a bit slack with the cleaning lately. Well, hardly slack, she realised. Dusting, vacuuming and mopping every day was not 'normal', according to 'people'. 'But I've been a bit more normal with cleaning,' she said aloud. 'Yessiree, Jackson. Walking around naked, talking to yourself . . . You are so normal.'

She stuck her head in the fridge, rifled around, trying to salvage something for lunch from her Scotty-plundered kitchen. God, it's good to be home, she thought, immediately noting the absence of the cask of wine, as she did every time she opened the fridge door. Undercover, three months ago in a rundown housing-commission flat, she'd had to have the wine waiting when her neighbours came to call, or they'd have thought her some kind of freak. Either that or a born-again Christian. Either way, that meant victim out there. The cask had seemed to squat there, malevolently, blighting everything else. And it had mocked her, taunted her, called to her at night. *Come and get pissed. I'm in here – might as well drink me. Who's gonna know? You know you want to.*

She grabbed a heavy head of iceberg lettuce from the crisper and what was left of the block of tasty cheese she'd bought on Monday. *How he isn't fat, I'll never know*, she thought, shaking her head and kicking the door closed. She opened the freezer to get some bread.

'No way,' she said, rummaging around. He'd eaten the whole loaf!

Laughing, Jill made a cheese sandwich with lettuce leaves instead of bread, smearing mustard straight onto the cheese. She remembered Scotty going backwards and forwards this morning for more toast, but she hadn't exactly been counting. She'd been kind of distracted by that bare back, those brown shoulders when he walked to the kitchen in his boxers. And then that chest when he walked back to join her on the lounge. A trill of pleasure fluted through her stomach, hurting.

Still smiling as she bit into her 'sandwich', she walked into her bedroom and pulled on shorts and a T-shirt. She then took her lunch out to the balcony.

Jill wondered whether there'd ever been a more beautiful day. Across the street, across the park, across the snowy sand and a smattering of sea-smoothed rocks, glowed the ocean. With every shade of blue and most of green, today the sea's opalescence was lit from beneath. The motes of sunlight skipping across its facets seemed as though they'd exploded from the waves. Billions of pinpricks of energy, bursting free to dance in the sun.

Shielding her eyes, Jill watched the gulls in the park. Every morning, a local baker dropped off the previous day's leftovers. When jogging this morning, she'd seen a riot of birds feasting on broken meat pies, donuts and custard slices. The Maroubra seagulls and pigeons had to have higher cholesterol counts than the regulars who waited each morning for the pub doors to open down the street.

Suddenly, a piece of blackness broke away from the birds on the grass and soared into the sky. The massive black crow caught an air current in line with her balcony, and she watched it, transfixed, as it hovered and surfed right in front of her, like a hole rent in the daylight, allowing a bird-shaped slice of midnight into midday Maroubra.

Jill's mobile rang and she picked it up. 'Jackson,' she said.

A throat cleared. Male.

'Hello,' she said.

'Ah, yes. Ah, Jill. This is Bert.'

Bert? Captain Andreessen? 'Bert?' she said.

'Yeah, Andreessen,' he said. 'I, ah –'

The phone became the world – there was suddenly nothing else. Jill's former boss never called her. He'd never used his first name in her presence. And now he was talking to her like a civilian. No – like a civilian about to be told something fucked.

'There's been an incident,' he said.

No no no no no no no. 'What?' she said.

Cassie, Mum, Dad, oh God, Lilly, Avery –

'What?' she said.

'It's, ah, Scotty.'

Andreessen always calls him Hutchinson, she thought. Jill pulled her knees up onto the chair and into her chest, freezing now.

'Where is he?' she said.

'We're at RPA, Jill.'

'I'll be there in twenty.'

'You want me to send someone to pick you up?'

'No.' Why? 'It's faster if I come now.'

'Just drive safely, Jill.'

He calls me Jackson, she thought. She dropped the phone and the shivering began.

Jill kept the bullshit up all the way to the hospital. He's going to be all right; he'll be all right. Whenever she stopped the mantra, the other thought rolled in, like a huge breaker, smashing her down: Andreessen used his informing-the-family voice.

When she reached the front of the hospital, she ripped up the handbrake in a police bay and wrenched the car door open. Almost screaming in frustration, she tried to get past a man pushing a woman in a wheelchair up to the hospital.

She saw them before they saw her. Waiting out the front. Andreessen, Emma Gibson. Jill understood everything from the way they stood there, scanning the heads for her. They wanted to tell her before she got in there.

Scotty's dead.

Andreessen found her eyes. He nodded.

She dropped.

14

Saturday, 27 November, 12.30 pm
Troy put the phone down. His boss, Caesar O'Brien, was taking things pretty well, considering. When Caesar had told him that his restaurant would be a crime scene for another few days, Troy had nearly crapped himself. He knew how much capital was tied up in Incendie; he knew how much it cost for the finest, freshest food they stocked each week; he knew what the staff were being paid; he knew the rent Caesar was paying in the hotel, and the amount he'd spent marketing the restaurant. Caesar did not like his money wasted. But his boss was seeing an upside.

'The name of my restaurant has been on the TV ten times a day for the past two days,' Caesar had said. 'Every news bulletin, on every channel, they're updating the case. They're all talking about the irony of the name.

Incendie, Incendie. The fine dining restaurant Incendie. They keep saying the name.'

'You're not worried about the fact that the name is now linked with a death?' Troy felt he had to ask. It was worrying the shit out of him.

'Not a death, Troy, my boy,' said Caesar. 'A murder.'

'I know.' Troy winced.

'No, it's good,' said Caesar. 'I mean, it's not good for Mrs Caine, poor bloody woman. And it's pretty terrible for her family, but it'll be good for business in the long run, you'll see.'

'How do you figure that?' asked Troy. Are you fucking crazy?

'Listen, a place has to have an edge these days. It's gotta have something else. They're going to catch the murderer, it'll be all over the news again, and then there's gonna be this curiosity factor. People are gonna want to come see where it all happened. And when that dies down, the restaurant will still stay in people's minds, and there'll be an edge of danger, of mystery. People love that shit! Crime in this country is the new celebrity.' Caesar laughed.

Troy shook his head. He knew he should be laughing with his boss at that point, but he couldn't bring himself to do it. 'Have you been in touch with the Caine family?' he asked.

'Oh, we're sweet there too,' said Caesar. 'My legals tell me that they won't be able to come after us. They can't sue – it's a criminal matter, and the restaurant had nothing to do with it.'

'Okay,' said Troy. That's not what I asked. 'Have you contacted David Caine?'

'I wanted to get the legal aspect covered first,' said Caesar. 'Can't go making apologies if your arse ain't covered – it can be used against you, believe me. But now we should let them know we feel for them. Would you take care of that, Troy? I'm flying to Melbourne tomorrow. Got some shit to take care of. I'll be back in time for the reopening, don't worry.'

'I think we should offer to pay for the funeral,' said Troy. 'Let them know how sorry we are this happened.'

'Great, good. Make sure there are a lot of flowers. See if you can't get some kind of wreath with our name on it. In case the cameras show up at the funeral.'

'I don't think that's a good idea,' said Troy.

'Tacky?'

'Tacky.'

'Well, I trust you, son. You've handled this shit well from the get-go. Keep me posted with things.'

'So, I'll let the staff know they're not needed for a couple of days at least?' asked Troy.

'Yep. Nothing else we can do with them. Don't pay the casuals, of course.'

'Well, we might not get them back when we need them. We're going to need all hands on deck if we want to be open in time for Chief Superintendent Norris's retirement party.' Troy's gut clenched at the thought. Half the cops in Sydney. In his restaurant. He almost prayed they wouldn't be back on deck by then.

'Oh, don't worry about that, Troy. We'll be open. You think the investigation team is going to risk stuffing up the send-off for the Chief? Hardly. They'll get the job done, pronto. And don't worry about getting the staff back either. They'll be back. Everyone needs money.'

Troy took a walk around the apartment, thinking about what to say to David Caine. He decided he'd better call him immediately or it would be too late to help with funeral arrangements. He wondered whether the police had updated Caine any further about the case. He guessed they wouldn't have told him much. They would have to have Caine on the radar as a potential suspect, even though he wasn't anywhere near his mother until she was on fire. What the fuck had happened in there? Every couple of hours, the same question pecked at him.

In the kitchen, Lucy sat at the table, a textbook in front of her. 'Was that your boss?' she asked.

'Yep,' he said.

'Did I hear you say you've got tonight off?'

'Uh huh.'

'Well, if you don't have to go to work tonight, could you run me over to Mona's?'

'Mona Caine? You hanging out with her again?'

Lucy shrugged. 'She just texted. Wants to know if I'll study with her this arvo.'

'She must be a tough little bugger,' said Troy. 'I'd imagine she'd be able to get out of her exams easily, with what's just happened to her.'

'I guess,' said Lucy. 'People deal with grief in different ways. She probably just wants to focus on something else.'

'Yeah, well, I was just going to phone her father. See if there's anything the restaurant can do to help. I'll see if I can speak to him in person. I'm ready when you are.'

Troy left without checking in on Chris. He'd bawled him out all the way back from the copshop last night and told him he couldn't go out tonight. But Troy would bet his arse he'd come home to an empty flat this afternoon.

'Are you coming in?' Lucy stood by the driver's window looking down at Troy, her backpack in hand.

'Do you think it's rude for me to just show up like this?' Troy asked his sister. 'Maybe I'm the last person this guy wants to see.'

'Maybe,' she said. 'Maybe not. Maybe he's not home. Maybe I'm going to grow old and die here, waiting for you to decide whether you're coming in.'

Troy stepped out of the car and walked with Lucy through the gate of the single-storey seventies-era home. With the brickwork rendered and newly painted grey, the little house should have stood proudly amongst its tired counterparts in this side street of working-class Rosebery. Instead, it seemed to absorb the bright sunlight around it, taking the shine off the summery Saturday.

David Caine answered the door. It turned out Troy needn't have worried about showing up like this. Caine seemed pleased to see him and waved him right in. When he'd offered a beer straight up, Troy took it. Habit. After Caine directed Lucy to Mona's room, he gestured Troy to a dining table just off a small kitchen. It seemed the renovation had ended at the front door. All the indoor surfaces shone with polish, but the paintwork looked original and the furniture was well worn, to say the least.

Caine accepted Troy's offer to pay for the funeral gratefully. He hadn't made plans yet; his mother's body hadn't been released from the coroner.

'It's strange here without her,' he said. 'Much quieter. Mona's a mouse, but I'm willing to bet that my mother talked straight through the day, even when Mona and I were out.'

'Sounds like she had a lot to say,' said Troy.

'A lot of bitching and moaning. Mostly the same stuff. You know how it is with women.'

Troy took a deep sip of his beer to hide his surprise. Caine seemed to be recovering from his grief pretty quickly.

'I shouldn't speak about her like that,' said Caine. 'Not now.' He sighed and leaned back in the wooden dining chair, running a hand through the remnants of his hair. 'It's just that my mother was a difficult woman. I loved her, God knows, but . . . My parents were both Holocaust survivors. You ever met one, Troy?'

Troy shook his head. 'I don't think so.'

'Well, they're very paranoid people. They don't trust anyone, especially the government. My mother got worse as she got older.'

'I guess you would have trouble trusting anyone after that,' said Troy.

'She thought everyone was after her in the end. She was always saying that the government was going to kill her one day, that people were monitoring our conversations, that they were saying our name over the radio. Sounds crazy, right?'

Troy considered another sip but saw that Caine's beer was still three-quarters full, and he just had a mouthful left. 'Well, I guess it does,' he said. 'But then this happened, so your mother was right that someone wanted to hurt her.'

'I can't believe this could be murder,' said Caine. 'How are they going to prove that? No one saw anyone set her on fire. You were the closest person to her, and you didn't see anything like that, right?'

'Well, I wasn't looking at your mum,' said Troy. 'I turned when she screamed.'

'It has to have been some kind of accident.' Caine took a sip of his beer. He stared at Troy through narrowed eyes. 'Have you heard of spontaneous human combustion?' he asked.

'I've heard it's a crock of . . . I've heard it's not real.'

'Well, whatever happened, the police won't be able to figure it out. Bunch of imbeciles.'

Troy coughed. 'Ah, I should tell you that I used to be a cop.'

'Well, sorry, mate. I shouldn't have said that, but at least you had the sense to quit. Why'd you get out?'

'Well, let's just say that when it comes to the people at the top of the police hierarchy, I don't exactly disagree with your last statement.'

'I'll drink to that.' Caine stood. 'Get you another?' he asked, on his way to the fridge.

'Better not,' said Troy. 'I've got to drive.'

'You're allowed two. You should know that, being an ex-cop.' He slid a fresh bottle across the table. 'The government says you're allowed three middies in an hour. They're supposed to know everything.'

Troy cracked it open. Habit.

'So, you married, Troy?' Caine asked.

'Nah. I was engaged but it didn't work out.'

'You're lucky. My bitch wife walked out on me and Mona when Mona was just four.'

'Yeah?' said Troy. 'My mum sort of let us kids down too.'

'Mona told me you've looked after your brother and sister for years. Not easy on your own, is it, mate?'

'You could say that,' said Troy. He found himself telling Caine about Christopher and his feelings of helplessness in keeping his brother out of trouble.

'I'm sure he'll be all right,' said Caine. 'Most boys have these periods, don't they? Didn't you go through a wild phase?'

Troy laughed. 'Definitely, but it was pretty brief. I had to look after the kids.'

'Cop any charges?' asked Caine.

'Just juvie.' Now Troy wanted to get out of this conversation. He really didn't want to hear the next question.

'What for?' Caine asked.

'It was a long time ago,' said Troy. 'I'd rather not get into it. I probably should get going.'

'Don't be a baby,' said Caine. 'It can't have been too bad or else they wouldn't have let you join the force.'

'Juvenile records don't count. You can get around it.'

'So what did you do?' Caine was still nursing his first beer.

Oh, for fuck's sake. Troy cursed himself for coming here. He could be at home watching cricket with his own beer and his hand down his pants. 'I set a fire in a school,' he said, and waited for the fallout.

Which wasn't what he'd expected.

Caine laughed. 'Well, isn't that priceless,' he said. 'Charged for fire-setting as a child, you run a restaurant named Incendie, and you're closest to my mother when she burns to death. The police are going to stick a microscope up your arse.'

Troy stood, swaying a little. What a fucking thing to say. And to laugh! This guy felt off. This house felt off. He wanted to get out of there, and he wanted his sister with him.

'Troy, Troy, I'm sorry,' Caine stood too. 'I'm not myself. It's just that the whole idea that my mother was murdered is so ridiculous to me, and I guess I'm not taking that angle of things seriously. I haven't really slept or eaten since this happened, and the beer has made me a bit stupid. Please, mate, sit down. Don't go like this. I'd feel terrible.'

Troy pulled at his lip. He still wanted to go, but he didn't want bad blood with this guy. He still had Caesar to answer to. Besides, the poor prick probably just wasn't thinking straight. Troy didn't think Caine was ever going to be his kind of guy, but he'd just lost his mother in a fucked-up way.

He took his seat again, smiled, uncomfortable. 'Sorry,' he said. 'Touchy subject. And what happened with your mum has shaken me up a lot too.'

'So, we're good then?' said Caine, offering his hand.

Troy took it, waiting for the next question he wouldn't want to answer.

Lucy appeared in the kitchen. 'I didn't think you'd left,' she said, frowning at the bottles on the table. 'I could hear you out here.'

'Everything all right, Lucy?' asked Caine. 'You girls want something to eat?'

'Mona's not feeling too good,' said Lucy. Troy stood again. Lucy's voice was tight.

'Everything okay, Luce?' he asked.

'Yeah. I think so. I think Mona just needs more time. I'm ready to go if you are.'

Oh, thank God. 'Sure,' he said. 'Okay.'

'Is this going to become a habit?' asked Lucy, first thing after strapping on the seatbelt.

He met her eyes, raised an eyebrow.

'The *beer*?' she said.

'I had two,' he said. 'I'm legal.'

She sighed and put her feet up on the dash.

'You sounded a bit, um, funny in there,' he said, pulling out. 'Is Mona all right?'

His sister didn't answer.

'Luce?'

'I'm just considering the question,' she said. She faced

the window. 'Mona's . . . well, she's a little disconnected at the best of times. I mean, I don't know her that well, but she's always been a little . . . ah, fringe.'

'Does she take drugs?'

'I don't know!' Lucy shot out the words with a whip of her head in his direction. She turned back to the window. 'Why is that the first thing you always think of? It's not that, anyway,' she said. 'Mona's just kind of alternative, I guess. She'd better not be like this next week – she's asked me to study with her each afternoon until the exams and today she didn't want to work. I mean, I don't mind if she wants the company but she didn't want to talk either.'

'It can't be easy now, just with her and her father. He's a little odd.'

'Yeah, and losing her grandma after losing her mother like that.'

'Has her mother ever been in touch?' asked Troy.

'Where from – the afterlife?'

Troy frowned. 'I didn't know she died. I just thought that after she walked out on them, she might have tried to get in touch.'

'What are you talking about?' said Lucy.

'What are *you* talking about?' asked Troy.

'Mona's mother never walked out on them. She was electrocuted in the bath. Mona saw her body.'

15

Sunday, 28 November, 4.45am
Jill's emotions had battered her before. Rolling storms of anxiety that would start before she'd even opened her eyes in the morning. Tornados of fear that would begin somewhere near the base of her spine, churn through her stomach, then gather momentum and hurtle up through her chest. Somehow, when she was about fifteen, after years of waking everyone in the house, she'd learned how to silence the terror as it screamed through her throat and broke free from her mouth.

But Jill had never imagined that emotions could make her feel the way she did now. Although always horrendous, her fear had become familiar. But this was nothing like fear and she knew she would never get used to it.

Right now, she believed this pain could kill her.

This time she'd been in the laundry, her eyes and nose

streaming. Walking from room to room seemed to keep her a few steps ahead of the agony. But when she stopped, sometimes unaware she'd even been moving, or that now she was still, she felt it coming. It stalked her. She'd hurry to the next room, wanting to run but lacking the energy for anything more than a flat pace.

Periodically, it caught up. Maybe five or six times so far in this space between sunset and dawn. This time it found her in the laundry. Jill dropped to the ground and scuttled to the nook between the washer and the sink. Curled in tight on herself. Kneeling, crushing her chest into her legs, her forehead on the tiles, her arms holding everything in. She couldn't see how she would not be ripped apart by this pain if she didn't physically contain it.

Jill screamed into the triangle between her knees and the tiles. Her tears smelled like blood. Surely she was bleeding somewhere? You couldn't feel this bad and not bleed, could you?

Scotty.

She'd never see him again.

Scotty on fire in the car, his big, beautiful body melting. She screamed with him, called to him as he called to her. He begged her to help him and she begged him right back.

'*Let me die!*' Jill screamed into the floor.

16

Sunday, 28 November, 9.30 am
In the captain's office, Emma Gibson couldn't even glance in Jill Jackson's direction. It had nothing to do with guilt.

Emma didn't feel bad about trying to take Scotty from Jill. She'd seen for years that he watched Jill in just the way she wanted him to stare at her. She'd seen Jill oblivious, in denial, or just not interested. Whatever the reason, Jill did not take what was there on offer. And Emma had wanted what was on offer. Whenever Jill was around, Emma found it impossible to get Scotty to herself, but when Jackson had gone undercover, Emma had known she had a shot. She'd coaxed him to apply with her for a training posting at the academy in Goulburn. And when he'd accepted, she'd felt that the planets were aligned again. Since sixth grade, Emma had always been able to have any boy she liked.

And for a while at the academy, she was winning. There'd even been that one night.

But it was during that night that she knew. Scotty hadn't gone to Goulburn to be with her. He'd come to the academy to distract himself from Jill. From worrying about Jill undercover. From worrying about Jill working with that Fed, Delahunt. Emma had never met Gabriel Delahunt, but she'd never forget his name. In Goulburn, Scotty spoke about both of them at least five times a day.

But Emma Gibson wasn't having difficulty looking at Jill right now because she felt bad about all that.

She couldn't look at Jill because it hurt to see someone suffering that much.

There were no tears. Jackson sat very still. But even though she angled herself to face another direction, Emma could feel Jill's despair. It was the way she held herself, tight and closed in. And her eyes, all but swollen shut.

Emma had cried last night for Scotty. All night. Her chest felt bruised, her throat as though she'd been punched in the neck. Emma knew she'd cry again – right now she felt the sobs trying to push their way through her swollen throat. But she also knew that, some day, she'd hurt less than she did right now.

Emma lifted her grey eyes and flicked them across Jill's bowed head. She couldn't imagine Jackson ever would.

'I want to know everything,' said Jill, her voice reasonable, flat, dead.

'It's pretty bad, Jill,' said Captain Andreessen.

She met his eyes. Said nothing.

'Right. Well, if you're sure,' said Andreessen. 'How would you feel about making this a full case briefing?'

'Of course,' said Jill. 'We've got to get the case moving as fast as we can.'

'Okay,' he said. 'Look, Gibson's here because she was the last to speak to Scotty. I thought perhaps you would want to hear things from just me and her. That's why we're in my office.'

Jill waited.

'But for a full briefing we've gotta move this over to the squad room,' he said.

Jill stood. Her captain stayed seated. Shifted a little, cleared his throat.

'It's just . . . Before we go over there, I wanted you to know that I've invited some others to the meeting.'

At that moment Jill thought it fortunate that she could feel absolutely nothing. When she'd woken at six this morning, still on the laundry floor, she'd known that something had broken inside her. The numbness was back, but now she couldn't imagine ever feeling anything again. Somehow she knew that had to be wrong, though, because impatience was tightening the small of her back, clenching the already aching muscles of her gut. Why doesn't Andreessen just get the fuck up and get on with this? She stared hard at him.

'Others,' she said. Who cares. Jill was vaguely aware that Emma Gibson was now also standing.

'Actually, they should be over there now,' said Andreessen, pushing hard on the arms of his chair to raise himself. He was out of breath just getting up. He stood there, an awkward expression around his grey, grizzled mouth. To leave the room and lead the way, he'd have to push past Jill, something he'd never had trouble doing before. If people didn't get out of his way fast enough he usually ploughed right through them. Hell, she'd once seen him use that barrel of a belly to literally bounce a techie out of his office when he'd stuffed up an operation.

Jill turned and walked from the room. She wasn't going to do some kind of politeness dance with her captain and Gibson. She had to learn everything she could about who had taken Scotty from her.

And then she had to find the motherfucker and kill him.

Just great. Three people Jill did not want to see.

Elvis, a Maroubra detective who hated her. And she hated him right back.

Her former commander, Superintendent Lawrence Last. She didn't need his grave, sympathetic nod right now.

And Gabriel.

Jill paused at the door to the briefing room. Eight or so men and one woman stared back at her. Gabriel jumped up off the desk he'd been perched upon and moved towards her. She took a step back, right into Captain Andreessen immediately behind her. Everyone froze.

'Ah, let's get in there, hey, Jackson?' said Andreessen, loudly. Closer to her ear he said, 'I'll fill you in straight away on why the Feds are here.'

Jill sensed the tension in the room but it meant nothing to her. She avoided eye contact and took a seat, second row from the back, closest to the wall. She squinted towards the whiteboard, then mapped the room, her eyelids so swollen that she could almost see them, a red frame around everything she looked at.

Superintendent Last stood next to Gabriel on the opposite side of the room. She refused to meet Gabe's eyes, continued her survey. Even with his stooped shoulders and hung head, Last was too tall. As in basketballer tall.

Andreessen had stopped on his way to the front and was speaking closely to a cluster of her former colleagues, Maroubra detectives. Moses, Elvis and Ray. Finally the conversation appeared to be over, and Andreessen moved to the front of the room. Moses and Ray turned in their seats to catch Jill's eye, all smiling sympathetically. Elvis kept his face forward. His real name was Eddie Calabrese but he loved the nickname – he also referred to himself as King. Gag. Jill liked the nickname too – the fat fuck looked just like Elvis in his final days. He'd given her hell when she'd first started here. Spread rumours that still outran her when she visited copshops around the state. He could never get over the fact she'd put his baby brother, Luca, in prison. Well, that's what you get for being an outlaw bikie, she thought.

Jill sensed Gabriel approaching from behind her. Without looking, she knew who it was – no one else in this room could move so quietly. He slipped into the seat on her right.

Andreessen cleared his throat. 'First of all, I'm going to say that losing Scotty like this is fucked,' he said. 'Every one of us here in this station loved him. Big bastard was like a son to me. But Scotty has a father. He has a mother and a stepfather and a sister, Rhiannon.'

Silence.

'Now, I know all of you want to get out there and find the cunt that did this,' Andreessen went on. 'I know most of you know what happened now, but we're going to go through it again, adding in some new findings. This shit is hard to say, and it's hard to hear. We've got the shrink coming in this arvo to talk to all of us. She'll be here, in this room, at three.'

Groans.

'That's bullshit, Captain,' sang out Moses. 'How we gonna work if we've gotta be back here at three?'

'Make yourselves available,' Andreessen said. 'Superintendent Last is going to conduct the briefing, but before I hand over to him, I just want to welcome one of our federal cop brothers . . . ah, colleagues.' Andreessen cleared his throat again and nodded in Gabriel's direction. 'This is Special Agent Gabriel Delahunt.' Heads swivelled. Jill studied the desk. 'The Feds will be working with us on this one because of the similarities of this murder with the Caine murder at Incendie last Thursday.'

But why bring the Feds in? wondered Jill. Two possibly related murders didn't automatically mean they had to be involved. These weren't crimes against the Commonwealth. Was there some organised crime component here? She watched Last shuffle his way to the centre of the room. Organised crime? What would they get out of a hit on an old woman? Was she the wrong person's mother? She'd met David Caine. No way he was mobbed-up. And Scotty said he had no sheet.

She snuck a peek at Gabe. He was watching her. Lawrence Last began to speak and she faced the front.

'I'd like to offer you detectives my heartfelt condolences on losing one of your own,' began Superintendent Last. 'I am really terribly, terribly sorry. I promise you we will deploy any and every available resource to deliver justice to Detective Hutchinson's family, friends and colleagues.'

Jill remembered feeling surprised when she'd first heard Last speak. She'd expected a lot of noise from someone so tall. But Last's quiet, mannerly voice carried, even in the large briefing room. She'd never heard anyone try to interrupt him. He cleared his throat and took a sip of water.

'This is very difficult for me to say, and it will be hard for you to hear,' said Last. He paused, the room completely silent. 'Yesterday, at eleven hundred hours, Detective Hutchinson was stopped at the lights on the corner of Anzac Parade and Maroubra Road, on his way back to Maroubra Area Command. While he was stationary, an improvised incendiary weapon, most likely a Molotov cocktail, was thrown by an unknown suspect through the open passenger-side window of his vehicle. Burns evidence suggests that the device landed in Detective Hutchinson's lap and exploded, igniting his clothing.

'It appears Detective Hutchinson may have reacted in shock or passed out, or his foot has slipped onto the accelerator. In any event, witnesses report that his vehicle ran the red light, and a city-bound bus collided with it, the impact point being the midsection of the car, passenger's side. This impact rotated the vehicle one-hundred and eighty degrees, propelling it into oncoming traffic on Anzac Parade, resulting in a head-on collision with a sedan. Detective Hutchinson and the civilian were both trapped, but it's believed that Scotty most likely lost his life when his vehicle was hit by the bus.

'A passerby has used the fire-extinguisher from the bus to put out the fire in Hutchinson's vehicle within five minutes of the cars coming to rest. The civilian in the passenger car, a young woman, is in a satisfactory condition in the Prince of Wales Hospital with leg injuries. The bus driver and two passengers were admitted briefly and released, following counselling. The citizen who tried to assist Detective Hutchinson will be recommended for a bravery award.'

Jill shook her head a little. Why didn't someone say something about the noise? If they could get someone to stop those drums playing so loudly she'd have a better chance of hearing the superintendent. For fuck's sake, it's only getting louder and faster; you can't have a meeting like this. She pushed her fingers into her ears. The noise dulled a little, thank God. But, funny thing, Jill could suddenly hear Last's voice more clearly, like it was being miked right into her head. She pushed her fingertips deeper. His voice sounded different this way, though, kind of tinny.

'You're a weak piece of shit, Jackson,' Last said, straight into her ears.

What?

'And you're a dirty little whore.'

What? Don't say that. Jill shook her head again.

'You're a weak piece of shit and a dirty little whore, and you've never been anything but a failure.' Last spoke calmly, reasonably, deep inside her head. He told the truth.

'I know,' she said. She nodded.

'Jill.' She felt Gabriel grab at her hands, trying to pull her fingers from her ears. 'Jill,' he said. 'Open your eyes.'

'What a waste of space you are, Jackson,' said Superintendent Last. 'You're so fucking weak you couldn't even protect your partner.'

'It's true,' she said.

'And you were fucking him. Whore.'

A deep sob escaped her. Jill couldn't help it. She hung her head.

'Jill! Stand up.' Gabriel was tugging at her now. She could feel him struggling, trying to manoeuvre his arm under her elbow to lift her from the chair. She pushed her elbows even more tightly into her sides. 'Shut up!' she hissed at him. 'I've got to listen to this.'

'You should have killed yourself a long time ago, Jackson,' said Last. 'Dirty little whores like you shouldn't take up any more space.'

He's right. Jill nodded again. 'You're right,' she said.

'I can't hear you, Jackson,' said Last. 'Speak up, whore.'

'You're right,' she said more loudly, shrugging out of her jacket as Delahunt tried to drag her to her feet.

'I've got her,' she heard Gabriel say. 'Just back off. I've got her. Jill, it's Gabriel . . . Open your eyes!'

'*Let me go!*' Jill opened her eyes. She saw everyone in the squad room, too close now, and getting closer. She dropped to the floor, scuttled under the desk. Curled in tight. She could hear it coming, running now, flat-footed. Laughing.

She began to scream.

17

Sunday, 28 November, 9.50 am
Troy had a bad feeling, and it was more than just the hangover. It was also more than just the memories of Miriam Caine on fire in his restaurant; more than the investigators who'd eyeballed him too closely at the scene. It wasn't helped by his brother being out until fuck knows when last night, but it was more than that too.

Why would David Caine lie about his wife?

Not just lie about the fact that she'd died – that, he could understand; maybe he just didn't want to talk about it. But why would he speak so viciously about her supposedly 'leaving' him and Mona if she'd actually died in an accident?

Driving through Mascot, Troy turned left on Hatfield Street, sticking to the speed limit. The library opened at ten, and he wanted to know more about this guy.

Only two other cars in the council carpark. Good – he'd have the library to himself, then. There were still five minutes before the doors opened, so he debated waiting in the car and catching the news or crossing the road for a coffee. He got out of the car.

Fifteen minutes later, brushing custard tart crumbs from his T-shirt, Troy stepped into the silence and smells that seem to be reserved only for libraries. He took a deep sniff; he'd always loved the smell. But he could have saved himself the trip if he'd kept up with how to use the bloody internet properly.

First thing this morning he'd tried a Google search on Caine. There were so many hits that he abandoned the idea quickly. He decided to search the newspaper websites for stories about women electrocuted around twelve years ago, when Mona would have been about four. On one of these sites he found a tab marked 'Archives', and, relatively quickly, up popped the link to an article entitled 'Husband Urges Households to Install Safety Switches after Electrocution Death of Wife'. It was dated 14 June 1998, which seemed about right. Pleased with himself, he'd clicked the link. A box flashed up, informing him that he could view the article if he logged in or registered.

That's when the fun had started. He could not figure out how to log in to retrieve the article, and when his outdated laptop froze for the third time, he gave up in disgust. He wrote down the details of the article, grabbed his keys and got out of there. Now, with the familiar microfiche system in front of him, he trawled quickly until he found the article.

Husband Urges Households to Install Safety Switches after Electrocution Death of Wife

Finding his wife dead in the bath was the most terrible moment of his life, says David Caine, of Fortitude Valley, QLD, and today he urged all Australians to install safety switches to prevent such a tragedy happening in their homes. Last week's death of Louise Caine, 26, comes during a federal government drive to encourage householders to have the electrical circuit-breaker systems installed. This young mother's death was a terrible reminder of what can happen in unprotected households.

'We'd just put our daughter to bed,' Mr Caine said yesterday. 'My wife had given our daughter a bath, and then added more water for herself. When she got in, it overflowed. We always had the hairdryer on the platform of the bath – stupid, I know. It was plugged in, and the water on the platform became live, killing my wife instantly. That's how easily someone can die. Police have told me that Louise would be alive today if we'd had a safety switch. Do a better job of protecting your family. Don't let this happen to you.'

Troy printed the article and leaned back in his chair, absently rubbing at the stubble on his chin. What does this prove? he asked himself. Well, it showed that Caine had once lived in Queensland. And one more thing. It showed that he was right about David Caine. The guy was off.

18

Sunday, 28 November, 4.12 pm
'I don't want to take it, Mum,' Jill said. She sat propped against the headboard of her bed, knees tucked up to her chest.

'It's only a Valium, Jill,' said Frances Jackson. 'I spoke to Dr Raj. He said it'll help you right now. You've got to get some sleep, honey.'

'Will it stop the rain?'

Frances Jackson sighed deeply and perched carefully on her daughter's double bed, reaching out a hand towards her. 'It's not raining, baby,' she said.

'It sounds like it,' said Jill. It was all she could hear clearly. Her mum's voice was muffled, distorted.

The doorbell sounded. Frances Jackson stood.

'No!' said Jill. 'Don't let anyone in here, Mum.'

'It's okay, Jill. It's just Gabriel. I sent him out to pick

up the script, remember?'

'I don't want to see him today.'

Frances paused in the doorway, her smile gentle, her eyes terrified. 'Jill, honey. He's only been gone ten minutes.'

'He was here today? Why?' I wish the goddamn rain would stop.

The doorbell sounded again. Frances spoke over her shoulder as she moved to answer it. 'He brought you home from work, darling. After the meeting . . . about Scotty.'

Images flashed into Jill's mind: Andreessen, Lawrence Last, Elvis, Emma. The briefing. The bus. Scotty on fire. Under the desk, screaming. She scanned through the pictures quickly. She couldn't remember coming home. She couldn't remember seeing Gabriel today. She couldn't feel the fresh tears wet upon her face.

'Hey, Jackson. Got your chill pills.' Gabriel Delahunt walked into her bedroom. He tossed a paper bag onto the bed.

'I don't want them,' she said.

He shrugged, dropped down onto the end of her bed. Bounced up and down a couple of times. 'Not bad,' he said. 'It's not latex, though.'

She stared at him through the hills of her knees. He wore a grey T-shirt and cargo pants. No cap for once. His dark curls hung in his eyes. She was sure she hadn't seen him today.

'You should get a latex bed,' he said. 'It retains your slumber signature.'

She blinked.

'You done any packing yet?' he asked.

Frances Jackson appeared in the doorway, holding a tall glass of water.

'We haven't talked about that since you left, Gabriel,' Frances said, walking around him towards Jill. 'Have we, honey?' She placed the glass on the sideboard and picked up the package from the bed. She opened the box and popped a small blue pill from its blister pack. 'They're so tiny,' she said. 'Look, Jill. It's nothing at all.'

Jill took the pill from her mother, suddenly so exhausted she felt she would pass out. She took a sip of water and swallowed.

'We'd better get some of your stuff together before that hits you,' said Gabriel.

'What stuff?' said Jill. The rain sounded more like static from a TV test pattern now. She was missing every second word Gabriel said.

'For the psych hospital,' he said.

Jill knew she didn't hear *that* right. She waited for Gabriel to say something else so she could understand his real message. She felt her mother watching her worriedly, but she kept her eyes on Gabriel's mouth.

'It doesn't get too hot down there,' he said. 'It's set in a kind of forest. You probably want to bring some jumpers and shit, 'cause it can get cold at night.'

'What are you talking about?'

'We've been through this, Jill,' he said. 'Me and your mum told you we've arranged for you to go to Bendigo for a week to get some help coping with Scotty's death. You flipped out, screamed and shouted, and told us you're not fucking going.'

The conversation returned. She remembered. 'I'm not fucking going,' she said.

Frances Jackson winced.

'Yeah, we moved past that bit,' Gabriel said. 'Try to keep up, Jackson. I told you what you did back at the station, and that you're now officially on sick report.

They want you to get counselling up here, but I told them I'd handle it. Then you started crying.'

Jill started crying. 'I don't want to go,' she said.

'Jill, honey. We've got to get you some help,' said Frances. 'This place is supposed to be beautiful. It's only for a week.'

'I can't go to a psych hospital, please, Mum,' Jill pleaded. 'I'll be okay!'

Frances Jackson smoothed her hand over Jill's hair.

Jill tried Gabriel. 'I can't go anywhere,' she said. 'I have to find out who killed –' Her voice fractured.

'No one will let you near the case now, Jill. Not after what happened today,' he said. 'They wanted you off this thing altogether, but I got Last to promise me that he'd let you back on if you have a week of intensive treatment. That's if we haven't caught the prick first, of course.'

'I can't go, Gabe,' she said, her voice tiny. 'Every cop in New South Wales will think I've gone mad. No one will work with me again.'

'That's why you won't be in New South Wales,' he said. 'I said the place is in Bendigo, remember? In Victoria. It's not gonna affect your career.'

'Well, what if I just take a week away from work. I can stay here,' she said.

'No, you can't, because you're going mental,' he said.

Frances Jackson made a choking sound.

A lead blanket of fatigue pushed Jill's head back against the headboard, pressing her eyes closed.

'How will I get there, then?' she asked.

'I've got a flight booked for early tomorrow morning, Jill,' said Frances. 'I'm coming down with you.'

Jill snapped her eyes open and shot bolt upright. 'I can't get on a fucking plane like this!' she yelled. 'I'll have a panic attack in midair. I can't! I can't!'

'Shh, Jill. Okay, okay.' Frances pulled Jill into her arms.

'You can take a Valium,' said Gabriel. 'You'll sleep the whole way down.'

Jill pulled herself from her mother's grasp, boring her eyes into his. The memory of last night, being hunted and raped by those panic attacks, gave her voice a cracked edge. 'You'll have to shoot me to get me on a plane, Delahunt.'

'Shh, it's okay, honey,' said Frances. 'We'll think of something.'

19

Monday, 29 November, 7.50 am
'Callie, please, honey – would you hurry? We're going to be late again!' Erin Hart stood in the hallway of her renovated terrace house in Glebe and took a deep breath. Her voice had become louder and shriller with every word she'd called up the stairs.

Erin opened the door to the cupboard under the stairs and groaned. She began picking up the jumble of shoes on the floor, hurling them one by one at the shelves at the back that were designed to hold them neatly. She couldn't scream at the kids for this one. A good half of the shoes were hers. Tangled in with the pile was a pair of rollerblades, a backpack, a remote control for a toy car that had gone missing months ago, and a string of indoor fairy lights. She would never have listed 'good housekeeper' on her résumé, and most of the time she was proud of the deficit. She earned enough as the local member for Balmain to pay for a cleaner, but she didn't expect the woman to clean her cupboards.

She found a pair of pumps that were not what she'd been looking for, but which would do. Several other repositories for shoes and useless refuse existed in her home, but Erin had no time to search them now. She went back to the kitchen and messed up her twelve-year-old son's hair.

'What if I'd just brushed it?' he said.

'I'd have noticed and fainted,' she said.

Reece kept his eyes on his laptop. It sat where his breakfast should have been. His plate, containing toast and a boiled egg, was pushed to the side.

Erin grabbed the All-Bran from the cupboard and the scales from next to the toaster, then measured out thirty grams of the cereal. She added skim milk and a chopped banana and sat down next to her son.

'What would it cost me to get you to eat your breakfast and brush your hair every morning without me asking?' she asked.

'A hundred bucks a week would do it,' Reece said, typing.

'A hundred, huh?' she said. 'And what about your sister? How much would I have to pay Callie to be down here by seven-thirty each morning?'

'The money wouldn't work with her,' Reece said. 'I mean, she'd take your cash, but she'd still sleep in.'

'What would you recommend?' Erin asked, chewing.

'Another fifty for me,' he said. 'I'd tip her out of bed every morning at seven.'

'You'd do that for me?'

'For a hundred and fifty, you can have all that.'

'You're a good child,' she said, and yawned.

Callie appeared in the doorway, fresh-faced, fifteen, uniform pressed, big frown.

'All-Bran?' asked Erin.

'Very funny,' said Callie.

Callie dropped a slice of bread into the toaster and depressed the lever. Erin scooped up the last of her cereal and held the bowl up to her mouth, draining the milk. She took her bowl and spoon over to the sink.

'Cook you an egg?' she asked, smoothing her hand over her daughter's golden hair, which was pulled back neatly in a low ponytail.

'Ew,' said Callie.

'Can I cook you an egg, and eat it myself?' Erin said. 'I think that might be a loophole in my diet.'

Callie smiled at the toaster.

'There's my girl,' said Erin. 'I remember you. Gorgeous smiley thing, running around the house telling me how much she loves me.'

'I was five.'

'Well, what business did you have getting any older than that?'

Callie shot her the stare that all girls in Years Eight through Twelve had perfected. It could make a Year Ten boy run, and a substitute teacher cry.

'What's wrong?' asked Erin.

'I don't want to go to Dad's tonight,' said Callie.

Erin sighed and crossed the kitchen floor. 'Eat your breakfast,' she said to Reece. 'I told you, Callie, I have a meeting after work. It's going to run late.'

'Well, I shouldn't be punished for that,' said Callie.

'Yeah, can't we come home?' said Reece, dipping his toast in the egg.

'Don't you two want to see your father?' asked Erin.

'It's a big hassle going there after school,' said Callie. 'All our stuff's here.'

'Yeah,' said Reece. 'He's the one who left us. He should

go out of his way to see us, not the other way around. He can come here and look after us while you're out.'

'I don't need looking after!' said Callie, banging her knife down on the bench.

'Let's not do this today, guys,' said Erin, tiredly. 'If you don't want to go to your father's this afternoon you can come home. But straight home, no friends over and don't open the door for any reason.' Erin grabbed her handbag from the lounge. 'And you can both call your father in your lunchbreak. I'm not telling him you don't love him anymore.'

'Oh, you're very funny, Mum,' said Erin.

'Don't say that,' said Reece.

'Sorry, baby, just joking. Now, bring whatever you haven't eaten out to the car. I've set the alarm. You've got two minutes.'

'Mum!' A chorus.

After dropping the kids at school, Erin parked her Prius underground at the Broadway Shopping Centre carpark. She walked back through the centre, ignoring the gorgeous coffee smells from what seemed like every second shop. The coffee was diet-legal, but the food pornography on display alongside it was too much to resist right now.

'I love the sound of my stomach grumbling,' she muttered quietly to herself. I could slaughter some cannoli. She shook the thought away. The scales had shown a three-kilo drop this morning. She'd soon be able to wear more than ten per cent of her wardrobe again if she kept this up.

'Morning,' Erin said, walking in through the door of her office shopfront on Parramatta Road. The blow-up photo of her face on the front window was eight years old, and taken before she was even elected, but she wouldn't let go of it easily. In it she looked streamlined and taut, her eyes happy and secure in the knowledge that she had the best family in the world and a great career ahead of her. Those eyes knew her husband found her fuckable. In all the photos she appeared in now, her smile was too bright, and her eyes told everyone she was forty-five and unfuckable. Her eyes in photos now grieved, betraying her every time.

'Hi, Mrs Hart,' said Hamish from behind the front counter. His jet-black hair hung across his eyes, and she was certain he'd used a straightener on it. When paying at the hairdresser last week, she'd remarked at the micro size of a hair-straightener on sale at the counter. 'Who'd want one so tiny?' she'd wanted to know. It'd take you all day to do your hair. 'They're for guys,' the girl at the register had told her.

'Hi, Hamish,' she said. 'Remember I said to call me Erin?'

'Yes,' he said.

'So, call me Erin,' she said.

'Yes, Mrs Hart,' he said and smiled.

Oh, for fuck's sake. Erin smiled back, and Hamish thought the smile was for him. Actually, she'd smiled because she'd been thinking in text-speak lately. 'For fuck's sake' was being abbreviated in her mind to 'FFS'. She'd found herself thinking 'LOL' when she was watching telly last night. She'd have to ask Callie whether kids actually used these words verbally. If *she* was thinking this way, she'd bet they did.

Erin put her lunch in the bar fridge in the kitchen, then swung her bag onto a chair in her office, sending a file skidding. She stuck her tongue out at the file and dropped into the seat behind the desk. She logged on to her computer and opened her diary before surfing all her usual junk sites. Great. First goal met for the day. She took a look at her nine o'clock appointment, groaned, closed the diary and opened Yahoo. She followed her ritual surfing pattern, beginning with her horoscope.

By lunchtime, Erin had met with a man who came in to see her almost every week to complain – about the lack of flashing lights around school zones, the need for speed humps in his street, people who park in the bus zones on Glebe Point Road. Today, it was a faulty electronic speed sign at a roadworks site. He'd been doing forty, he told her, that vein throbbing on his forehead, and the sign flashed up that he was doing fifty and told him to slow down! She'd also met with a single mother who was being told by Centrelink that she had to prove she was trying to find a job when she had two kids with ADHD, a mother with dementia, and an ex-husband who still thought he could come over once a fortnight and smack her around.

Her next meeting had been with a Sri Lankan girl who'd met the government's refugee criteria, but whose family was still waiting. The Tamil Tigers had seized her parents' home, she told Erin. Her parents and little sister now lived in a refugee camp; her father had cancer and her sister was being lined up to service the visiting guerrillas. A complaint about the screeching of a neighbour's cockatoo was next, and then a man had wanted her to inform the people in the flat below his that they could not smoke on their balcony because it was poisoning his lungs and preventing him from being able to open any of his windows.

Now, with thirty minutes free, Erin thought about lunch. A hamburger with the lot could have made that morning a little less hideous. For a chicken schnitzel and melted Swiss cheese focaccia, she'd do it all again. Right now, she'd give a massage to the man with the vein on his temple if someone would feed her a plate of lasagne and garlic bread. Instead, she walked to the kitchen and nuked her Lean Cuisine. She ate it standing by the sink, staring vacantly at the biscuit jar.

She poured yet another glass of water to fill her stomach – who the hell came up with bullshit like that? – and stuck her head through the doorway to the office.

'Who's confirmed for the meeting tonight, Hamish?' she called.

He read out the list and she thanked him, her shoulders dropping with the missing name. Everyone would be there – except Sheila McIntyre, and she'd never be there again. Erin walked back to the office, shaking her head. What a waste for Sheila to die in such a senseless accident. Missing her footing whilst being jostled, waiting for a train.

The guilt left Erin longing for a biscuit. If she hadn't asked Sheila to be involved in the CCTV committee she would still be alive. Erin always wanted to eat when she felt guilty. And when she felt sad. And angry, embarrassed, excited, happy or hung-over. Oh, and when she was drunk.

In the afternoon she tried to concentrate on her paperwork, but she found herself more often lost in thought. She hated when that happened – sitting at her desk, in front of the computer, unfinished reports and files everywhere, and she couldn't focus. The problem was that she felt just as tired at the end of the think-session as if she had actually ploughed through the real work. And what was worse, most of the thoughts were about Shane, as usual. Why he'd had to be so clichéd as to go and have an actual midlife crisis, she would never understand. It was very Shane, though, to follow every rule set by pretty much all of his peers: go to uni and get an economics degree; marry a doctor's daughter; have two children – a girl and a boy; renovate a period terrace house; climb the ladder in the bank to senior management; buy sports car; get fit; get a tattoo; fuck a new graduate on the rise in the bank; rent a city pad and dump his wife.

FFS, didn't he have enough? His kids – bright, healthy, considerate – they loved him; great home; great friends; holidays; her. Oh no, not more tears. Erin tiredly pulled out a tissue. It was a wonder she didn't have RSI from that movement. Her. That was the problem. She hadn't been enough. Or maybe she'd been too much: too much bottom, too many chins, too many laugh-lines concertinaed around her eyes. When he'd first come out with his ridiculous, embarrassing, heart-shredding news, she'd put it all on him. Of course this was all about his own inadequacies: he wouldn't grow up and face his mortality. It was an existential crisis. It was pure vanity. His dick was too small. He was so shallow and materialistic that he couldn't see that true value existed in relationships forged over years. But as the calendar had clicked over and his changes and revelations had continued, Erin's doubts about herself had festered in her gut, bubbles of them rising up and bursting as reflux in her throat at night. She'd wake choking on the acid of her insecurities.

Erin stood from her chair and stretched her arms above her head. Her blouse pulled free of her skirt, exposing her soft white belly. She tucked her shirt back in. The worst thing about these kinds of thoughts was that she knew they were wrong. Her first thoughts about Shane's actions were the correct ones. But while she understood in her head that they were the facts, she still believed in her heart that it was all about her. The acid had corroded, eaten away at her self-esteem, and she was now just a mother in a suit with a good job. She'd lost Erin.

Four-fifty. 'I might as well have gone for a swim,' she said to Hamish, who was packing up at his desk. She stared across the peak-hour Parramatta Road to the park and the Olympic-size pool within it.

'How come?' asked Hamish.

'Oh, I just didn't get a lot done this afternoon, Hamish.'

'It's hot out there,' said Hamish. 'You could still go swimming later tonight.'

'You know, I think I'm going to do that tomorrow – swim after work,' Erin said, the thought cheering her. She hadn't been swimming in three years. There was no room for a pool in her backyard, and she'd been too embarrassed to put on her swimsuit at the beach when she'd taken the kids. Even on holidays, she'd stayed in a sarong. Next year, she'd always promised herself. I'll lose weight, and I'll go in next year. Well, fuck it, she thought now. I love swimming, and I'm sick of worrying what people think.

'What are you doing tonight, Hamish?' she asked.

'I met someone last night,' he said, smiling, angling his face to hide behind the curtain of his hair. 'We're having a drink.'

'Ooh, lucky you,' she said. 'What's his name?'

'Michael,' he said, standing and shrugging under the strap of his shoulder satchel. 'I think he's the one.'

Erin threw her head back and laughed. 'Oh my God, Hamish. You're hilarious. Still, I hope he is. See you tomorrow.'

'Have a good meeting, Mrs Hart.'

Erin locked up the minute Hamish stepped out the door. First thing on the agenda for the CCTV committee meeting tonight was a discussion of the threats they'd been receiving recently. She had to get some more information out to the press about the benefits of their plan. It'd never stop the threats from the loonies, but Erin wanted public opinion on her side. She'd have the committee okay some funds for the spin-doctors.

20

Monday, 29 November, 3.36 pm
'Don't you leave me, Bec. You promised.'
　Watching the girls from the public school, Haley Browne tried to hitch the skirt of her private-school uniform a little higher. How was she supposed to compete with that? A rangy, auburn-haired girl in a school tunic that barely covered her knickers chased her plumper, dark-haired friend across the food hall. Brown-limbed, kohl-eyed, lip-gloss-smeared, and working push-up bras and bed-hair, they were being watched by half the males in Westfield Eastgardens – a fact of which they seemed very much aware. Although they were probably in Year Ten just as she was, Haley felt the public-school girls were as different from her as she was from Lindsay Lohan.
　'I'm not going anywhere, Hale,' said Rebecca Smart, Haley's best friend since Year Three. 'Hey! Put your

hat back on, you idiot. You'll get suspended if anyone reports you.'

Haley loosened her ponytail a little, dragging a few tendrils onto her shining face. 'Oh, Rebecca! I told you we should have brought some clothes to change into. How am I supposed to compete with them?' She sighed.

'Right,' said Rebecca, 'so we were supposed to change out of our uniforms to talk to him, and then put them back on before we get home? *And* hope and pray that no one who knows us sees us in those clothes and tells our parents or the school. Anyway, he said he'd meet *you* here, didn't he?' she asked. 'Not them. He wants to talk to *you*. He's going to ask you out, I swear –'

'Oh, fuck, Bec. It's him! Don't look, don't look! Come on, let's go. It's not too late to go.'

'Shh, calm down,' said Rebecca, laughing. 'Just be cool. You're gorgeous. He's . . . oh my God, *he's* gorgeous! And he's got that guy who was with him last time. The cute one.'

'I swear to God, Bec, I'm gonna spew.'

Rebecca laughed again, throwing back her head. Her school-issue straw boater flew off and scuttled across the floor of the plaza. The shorter of the two youths walking towards them scooped it up.

'Thanks – quick, give it to me,' said Rebecca to the boy. He wore the male version of the uniform of the two girls across the food court. Rebecca noticed that the girls had stopped running and were watching them.

'You look better without it,' he said to her. 'It hides your pretty face.'

Where was a freezer when you needed it? Rebecca felt her cheeks burning. 'You'd better give that back. If I get caught without it, I'm gonna get busted.'

'Your friend doesn't have hers on,' said the boy.

The taller boy spoke for the first time. 'She definitely shouldn't wear anything to hide that face.' He took a step closer to Haley and stared down at her, his mussed-up, dirty-blond fringe hanging in his eyes. He reached forward, and with a finger, tucked the errant hair behind her ear.

'Hey!' said Haley.

'Hey,' he said.

'I don't even know your name,' she said.

'Which is going to be a problem when you're putting my number into your phone,' he said.

Haley pulled out her iPhone.

'Fuck, sweet phone,' said the darker-haired boy.

'I'm Connor,' his taller friend said, and recited a number. Haley thumbed it in.

Later, when she was finally able to speak of these events, Haley would tell people that, in the next split-second, she thought the world had ended. Depending to whom she was speaking, she would add that she wished it had.

It began with a crash and screaming. Haley screamed first from the shock of the noise. And then the pain had set in. She didn't stop screaming until the ambulance officers had sedated her with morphine.

From a shattered bottle, dropped from two floors above, concentrated nitric acid splashed upwards and outwards in a seventy-centimetre arc. The acid sprayed from the glass in an explosion of droplets, and every millimetre of flesh they landed upon received full-thickness burns.

Rebecca Smart was hit by three droplets – one on the back of her hand, one on her calf and one on her knee. After falling to the ground, screaming, she leapt up and sprinted to the nearby Donut King, where she was ushered in by staff. She climbed onto the sink and ran the wounds under water, sobbing.

Connor Stalls was struck by a whip-like line of acid that shot up his calf, instantly dissolving the skin it touched, and eating down through layers of flesh.

The spray completely missed Connor's friend, Trey Doncaster, who dragged Connor, screaming, to the McDonald's counter, where staff used the sink hoses to spray water onto the jellied line on Connor's leg.

Jason Dunstan, shopping for dinner for his pregnant wife, desperately wanted to help the last girl left on the ground, but when he saw what was happening to her legs he couldn't move. He shouted for help, and Alexander Compton, who was grabbing a late lunch before his night classes at uni, came running. Alexander took a look at the girl on the ground and vomited onto his shoes. It took Mrs Anita Singh, sixty-four, to start dragging the writhing girl by her school blazer, before several other shoppers assisted and pulled her over to the McDonald's.

The jets of water weren't enough to stop the third-degree burns that ate through Haley Browne's calves. What she didn't know then was that, for the next month, under the direction of the best burns team in the country, she would endure daily dressing changes of the open wounds, while granulation tissue was prepared for surgery and split-thickness skin grafts were harvested from her anterior and lateral thighs.

It was probably best for Haley's sanity that she also didn't know that, for the rest of her life, beetroot-coloured gouges extending across an area as big as a dinner plate would mar her once-perfect legs.

21

Monday, 29 November, 6.34 pm
'Mummy, what's wrong with that lady?'

'Bindi Graham, I've told you not to say things like that.' Sybil Graham ushered her five-year-old daughter to a seat away from the two women huddled together by a pylon. She gave the older woman an apologetic glance, then curled her arm around little Bindi. Bindi's white-blonde hair was the same shade as the hair of the younger woman, who was wrapped in a blanket. A matted tangle of her hair hid the young woman's face and eyes, but Sybil was certain she must be the older woman's daughter. Only a mother would watch over her with such a look of heartbreak and helplessness.

I wonder what happened to her? Sybil thought. Probably drugs, or maybe mental illness. So sad. She rubbed her daughter's sunny knee next to her own, trying not to stare at the women. Bindi's little red shoes swung backwards and forwards above the grime of the floor of Central Station.

The station walls around them grumbled and yawned as the next train pulled in. Sybil checked the timetable in front of her. The Melbourne XPT. Two trains to go. She watched the older woman release the handle on the wheel-bound suitcase next to her daughter, hooking her other hand into the crook of the girl's arm, over the blanket. 'This is our train, darling,' she heard the lady say. 'Come on, Jill.' When the doors of the CountryLink train wheezed open, the woman guided her daughter inside, dragging the suitcase along behind her.

'Poor woman,' said Sybil.

'What's wrong with her, Mummy?' whispered Bindi.

Jill curled up on the seat closest to the window on the train, staring blankly around the private cubicle. She watched her mother slide the doors closed, then she pressed her forehead to the glass of the window. Miranda Kerr smiled back at her, the Australian supermodel just barely wearing a bra and knickers. Jill recognised the poster as the same as the one at the bus stop at Coogee.

'Are you all right there, darling?'

Jill supposed she should answer her mum. But what would she say? *Are you all right, darling?* The sentence didn't seem to make sense. The constant shooshing noise in her head made everything sound garbled.

The train began moving and Jill blinked in the dying sunlight. Through the shooshing noise, she heard her mother's phone ring. 'Hi, Cass,' she heard her mother say, quietly. 'No, she's still the same.'

Jill listened to the stops and starts of her mother's conversation. Like Morse code.

'It takes about ten hours to get to Melbourne, then another train ride and the final leg by taxi.'

Stop.

'No, she wouldn't get on a plane.'

Stop.

'We'll be all right, darling. Don't worry. If you could just keep your father busy for a couple of days . . .'

Stop.

'No, I'll fly back, once we've settled her in.'

What with the shooshing and the bumping of the train, her mum's whispers over the phone to her sister, and the trees and buildings flicking past in the last of the afternoon sun, Jill was beginning to feel sleepy. She tried to remember how many nights had gone by without sleep now. Two? Three? Was there some kind of record out there?

She leaned back into the headrest and closed her eyes.

The trees and buildings still seemed to flicker past behind her eyelids; the rhythm like a big animal loping through the forest, flat-footed, hunting. Hunting her.

She snapped her eyes open before the screaming could set in.

22

Monday, 29 November, 6.45 pm
When he heard the key in the front door, Troy decided that he would not fight with Chris tonight. It wasn't yet seven, and despite the fact that Chris was supposed to be home at four, at least he was home. And Troy acknowledged that his brother knew he was not at work today and so would be here with Lucy. Not that that had been a consideration for Chris in the past. Troy adjusted his attitude and prepared to greet his brother as he opened the door.

But when he saw Chris, he immediately asked, 'Where'd you get the iPod?'

'It's a friend's,' said Chris. He wore another new hoodie, white iPod speaker lines bright under the shadow of the hood. He pulled them out, letting them hang.

'Your friend doesn't need his iPod?'

'He's got two.'

'How was school?' asked Troy.

'Whatever.'

'You need help with your homework?'

'I'm thinking of quitting.'

Troy groaned. 'What would you do?'

'I want to be a DJ,' said Chris.

'You need money for that. To get the equipment.'

Chris came over to the table, dropping his backpack by his feet. He sat down. Troy figured it was about a year since Chris had sat with him this way.

'I was thinking you could help me get set up,' said Chris. 'Like, with a loan. And then when I was making money, I could pay you back.'

'That shit's expensive, isn't it?' asked Troy.

Chris bent to his bag, unzipped it and pulled out a glossy black flier. 'This place has some sick shit – like, at clearance prices,' he said. 'I made a list.' He pulled a folded piece of paper from a pocket near the knee of his jeans. 'I don't need everything right away. I'll only need a mixer, turntables, speakers and a mike to start off with.'

'How much?' asked Troy, flicking through the catalogue. He couldn't figure out what any of the electrical-looking boxes were. And there were no prices.

'Between two and three.'

'Hundred or thousand?'

'Aw, come on man. Thousand.'

'So you want to borrow between two and three thousand dollars?'

Chris tilted his head and looked up at him from under his hood.

'*And* you want to leave school?' said Troy.

Chris nodded, once.

Troy blew out a sigh and leaned back in his chair.

'Do you even know how to use any of this shit?' He tossed the flier onto the table.

'Yeah, man. I'm fucking good, too. Jayden's got a mixer and turntables, and I can fuck that shit up,' said Chris.

'That Jayden's a little prick,' said Troy.

This time Chris sighed. 'Oh, man. He's all right.'

'So why don't you use his stuff?' asked Troy. 'Go in this together?'

'His shit is shit.'

'His shit is shit?'

Chris smiled. 'You know, man. It's all old and shit. It won't get me a gig in a club.'

'And how would you get a gig in a club? How would you even get into a club? You're only sixteen.'

'There'll be parties first. I'll get some money together and get a van.'

'You've been thinking about this a lot, haven't you, Chris?' asked Troy.

'Always,' said Chris.

Troy clapped his hand on his brother's shoulder. 'Tell you what, bro,' he said. 'Give me a couple of days to think about it. I've got a lot happening right now.'

'When can you tell me?' asked Chris. 'It's just that I was thinking of asking Mum for the loan if you said no.'

Troy's face darkened, and then he laughed. 'You little scamming fuck,' he said. 'You know I don't want you going round there, so you drop that on me?' Chris wore a small smile. 'Tell you what,' Troy said. 'Give me till the end of the week – I'll have a look into this equipment, understand this DJ thing a bit better, and in the meantime you keep going to school.'

'Till Friday?' asked Chris.

'Friday,' said Troy.

This time Chris's smile split his face, and he reached

forward and grasped Troy in a brief hug. 'Thanks, bro,' he said.

After four years of working nights, these unscheduled days off had left Troy out of step with his usual routine. Ordinarily, he'd watch a mid-morning news bulletin before getting ready for work, but today he'd used the morning to shop and the afternoon to clean the apartment. He got antsy every time he stopped working. And he wasn't in the mood for company, either. He didn't want to distract himself by socialising. He felt as though he had a weight on his head and shoulders, pushing him down. Everything felt wrong, and yet nothing tangible was happening. He waited, knowing something was coming, feeling that the events of the last few days were not the past, but the beginning of something. He waited, and while he waited he tried to stay busy. But at ten-thirty, four beers in and the kids in their rooms, there was nothing left to clean, no one he wanted to ring and nowhere he wanted to be. He switched on the television.

Troy missed the coffee table putting his beer down when he saw the first news item. The bottle fell to the rug and fizzed, unheeded.

Scott Hutchinson was dead. Murdered! What the fuck is going on here? Troy watched, his hands clasped, leaning forwards on the edge of the couch, as reporters fleshed out what they had learned since the detective was killed on Saturday. A computer-generated recreation of the events showed a blank-faced simulation of a person throwing a petrol bomb into Hutchinson's car. Someone had set him on fire!

How could this fucking be? Miriam Caine, burned to death on Thursday, and the cop investigating her murder attacked with a petrol bomb on Saturday. Could these things be connected?

The news item ended and Troy fell back against the cushions. He noticed the beer bottle, now empty, and the rug soaking. 'Aw, fuck,' he said. He walked into the kitchen; the pressure over his head stooping his shoulders. He reached the sink, aware he'd gone there for a reason but unable to think what it was.

Troy paced, rubbing his hand where his fingers should have been.

Hutchinson had seemed a good bloke. Troy thought about the people out there hurting tonight, lost without him. He wondered whether Scotty had kids, a wife. Troy had tried to keep in touch with Jonno's wife, after the shooting, but she'd wanted nothing to do with the service then. She hated all of them for taking him from her. He couldn't blame her.

On his third lap around the kitchen table, Troy stopped at the fridge. He opened it, then remembered. Oh, fuck – the beer. He grabbed a fresh one and a roll of paper towels, then headed back to mop up the spill.

On his knees by the couch, he sighed. He'd never been seriously worried that he'd become a real suspect in the murder at Incendie, but now he felt a guilty sense of relief that Hutchinson's murder would surely count him out as a suspect. The two deaths had to be related, didn't they? And if they were connected, then they had a real lunatic out there to catch.

An image of David Caine came to Troy's mind, and he wondered again why he found him so odd. It wasn't just the lie about his wife. It was his whole reaction to his mother's death. If it had happened to someone Troy loved, he'd want to know exactly what had happened and what the police were doing about it. Caine just seemed convinced that it couldn't have been a murder, and that the police wouldn't get anywhere anyway. Troy remembered a prosecutor with the DPP who once told him that he knew when to lean on a suspect in court. It's all in the affect, he'd told Troy. If a person's affect doesn't match what they're saying – if they're too emotional when they don't need to be, or not emotional enough, if they're smiling when they should be worried, or crying too hard, then you lean, he'd said. It seemed to Troy that in almost every interaction they'd had, Caine's affect had seemed odd.

But he couldn't see him as a double-murderer. He'd been starting to think that the fucker might have killed his mother – someone did – and murders were usually personal. He had no idea how he could have done it, but then again he had no idea how anyone could have done it. But to take out a cop? Troy couldn't see it. Caine just struck him as a socially ineffective whinger who resented people with more power than he had. There was a Caine on every street and in every office in Australia. Shit, probably on every street and in every office in every country in the world.

Suddenly Troy froze. Caine couldn't possibly have killed Scotty. Troy had been over at Caine's home Saturday, drinking beer with the bloke in his kitchen. Maybe Caine had nothing to do with either death. Maybe the deaths weren't connected. Who the fuck knew? Troy felt as though a bee had flown into his ear and was putting up a shit-fight to get out again. He pulled himself up onto the lounge, took another slug of beer.

Someone out there knew what was going on, and Troy hoped they found him soon. Death had walked into his world twice in just one week, and all this crap felt too close for comfort.

23

Tuesday, 30 November, 6.12 am
'Good morning, darling.' Jill's mother was next to her on the train seat, smoothing her hair. Jill sat forward. Remembered. A fat tear overflowed, sliding down her face and into her mouth.

'I'm so sorry, Mum,' Jill whispered.

Frances Jackson wiped the tear with her palm. 'Don't be silly, honey. There's nothing to be sorry about.'

'Do I have to go?' Jill asked.

'We're nearly there now. It's supposed to be the best ... place to recover in Victoria. And no one there will know you. Gabriel said it would help, you remember?'

'What time is it?'

'It's just past six. You slept through the whole night.' Frances tried straightening Jill's collar. Jill scowled. Her mother smiled. 'You look so much better.'

Jill realised that the noise in her head had stopped. 'Did you get any sleep?' she asked.

'Oh, bits and pieces. You know I don't sleep as much as I used to anyway, darling.'

Well, two fuck-up daughters will do that to you, I guess, thought Jill. She straightened in the seat, pulled the blanket off and began to fold it.

'I'll do that, darling.'

'I'm okay now.' Jill stood, stumbling a little, then her feet found the rhythm of the carriage. She took the blanket over to the suitcase.

'I'll stay as long as I can handle it, Mum,' she said, squatting by the bag. She looked back over her shoulder at her mother. 'But I'm not promising anything.'

'Give it a week, Jill. You need it. Please.'

'We'll see.'

She took a walk through the hallway of the train, stretching her neck from side to side. Everything felt bruised, especially her chest, as though a horse had stood on it for a couple of days. The meeting at the station was a blur. She didn't really remember much after she'd backed into Andreessen before the briefing had even started. But she recalled the last of the conversation with Gabe yesterday.

'I've got to find who did this to him,' Jill had said.

'You can help when you get back,' Gabe had told her. 'If I haven't caught the cunt first.'

Her mum had walked away when he'd said that bit. She remembered now.

'You're no good to me like this,' he'd said.

'It's a fucking loony bin,' she'd pleaded.

'I went there,' he told her. 'When Abi died.'

Abi, Gabriel's wife, had been killed by a drunk driver when they were on the job together in Canberra.

The fact that Gabriel had been through this too had melted some of Jill's resistance.

'Well, I'll go only if you promise me one thing.'

'What?'

'You have to call me every single night and brief me on the case.'

'No.'

'Then I'm not going.' Jill had stood up. 'And you can get out.'

'You need some time away from all this.'

She pointed at the door.

'Okay,' said Gabriel. 'I'll call you every day.'

Jill remembered that when Gabe had left, she'd tried to help her mother pack, but she'd found a sock of Scotty's under her pillow and the raining in her head had become a hurricane.

Now, she made her way back down the train towards their cabin. The other occupants of the train seemed to be waking too. Most of the shutters in the individual cabins were up as she walked past. She felt people staring at her but kept her eyes dead ahead.

'Mum,' she said, sliding open their door. Frances Jackson looked like she'd just had a shower and dressed nicely for the day, instead of having sat on a train seat all night watching over her lunatic daughter. Jill noticed that only the skin of her face was rumpled. More so than ever.

'Yes, honey?' Frances smiled, but worry crouched in her eyes.

'Mum, I want you to take a cab to the airport when we get to Melbourne.'

'No, Jill –'

'Listen to me, please. You've got to get home. I'll catch the train to Bendigo, and I'm fine to catch a taxi out to the hospital. I want you to get back to Dad and Cass.' She threw her sister's name in to ramp up the guilt factor. Cassie had only just been released from court-ordered rehab. 'You can call Dad from the airport and get him to pick you up. You can be back in Camden in a few hours.'

'No, Jill. I've got to see you get there okay.'

'Mum, I'm a cop. I'm thirty-four years old. I'll be fine.'

Frances frowned.

'To be honest,' Jill said, 'I don't want to show up at this mental hospital with my mummy. And where are you going to sleep, anyway? This place costs a grand a night.'

'It's a specialist health retreat, Jill, not a mental hospital.'

'So you'll go home?'

'You'll go straight to the retreat?'

'Deal.'

24

Tuesday, 30 November, 6.15 am
Erin switched the alarm off before the radio had a chance to play. She didn't care how great the song was – she hated any sound coming out of that thing. She didn't have a good relationship with anyone or anything that woke her up. This was not a problem this morning, though. She'd been awake since five.

She sat up and glared balefully at the Concept2 rowing machine by the window. Who, in God's name, had devised such a tortuous device? It was the most efficient piece of exercise equipment available. And it wasn't just the musclebound salesman with a neck as thick as her thigh who'd told her this – she'd researched it. But, oh my God, half an hour on that thing rendered her almost demented. It was the boredom – the repetition, sliding backwards and forwards, ripping her arms from their sockets and the breath from her lungs. She'd spent thirty minutes on it yesterday, constantly willing the clock to go faster; every five minutes felt like fifteen.

Erin decided she'd put the morning to better use. Lying in bed this past hour, she'd been thinking of what to tell the PR agent about the CCTV committee plans. The committee had agreed that she would attempt to garner some public favour – each of them had recently copped flack about their involvement. She pulled her laptop out from under the bed, propped some pillows up behind her, and prepared a brief for the agent.

Extension of the Street Safety Cameras Campaign: Glebe, Pilot Program Area
There are currently eighty closed circuit television (CCTV) cameras in operation in known high-crime locations in the Sydney CBD. Over the past five years, there has been a thirty per cent reduction in crime in these locations.
A committee has been formed to oversee the development of a pilot program to dramatically increase the use of CCTV cameras in the Glebe area. The pilot program will implement several key changes to the current system in order to overcome some of its current limitations. These include:
- The cost of monitoring the cameras: currently, the cameras are at their most effective only when being monitored. A dramatic increase in such a system would be cost-prohibitive.
- The quality of the images captured: currently, the cameras rely upon an operator to zoom in on suspects in the process of committing an offence. Where this does not occur, the images captured

are often unusable for the identification and prosecution of offenders.
- Privacy concerns: civil-liberties groups and other sections of the public are concerned about ordinary citizens being constantly monitored while going about their everyday business.

Extension of the Street Safety Cameras Campaign
The Glebe Area Pilot Program plans to implement and evaluate the effectiveness of the following measures:
- All businesses with street-front premises to have a CCTV camera installed which oversees entry to the business and its immediate street frontage.
- All cameras to be current technology, with high resolution, autofocus ability, and motion-activated sensors.
- Footage from all cameras to be stored at Glebe Police Station. The cameras will not be monitored, and footage will only be accessed when a crime has been reported; it can then be used for identification and prosecution purposes. Footage to be stored for a maximum of thirty days.
- If police are advised that a crime is in the process of being committed, live footage from the cameras can be immediately accessed.

The Committee wants the benefits of this system to be clearly explained to the public. These benefits include:
- Increased protection of citizens and property from crime: reduced rates of crime.
- Improved identification and prosecution of offenders.
- No monitoring of private citizens at any point: footage will only be accessed when a crime has been or is being committed.

Erin saved and closed the document. She really couldn't see why anybody except offenders would have a problem with this plan. It made perfect sense to her, and she had no doubt that all the other councils would follow suit when they saw the reduction of crime in her district. The PR consultant had promised to distribute the information quickly, which she needed in order for people to be better informed before the first town meeting at the end of the week. She imagined there would be a lot of questions, but she really felt that the privacy people would come on board when they saw that access to the footage would be subject to the same regulations as all other information held by the police. All access to the system would be monitored.

Erin opened her email and sent a copy of the document to her office, then scanned through her new mail. Five minutes later she pushed the computer from her lap. The privacy people were one thing, but no amount of spin was going to tame the crazies. She had four new emails from people believing that the cameras were going to monitor their brainwaves or broadcast their thoughts around the world.

She wondered whether she could get the committee to approve a budget for the increase of antipsychotic medication in her district.

25

Tuesday, 30 November, 9 am
In the front seat of the cab, Jill remembered the last time she'd driven along the winding driveway of a rural psychiatric hospital. Richmond, New South Wales. The Sisters of Charity. On her way to interview the shrink, Mercy Mellas.

Scotty had been driving.

Jill forced herself to focus on the scenery, when the memory of him next to her stabbed a knitting needle through her heart. This time there was bush around her, instead of the ambling cows and river at the hospital in Richmond. She heard a lyrebird's whistle-crack, then saw something fat and furry scramble through scrub at the side of the dirt road.

'Was that a wombat?' she wondered aloud.

'Probably,' said the driver. 'You see one squashed

every day when you go up the road to the top of the mountain.' It was the first exchange they'd had since Jill had stepped into the cab at Bendigo Station, when she'd told him where she was going.

'You visiting someone out here?' he asked now.

He knew she wasn't. He'd helped with the bag.

'Nope,' she said.

'Supposed to be a nice place,' he said.

'Looks pretty so far,' she said. The road continued to snake through overgrown tree ferns, the thick forest pressing up behind them.

'God, it's a long way in, isn't it?' she said. The gates had been a couple of kilometres back.

'Another click to go,' he said.

Jill swallowed. What the fuck am I doing here? What the hell has happened to my life? A week ago she'd been taking notes in Gamble's psychology class, and now here she was, a psych patient herself.

The taxi rolled along, crunching over stones and negotiating deep ditches.

26

Tuesday, 30 November, 9.10 am
As soon as he opened the door, his toothbrush still in his hand, a tic began above Troy Berrigan's right eye. He stepped aside to allow Detective Eddie Calabrese and Federal Agent Gabriel Delahunt into his three-bedroom unit in Waterloo. He hadn't been able to sleep for hours last night, thinking about Hutchinson and reliving his last moments with both Jonno and Miriam Caine, and he'd again not woken in time to help Lucy and Chris get ready for school.

The officers walked into the unit and Troy held up his toothbrush. 'Gimme a minute,' he said. 'Go through to the kitchen.'

On his way back to the kitchen, Troy kept close to the wall, taking the opportunity to observe his visitors. The floor plan of the unit was odd, with bathroom and laundry off the hallway by the front door. The hall continued past the three bedrooms and opened into a lounge, kitchen and another living area.

Calabrese was a walking advertisement for reducing one's beer intake. He'd seen this bloke before – he used to drink with Herd and Singo over at Redfern. He'd stacked on the weight since then. His gut overhung his chinos like he had a breadbin down his shirt, and he had a good glow going on across his cheeks and nose. Troy promised himself an extra two kays on his run this morning. He upped it to five when his attention turned to Delahunt.

This guy he'd never seen before. In a trucker cap, black boots and combat pants, Delahunt was squatting in the kitchen. Shrek, his tail at ninety degrees, bashed repeatedly into Delahunt's knees to take maximum benefit of the pats he was offering. Troy was pretty sure if he was in a squat that deep, he'd have been on his arse with that truck of a cat bowling into him. Delahunt just smiled at the cat, his back straight, his black T-shirt loose where Calabrese's strained for mercy, but snug across the chest, biceps and delts. This is fucking yin and yang in my flat, Troy thought.

'Sorry about that,' he said, as he emerged from the hallway.

'No problem, Mr Berrigan,' said Calabrese. 'Thanks for inviting us in.'

Delahunt remained in the squat, really working Shrek's cheeks and ears now. A string of drool connected the cat's chin to the kitchen floor. He mewled like a budgie on steroids.

'Call me Troy,' he said. 'You want a seat?'

'Troy. Righto, we'll get right to it, then,' said Calabrese, scraping back a chair at the kitchen table and falling into it. 'We're investigating the death of Detective

Scott Hutchinson, and we believe it could be connected to the murder at your restaurant.'

'It's fucked,' said Troy. 'I can't believe it. I saw it last night on the news. I thought they might have been connected.'

'And why's that?' asked Calabrese.

'Well, fuck, two people burned to death in a week? That just doesn't happen.'

'No, it doesn't,' said Calabrese. 'Not to mention the fact that there were certain substances in common at each crime scene. Federal Agent Delahunt and I are here as part of a joint investigative taskforce which has been established to investigate both matters. We've got your statement here about the events at Incendie last Thursday, and we'd like to go through it in more detail with you.'

'No problem,' said Troy. 'Of course.' He picked at a little loose skin on his lip. The mismatched double-team were ramping up the tempo on his eye tic. Calabrese had a shiny sweat going that smelled faintly metallic; Troy recognised it from the drunk cells. The liver gets overburdened, tries to excrete toxins through the skin. Meanwhile, Delahunt showed no intention of standing. Troy's thighs would have been screaming by now. Shrek had collapsed in ecstasy at his feet, a giant orange puddle. Troy pressed his right forefinger into his eyebrow, trying to stop the tic. Shit, wrong hand.

Calabrese stared.

'I remember responding when your partner was shot, Troy,' said Calabrese, pointing his chin towards the place Troy's fingers should have been. 'They called in all units, but we were out Leichhardt way, and by the time we got there you were in the ambulance and we weren't needed. That was a good head-shot you made there, son.'

Troy said nothing. What do you say to that, anyway?

'You must be pretty pissed off about losing your fingers that way,' said Calabrese.

'Well, I'm not thrilled about it,' said Troy. 'But I still have my head.' Troy thought Delahunt might have laughed, but the sound could have come from Shrek, who had an open-mouthed purr thing going that Troy had never seen before.

'Can I get you a drink?' asked Troy. A change in activity might change the subject.

'I'll take a coffee,' said Calabrese. 'White with three, if that's okay. We could be here a while.'

Troy looked down at Delahunt expectantly.

'You've got a nice cat,' said Delahunt.

'I think he likes you,' said Troy. 'Drink?'

'Cats pretty much always like me,' said Delahunt.

Okay. Troy walked over to the bench and put the kettle on.

When he came back with the coffee, Calabrese launched in, putting his notepad next to his coffee cup, his pen in one hand and Troy's police statement in the other. 'So, you say in here, Troy, that you heard a scream –'

'I think I'd like juice,' said Delahunt.

Calabrese stared at the Fed as though he'd just stripped naked and done a lap around the kitchen.

'Ah, I'll see what we've got,' said Troy. From the open fridge door, he called, 'We're out. I've got Coke, water or milk.' No answer. 'Or tea, coffee . . .'

'You got any green tea?' asked Delahunt.

'Um . . . No, no green tea. I've got English Breakfast.'

'What about Milo?'

'Are you fucking kidding me?' said Calabrese. 'Milo? What the fuck?'

'No Milo,' said Troy.

'Chocolate topping?' asked Delahunt.

Calabrese made a sound like air shooting out of a stabbed tyre.

Troy opened a cupboard, rummaged around, right to the back. 'We've got chocolate topping,' he said, turning around with the bottle in his hand, a bemused smile on his face.

Delahunt grinned widely, then walked over to the fridge and grabbed the milk. 'You having one too?' he said to Troy.

'Yeah, why not?' said Troy.

Delahunt cracked the freezer. 'You want ice-cream in yours?' he said.

'Okay,' said Troy, giving a laugh.

Calabrese scraped back his chair, muttering, 'Chocolate fucking milk.' Then, 'Bathroom down here?' he called, already pretty much there.

'On your left,' said Troy.

Delahunt pulled open a couple of cupboards.

'What are you after?' asked Troy.

'Stick-blender.'

Troy pulled a hand whisk from the third drawer. 'This do?' he asked.

Delahunt frowned. 'You don't have a lot of foodie shit for a restaurateur,' he said.

'I'm not a cook,' said Troy. 'But I'm a great manager.'

'They're gonna get all up on you for the Incendie murder,' said Delahunt.

'What?'

'Elvis has a hard-on for you.'

'Elvis?'

'Yeah. Calabrese, using your shitter in there.'

'What the fuck? That's fucking stupid,' said Troy. 'Why me? What have I got to do with murder?'

'The arson profile,' said Delahunt. 'Come on, you'd have studied this at some point. Arsonists are often emergency services, or they once were. Check. They worm their way into an investigation. Check.'

'Hang on a fucking minute,' said Troy. 'I didn't worm my way anywhere.'

'Scotty and Gibson should have got you off the crime scene immediately,' said Delahunt. 'What're you gonna do? Anyway, back to the list. Arsonists are usually socially isolated. You're not exactly flush with friends, Troy.'

'Hey! You try looking after two kids and working. See how much time –'

'Back to the list. Arsonists are disgruntled with authority and might feel inadequate.' Delahunt reached out and grabbed Troy's right hand, holding it up. 'Check.'

Troy ripped his hand away.

Delahunt started scooping vanilla ice-cream into a big plastic jug. Kept talking. 'Oh, and active arsonists have usually been busted for arson in the past. Check.' Delahunt glugged chocolate syrup into the jug. 'We pulled your juvie files. And this is to say nothing of the fact that you were the closest to the vic when she went up.'

'That's ridiculous!' said Troy. 'I was a kid! And you're not just talking about arson. This is murder here.' Troy started to pace. 'This is a fucking joke. You people are so wrong.'

'I know. You only fit the profile on the very surface. There's a lot more to murder than checking boxes, especially with this case,' said Delahunt. 'Word to the wise. Elvis will be back here in just a sec.' The toilet flushed. 'He wants you jammed up for this, and he'll try to cram your arse into the Scotty thing too. But in the end, that shit's never going to fly. You know it, I know it. But you can't overreact here, get yourself arrested. He's going to draw this out, go through details. He won't accuse you of anything. Not now. But you've got to stay cool, not get offended. You've got your brother situation going on, your sister's got exams. You've got your job to keep.'

'What don't you know about me?'

'Not a lot.'

Troy stared, eyes hot, fists clenched by his side.

'Play the game, Troy,' said Delahunt. 'You know the game. This fat fuck's going to go nowhere with this shit, but it's gotta play out. Right now there's a dead cop and people out there pissing blood to crack this, to make it their career case. But Elvis and Co. aren't the only ones out there hunting.'

The bathroom door closed. 'Play smart,' said Delahunt, whisking.

Elvis shuffled back to the kitchen table. 'You done making cupcakes, girls?' he said, eyeing Delahunt with the whisk.

'Chocolate milkshake, Elvis?' asked Delahunt.

27

Tuesday, 30 November, 9.45 am
Jill perched at the edge of the freshly made single bed. It had been fifteen years since she'd slept in a single bed. Well, except for Gabriel's fold-out that one night last year. Bloody Gabriel. Why had she listened to him? What the fuck was she going to do here? She reached over and slid out the top drawer of a nightstand next to the bed. Empty. She wiped her forefinger across the bottom of the drawer. Clean. Huh. Jill stood and moved to the large framed window that took up most of the back wall. Well, that's pretty spectacular, I have to admit, she thought.

She had been guided by a nurse in civvies from the luxurious reception area through high-ceilinged meeting rooms, past closed office doors, and through a large, sunny dining room. Jill had gasped when they'd exited the building into a glass-enclosed outdoor corridor, which stretched through the sky to another building opposite. To the right, one floor down, was a cobblestone courtyard. Sandstone benches squatted around a gently playing fountain. Three tiny potbellied birds with iridescent blue chests chirruped and washed in the water. To her left, an impeccably tended emerald lawn rolled down the hill to the forest.

The nurse had smiled. 'Not bad, huh?' she'd said.

'Mmm,' said Jill.

'That's you over there.' The nurse pointed with her chin. 'You're in Lyrebird.'

'I'm in Lyrebird,' said Jill. Whatever that means.

'Yep,' said the nurse. 'Lyrebird Unit. For the worried well. We just came through Platypus – that's for people suffering a psychotic mental illness. Up closer to the gatehouse you've got Kingfisher – D&A. Then we've got Rainbow Bridge right behind us – Palliative Care.'

Jill followed the nurse over the walkway, wheeling her bag. 'So, I'm the worried well?'

'Yeah. Look, Lyrebird is for people with depression or anxiety. Or both. We've had quite a few cops come stay with us. It's nice over here.'

The corridor led them into an open foyer. The floorboards beneath them extended straight out to a huge timber balcony. The balcony perched in the forest. The trees extended right up to the wooden railings, and colourful birds flitted from the branches to the two huge hanging birdfeeders suspended from the balcony's roof.

Along with some mismatched fabric armchairs and cushions, the birds were the only occupants of the spacious balcony.

'Wow,' said Jill, walking over to the railing. The forest floor below was only around a two-metre jump down, but the leafy ground dropped away sharply, leading into a deep tangle of inky greenness.

Now, at the window in her bedroom, Jill stared out into the forest. Scotty stood behind her. She leaned her head into his chest and closed her eyes to heighten the illusion. He trailed his hands lightly over her hair and she stiffened. Shh, he told her. It's okay. He smoothed his fingers over her forehead, smudged his thumbs across her eyes and out to her temples, her earlobes. No one had ever touched her like that. Scotty wrapped his huge arms around her chest, trapping her to him; his heart was beating against her spine.

'Um, are you okay?'

Jill spun towards the voice, flattening her back against the window.

'Hi. I mean, hang on a sec, I'll get you a tissue.' The young woman in the doorway moved over to the other bed in the room and grabbed a box from the nightstand. 'We go through a lot of these here,' she said. She moved towards Jill with the box.

Jill took a tissue.

'Hi, roomie,' the dark-haired girl said. 'I'm Layla. I've got bipolar disorder. I'm coming out of a manic phase right now, so if I talk your ears off you're gonna have to forgive me.' She turned her back on Jill and opened her top drawer. 'Raspberries or frogs?' she said, turning back with a bag of lollies in each hand.

Jill wiped her nose.

'You're right – chocolate, of course,' said Layla, dropping the lollies back in, and pulling from the drawer a family-sized block of Caramello.

'Quite a stash,' said Jill.

'I just stocked up – you're lucky,' said Layla, snapping off two rows of the chocolate and offering them to Jill.

'No, thanks,' Jill said.

'What's your name?' asked Layla, around a mouthful of chocolate.

'Jill.'

'What's wrong with you, then?'

'I'm the worried well.'

Layla laughed. 'It doesn't sound too bad, does it? You signed up for groups yet?'

'I don't like groups.'

Layla studied her with green eyes, her head askance. 'Well, you got no choice here. The groups are compulsory. Mornings and arvos, two hours each. And you gotta have one-to-one twice a week.'

'One-to-one?'

'Yeah, you know, see your counsellor.'

'What if I don't?' said Jill.

'Well, you'd hafta leave,' said Layla.

That's the most sensible thing I've heard all day.

'It's a voluntary hospital – you know that, don't you?' said Layla. 'Anyone can leave whenever they want, or they can make you leave whenever they want. They don't let any really high-risk patients stay here.'

'Yeah, I know.'

'Well, we gotta get you signed up into groups right now, Jill, on account of if you wait much longer, you're gonna get stuck in John Jamison's group.'

'And that would be bad?' asked Jill.

'John Jamison is the most boring motherfucker you ever had to listen to in your life, I swear to God,' said Layla. 'Only way you wanna go to one of his groups is if you got insomnia real bad and you got no Valium PRN.'

Jill glanced at her luggage bag near her bed.

'I'll help you unpack later,' said Layla, walking over to the door. 'Come on.'

'You see what I said, Jill?' said Layla, reaching up with a pen to the list pinned to the noticeboard. 'I just saved your arse from a fate worse than death. One spot left in Clarissa's group.'

'Who's Clarissa?'

'This witchy, hippy counsellor. She's pretty cool. You get to do a lot of meditation, tai chi and shit with her, and she don't go on and on about praying all the time, like John Jamison does. What's your last name?' Layla turned, pen still in hand. Her lime-green hoodie had ridden up, and a bellybutton ring dangling a smiley charm jiggled above her low-rider jeans. That wasn't the only thing jiggling above her jeans, Jill couldn't help but think. She mentally bitch-slapped herself.

'Jackson,' she said. 'Jill Jackson. Thanks, Layla.'

'Cool. Come on. There's still an hour before group – I'll show you around.'

Layla led Jill around the hospital grounds, chattering all the way, seemingly unconcerned that Jill barely spoke a word in return. Jill was surprised to find that the beautiful grounds, the constant babble of language from the girl next to her and the aimless dawdling was loosening the fist that had been squeezing her insides for the past few days. She tuned in and out of Layla's conversation. She learned that Layla had recently been transferred from the Platypus Unit. 'I thought I was the Virgin Mary when I got in here,' she'd said. 'Only problem with that is the virgin part, on account of when I'm manic, I'm randy as hell.' Also that she'd done a stint in Kingfisher too: 'Tell you what, Jill Jackson. You need extra meds, some pot or booze, you pay a visit to Kingfisher. Those rehab motherfuckers got so many stashes around the hospital grounds it's a wonder all the wildlife ain't poisoned.'

Layla told Jill that when she wasn't a resident here, she was an apprentice hairdresser, twenty-five years old, who lived with her parents. 'It's lucky they got me on their health-insurance plan,' she said. 'You ever been on a state-run psych ward, Jill? Damn! This hospital is paradise, I'm telling you, compared to a real psych unit.' Jill also learned who the 'cool' nurses and counsellors were, and who to avoid; who was doing whom at the moment amongst the inpatients and staff, and that she definitely had to stay away from 'Fast Fingers' Anthony.

'Now, Fast Fingers Anthony is gonna get up real close as soon as he sees you, Jill,' Layla said. 'What you gotta do is keep your back to the wall when you're in the same room as him, and if he approaches, you gotta tell him to step the fuck back. Either way, though, get used to the fact that you're gonna get goosed at some stage by Fast Fingers.'

'Goosed?' Jill said.

'Yeah, you know – he tries to get his fingers up your crack.'

Jill blinked. Fast Fingers would have some broken fingers if he got within a metre of her.

Jill followed Layla into the dining room. Jill guessed that whoever had designed this hospital had reasoned that a lot of light would be therapeutic. The dining hall was like an atrium – huge French windows and doors let in the garden views, and, from above, sunlight and blue sky shone through two room-length skylights. The designers may have been onto something, Jill thought. Depression felt like being in the deepest, darkest tunnel in the world, and to be constantly confronted by sunshine definitely seemed to counteract the illusion a smidge.

'You want a juice?' asked Layla.

Suddenly starving, Jill nodded, and Layla handed her

a glass from a gleaming stack next to four water and juice dispensers. She filled her glass with apple juice and grabbed an apple and a couple of packets of cellophane-sealed cream biscuits from bowls next to the juice.

'Eat on the way,' said Layla. 'We gotta get to group.'

28

Tuesday, 30 November, 10.50 am
Troy closed the door behind Delahunt and Elvis. He slid down the wall and sat on the floor in the hall with his knees up. What the fuck is going on?

He had no reason at all to trust the Fed, but he hadn't seen any other way to play it than what Delahunt had suggested, and he'd had no time to plan otherwise. When Delahunt told him he was suspect number one in two murders, he'd simultaneously wanted to laugh, vomit and kick someone's arse. But then Elvis had returned and he'd decided to play it out, to see where the questions went.

Elvis had clarified every point in his Incendie statement, unpacked each detail, asked for fuller perspectives on what he'd seen, heard and thought throughout the incident. A civilian would have thought that Elvis was just being thorough. But even without Delahunt's heads-up, Troy knew that Elvis was trying to set him up in a lie. He knew that when a perp bullshitted about a crime scene, he'd get deeper and deeper into his fabrications until eventually the inconsistencies began to show. The more lies you tell, the harder it is to remember all the shit you've spun. In subsequent interviews, the questioner would twist small, incidental parts of what you'd said and selectively feed it back to you as though they were the facts. Troy had seen guilty suspects get so confused going over and over the bullshit that they'd have sworn day was night and that they walked with their arsehole pointing at the ceiling. Eventually, they'd blurt out a confession just to stop the brain pain.

So did this fat fuck really think he'd done it? Or was this all the federal agent's game plan? An elaborate good cop/bad cop routine, to make him think he had a friend on the inside? He'd never heard of a fellow officer deliberately sabotaging another's case, aligning himself with a suspect. How could he trust this Delahunt fucker? Maybe they didn't have enough evidence to execute a search warrant and Delahunt was trying to rattle him, scare him enough to do something stupid – maybe to try to dump evidence.

If that was the case, they'd have a tail on him at all times. Fuck, even if Delahunt was playing it straight, they'd still be watching him.

Troy leaned his head back against the wall. Why the hell did they think he would be capable of killing a cop? Or an old woman, for that matter? It was just fucking ridiculous. But when Delahunt had laid out the bullshit profile, Troy realised he'd have suspected himself if he'd woken up with amnesia for memories of the past week.

But he remembered everything.

And he knew that he was in this shit because he'd been too close to Miriam Caine. Troy was starting to believe that being too close to a Caine was bad for your health.

He crossed his legs and thought carefully. Took it back to the beginning. Most murders are crimes of passion, committed by someone who knows the vic. Troy had no idea why Caine might have done it, and no inkling of how, but he was really starting to believe that the man had murdered his mother.

And if he'd murdered his mother, then maybe he'd murdered his wife too.

If the cops were going to waste their time looking up Troy's arse, then he was going to try to find out some more about David Caine.

29

Tuesday, 30 November, 11 am
There had to be twenty people in the group room. Jill checked for the exits first, then did a quick headcount. Eighteen, including her and Layla. Too many people. The fist in her belly squeezed tighter.

A wild-haired woman in multicoloured tights and a tie-dyed, oversized T-shirt stood in front of the whiteboard at the head of the large room. The room appeared to be some type of gymnasium, but there was no equipment around.

'We got a couple of minutes,' Layla whispered. 'I'll give you a run-down on who's here.'

'Clarissa, the counsellor,' Jill interrupted, pointing with her chin to the woman by the whiteboard. 'Fast Fingers Anthony,' she said, nodding backwards at the man who'd just walked in the door behind them.

'Right and right – how'd you know?' asked Layla.

'Fuck off,' Jill said loudly to the balding new entrant to the room. He stopped midstride on his way over to introduce himself.

Layla laughed. 'You heard the girl, Anthony. Get.'

Jill dropped into the seat nearest the door at the back, next to a heavy-set woman in sunglasses and a zipped-up khaki bomber jacket. She had to be boiling.

'Nah, Jill, we sit over there,' said Layla, putting a hand onto Jill's arm. Although Jill made no perceptible movement or sound, Layla pulled her hand back quickly. 'Or we can sit here,' she said.

With a fifteen-minute break halfway through, Jill and Layla spent the next two hours learning about the 'Seven Deadly Sins of Thinking': Catastrophising – making mountains out of molehills; Selective Attention – only noticing things that fit your negative view of the world, and ignoring anything that didn't; Black and White Thinking – everything had to be one hundred per cent perfect or it was a total failure; Personalising – feeling that everything bad that happened had to have something to do with you; Fortune-Telling – imagining the worst possible outcome in a situation, even when you had no idea what would happen; Hindsight Bias – judging yourself negatively for past behaviour based upon knowledge that you have now but didn't have then; and Should-ing – constantly berating yourself for not doing enough, and ceaselessly telling yourself you *should* do more. Jill reckoned that every one of these 'flaws' of thinking had kept her alive in her job for the past decade. But she also recognised that they kept her miserable as well.

Better miserable than dead? Sometimes she wondered.

After the group, Layla didn't wait with her for the queue to die down in the lunchroom, but Jill made her way over to Layla's table when she'd selected her meal. It was hard not to – Layla was waving and calling loud enough to be heard back on the ward.

'Oh my God, Jill, you took *forever*!' said Layla. 'I'm going to have to teach you the way things work around here. Look, everyone in Lyrebird's gone back already. They're gonna get the best chairs on the veranda. Good thing I wanted some more of that apple crumble, or I'd have left you here to eat with the Kingfishers, and they're some noisy fuckers.'

The warm fish and salad was actually pretty great. Jill had started on her apple crumble before she remembered that Scotty had once told her it was one of his favourites. She pushed the plate away.

Layla cocked an eyebrow. 'Now, that's just wasteful, that is,' she said, and swapped Jill's spoon with her own. She waded in.

Back on the unit, Jill told Layla that she wanted to unpack and lie down for a while.

'Don't you want to come out on the veranda to meet everyone first?' asked her roommate.

Actually, I'd rather stick a fork in my eye. 'Later, Layla. I don't feel like it right now.'

Curled on her bed, Jill reasoned that the hardest thing she was going to have to get used to in here was the lack of a bedroom door.

'All psych units are like that, Jill,' the nurse had told her that morning.

'But where am I supposed to get changed?'

The nurse had walked over to the handle-free door at the side of the room and pushed it open. 'Bathroom.'

'If someone was going to off themselves behind closed

doors, they could just do it in there then,' Jill grumbled.

'You gonna off yourself, Jill?' the nurse had wanted to know.

'No.' Exactly what Jill would do after a couple of days with no sleep in here, she couldn't determine. No way she'd be able to go to sleep without a door. She pictured the specially constructed metal front door – with multiple locks – in her flat in Maroubra.

'There are no doors because we nurses have to do the rounds five times a night – to check you guys are okay,' the nurse continued. It sounded as though she'd given this explanation a couple of dozen times. 'Opening and closing doors all night wakes everyone up.'

Birdsong as perfect as any new-age CD fluted in from the open window behind her, along with soft green light and fresh air. Jill uncurled her knees and rolled over onto her back, her eyes on the ceiling. Scotty smiled down at her. When the tears had made the back of her hair wet, she got up off the bed and started to unpack.

The tension in her stomach was back, as full-force as ever. She had to get rid of some of this adrenaline. She'd take a run as soon as she put her stuff away.

Layla appeared in the doorway.

'Hey, I'll give you a hand,' she said.

'That's okay, I got it,' said Jill, voice thick.

'No, you don't get it. I want to see all your shit.' Layla sat down at the base of Jill's bed and peered up under the sheet of hair hiding Jill's face.

'Hey. You need some more chocolate, Jill Jackson,' Layla said, jumping up from the bed and dashing across the room. 'Goddamn it!'

'What?' said Jill.

'Someone's been in my lollies again!'

'It wasn't me.'

'I know,' said Layla, her arse in the air as she rummaged through her drawer. 'It's that fucking Justin Cuthbert. Every time some of my stash goes missing, I see him eating lollies. Fucker's even offered me some.'

Jill tucked her ironed T-shirts into her bottom drawer. 'So, if you know he's taking them,' she said, 'why don't you just tell him off? Tell him you'll report him for stealing if he does it again?'

'Because every time they go missing, the bastard's been accounted for. He's been in group with me, or on the veranda.'

'So it can't be him, then,' said Jill.

'That's right,' said Layla. 'Except it is.'

Jill shook her head. 'I've got to get out of here,' she said.

'What do you mean?' Layla snapped her head around.

'I mean, I've got to go for a run.'

'Now that is something I'll never understand,' said Layla, reclining back on her bed, one arm behind her head. 'Why in hell someone would want to go for a run. Best day of my life was when I left school and realised I'd never have to do a cross-country again.'

'Yeah, well, it's how I stop myself completely going mad,' said Jill, and then realised what she'd said. 'Sorry.'

'It's okay. You use running, I use Lithium.'

Jill smiled.

'You're out of luck though, Jill,' said Layla. 'It's why I came back in the first place. I forgot to tell you – you got a one-to-one with Sam Barnard.'

'Look, no offence, Sam,' said Jill sitting in a big green armchair opposite the young man in a matching chair.

'It's just that me and counselling don't work so well.'

'Have you had some bad experiences?' asked the psychologist.

Jill studied him, wondering how to answer. Well, we could start with the ten or so therapists I saw to try to get me to stop carving my thighs up as a kid, she thought. Or maybe we could talk about Mercy Mellas, probably the best counsellor I've ever seen, who also turned out to be a serial killer of paedophiles. Or maybe my last psych – paid for by the service, but only there to ensure she was covering her own arse. Jill sighed and decided he didn't need to hear all that. He looked about four years younger than her, and his hairline was already working its way backwards fast.

'Look, I just need to run right now,' she said.

'We all feel like that sometimes, Jill,' he said. 'Especially in times of pain, but it's important to stay with the pain. To work through it.'

'No, Sam,' she said, the vice of tension working its way up her spine. A spasm in her shoulder felt like it was pulling her head down to her neck. 'I mean I need to go for a *run*.' She made a walking motion in the air with two fingers.

'Oh,' said the counsellor, blushing. 'I understand. It's just that it would be better if you could do that afterwards, because we're scheduled to talk right now. You haven't been properly admitted until we've had our first meeting. I need to make sure you're –'

'I'm not suicidal,' she said. And if I was I wouldn't tell you.

'Well that's one part of it, but –'

'Look, you don't get it,' said Jill, the adrenaline making her stand. 'When I feel like this I've got to do something physical. Running is how I cope when I feel this way.'

'There are other methods you can learn.'

Her voice completely flat now, Jill said, 'Have you read my file?'

'Yes.'

'So, you know about what happened to me when I was a kid? Did they write in there what they did to me?'

'Yes. I'm sorry. It was terrible –'

'Yes, it was terrible,' she said. 'And most people would be completely fucked after living through that. I'm only partially fucked. I have been all the way there, but I got myself back again on my own. The way I keep my shit together when I feel out of control is to run. I don't do out of control. So we can talk later.' She moved to the door, 'Or not. You can do what you gotta do.'

'Well, can I at least run with you?' he asked.

Jill flicked a glance up from his shoes to his eyes. 'You can try,' she said.

30

Tuesday, 30 November, 3 pm
To give him credit, the counsellor did keep up for the first lap, and she figured that was a good three kilometres. When they got to the gatehouse he gave her a hopeful look – *Is that it?* Jill grinned and put on an extra burst. Sam Barnard dropped to the grass and gave her a salute. When she looped the gatehouse the third time, he was gone.

Now, her face angled into the shower spray, Jill wondered how she was going to get through a week here. She was furious with Gabriel. He'd called today, as promised. She was stunned when a nurse had told her he was on the line and had transferred it through. She hadn't been expecting the call until tonight. But he was maddeningly scant on details of the case. He promised her he would tell her more as soon as he knew, but she didn't feel she could trust him to do that. She knew that he believed that she'd be better off concentrating on grieving and recovery. She should never have agreed to come here. Still, Gabriel had promised he'd know more tomorrow. She told him he'd better, or she'd come back and find it out for herself.

Towelling her hair, Jill wondered whether she should contact Scotty's mum and sister. She couldn't imagine how hard it would be to make that call, but seeing them for the first time at the funeral would be even worse. It was scheduled for the day she was supposed to be back in Sydney. *How am I going to get through that?* Whether she lasted here or bailed early, she had a week to figure that one out.

Jill was grateful that the ward had been deserted when she'd come back from her run. One-to-one sessions took precedence over groups, so she'd also missed the afternoon session. She pulled on a pair of yoga kick pants and a long-sleeved tee and left the bedroom. She stopped at the communal ward kitchen, a small but well-equipped coffee-making hub, and made herself a green tea. She took it out to the balcony.

She selected a chair she'd seen vacant earlier. That'd reduce the chances of being caught up in some chair turf war when the others got back. She figured she couldn't avoid them the whole week if she was going to stay. She sighed. It had been easier to speak to people over the past year than any time since she was a child. Working with Gabriel and the taskforce to catch Cutter and Co., going undercover and surviving by making social connections, interacting with other cops at the college – it had all helped with the dreaded communication thing. But with Scotty, Jill had really begun to thaw, to trust, to be able to say things that she didn't even know she was feeling.

He'd been like a bridge for her – a bridge from a frozen wasteland towards a warm, sunny world.

And now the bridge was gone. It felt like she'd come too far across to get back again, but Jill had no idea how she was going to move any further forward. She pulled her legs up onto the chair and rested her chin on her knees.

A brilliant red-feathered bird cracked seeds on the balcony railing, watching her, spitting his seed casings over the edge. She could see she was the entertainment while he ate his snack.

Voices, footsteps and laughter signalled their approach. Jill stood. Sat down again. Leaned back in the chair. Perched on the edge. The bird watched her, head askance, spat seeds.

The first to arrive was a surprise. A barrel-bellied golden Labrador ambled across the floorboards straight to her feet. She plonked her broad backside by Jill's chair and stuck her blonde muzzle into Jill's waiting hand. The dog smiled, her pink tongue lolling.

'Yuck, dog germs,' Jill told her.

The dog yawned cavernously, then stretched her paws forward and dropped her chest, deadweight, onto Jill's feet. She patted her back.

'I see you've met Fatso.' A grey-bearded man took the seat next to Jill. He reached out a sandshoe and scratched at a spot near the dog's tail.

'Good name for her,' said Jill. 'I could use her back as a coffee table.'

Jill recognised Layla's laugh behind her. 'A coffee table! You could seat a family of four down to dinner around that body, baby.'

Jill smiled tightly. Seven other people dropped into chairs around the veranda.

'All right, who reckons they can get everyone's name right first go?' asked Layla. 'We gotta introduce everyone to Jill, here. I'd give it a go but I'll fuck it up. I've only been over here a couple of days. Lollies for the person who can name everyone.'

'I'll give it a go,' said a skinny blond-haired man with a goatee and a baseball cap. Jill guessed him for around twenty-five.

'Seems to me you've always got plenty of your own lollies, Justin,' said Layla. 'Or someone's lollies, anyway.'

The guy grinned. 'That's Kaitlin, Camilla, Brian, Doug, Lynne, and, um, June, isn't it? And you're Jill?' asked Justin.

Jill nodded.

'And I'm Justin, and that there's the lovely Layla.'

'You forgot the dog,' said Layla, sullen.

'She's met the dog,' said Justin, grinning. He held out a hand. 'Got any jelly babies?'

'Don't worry about those two, Jill,' said the bearded man next to her, Doug. 'They're always fighting. We all think they love each other.'

'Fat chance!' said Layla.

'Speaking of fat, I have to get this dog off my feet,' said Jill. 'She weighs a tonne.'

'She's so spoiled,' said Camilla, who looked to be a well-preserved forty-five, or a downhill-fast thirty-five.

'We're not supposed to feed her,' said Lynne. She's gotta be fifty, thought Jill. Ouch, those fingernails have to hurt. What was left of Lynne's nails was surrounded by chewed, shredded skin. A couple of fingers looked to have nothing left but bloodied cavities. Jill looked away.

'That dog is not supposed to be on the unit, you know,' said June, the woman with the bomber jacket and sunglasses from group this morning; the outfit was still intact.

'She used to belong to Billy Broken Back on Platypus,' said Layla.

'Don't call him that,' said June.

'He was in a wheelchair,' explained Camilla.

'Poor Billy spent more time in this hospital than out of it,' said Doug. 'They couldn't get his meds right. He was always talking to himself.'

'He talked to others too, if you ever listened,' said June.

'And he loved Fatso,' said Layla. 'Everyone got to know her over the years on account of Billy Bro– on account of him getting worse if they didn't let her come and stay with him when he was admitted.'

'And then when he went over the Rainbow –' began Camilla.

'That means when he died,' said Layla. 'The hospital just kept Fatso. Billy didn't have anyone else out there.'

'Except she's not supposed to be on the wards,' said June.

Fatso yawned again and rolled onto her back.

31

Tuesday, 30 November, 3.15 pm
When they pulled up in front of David Caine's home, Emma Gibson reached under the seat for her handbag.

'What do you need that for?' said Eddie Calabrese, cracking his door. 'I've got the recording equipment. You only need your notepad.'

'Ah, thank you, Elvis,' she said, unclipping the bag. 'I can figure out what I need to bring. Can you just give me a sec?' She rummaged through the bag until she found the flat package she was looking for – paracetamol. She'd taken two every four hours since she'd woken with the alarm and a bitch of a hangover. She swallowed these two a little early with a swig from her water bottle.

Emma rarely drank alcohol – well, maybe a glass of champagne on her birthday – and she never drank alone. She didn't like the taste at all. Over the years, many dates had insisted she try a glass of the triple-digit bottle they'd bought, trying to impress her. It was all she could do to not grimace with her smile over the rim. And she was certain that if her girlfriends were being honest, they'd list 'most reliable designated driver' as their favourite quality of Emma's.

But last night the pressure of the investigation had left her completely unable to unwind. As the team had further unpacked the full horror of what had happened to Scotty, she'd developed an unrelenting pain in her stomach. She figured it was all of the unshed tears, as she'd been unable to cry for Scotty since Jackson had broken down at the briefing. The power of Jill's distress had seemed to blast her own deep inside her somewhere, leaving just the ache in her gut, which last night had left her moaning and rocking on the couch.

Knowing she had to do something to relieve the tension, she'd tried Pilates and tai chi, and then back-to-back reruns of *Gossip Girl*. Nothing helped. At eleven-fifteen, standing on a footstool in front of her pantry, she'd searched every corner for a leftover chocolate bar or sweet of any description. Three times she'd pushed aside the almost full bottle of brandy she had bought to make a Christmas cake last year. On the fourth sweep, she held on to it, pulled it down and, standing there, took a deep swig from the bottle.

It was the most hideous thing she'd ever tasted in her life. Swearing, she recapped it and pushed it right to the very back of the cupboard. Ugh!

Five minutes later, she dragged the footstool back to the pantry. For the first time in three days, the knot in her stomach was gone. She drank her first-ever glass of brandy in big gulps, holding her nose and shuddering after every taste.

And now here she was, experiencing the after-effects of finishing half the bottle, partnered with freaken Elvis, something she'd managed to avoid since becoming a detective at Maroubra.

'I don't know why Delahunt didn't come here himself,' she said, eyeing the recording equipment Elvis had brought for the interview. *Why couldn't I be partnered with Gabriel instead of this lug?*

'He's with crime scene. I already told you. Andreessen reckons he's a bit of a buff with forensics. All we got is all this camera equipment. I hope you were listening when Delahunt went through how he wanted this shit set up, because I certainly wasn't. Fucking Feds – they all think they're James Bond. Can we get in there now? I want to get this over with, so I can get back to looking into that Berrigan rat-fuck.'

Emma pushed her bag back under the seat, then got out of the car. All the way here, Elvis had been listing every reason he thought Troy Berrigan had killed the Caine woman and Scotty. It made no sense to Emma – mainly because she couldn't wrap her mind around anyone wanting to do things like this. She'd been involved in a few murder investigations, and the motives then had made sense. Revenge, sex and greed. What had happened here didn't seem to fit any motive. She'd known Scotty for years, and she could see no connection between him and the Caine woman. And there was no way she could see that anyone could profit from killing a cop and an old lady. It seemed the only motive left here was thrill-killing, and she just couldn't make her mind understand what sort of a person could get a kick out of this.

The more Emma thought about it, the crazier it seemed to jump to the conclusion that the murders were even related. If you left the two unconnected, it still would leave the Big Three motives as possibilities for both killings. Like revenge: someone may have had a long-held reason to kill Miriam Caine. What was in her past or in her family that could have led to this? And as to Scotty – well, all cops knew they had a target on their back, whether from a specific squirrel they'd locked up, or just some demented psychopath with an itch to slaughter a pig.

But Delahunt reckoned preliminary evidence had connected the scenes, so Emma was looking forward to that briefing tomorrow morning. Confirmation that they were looking for the one killer would eliminate eighty per cent of her suspect hypotheses. But the ones she'd be left with were baffling to her.

Emma shook her head and followed Elvis through the low gate that separated David Caine's sparse garden from the street.

After setting up the recording equipment according to Delahunt's specifications, Emma allowed Elvis to conduct the interview. The few questions she initially tried to put in were either cut off or not followed up by Calabrese. Besides, she found that she was gaining more by watching the interaction.

When Emma had been part of Caine's first interview with Scotty and Jill, she had agreed with Scotty that he did not seem to react as she would have expected the day after his mother was set alight. But she'd seen all kinds of weird reactions by loved ones following deaths. Still, it appeared that Miriam Caine had been murdered, so she and Scotty had dug deeper into Caine's past to rule him in or out. Only one feature of his life had blipped on the radar – the electrocution of his wife in the bath. She and Scotty had pulled the records. Caine had been looked at hard over that, but the death was ruled accidental, with their child as a witness and nothing to suggest Caine had been involved. Since then, he'd raised his kid and lived with his mother in four different states. Paid taxes every year. He'd had steady work with a national cleaning company that had allowed him to transfer to different working-class suburbs; he'd been in this one for the past two years.

Elvis took Caine through his Incendie statement again, and Emma thought that the man again seemed pretty relaxed about the whole thing. She couldn't pick up any great anxiety or frustration. Emotionally, he seemed kind of . . . blank.

When they reached the end of the statement, Elvis closed his notepad and leaned back against the kitchen chair; he quickly sat forward again when it groaned. Emma took the opportunity to jump in.

'Mr Caine, can you tell us where you were last Saturday at eleven am?' she asked.

He turned to face her. 'The day Detective Hutchinson was killed? I've been meaning to say to you that I'm very sorry that happened. He seemed like a good bloke.'

'Thank you,' said Emma. She swallowed. 'He was.'

'Well, I'll tell you where I was,' said Caine, 'but I'm not sure why you want to know. I was here.'

'Was anyone here with you? Do you have any way of proving that you were here?'

'Why the hell would I have to do that?' said Caine, showing the first sign of elevated emotion she'd seen from him all afternoon. His face flushed, his breathing quickened and he spoke loudly, his hands flat on his kitchen table.

'Hey, take it easy, Mr Caine,' said Elvis. 'We think there might be some connection between the death of your mother and the death of our colleague.'

'That's impossible,' said Caine.

'What makes you say that, Mr Caine?' asked Emma.

'Look, I'm not convinced you people know what you're doing, to be frank. I can't see why the death of a cop and the death of my mother would be related in any way. What connection did you find?'

'There was –' began Elvis.

'I'm afraid we don't have all the evidence together just yet,' said Emma.

'Well, what have you got that makes you think there's some kind of link?'

'We're not at liberty to discuss that,' said Emma quickly. 'We do, however, still need to know where you were on Saturday. This is a standard procedure when there's a possible link between crimes.'

'Well, like I said,' said Caine, standing. 'I was right here, with my daughter. You can ask her.'

'We will. Thank you,' said Emma.

'And you can also ask that restaurant manager, Troy Berrigan. He was here too. We were sitting right here at this table, half the day.'

Emma whipped her eyes to Elvis, who sat grey-faced and open-mouthed. Berrigan was here on Saturday?

Their two main suspects had just alibied one another.

32

Tuesday, 30 November, 11.50 pm
'You'll get used to it,' said Layla quietly, as Jill rolled over in bed when footsteps sounded again in the corridor.

Jill punched her pillow into some kind of shape that might work. 'Sorry,' she said. 'Did I wake you up?'

'Nah. Still coming down off the mania. That shit don't let you sleep. I've done three days straight in the past.'

Yeah, I feel ya, thought Jill.

'How many times have you been admitted, Layla?' said Jill. She rolled onto her side, tucking the light blanket under her chin.

'Eighteen.'

'Oh my God. I mean, sorry.'

'Yeah. It's pretty shitty. I mean I like it here, but I'm not like Lynne and Camilla. Fuck knows how many admissions they've had. No sooner they're out than they're threatening suicide to get back in. The place can become addictive, I guess.'

'So, is it mania each time you're admitted?' asked Jill.

Layla propped herself onto an elbow and leant over to her drawer. When she opened it she sighed hard. 'Fucken thief.'

'Again?' said Jill.

Layla nodded in the deep blue light, a sardonic smile on her face.

'But that had to have happened when we were at dinner,' said Jill.

'Uh huh,' said Layla.

'Well, everyone from Lyrebird was there, so it has to be someone from another ward,' said Jill.

'It was him,' said Layla.

Jill figured that the mania must come with paranoia for poor Layla.

'It's not always the mania,' said Layla.

'Huh?'

'That I get admitted for. Sometimes I get psychotic with it, like last time. A coupla times it's been depression. But mostly it's the mania.'

'What happens?' asked Jill. 'I mean – don't tell me if you don't want to. Um, sorry.'

'It's sweet. I don't mind,' said Layla. She bit the head off a jelly snake, grabbed a handful from the packet and lobbed the rest of the bag to Jill. Strings of coloured jelly flew from the bag onto Jill's bed. She gathered them up, then bit into a red snake.

'I stop going to TAFE and start spending money all over the place,' said Layla. 'I can't sleep, and I get these crazy ideas, which seem really smart at the time. Sometimes I go out and score speed, and then the shit really hits the fan. I have sex with just about anyone who feels like it. Usually I don't come home for a couple of days, and Mum and Dad start looking for me. They found me in our local supermarket carpark this time. It was three in the morning and I was giving the stray cats a sermon about Jesus Christ our saviour.' She laughed. 'Fucked up, hey?'

Jill didn't know what to say. 'So you're studying hairdressing, right?' she tried. Lame, Jill.

'Yeah, for ten years!' Layla laughed. 'The people at college have been cool, though. Each time I drop out, they let me back in. One of my teachers resigned, though, when I stripped naked in her class, and they still wouldn't kick me out.'

Layla was on her stomach now, her head down the end of her bed, closest to Jill's. Her knees bent, she kicked her feet behind her in the air. 'Hey!' she said. 'You want me to do your hair?'

'What? No. What?'

'You know, cut it. I'm really good.'

'I have a thing about people standing behind me with scissors, Layla. I've been going to the same hairdresser since I was fifteen.'

'Whoa. She must be an old bat by now.'

'Thank you very much.'

Layla laughed. 'Oh fuck, sorry, I didn't mean it like that. How old are you anyway?'

'Thirty-four.'

'And why are you here?'

Jill sat up, pressed her back into the headboard, her knees into her chest. 'I'm a cop.'

'Well, shit, I knew *that*. I come from a great family, but I grew up in a pretty rough place. You get to be able to spot police.'

'So, it's really that obvious, even here?'

'I don't know – I could have said army, maybe. You're pretty uptight.'

'Yeah. Well, I'm here because my partner just got killed.'

'Your partner or your *partner*?'

'Both.'

'Damn. That's fucked.'

'Fucked.'

'How did he die?'

Ohgodohgodohgod. 'Um, burned to death.'

'Oh, fuck! I saw that on the news. Someone killed him. Set him on fire!'

'I really don't think I can –'

'Why aren't you out there looking for who did it? Oh, sorry – Jill! Wait!'

Jill took the first exit available. Before Layla had even made it out of their room, she'd climbed the railing and dropped from the edge of the veranda. One bare foot caught something hard underneath the leaf matter and Jill stifled a shout. With no other thought than to get away from the image of Scotty melting, she bolted into the forest.

33

Wednesday, 1 December, 12.03 am
The forest floor dropped sharply away from the hospital unit. With her foot throbbing, Jill half-fell, half-ran down the incline, grasping at bush branches as she tumbled, trying to slow her pace. The darkness was as complete as anything she'd ever experienced. Blind. Again. Her chest heaving, eyes wide, trying to see something, anything, she tumbled down the steep slope.

Jill sat up.

Vomited.

Put her hand to her head in the dark.

Lay down again.

What's going on?

She began to whimper, remembering. She must have slammed into a tree, knocked herself out.

'Why is my life such a fucking mess?'

She curled up in leaves and dirt and sobbed.

Shivering, Jill prepared to climb back up the hill. She would much have preferred to have spent the night down here, waited until light, then found a way through the forest, around the hospital and out to the main road. She seriously considered it. Two points changed her mind. Number one, the nurses in Lyrebird would soon be getting other staff involved in trying to find her and, when they couldn't, they'd call in the cops; her family would be informed she was missing; their cops would call her cops, and fucking forget it. Number two, even if she managed to make it to the road without anyone spotting her, what kind of freak motorist would stop to pick up a woman in pyjamas hitchhiking out the front of a psychiatric hospital?

Nope, she had to get back up there soon, and face all those people, feeling like a complete dickhead. Like a psych patient, for God's sake.

Wet and cold, her foot and head throbbing, she scrambled back up the stupid hill.

34

Wednesday, 1 December, 10.10 am
Troy stared at the ringing phone. What new misery would this bring? The possibilities ran through his head. Would it be the cops calling to tell him Chris was locked up again? After not coming home last night, Christopher had finally called to say he was staying at Makayla's. Telling Chris that was not okay had made no difference.

Or would this be Elvis, asking him to come in for another interview? Troy knew the cops' strategy would be to now ramp up the pressure.

Maybe it would be his mother, phoning for money. She always chose the most fucked time possible to call.

Troy picked up the phone.

'Troy, my boy!'

Caesar O'Brien. His boss.

'Hail, Caesar,' said Troy.

'Guess where I am?' asked Caesar.

'The White House?' said Troy.

Caesar laughed. 'The restaurant, you idiot. They've packed up their shit.'

'Really? When are we opening?'

'Friday night, but I'm going to need you in here tomorrow, to sort shit out.'

Troy sighed, thinking about everything going on right now. 'Wouldn't that be great.'

'What?'

'To sort shit out.'

'Yeah, well, that's your job, Troy, my boy. I want the kitchen cleaned, rosters drawn up, arses on seats for the weekend. You'll have to call everyone on the reservations list, make sure they're still coming. No one will know for sure whether we're open or not,' said Caesar. 'You get any drop-outs or doubtfuls, you call people from the list from the night of the fire. Offer them their on-the-house meal. Mrs Caine is costing me a fucking fortune,' he said. And I hope she's not going to cost me a hell of a lot more than that.

After ending the call with Caesar, Troy wondered what to do next. Last night's conversation with Lucy hadn't gone down too well. He'd decided that he didn't want her studying with Mona Caine at her house, and he'd asked Lucy if she was thinking of working with Mona again. When she'd said they had plans for this afternoon, he'd asked her to study here instead. Lucy had become all super-snoop immediately; flustered, Troy could think of nothing to say to explain his request. He didn't know what to tell her about her friend's father – there was nothing concrete he could really say. And he didn't want to tell her the rest of the whole hideous story. Lucy was an expert at wheedling things out of him. And despite the fact that she was more sensible than any woman his own age, she was still only fifteen, and he couldn't tell her that he was suspected of two murders.

How ridiculous. He had the same thought every time he considered Elvis's suspicions.

'No – tell me, Troy, why don't you want me to go there?' Lucy had demanded last night.

'I just think her father's a bit weird, that's all,' said Troy. 'I'd feel better if you were here.'

'Well, if that's it, you don't have to worry,' she'd said. 'Mona's father works nights. Yesterday he'd left by the time I got there.'

'Okay, cool, then,' said Troy. That would have to do for now, until he thought of a better explanation to keep her away from Caine. 'Do you know what he does?'

'Contract cleaning. He cleans office buildings,' said Lucy.

'How do you always know this stuff?' he'd asked.

'It's a social thing,' said Lucy. 'When you speak to people, you ask them things about their lives and you tell them things about yours. It results in the formation of a thing called friendship. You really should read up on the concept.'

'You don't need any more school,' Troy had replied. 'You're too much of a smartarse already.'

Now, in the kitchen by the phone, Troy considered that he might take Lucy around to Mona's today, after all.

35

Wednesday, 1 December, 10.45 am
'You're going to be late for group.' Sam Barnard stood at the foot of Jill's bed.

'What? I'm not going today.' She put her pillow over her head. 'Everything hurts, and I only just got to bed.' She spoke through the pillow.

'Do you really think I could hear any of that?' said Sam.

Jill removed the pillow. 'I said, everything hurts and I only got to bed an hour ago.'

'I know,' he said. 'I heard you the first time.'

Jill threw the pillow at him.

'You have to go to group,' he said. 'We've only got you for a week, and you obviously need to get something out of being here. Besides, it's the rules.'

'Well, get out, then, so I can get dressed.'

With an eyebrow, Sam gave her a you-don't-have-to-be-rude look.

'Please,' said Jill.

'See you at two,' he said. 'My office. You'll be skipping the afternoon groups all week. I've cleared an hour for you each day.'

Jill groaned.

With still an hour before she had to see Sam, Jill sat alone on the veranda. No point going to her room now – she'd only fall asleep. The other Lyrebirds were fixing after-lunch coffee and tea. She'd already noticed that people in here drank as many hot beverages as they did in gaols.

She stretched. She was glad she'd gone to the group this morning. It had been pretty great, actually, which was a big surprise. Progressive muscular relaxation, they called it – PMR. Years ago, Jill had tried meditation, but as soon as she'd started to let go of her tension a feeling of terror would strangle her and she'd have a full flashback. Twelve years old, blindfolded in the basement, her vagina in agony from the last rape, the smell of her nipples being burned. The meditation teacher had called an ambulance.

So, she'd not been exactly thrilled when she entered the gym and had seen the three words on the whiteboard. She just figured she'd fake it. Hell, maybe she could even get some sleep. But Clarissa had asked them to focus, not to let go. The aim was to concentrate on each muscle group, tensing it, noticing what the tension felt like, and then releasing the tension, feeling it leave, noticing the sensations in as focused a way as possible. Jill was good at focusing minutely. And at instructions. She'd tried it. It was fucking great.

They were supposed to practise. So, now, she squeezed her left hand into a fist, remembering Clarissa's instructions. She stopped when Justin walked onto the veranda, a bottle of water in his hand, and took the seat next to her. Fatso suddenly skidded around a corner in the hall behind them, lolloped across the deck and barrelled straight into Justin.

'Oof,' he said. 'Good girl, good girl.' He rubbed at her nuzzle.

'She really loves you, doesn't she?' said Jill, giving the big dog a scratch.

'All dogs do,' he said. 'I've got three at home. Sometimes they're the only reason I keep going.'

'Well, all I can say is that I'm glad it was you rather than me she ran into just then. I couldn't take another beating today.'

'You do look like you got bashed, you know,' he said. 'You sure you didn't have a bitch-fight with Layla and made up the whole story about your run through the forest?'

'She'd look a whole lot more fucked up if that were the case, smartarse.' Layla had arrived.

Justin laughed. Jill smiled. You have no idea, roomie, she thought.

Layla held a backpack. She dropped it onto her favourite chair. 'Don't let anyone sit there, Jill,' she said. 'I'm just going to grab a coffee.'

Camilla, June, Doug and Lynne arrived together and found their seats. June still had the sunnies in place; she hadn't even taken them off during PMR.

'You feeling any better, Jill?' asked Camilla, lighting a cigarette. 'That's a horrible scratch on your forehead.'

'I don't know how you didn't break your neck, jumping off here like that,' said Lynne, nodding at the railing. 'Look how high it is.'

'Lots of people have done it,' said Camilla. 'This used to be the Kingfisher Unit, but they were making so many trips out to the bushes every day to get their stashes of booze that they swapped units.'

'No shit?' said Justin.

'Why did you jump?' said Lynne.

Jill's pulse began to beat loudly in her ears. *I cannot discuss Scotty with these people.* 'Ah –' she said.

Layla walked over to her seat and put down her coffee cup. 'You want to do it now, Jill?' she interrupted.

'Do what?' asked Jill.

'Your haircut.'

'Um, no. I said no last night.'

'Yeah, but you weren't thinking straight then,' she said. 'Well, obviously. Besides,' Layla dragged an upright chair over to the edge of the veranda, 'I told you all about my sad story and how hard I've had to fight to become a good hairdresser. You're not going to reject me now, are you? That could devastate me.' She picked up the backpack and dropped it next to the chair. Justin laughed. 'Come over here, Jill,' said Layla. 'A haircut will make you feel better.'

'She really is good,' said Camilla, blowing smoke with the wind, away from the group. She seemed practised at the gesture.

'Actually, she's great,' said Lynne. 'Half the nurses come around here to get their hair done when Layla's admitted. Remember that nurse, Deanne Reynolds, Camilla? She came here the morning of her wedding. Got her hair done and all of her bridesmaids'.

Justin watched the conversation with a smile, his eyes dancing under his ball cap.

Layla had dragged a coffee table next to her chair, and on it she unpacked a towel, a comb, spray-bottle and three pairs of scissors.

Jill watched her in horror.

'Do it,' said June, lifting her sunglasses to look Jill in the eye.

'You've gotta be fucking kidding me,' said Jill, standing and making her way over to the chair.

Fatso barked.

'Wow. You look different,' said Sam Barnard, closing the door to his office behind Jill.

'Yeah, I guess,' said Jill, dropping into the green chair. That was an understatement. She'd often asked herself why she even bothered to visit her hairdresser every couple of months. For twenty years she'd been wearing her blonde hair just past shoulder length, but almost always pulled back in a ponytail. That wouldn't be happening for a while.

The Lyrebirds had kept up a constant banter while Layla snipped away behind her. At first she'd used PMR to try to forget about what was happening, but she soon found herself laughing and listening to the others. And when Lynne had asked Justin why he was first admitted to the hospital, she waited keenly for what he would say. It seemed remarkable that so many people here could tell their stories so easily, and even more remarkable that others would come straight out and ask them about it. But it was obvious that Justin hadn't told his story before. The conversation faltered; the snipping stopped.

Justin's cap hid his eyes. He continued to nuzzle Fatso's belly with his foot.

'Sorry, Justin,' said Lynne. 'I shouldn't have asked.'

'It's okay, Lynne,' said Justin. 'Sam reckons I should be talking about it, anyway.' He stood. 'Be easier if I show you first, though.'

Justin wore a football jersey and baggy jeans. For the first time, Jill wondered whether he might be hot in those clothes. The weather had been beautiful here throughout the daylight hours. 'I'm warning you, though, it's not pretty,' he said. He lifted his jersey.

Lynne gasped, and Jill heard Layla's sharp intake of breath behind her. A raised white scar the width of a thumb ran from Justin's breastbone down the centre of his torso and disappeared into the waistband of his jeans. Jill noticed how skinny Justin was under all those clothes, and then she spotted the other scars. They were much smaller, but at least six or seven of them covered his stomach and chest. Justin swivelled and Jill saw three more scars marking his back.

'I got stabbed,' he said. 'Twenty times.' Justin dropped his jersey. Nobody spoke. 'I was out with a girlfriend I had at the time,' he went on, staring out into the forest. 'It was a birthday party for one of her friends, Phillip. He was turning eighteen. I'd never even met him.' He shook his head. 'I'd had my own eighteenth the month before. Some dickheads had crashed my party, but we were able to kick them out without a big problem.'

Justin sat back down in his seat. Fatso plopped down onto his shoes. Justin fondled one of her ears. 'There were only these three guys, but they were really pissed and Phillip's dad wanted them out. Phillip and two of his mates sort of pushed them out the side gate onto the front lawn. I went along to watch.' The rim of Justin's cap dropped increasingly lower, along with his voice. 'That's when the other cars pulled up.'

'Oh, shit,' said Doug.

'Yep,' said Justin. 'About twenty blokes poured out. They just ran in and started bashing the shit out of Phillip and his mates. His dad came out and they got him on the ground and started kicking him in the head. I couldn't just stand there. I tried to drag this bloke off the dad and I felt myself getting punched in the back. I turned around and this Kiwi bloke was standing there, swinging punches. At least, I thought they were punches. Everyone started screaming and I woke up four days later in the ICU.'

'That's horrible,' said Layla. 'Sorry, Justin.'

'So, that big scar – what the hell did you get stabbed with?' asked Camilla.

'No, that's from the operation. They had to open me right up to sew up my insides, stop the bleeding.'

'Fuck,' said Layla.

'Sorry, Justin,' said Jill.

'And that's my happy story,' said Justin. 'The doctors fought so hard to save my life, but sometimes I wish they hadn't.'

'Don't say that,' said Layla. 'We're glad you're here. Well, not here, but you know –'

'Actually, I've been getting better,' said Justin. 'This place has really helped. I've had four admissions, and I was much worse when I first came in. I came back this time because it's around the time it happened. The anniversaries fuck me up.'

I hear you, thought Jill. Camilla nodded. June dropped her head.

'Right, well. That's not fucking fair at all, but I'm glad you told us, Justin,' said Layla. 'Maybe now when I catch you stealing my lollies I won't kick your arse so hard.'

Justin smiled, his face pale.

'That shit again?' said Camilla. 'They'd better up your Lithium, Layla. I reckon you just eat them all yourself.'

'One day I'll catch you, Justin,' said Layla.

'Can't wait,' said Justin.

The snipping began again. Startled, Jill turned around.

'Hold still,' said Layla. 'I'm almost done.'

Jill froze. She'd just noticed the deck covered in her hair; it was not so much the amount, but the twenty-centimetre lengths that floored her. *Oh, fuck.*

But it was the girl in the mirror that shocked her the most. She burst into tears.

'Oh, no! Do you hate it?' asked Layla, behind her in their bathroom. 'Everyone thinks it looks great.'

'It doesn't look like me.'

'Well, it is you. You look great.'

Jill fingered her fringe. She'd never had a fringe. Now her hair brushed her eyelashes.

'Too long?' asked Layla. 'I can trim it, but I love long fringes. More mysterious,' she said.

Jill plucked at the hair curling around her ears, reached around to the base of her neck. She felt completely naked. Her hair fell just to her collar.

'What's with the curls?' Jill said. 'My hair's straight.'

'With the length gone, the weight's gone,' said Layla. 'It just lets your natural kink through.'

'My natural kink.'

'Yeah,' Layla laughed at Jill's flat tone. 'And they're not curls; it's more just a bit of feathering. It frames your face. You look great.'

'It makes my freckles stand out more.' Jill smudged her thumb across her turned-up nose.

'They're cute.'

Jill sighed. Cute. Fucking hell, she did look cute. She also looked more like her sister Cassie than she ever had in her life. But cute? Cute meant innocent, and innocents get killed. She stepped on the thought – she wasn't going to die because she'd had her hair cut. 'I've still got my gun,' she said.

'Okaaay,' said Layla. 'God. I've never had someone hate a haircut that much.'

Jill laughed. 'No, I don't hate it, Layla. Thanks for doing it. I think I'm probably going to like it. I just have to get used to it.'

36

Wednesday, 1 December, 4.30 pm
'Don't forget, today's the last day I can drop you round here, Luce,' said Troy, as they pulled up in front of the grey house on Tramway Street. 'And while I'm at work, I want you home, okay? It's bad enough I have to worry where Chris is all the time – I'm not going to be stressing about you all night too.'

'Okay, okay,' said Lucy.

'So if Mona can't come and study with you at our flat, you'll just have to go it alone.'

'I get it, Troy. Sheesh. You act like you're my big brother or something.' She punched him in the arm. 'Look – your best friend's leaving for work.'

Troy turned and watched the garage door rising. A Toyota Liteace backed out. Fuck. Caine. He rolled his car a little further forward so he wasn't blocking the driveway. Please, let the prick just keep going. Troy didn't know how he was going to speak to this guy with the suspicions he had.

The van pulled over at the curb behind him, and from his rear-view mirror Troy saw the driver's door open. Caine stepped out, smiling.

Lucy watched her brother's face and laughed. 'Oh my God, he can't be that bad, can he?' she said.

Well, that's what I'd like to know, Lucy.

She got out of the car as Caine walked towards his window.

'Call me when you're done,' he said to his sister. He watched her walk through the gate, then buzzed his window down.

'She's a good kid, isn't she?' said Caine, bending to speak through the window, one hand on the car, the other shielding his eyes from the afternoon sun.

'Very,' said Troy.

'It's a comfort to know she's in there with Mona at this time. Poor kid's still so upset.'

'You're back to work then?' said Troy. 'I guess you have to get on with things at some stage after something like this.'

'Yeah. I went back on Monday. My mother wouldn't have wanted me lying around doing nothing.'

'Mmm. I'm back tomorrow. The crime scene is done, over at the restaurant.'

'They've had it shut down this long?' asked Caine. 'It's a week tomorrow. Bloody Australian police. Bet they're the slowest investigators in the world. Oh, sorry, mate. Forgot you were a cop.'

'That's okay,' said Troy. 'I'm beginning to wonder whether you're right about these guys.'

'Told you they'd come up with nothing,' said Caine.

'Sometimes things just aren't explainable. Terrible accidents can happen. My mother probably spilled something on herself before we left for dinner. I've got all sorts of solvents in there, and you could see she's a clean freak. She must have got too close to a naked flame, and boom. A terrible accident. Not everything is a bloody conspiracy, is it, Troy?'

'Not everything,' said Troy.

'Idiots came over the other day trying to tell me my mother's death was related to the detective's, Hutchinson's.'

'Yeah, I heard.'

Caine snorted. 'Anyway,' he said, thumping once on the door, 'I'd better get moving. Make some money.'

'Righto,' said Troy. 'Have a good one.'

He waited for Caine to drive past him, gave him a wave, and then pulled a U-turn across the street. He drove back down Tramway Street, and turned left on Botany Road towards the Mascot shops. Rather than stay on Botany Road, however, he pulled into a side street and waited ten minutes, watching the traffic, then he got out of his car. He went into a milk bar and bought a carton of vanilla milk and a packet of Twisties. He took them back to the car and ate them. When half an hour had gone by, he pulled back onto Botany Road, and made his way back towards Tramway Street. He drove straight past Caine's road and took the next left. He parked the car near a walk-through alley and got out.

Troy took the alley back to Tramway Street. Nothing moved on the dispirited road. Even the few trees were still, exhausted in their attempts to cheer the lifeless region. He crossed the road to the little grey house, stepped over the fence and knocked on the front door.

Mona cracked the door and stared at him from black-rimmed eyes.

'Mona, hi. Sorry, I've been a dick. Can I come in?' he said.

'Why?' she asked.

'I . . . uh . . . I locked myself out of my car. Over at Mascot. I was hoping you wouldn't mind me having a look for something that'll get me back into the car.'

'We don't have anything like that.'

Troy gave a quick laugh. 'You'd be surprised. I know just what I need – something flat and thin, a piece of packing strap would do, or a wire coathanger.'

'Who is it, Mona?' Troy heard Lucy from behind the door.

'Your brother,' said Mona, swinging the door open.

'Hey, Troy. What's up?' said Lucy.

'Locked the keys in the car,' he said.

'What? Where?' asked Lucy.

'Mascot shops. Look, girls, is it okay if I come in and try to find something to get me in the car?'

Lucy and Mona stepped aside.

'He'll find something quickly; don't worry about it, Mona,' said Lucy. 'I remember about five years ago we had an even crappier car than we have now. I could never get into it without waiting for Troy to unlock it from his side.'

'The passenger lock was broken,' said Troy.

'Shit car,' said Lucy. 'Anyway, one day I left my schoolbag on the front seat, even though Troy had always told me not to, and someone broke in to get it.'

'Wrecked the driver's lock too,' said Troy.

'So for about six months, we had to break into the car every day just to get into it. Troy taught me how to do it and I'd be in after about thirty seconds. I was faster than Chris.'

'There's a sweet spot,' said Troy.

Mona rolled her eyes and turned away.

Troy bent his head to whisper to his sister, 'Friendly girl.'

Lucy gave a crooked smile. 'Why didn't you call for road service, anyway?' she said.

Mona glanced back over her shoulder.

'I did,' he said. 'They told me it'd be an hour wait. It was a five-minute walk back here, so I figured I'm better off this way.'

Mona waited in the kitchen, arms folded. Troy walked to the kitchen drawers, opened each and searched through.

'Nothing here,' he said. 'Why don't you girls get back to work, and I'll give you a call when I've found something.'

'Come on, Mona,' said Lucy. 'I'm going back to it. After these summaries, I've got an assignment to finish.' Lucy walked down the hall.

Mona didn't move. 'What did you say you're looking for?' she asked.

'Just something flat and flexible,' said Troy. 'I'll know it when I see it.'

'I'll have a look around,' said Mona. 'You stay here.'

Mona left the room and Troy quietly opened the back door. He'd spotted the shed from the kitchen window the last time he was here. He crossed the scrap of back lawn quickly, but even from here he could see the padlock on the door. Huge. He rattled it anyway in frustration. He didn't know what he hoped to find on Caine, but he knew that he wanted to get a better look into his life.

The shed was a two-by-three-metre Colorbond box. Troy moved around its perimeter towards the back fence. The corridor between fence and shed was striped with shadow. He sidled through, and there it was – a window.

But it was installed too high up in the wall to see into the shed. Troy whipped his head around, searching for something to stand on. There – a milk crate near the clothesline. He dashed across the yard, picked the crate up and ran back; then he used it to step up high enough to see through the sliding double-window. But with the last of the daylight quickly evacuating the space between the fence and the shed, details of the interior were hidden from him. Troy could make out boxes and shapes, but nothing clearly. He grunted in frustration and tried to wipe the dusty window. It moved.

Without another thought, Troy slid the window open and boosted himself up into the space. On his belly on the windowsill, his legs in the yard, his head and chest in the shed, he wondered what the fuck to do next. The drop was too high to fall hands-first. He'd break his neck. He rocked in the window a moment, and then eyed the boxes to his left. He inched his way forwards, scraping his belly over the edge of the sill, trying to balance like a fulcrum with his hands against the shed wall. When he was in up to the hips, he swung his legs hard to the right, propelling the top half of his body to the left. His arms splayed against the wall, he tried to regain balance, but he was leaning too far forwards. He felt himself sliding. Troy scrabbled with his hands down the wall as he fell. Through his jeans, the windowsill carved into his knees and shins, and he stifled a cry. The floor coming up at him, Troy hooked his ankles at the last moment against the windowsill, slowing his momentum, and managed to swing himself to the left. He came down on the edge of a box, hard on his shoulder, feeling something give.

'Fuck, fuck, fuck,' he muttered, rolling over to sit on the floor. He clasped his hands behind his neck and pulled his elbows into his head. 'Fucking *ow*,' he said into his lap. He stretched his neck carefully, grimacing, and peered to his left. The corner of the cardboard box he'd landed on was crumpled, but it had stayed upright. There was definitely something harder than him in there. Gingerly, he rolled over onto his knees and pulled at the top flap of the box. He lifted a heavy plastic container from the box, and with the last of the light in the shed, he read the label: CH_3OH. Methyl alcohol. Huh.

Troy let the bottle slip back into the box. He stayed on his knees and felt about in the near dark. More boxes, more bottles, other shapes in the corners of the shed.

Suddenly, he dropped to his stomach. The clank of the padlock at the door. With the sound for cover, he pulled himself forward on his belly, into deeper shadow. He rolled over to watch the door opening, his blood rushing in his ears. Could it be Caine?

It was Mona. She stood peering in, silhouetted in the late afternoon light. From here he could see her black boots, tights, tartan miniskirt and the bottom of her black T-shirt. He could not see her face. Could she see him? Should he stand? What would he say? If she'd spotted him from the house, walking around the shed, she might have wondered where he'd got to. He was pretty certain she wouldn't have imagined he'd climbed in here – only a lunatic would do that. But if he stood up now, he'd scare the hell out of her, and she'd tell her father. He stayed where he was. If he was caught, he was caught, on his feet or on his arse.

Mona stepped further into the shed. Troy held his breath. After a few shuffling movements, however, the space became fully dark as Mona left, pulling the door closed behind her. Troy heard the key turning in the heavy padlock.

He felt a moment of claustrophobia. Locked in, in the dark.

It's the same shed it was a moment ago, you idiot, he told himself. And there's a window open behind you. Troy reached up to the window with both hands. There was no point being in here a minute longer – Lucy and Mona would be wondering where the hell he was, and he couldn't see anything in here, anyway.

Fortunately, getting out was a lot easier than getting in. He pulled himself up onto the windowsill and used the back fence to negotiate his way back into the backyard. He dashed across the yard to the back door.

Lucy opened it, arms folded. 'What are you doing?' she asked.

'Looking for something to break into the car,' he said. 'What do you think I'm doing?'

'I think you're running across the backyard like you're in a spy movie. Are you hearing voices?'

Even with his heart still hammering, Troy had to smile. 'You're an idiot, Lucy.'

Mona walked into the kitchen holding a blue nylon packing strap. 'Is this what you mean?' she asked.

'Perfect,' said Troy. 'Where'd you find it?'

'The garage,' said Mona. 'But I thought there might have been something in the shed.'

Troy met her eyes. She held the stare. Finally, he dropped his eyes to the strap in her hand, reached out and took it.

'Well, anyway. Thanks, girls,' he said. 'Sorry to have been such a pain in the arse. Give me a call when you're ready to come home, Luce.'

He left the kitchen and made his way out of David Caine's house.

37

Wednesday, 1 December, 8.26 pm

'Jill. It's for you,' said Layla. 'Gabriel someone.'

Jill rocketed up from her bed, crossed the bedroom in a bound and took the phone from Layla. She covered the mouthpiece.

'Layla, is it all right if –'

'I'm on my way,' said Layla. 'You want me to bring you back a Coke?'

Jill shook her head, and walked with the handset towards the window at the back of the room. She uncovered the mouthpiece.

'So, what's happening?' she said.

'Hi, Jill,' said Gabriel.

'Hi.' she waited.

'Well, I'm concentrating on forensics. We're testing the chemical components of the firebomb.'

'How's that going?'
'Ongoing.'
'Any link to Incendie yet?' she asked.
'Not conclusive.'
Jill sighed. 'Gabe. What does that mean? Please. Are we looking for one killer or two?'
'Look, Jill. I think there could be a link between the crime scenes. The preliminary tests indicate that at least one of the substances used is the same in each case.'
'There you go then. So the person who killed Scotty was at Incendie. And we know everyone who was at Incendie. It's a matter of time. What are you doing about interviewing the staff and diners?'
'Well, firstly, I think your conclusion is precipitous.'
'Precipitous.'
'Yeah, you know. Rash, impetuous.'
'I know what you mean, Delahunt. And what are you, a thesaurus now? Is there a link between the crimes or not?'
'Probably. Maybe. Maybe not. I'm not trying to be a pain in the arse here, Jill. It's just that I get a different vibe from each scene.'
'Well, you explore the vibe. What are the others doing about the Incendie people?'
'We've reviewed all the statements. Emma and Elvis have reinterviewed Caine, and Elvis and I have been out to see Berrigan, the manager, again. It looks like he's the one who did it.'
'What! What did you just say?'
'I said that it looks like Troy Berrigan killed Scotty and Miriam Caine.' He paused. 'But I don't think he did.'
Jill's heart scudded. Fuck you, Gabriel. 'Why do you always speak in riddles?'

'The whole thing is still very fluid, Jill. You want answers now. So do I. Believe me, we all do. We'll know more tomorrow. I know how frustrated you must be. But listen, if we haven't caught the fucker by the time you come home, you'll be a part of every aspect of the investigation, so I need you to get well.'

Jill tried to catch her breath.

'How you going with that part, Jackson?'

'Okay.'

'Have you heard any more voices?'

'No.'

'Drums?'

'No.'

'Rain?'

'Fuck off.'

She felt him smile through the phone.

'It's a complicated grief reaction,' she said. 'So they tell me. Apparently, I have chronic and complex post-traumatic stress disorder.'

'Doesn't everyone?'

She grimaced. 'So, with my complex PTSD, the death of my lover apparently triggered a brief psychotic break,' she said. She'd memorised the terms.

'So he *was* your lover,' said Gabriel quietly.

They breathed together for a few beats. 'I'm so sorry, Jill,' he said finally.

The blackness of the forest outside was liquid ink through her tears. She could find no voice. No words.

'You're coming home Sunday, Jill,' said Gabriel. 'Get better, honey.'

38

Thursday, 2 December, 12.34 pm
Naked, Troy stood with one foot inside the shower cubicle, the other on the bathmat. Fuck it, he thought, deciding to ignore the phone ringing. He stepped under the cool water and lathered off sweat. His run today had done nothing to free the tangle of thoughts in his mind.

His first idea had been to take the information about the methyl alcohol in Caine's shed to the Fed, Delahunt, but he wasn't even sure how to contact him. He knew he could ask around, seek Delahunt out, but he worried that word might get back to that fat fuck Eddie Calabrese. Why he should be worried about this he was increasingly unclear, but having a secret conversation with a federal agent while the man's colleague was in the toilet had shaken him. Troy had had no chance to ask questions, to understand what was going to happen next – he'd just been left hanging. One thing he was sure about was that he didn't want any of his actions to compromise whatever Delahunt was doing to nail the real killer.

Troy had briefly considered taking the chemicals information straight to Elvis himself – maybe the guy could look into something that mattered. But then Troy thought about how breaking into other people's property would fly with his arson profile. Ludicrous as the possibility was, he didn't need his actions to completely backfire right now and cost him a break-and-enter charge. And he knew that what he'd found in there wouldn't put anything hard on Caine. Caine worked as a cleaner, and one of the first hits Troy had got when he Googled 'methyl alcohol' described its use as a solvent and cleaning agent.

Troy finished his shower and wrapped a towel around his waist. Thank Christ he had to go in to work today. It would keep his mind off all this shit. He hated having no control. On the way to his room, he saw the answering machine blinking.

It was Caesar, letting him know he'd arranged for James and Dominique to come in with him today, to get things sorted before they reopened. It was now one week exactly from Miriam Caine's death, and Troy was as confused about the whole thing as ever.

Troy entered the hotel lobby and spotted his sommelier, Dominique, by the elevators. Although they'd spoken twice by phone, he hadn't seen her since the fire.

He moved across the foyer quickly. 'Hold up,' he called, when the lift light signalled. Dominique turned towards him and smiled, her long blonde hair slicked back in a bun.

'Hey, Troy,' she said.

'Hi, Dominique,' he said. 'Back to it, then?'

'Yep.'

'How are you feeling about seeing the place again?'

Her bright eyes clouded for a moment. 'I'm okay,' she said. 'It was a terrible night, but we've got to get on with things now.'

He nodded. 'Yeah. I think so too. So, you're ready to work?' he asked.

'Always,' she said.

They entered the lift together.

'They're done up there, huh?' she asked.

'I can't believe it took them this long.'

'Caesar told me they haven't even been near the place the last three days. Apparently they just needed to keep it untouched in case they found something in the lab.'

'You know more about this than I do,' said Troy.

'Well, I've had to be in touch with Caesar,' she said. 'You know he asked me to call the guest list to cancel each night?'

'Uh huh. That's it, huh? That's the only reason you've been in touch with the boss?' He'd seen the way Caesar had watched Dominique.

Troy's mouth twisted when Dominique smiled and dipped her head. Fuck it. Why did he think he'd even had a chance with a girl like this, anyway?

'Well,' said Troy. 'I hope you know what you're doing.' The fact that his boss was twenty years older and a whole lot more married than Dominique was none of his business. It'd never stopped Caesar before. He had to hand it to his boss. Caesar had a type: Bond-girl beautiful, intimately aware of the finer things in life, but unable to reach them on her salary. Caesar got into their panties and they got into the world they felt they belonged to.

Dominique blushed. Troy sighed.

'Did Caesar tell you anything else about what the investigators found?' he asked finally.

'They haven't told him anything about their findings,' she said. 'The whole thing is pretty bizarre, huh?'

'You could say that,' said Troy.

He followed Dominique out of the lifts. A cleaning crew waited at the locked glass doors. He let everyone into the restaurant. It seemed the cleaners wouldn't have a lot more than their usual work to do. Troy wished he could say the same for himself. The kitchen would need an overhaul, he had so much ordering to do, and he needed to get Dominique onto the reservations – he had to get arses on seats for tomorrow night.

Everything else was way behind too. Troy knew he should be revamping the menu by now, getting the summer holiday vibe going. Whatever happened with the whole Miriam Caine thing, he was just going to have to let it go and trust that it would work out okay in the end. Frustrating as it was, there was nothing really he could do right now but wait and see how everything played out.

He found Dominique at his desk. She had the guest book open.

'Hey,' she said. 'I've been meaning to ask you – what did that woman's son want with you that night, anyway?' She looked up at him with big blue eyes.

'What are you talking about?' he said. 'You mean David Caine? What do you mean, what did he want with me?'

'You know, when he called you over. Just before his mother got, um, burned.'

'He didn't call me over, Dominique. I was already over there, talking to table fourteen.'

'Oh,' she said.

'Why did you think he called me over?'

'Well, it's just that he caught me when I walked past. Said he'd like a word with the manager. I was dealing with an order, so I told James to tell you.'

'Well, James didn't,' said Troy. 'But that doesn't make any sense. Caine wasn't even at the table when I went over there.'

'I know,' she said. 'The whole night was just weird.'

39

Thursday, 2 December, 3.50 pm
Jill took a seat in her counsellor's office. She reclined back into the green leather armchair. It was really very comfortable.

'How are you today, Jill?' asked Sam Barnard.

'Three days to go,' she said.

He smiled. 'Do you know that a countdown of your days remaining has been your response to that question every time I've asked it?'

'And what does that mean about me?' she said.

'It means that you want to go home. Has it been that bad here?'

Jill sat a little straighter in the chair, shook her head. 'Look, Sam. It hasn't been bad here. I think I've learned some helpful things, and the people have been great, but you've got to understand that it's almost impossible for me to sit here doing nothing while . . . that person is still walking around.'

'The person who killed Scotty.'

She nodded.

'You should say the words. You should try to speak about it as often as you can, Jill. In the long run, it will help you to process what's happened if you don't skip over the painful words, and don't push away the painful memories.'

'Yeah, well, sometimes that's impossible for me,' she said, flatly.

'How do you mean?'

'Well, like the memories of when I was twelve.'

'You mean, when you were kidnapped and raped. You see, when you say "when I was twelve", you're glossing over what actually happened to you.'

Jill sat forwards in her chair, drilled her eyes into his. 'You know, this is why I've always hated therapy,' she said.

'Why?'

'Because some cleanskin dickhead tells me that I have to stop avoiding the memories.' She felt hot tears in her eyes. 'You just do not get it. When you say the words "kidnapped and raped",' she parodied his tone, 'you don't get flashes of two old men sticking things inside you, up your arse, in your mouth, burning you with cigarettes. You don't feel the terror of knowing you're gonna die, and then of praying that you actually would.'

Jill could feel her breathing ramping up; she coughed, gripping the arms of the chair. 'How would you like to see and feel that every day for twenty years? Don't you think you'd want to fucking *avoid* it?'

She stood and paced, coughing. She couldn't catch her breath.

'Use your breathing, Jill,' said Sam calmly. He stood and walked next to her as she paced, counting quietly as she sucked in air, trying to slow her breathing with his measured voice.

Five minutes later, Jill returned to the chair, the tissue box on her lap.

'Sorry,' she said.

'You don't have to be sorry,' he said. 'You did great. You see, those memories, that bottled-up emotion, is toxic inside you. You just let some of the poison out. And you didn't run. You didn't die. Nobody got hurt.'

'You think that didn't fucking hurt?'

'Now it's my turn to say sorry, Jill. I know that hurt – I could feel it – but fairly quickly you were also able to reduce your distress using your techniques, and in the meantime you processed some of that pain.'

She wiped her nose.

'And when you can express the pain and then regain control, you're healing,' he said.

She leaned back in the chair again, suddenly very tired.

'Sometimes you have to let go of your control in the short term to regain it in the long term.'

'How Zen,' she said dryly, but with a small smile.

'Speaking of which, how did you go with your homework?' he asked.

'Do you really have to call it that?' she said. 'That's another reason I hate therapy.'

After the session, on her way back to the unit, Jill heard her name called from the nurses' station. She made her way over.

'Phone message for you,' said a heavy-set woman, holding a slip of paper above her head as she bent over a file, continuing to write notes.

'Thanks,' said Jill, taking the paper and scanning it quickly. Shit. She'd missed Gabe's call. She glanced at her watch. It wasn't even five yet. He'd never called at the same time twice. She pulled out her mobile and scrolled for his number. Patients weren't supposed to use mobiles in here, instead making and receiving calls via landlines to avoid phones going off during group and therapy sessions.

'Damn!' she said, when she got his answer service. She'd just have to keep trying.

The moment she woke each morning, Gabriel's debrief call was the first thing on her mind.

By eight pm Jill was in a foul mood. She'd been quiet over dinner, and had avoided the veranda altogether. She'd tried running the shadowy three-kilometre hospital driveway, but had been sent back to the unit by a nurse leaving for the night.

She'd tried Gabe's phone every half-hour. Nothing. The more she thought about it, the more she felt sure that Gabriel had called at a time he knew he'd miss her, in order to avoid the debrief. Why wouldn't he want to talk to her? Maybe something had gone wrong with the case? Maybe they'd arrested someone but he didn't want to get her hopes up?

She sat cross-legged on her bed, wondering what she could do. There was no way she could sleep tonight without talking to someone from the real world. For the first time since the first night, she seriously considered packing up and getting out of there. She could call a cab to get her to the airport. She didn't think she'd have any trouble on a plane now.

She ripped at a thumbnail. What should she do? Who else could fill her in on what was going on? She wouldn't dream of calling Andreessen – he wouldn't speak about the case to her when she was non-operational – and she wasn't quite up to speaking to him since her outburst last week. There was a remote chance that Lawrence Last might fill her in on what he knew, but he wouldn't be as up-to-speed as the key investigators. She also thought that his most likely response to her call would be to tell her to 'get some more rest'. She knew she'd smash her phone to pieces if she heard that tonight. Not a chance in hell she'd call Elvis. He wouldn't give her the time of day, let alone a debrief. He'd be well-pissed by now anyway.

That left one person. She had the number stored. She scrolled for it.

40

Thursday, 2 December, 8.10 pm
'Damn it! Sorry, Cecily, I have to take this.' Emma Gibson let the easy racquetball shot glance by her and pulled her mobile phone from her gym shorts.

'That's okay,' said her friend, walking to her corner and picking up her towel. 'We've only got the court for another five minutes, anyway. We'll call this a win for me.'

Emma laughed and answered the phone.

'Hello,' she said, walking back to her corner.

'Ah, hi, Emma, this is Jill Jackson.'

Emma stood still. She saw Cecily watching her and waved to her friend to go on without her. 'Jill?'

'Yeah, look, I hope you don't mind me calling you. Are you busy right now?'

'No. Not really. No, it's fine. Are you okay? Where are you?'

A pause. 'Um, my parents' house out west. Just taking some time, you know.'

'Yeah, of course. I mean, that's good that you're looking after yourself and you've got family around.'

'How are you going, Emma? I know you cared a lot about . . . about Scotty too.'

Emma was surprised to find her tears welling so quickly. She hadn't cried since that first night. She had to swallow hard before she could speak. 'I'm okay.' She sounded choked. Keep it together, she told herself. Jill doesn't need you blubbering right now. 'What about you?'

'Well, I'm a lot better than the last time you saw me,' said Jill.

'Well, that . . . that was a bad day.'

'A really bad day.' Jill cleared her throat. 'Listen, I don't know whether you've heard, Emma, but I'm coming back on the job on Monday. I'll be back on the team trying to find this fucker. Anyway, I just really need to know what's happening at the moment. I've tried calling Gabriel Delahunt but he's not answering his phone.'

Emma paced the racquetball court, her thoughts racing. What should I do here? Am I supposed to tell Jill about the case? How can I not – I mean why wouldn't I? But can she handle this right now – she completely flipped out during the briefing.

A knock sounded at the door to the court, and a balding man wearing a headband poked his head through.

'Oh, shit. Can I call you back, Jill? I'm on a racquetball court and I've got to pack up my stuff for the next players.'

'Sure, okay. Emma?'

'Yeah?'

'Will you call me right back?'

Emma skipped the changerooms and headed straight to her car. She locked the doors and called Cecily, letting her know she was heading home to shower. She then stared at her phone. Jill had sounded okay, but so desperate for news. Emma hit the return call button.

Jill answered on the first ring.

'So, can you fill me in, Emma?' she said.

'To be honest, Jill, I wish I could give you better news. This has just been the most frustrating case. Nothing seems to make sense at all.'

'Are you still running with the theory that the murders are linked?'

'Well, we are, technically. But I just don't know. I mean, there's prelim evidence that there were similar types of fuel used, but most arsonists use the same sorts of materials. Troy Berrigan was at the Incendie scene and had contact with Scotty afterwards, and he has a history of arson.'

'You are shitting me!'

'I know. But it's a juvie record, Jill, and I just don't know. David Caine seems like much more of a squirrel to me, but we really have nothing solid on either of them. And if they're telling the truth about where they were on Saturday, it's almost impossible either one of them did it.'

'How come?' said Jill.

'Apparently, Berrigan dropped his kid sister around to study at Caine's house on Saturday. They had a drink together.'

'They're friends?'

'No. They just met the night of the Incendie fire, but Caine's kid goes to the same school as Berrigan's little sister.'

'So they've got alibis for when Scotty was killed.'

'Almost. Elvis still thinks Berrigan's the one. He's done a timeline and figures Berrigan could have killed Scotty, picked his sister up and gone around to drink beer with the man whose mother he murdered. He'd have to be a hell of a hardarse to do that.' There was silence on the other end of the phone. 'Jill?' Emma said.

'Sorry. I just don't know what the fuck's happening. It's so frustrating being here.'

'Why don't you come back?' God knows, we could use the help.

'I kinda promised I'd wait until after the . . . funeral.'

Emma heard the pain in the words. She felt it too. 'So, anyway,' she continued, 'we've also been interviewing the public who were anywhere near the scene on Saturday. Everyone saw the accident, of course, but no one saw what happened just before it. That's another similarity with Incendie, I guess.' She paused. 'And that's pretty much where we're at.'

'Thanks, Emma,' said Jill. 'It's really helped to talk to you.'

'Of course,' said Emma. 'No worries. While I've got you, can you think of any of Scotty's past busts who might have wanted to do this? I mean, supposing that this didn't have anything to do with Miriam Caine's murder.'

'I've been thinking that through too. But no one I can think of jumps up as some psychopath arsonist. Have you gone back through his cases?'

'Yeah, a couple of times. No reason to call anyone in.' She sighed. 'It'll be great to have you back here, Jill.'

'Thanks, Emma. I also wanted to say that I'm sorry –'

'Don't be sorry for anything. Just feel better, Jill. And I'll see you Monday.'

41

Thursday, 2 December, 10.04 pm
Frank Vella didn't bother waiting for the walk signal before crossing Elizabeth Street. The intersection with Goulburn Street was as deserted at ten pm as it was packed during business hours. He could clearly hear what his wife, Mary, would have said about that. *All the real businessmen are at home by this hour. If you looked for a better job, or you stood up to your boss, you could be at home with your family at night. Carmel Pezzina's husband just got another raise; they're going to Canada on a cruise. I told you he bought her a Mercedes, didn't I?* Whenever he wasn't super-busy or asleep, Frank had a soundtrack of her bitching and moaning. She didn't even need to be there – if it wasn't coming directly from her, he'd heard her nagging and putdowns so many times over the past nineteen years that her voice was indelibly

etched in his own thoughts. Everyone had an inner critic, but Frank's had a name: Mary Vella.

Carrying a cumbersome cardboard box, Frank limped across the intersection, wincing. His shoes pinched and squashed his pinkie toes; he would swear the skin on his left one had been chafed off completely. He could feel raw flesh rubbing against his sock with every step. He'd rather lose the toe, though, than tell Mary. She'd drag him out shopping for new shoes.

Come to think of it, he'd sacrifice the foot completely rather than enter a shopping centre with her. First, the kids would have to come. Bony through nerves and obsessive housework, and standing only as tall as their thirteen-year-old daughter, Mary nevertheless had a voice that would carry clear across the food court of Ashfield Mall. And she would use it, bawling out constant instructions to their four kids, one or all of whom would invariably be crying at some point between getting into the car to get there and arriving home again.

Sitting in the car with Mary was the most difficult part. Frank had never hit a woman in his life, but when trapped with his wife in their Pajero, and trying to find a parking spot, sometimes the carpark disappeared and all he could see was his arm swinging hard across the seat, his elbow connecting with her jaw. Frank didn't know what he hated more about that image – that he could even think that way about his wife, or that he knew that if he actually followed it through, their kids would probably cheer.

The thing was, though, it wasn't always that bad. Maybe the main reason Mary's criticism of his job hurt was because he actually *wanted* to be at home at night with his family. At least a couple of times a week Mary would forget what she was mad at him for, and after one of her great meals she'd stop tidying long enough to let him pull her onto his lap, and they'd watch TV with the kids. These moments with them were the reason he did all this.

His brother-in-law Joe, on the other hand, thought Frank was the luckiest bastard alive. Married to Mary's sister, Joe knew a thing or two about the nagging himself, and he would say having to entertain clients in restaurants two or three nights a week was a 'get out of gaol free' card. But Frank had got over the rich restaurant food and having to ingratiate himself with the city's doctors long ago. As a pharmaceutical representative, he had to get his company's drugs on their prescription pads or his arse was grass. And that meant lavish dinners with personal attention. Frank needed to know that Dr Chu ordinarily didn't eat pork, but that he'd protest if he didn't get crispy prosciutto on his risotto when everyone else had it. He had to make sure Dr Holland was seated nowhere near Dr Wendell – after too many pap smears through the day and Chardonnays over dinner, these women were not above a scrag-fight at the table. And he had to keep the red wine flowing for Dr Mendel, and the Scotch for Dr Aziz.

Approaching the carpark, Frank shifted the box in his hands. Most of all, he was sick of the endless objects of marketing junk he had to lug around to these events. Pens, squashy stress balls and post-it notes were so passé. Nowadays, he'd bring everything from laptop bags and brass letter-openers to manicure sets, dress watches and electronic organisers. With everything covered in the company logo, of course. So much useless junk. And the way the doctors would just load it up, shoving fistfuls of the plastic-wrapped crap into their handbags and briefcases. Frank couldn't blame them – Lord knew these doctors had a shit job, every day writing scripts for – or copping abuse from – the Valium-shoppers; being coughed on and bled over; fingering arses, fondling lumps and shoving speculums up vaginas. And it wasn't like the pay or respect was there like it had been in the old days. Hell, Frank would take his crappy job over theirs any day.

He hobbled over to the entry ramp, the most direct route into the carpark. He heard footsteps behind him but didn't pause or turn. Some other poor bastard just trying to pick up his car on a Thursday night, he figured.

Frank definitely paused when he felt the first blow. He would've said something, offered his wallet, but his left lung was sucking air through a hole in his back and was in the process of collapsing. He couldn't get any words out. With the next blow, Frank Vella fell to his knees, doing his best on the way down not to tip the box; this one held company coffee mugs, and he knew they wouldn't survive the fall. The box probably saved Frank a broken nose, because with the third blow – to his neck – he pitched forwards, chest-first, onto the box. Still unable to get a word out, Frank thought that maybe, if he could just get a look at the guy, he could show him with his eyes he was sorry, and maybe he would just stop the hitting.

Frank Vella managed to turn his head just enough to make eye contact with his attacker. Had Frank's lungs not been full of blood at that point, he would certainly have screamed.

42

Friday, 3 December, 12.30 pm
Erin stared out at her audience and decided it was a good thing she'd chosen to hold the lunchtime meeting about the CCTV proposal in the smaller of the two meeting rooms. At any rate, Hamish would have free lunches for as long as he wanted them. There'd be enough sandwiches left over for a few weeks, at least. She figured she'd let him take them all home – he'd spent the morning complaining about having only twenty dollars a week to live on after paying his rent.

'Well, that's just not sustainable, Hamish,' she'd told him. 'What are you going to do?'

'Live on credit, like everyone else,' he'd answered.

'You'll have to move, Hamish,' she'd said. 'You'll end up in big trouble.'

'Are you serious?' Hamish had said. 'Do you know

how hard it is to get a place in Surry Hills?'

'You could move further west,' she'd tried. 'The rent is a little more reasonable.'

Hamish had shuddered. 'Don't even joke about it, Mrs Hart.'

Now, he sat to her left at the table they'd set out at the front of the hall. She was glad she'd discouraged the other committee members from attending. She and Hamish had put out sixty chairs for members of the community. Five of them were filled. She hoped that more people showed up tonight for the evening meeting.

Erin gave her presentation as though the hall were crammed with people, with more waiting to get in the doors. An elderly woman in the front row stood and left when she was halfway through. A man in a coat she could smell from her seat slept through the whole presentation.

She wrapped up her speech and asked the three conscious people whether they had any questions.

'I have more of a comment than a question.' A dark-haired middle-aged woman with a European accent stood.

Erin forced herself to not sigh aloud. She'd allowed herself that pleasure when she'd first entered the hall and spotted this woman. 'Yes, Florence?' she said. Florence showed up at most town meetings, and she never left before monopolising question time with a rambling diatribe, always beginning with the same sentence: I have more of a comment than a question . . .

Florence wanted it noted that CCTV cameras were not always effective. She had heard that, in the majority of cases, either police couldn't use the images or the courts found their data inadmissible.

Despite the fact that Erin had just wound up a speech highlighting the fact that the new cameras were designed to reduce these problems dramatically, Erin patiently went over these points again, by which time another person had walked out. That left her and Hamish; Mr Stinky, still asleep; Florence, who still looked good to go; and an Asian man, who'd sat through the meeting listening intently. He was stiff in his seat and he periodically mopped at his forehead with a handkerchief. Erin smiled at him. He certainly looked as though he had something to say. Instead, he just stared, hard.

'Okay,' Erin said, standing. 'Thank you very much for coming. We value your involvement, and we'll continue to keep everybody notified at every stage throughout the project.'

The Asian man stood.

'Ah, it looks like we have a final comment,' said Erin.

'Why do you really put the camera?' he said.

'Ah, I think –' began Erin.

'You use these to spy,' he said. 'This is just like China. The government is spying. You have no permission for my shop. You stay away from my shop.'

'I'm happy to speak with anybody who has a serious objection,' said Erin. 'Maybe we could have a chat now? Why don't you come and have a seat?' She gestured to the chair next to her at the table.

The man swung his head from left to right, his eyes wild. He suddenly shoved at his chair, sending it flying, and bolted for the exit.

By the food table, Florence watched the show, then went back to picking over the sandwiches. Stinky-coat slept on.

'That went well, don't you think, Hamish?' asked Erin.

'Can I take some of those sandwiches home?' he said.

43

Friday, 3 December, 4.12 pm
'Oh my God. Would you look at this,' said Troy. 'You're not actually home on time, are you, bro?' He stopped lacing his shoes and looked up.

Chris Berrigan gave half a smile and dropped his schoolbag. 'You have to go back to work tonight,' he said.

'And when has that ever got your arse home from school on time before?'

'I wanted to catch you before you leave.'

'Oh. That,' said Troy.

'It's Friday. End of the week. You said you'd let me know about the DJ equipment.'

Troy exhaled and stood, hands on hips, facing his brother. 'Here's the thing –'

'Oh *bull*shit,' said Chris.

Troy laughed. 'I haven't said a thing, you idiot.'

'You're going to say no,' said Chris. 'You're going to say you haven't got the money to hook me up right now.'

'No, no, no, not exactly that,' said Troy, quickly rethinking his next words. 'I was going to say that money is tight, you know, but it's not about that. It's just that I don't know a lot about this DJ business.'

'You said you were going to check that out.'

'Yeah, look, Chris, I know I did. It's just that shit's been hectic this past week.'

'You haven't even been working! You've been here, fucking around.'

'Bro, what I want to say is this,' said Troy. 'I know you don't want to stay on to Year Twelve. I understand that. That's cool. But I don't want you out there at sixteen trying to get jobs in clubs.'

'I told you I'd work parties first.'

'See, that doesn't make me any happier, Chris. You're still a kid. And you're, what, gonna be out there at parties every night until three, four in the morning?'

'It's good money, Troy. It's what I want to do.' Chris spoke quietly, his eyes on the floor. Troy looked at his brother's buzz-cut haircut – Chris didn't have his hood up for once.

'I get that, Chris. I really do. I haven't seen you this into anything for a couple of years. If you want to do this, then I want you to do this. But I want you to do a course first.' He kept speaking when Chris threw his head back, made a dissing sound with his mouth. 'Like a sound engineer course, or some kind of music-industry course. If you can do that next year, I promise you that when you finish it I will buy you the equipment you need to set yourself up. And you won't even have to pay me back.'

Chris pulled his hood forward over his near-shaved scalp. 'I told you, *bro*,' he said. 'I'm done with school. And you might think that you're my fucken father, but you're fucken not. I'm my own man now, and you don't tell me what to do anymore. You can't flog me anymore when I don't do what you want.' Chris took a step closer and eyeballed Troy hard. 'But you can always fucken try.'

Troy didn't move.

'Didn't think so.' Chris sneered. He turned, picked up his backpack and left the unit.

44

Friday, 3 December, 6.33 pm
'How come you like cooking so much but you hardly eat anything?' Callie asked her brother, snatching a wedge of garlic-buttered roast potato from the oven tray. She tossed it from hand to hand and finally dropped it onto the travertine benchtop.

'Ow! Hot!' she said, at the same time that Reece cried, 'Mum! She's taking stuff when it's not ready!'

Erin clucked at her daughter and massaged the back of her son's neck. Still so soft.

'Don't complain,' she said to Callie. 'He's a great cook, isn't he? And if he doesn't eat a lot, it leaves more for you and me, right?' She turned off the oven and slid out the tray of pan-fried, cheesy-crumbed, flattened chicken thigh fillets – Reece's specialty. 'Grab the plates, Cal,' she said.

'Two, please,' said Callie, holding out her plate, which was already mounded with potatoes.

'One and some salad,' said Erin.

Callie stuck out her tongue.

'Half, please,' said Reece, holding out his plate.

'One and some potato,' said Erin.

Erin lifted the foil draped loosely over her fillet of deep-sea perch. While she could easily have eaten the rest of the cheesy chicken thighs and all of the potato, the steamed fish looked great too. She was absolutely starving. She slid the fish onto her plate and then stacked it in salad. She worried a little about how much her mouth really watered when she unscrewed the ice-cold bottle of Sauvignon Blanc.

'At the table tonight, everyone,' she tried.

'Can't,' said Callie, her mouth full, on her way to her room. She swallowed. 'I've got a group assignment due and we agreed we'd talk online now.'

'At six-thirty?' said Erin.

'Uh huh.' Callie grinned, waved her fork and closed her bedroom door.

'What about you, my baby boy? You want to watch some TV with your mum?'

'Okay, first of all, Mum, if you ever call me that when we're in public, you'll get a call the next day telling you to pick me up in Emergency. Second, I'll sit in there with you as long as I can work on my programs.'

Erin waited. 'Is there a third condition? You look like you're not done.'

'Third,' said Reece. 'Don't get too drunk and start talking about what the world's coming to and what it was like back in the day.'

'Well, just for that, we're watching the news,' said Erin, thumbing on the plasma.

'Can you turn it down a little?' asked Reece from behind his laptop, his dinner untouched on the coffee table in front of him.

'Shh, in a second, honey. I want to hear this.'

'*Police are tonight urgently appealing for public assistance to determine who committed the brutal stabbing murder of Frank Vella, forty-three, of Ashfield in Sydney's inner west. Although we will not be showing the full attack, which was captured entirely by a city carpark CCTV camera, please be warned that the footage we will display may be disturbing to some viewers.*'

Erin leaned forward on the lounge.

The footage was very brief. Black-and-white, and just a little grainy – one of the older cameras. At first, just a person in a coat, back to the camera, leaning over a body on the ground in front of him, which had been pixellated.

And then the person turned around and directly faced the camera.

Erin stifled a scream, her hand over her mouth. Capering grotesquely, swinging what appeared to be a screwdriver, was a man in a cartoon mask.

'Isn't that a Ninja Turtle?' asked Reece.

The man brandished the weapon like a sword and then raised his other hand. Although again pixellated, there was no way of missing that he had raised his middle finger.

Just for the camera.

45

Saturday, 4 December, 12.20 pm
Despite Jill's frustration at being away from the investigation, the past three days at the hospital had flown by. She'd found that she'd learned something useful during each meeting with Sam, and the groups always gave her something to think about. The 'veranda therapy' on Lyrebird was also something she enjoyed, and Jill even found herself joining in and giving advice when the others had problems.

And she was always up too late at night with Layla, Layla doing most of the talking, and Jill a fair bit of laughing. She felt guilty almost every time she smiled, but Layla was great at distracting her. Jill's heart was still a heavy boulder, which rose to her throat several times a day, making it hard to swallow, but the flat-footed hunter – her panic attacks – had at least found someone else to stalk.

She stayed away from the lounge rooms each evening. One thing she did not want to do was sit and watch when news programs commented about Scotty's death. She just couldn't break down in front of everyone here.

After morning group on her second-last day, Jill sat on her bed, folding her clothes and packing them into her bag.

'What're you doing?' asked Layla from the doorway.

Jill gave her a I-would-have-thought-that-was-obvious look, and continued packing.

'You've got another day and night here,' said Layla, plonking down on the end of Jill's bed.

'I'm leaving at lunchtime tomorrow,' Jill said.

'How're you feeling about the funeral?' asked Layla.

A tear welled. 'Well, I'm feeling,' said Jill. 'And Sam reckons that's a good thing.'

'What would he know?' said Layla. They both laughed a little.

'You'd better leave the packing for now and come over for lunch. You gotta do your exposure therapy.'

Jill groaned. When she'd told Sam about her fear of queues and crowds, he'd given her more homework: she had to line up with everyone else for lunch, in the middle of the press of people. She'd coped.

'Well, you've got to leave the lunchroom with me at twelve-forty, all right?' said Jill.

'What for?' asked Layla. 'We're never out of there before one.'

'Exactly,' said Jill.

'Huh?' said Layla.

'What would you say if I told you I've solved the extraordinary mystery of the Lyrebird lolly thief?'

'You're shitting me!'

'I shit you not.'

At twenty minutes to one, Jill and a grumbling Layla left the dining room. Their fellow Lyrebirds watched them leave.

'Something to do,' said Jill, in reply to Camilla's question about where they were going.

'I got no dessert,' said Layla. 'I'm not myself when I get no dessert.'

'We have to hurry,' Jill said. 'We have to get there first.' She dragged Layla across the covered walkway at a jog. They ran past the veranda and approached the entry to their room.

'Slow up a little,' said Jill. 'We don't want to scare her.'

They sidled up to the doorway.

'Fatso?' said Layla, looking in.

'Shh,' said Jill. 'Watch.'

Together they watched Fatso at Layla's nightstand. The dog's head was level with the top drawer. She put her paw up on the handle and scrabbled. The drawer slid open. She then walked around to the side of the nightstand, facing Jill and Layla. She reached in with her muzzle, grabbed a bag of lollies and pulled them out.

'Good girl,' said Jill, quietly.

'Fat bitch!' said Layla, a little louder.

'Shh, stand back a bit,' said Jill. 'The show's not over yet.'

The golden Labrador sauntered from their bedroom, the bag in her mouth, and made her way casually down the hallway. They followed her swaying backside, remaining a few steps behind.

'Where is she going?' asked Layla. 'Oh, you've got to be fucking kidding me.'

Fatso ambled into another bedroom and Jill and Layla followed. Justin sat in the middle of his bed, grinning.

'Good girl, good girl,' he said to the dog, who'd dropped the bag on the floor and had her two paws up on Justin's bed.

'Just open your hand before you pat her, Justin,' said Jill.

'Yes, Detective,' he said. Still smiling, he opened his palm. A dog treat sat in the middle.

'I fucken knew it!' said Layla. 'You trained her to steal my lollies.'

'Pretty good, huh?' he said.

'Not bad,' said Layla, plonking down at the end of the bed.

'Not bad? That was genius. You want a snake?'

'With all her slobber on it? I don't think so,' said Layla. 'Gimme the bag. I'll check.'

'I'm going back to pack,' said Jill, and left them to it.

46

Sunday, 5 December, 9.57 pm
'Troy, a moment,' said Dominique.

'Please excuse me, Mrs Garofali, Belinda. I hope you enjoy your fish, but save some room for dessert. You know we're famous for it.' Troy left the mother and daughter with a special smile for Belinda. With Dominique's assistance, Belinda had earlier ordered a one-hundred-and-ninety-dollar bottle of wine.

'Phone, boss,' said Dominique, smiling, gliding graciously through tables.

Troy took the call in the kitchen. He never used his mobile when on the floor.

'Don't freak out,' said Lucy, on the other end.

'Then tell me now, or I will,' he said.

'It's Chris.'

'Well, of course it is,' he said. 'Is he okay?'

'He got arrested again.'

Troy took the phone away from his ear and made a hammering gesture with it against the wall.

'You there, Troy?'

'Here. What'd he do?'

'They wouldn't tell me,' she said. 'But he's locked up.'

'Where?'

'Redfern.'

Of course. 'So the cops called, but you don't know what he did?'

Silence. Finally, Lucy said, 'Nope.'

'Well, he's going to have to stay locked up a while longer, Lucy. I can't leave now.'

'They told me to tell you they wanted to see you. It's just work, Troy – Chris needs you.'

'Yeah? Well, I need this fucking job to keep a roof over our heads.' Troy lowered his voice. 'And it looks like our brother needs to spend a bit of time locked up, the stupid little shit.'

'I'm hanging up,' said Lucy.

'I'll call you back later,' said Troy.

The phone rang again, and he answered it.

Redfern police.

Troy couldn't concentrate on anything other than Chris. Redfern lock-up was rock-hard. Chris was a juvie and they'd keep him in segro, but some of the kids who'd be in there with him had grown up fighting adults and would keep swinging until they lost consciousness. Chris pretended he was a gangster but he'd never been in a real lock-up or slept a day in his life on the street. Troy paged James, and his head waiter joined him by the bar.

'I have to go,' said Troy. 'Family shit.'

'Are you okay?' asked James.

'It's my little brother. He got himself locked up.'

'Go,' said James. 'We're down to eight tables. It's sweet. We'll be fine.'

'I owe you,' said Troy. He grabbed a beer for the road.

This time, it was more than just filling in some forms. Troy had to speak to the cops who'd collared Chris. One he'd never heard of, and one he had. McNaughton. Just what he fucken needed. Four years ago it had been Herd and Singo, him and McNaughton. After Jonno had been shot, they'd been a tight-knit unit. Brothers.

McNaughton hadn't said a word to him after he'd submitted his report on the kid blinded during the beating by Singo. When his senior sergeant told him that McNaughton had applied for immediate reassignment, he'd been hurt but not surprised. But when his sergeant also told him that he should watch his back in the alleys from now on, Troy knew he had to get out.

Now, Troy waited in the same interview room in which he and McNaughton had tuned up suspects and interviewed witnesses. His chair pushed back from the table, he leaned forward, elbows on his knees, wishing he had another beer – or that he had Chris in here to kick around the room. Chris had brought him again to the last goddamn place he wanted to be – Redfern, facing his hypocrisy. He knew that was the major reason the other coppers had hated him so much. He and McNaughton had never been known to back down from giving a flogging themselves in these rooms. But everyone in Redfern knew the game – you had to speak the same language as the players. For the Asians, you got an interpreter. For the Abos, you used your fists. After a while, everyone could understand each other.

But Troy knew that he and McNaughton had never been as heavy-handed as Herd and Singo, especially with kids, and he had definitely never gone to town on someone the way they had on those two boys. Still, he'd lost skin from his knuckles in this room plenty of times. And here he was thinking about beating Chris again. He hadn't laid a hand on him or anyone else since he'd put in the report, but maybe he hadn't changed as much as he wanted to believe. He leaned back in his chair and belched acid.

Movement outside. McNaughton walked in, flattening the door against the wall. 'Smells like piss in here,' he said. 'You haven't changed, Berrigan. Still a degenerate alcoholic.'

'What, so you've been to rehab have you, Naught? Done the Twelve Steps?' asked Troy.

'What I've done and haven't done has nothing to do with you,' said McNaughton. 'That's how this works in here now. You're a pissant civilian, guardian of a shitbag hopper, and I'm Senior Constable McNaughton, which is how you'll refer to me from now on.'

Troy spread his hands in a sweeping gesture. 'Well, welcome to my office, Senior Constable McNaughton,' he said. 'So, you got another stripe? Two stripes but no bar. Sounds about right. Hardly setting the world on fire with your rapid rise through the ranks.'

'We can't all go around setting things on fire, can we, Berrigan?'

'Go fuck yourself.' Troy folded his arms across his chest.

'Whoa. Hit a nerve there, did I?'

'You got my brother in here. What do you want to talk to me about?'

'You've done a great job raising him, by the way,' said McNaughton. 'What a great kid. We had him in here the other week, didn't we? Hasn't even been to court for that one yet.'

Troy kept his head down, massaged where his fingers should have been. 'What'd he do?' he said to the floor.

'My partner will fill you in on that one,' McNaughton said, as a woman walked into the interview room.

'Constable Megan Bell,' she said. Holding a folder, she didn't offer her other hand but just took a seat next to McNaughton. Trim, tucked-in and in her late thirties – Berrigan put her down as a mum with a career change, began her cadetship late in life and was now proud as punch to be a copper. She looked as though she'd usually be a pretty friendly gal; his reputation had obviously preceded him.

'Good to meet you, Constable Bell,' he said. 'My name's Troy Berrigan. I'm Chris Berrigan's brother and legal guardian. I'm pretty worried about him. Senior Constable McNaughton has told me that you'll let me know what's going on.'

'At sixteen-thirty this afternoon, your brother and a Jayden Green were apprehended in possession of a firearm –'

Troy stood. 'What?'

'Sit down,' said McNaughton.

'A firearm? It's that fucking Jayden. I told Chris to stay away from him.'

'I said sit down,' said McNaughton, also standing now, 'or I'm going to put you on your arse.'

'I'd like to see that,' said Troy, eyeballing his former partner across the table.

'Can we get on with this?' said Bell.

Troy dropped into his chair and wiped his hand across his brow. A gun? Fuck, Chris.

'He has been charged with possession of a firearm and with discharging a firearm in a public place,' said Bell.

'He *fired* it?'

'They both did,' said Bell. 'Two clips. In a disused railway shed down at the yards.'

'But no one was hurt?' asked Troy, his heart hammering.

'No one was hurt,' said Bell.

'Thank God! Can I get him out, then? Is he going to make bail? I mean, I know he's up on the vandalism thing, but there're no assaults, no drugs.'

'Weapons charge,' said McNaughton. 'No bail.'

'They probably just found the gun,' said Troy. 'They were just fucking around. I'll keep him straight now; I'll lock the little shit in his room. Come on, there's flexibility on this. You know I know that. This doesn't have to go to remand.'

'What makes you think they found the gun?' asked McNaughton, his elbows on the arms of his chair and his fingers steepled in front of his chest. 'Where might they have found it?'

'How the fuck would I know?' said Troy. 'Where does a kid get a gun?'

'Maybe from home?'

A cold wave surfed Troy's spine, raising all the hairs on the back of his neck. 'I handed in my service weapon four years ago, Naught. I haven't seen a gun since.'

'We're going to have to check that,' said Bell, opening her folder. She put a piece of paper on the table. Slid it over to him with a finger.

'What's this?' said Troy.

'Warrant,' said McNaughton.

The interview room door smacked against the wall again. A stomach entered the room first. Elvis.

'You want to search my home?' said Troy.

'Oh, we're doing that now, Troy,' said Elvis. 'We're over at your flat, doing that now.'

47

Monday, 6 December, 11.40 am
'Are you sure you don't want to go to the wake?' asked Gabriel. 'We could just go for half an hour and then I'll get you right out of there.'

Jill sat in Gabriel's car in the queue with other mourners leaving the cemetery. Her eyes were red and swollen, but dry.

'No, thanks, Gabe,' she said. 'I came to the funeral for Scotty. I said goodbye to him here. I'm not up to comforting his family and friends. That's why I wanted to come with you. I know my parents would have nagged me to go to the wake.'

Gabriel nodded.

'Thanks,' she said.

'Well, you have to deal with things your own way. Just because it's a social custom, you shouldn't do it for the sake of how it looks to other people.'

When Gabriel indicated to turn left onto Carrington Road, Jill said, 'Gabe, where are you going?'

'Taking you home.'

'Are you serious?' Jill swung in her seat to glare at him. 'I've been out of this investigation for a week because you and my mother forced me to be. I'm back now, and I'm back in. We're going to your place, and you're going to tell me exactly where this case is up to.'

'You hungry?' asked Gabriel, opening the door of his third-floor unit.

'No,' said Jill, entering behind him.

'I'll make you a sandwich,' he said.

Jill knew better than to argue with Gabriel. He had his own kind of logic. She found two plates, two glasses and some napkins in the third drawer. If they were going to eat first, she could at least try to speed up the process.

Gabriel pulled from the fridge a loaf of rye bread, a takeaway barbeque chicken, an iceberg lettuce and a jar of mayonnaise, and began assembling the sandwiches. His little grey cat, Ten, came running with the smell of the chicken. Jill found another saucer and took a piece of chicken breast that Gabriel had stripped from the carcass. Ten did figure-eights at her feet. She shredded the chicken onto the saucer and put it down onto the floor.

'Thanks,' said Gabriel.

Jill washed her hands, poured juice into the glasses and took them over to the kitchen table. She sat and waited for him, rigid in the chair. Whistling, Gabriel brought the plates over to the table, and then walked over to the glass doors of his balcony, sliding them open. By the time he sat down, Jill felt like the muscles in her neck had fused.

They started in on the sandwiches, still without speaking. Jill could hear every noise around her acutely. The sound of the leaves rustling in the huge gum tree that almost overran Gabe's balcony usually relaxed her, but today they sounded like test-pattern static on a TV turned up way too loud. Jill usually loved to watch Gabriel eat. He ate almost everything with his hands, and always with a devoted, concentrated focus. Sometimes he rocked or hummed or smiled with pleasure as he ate. Today, the sound of him chewing almost made Jill scream.

'Good, huh?' he said, his mouth full.

Jill had peeled a crust from her sandwich and tried to eat it. Instead, she'd torn it into tiny pieces and dropped it onto her plate. She stared at him. Great detective.

Gabriel finished the last of his sandwich and she leant forward. Finally. He downed half his juice, then reached over to her plate. He waggled his eyebrows at her as he took half of her sandwich.

'Fuck!' she said, pushing her chair away from the table.

He peered up at her, chewing, smiling.

She laughed once, and shook her head. 'How long are you going to take?' she said.

'What are you waiting for?'

'To talk!'

'So talk.'

She groaned. 'Delahunt, you drive me mad,' she said.

He grinned widely, already reaching for the other half of her sandwich.

'Please, Gabe. Tell me what's going on.'

'Okay, let's go through what we know of the murder at Incendie. Give me your summary.'

'Miriam Caine was burned to death,' she said. 'No one saw what happened. It was Scotty's last case. He wasn't sure whether it was murder or suicide.'

'Well, now we know for sure that it was murder. The perp splashed the blouse and face of Mrs Caine with two types of accelerant, and she was set on fire. We know that Troy Berrigan was the first to her aid; he got her down to the ground and put the flames out. According to the vic's son, David Caine, he was on his way back from the men's and a stroll around the restaurant. Says he saw what was happening and rushed over. The patrons were removed from the scene to the evacuation point outside the hotel.'

'I know all this,' said Jill.

'We need to be on the same page from here on in. And I don't know what you know. So, I'm going to keep going.'

She nodded. 'Sorry.'

'The patrons' names were taken and we've done follow-up interviews with all of them,' he said. 'Many of the prelim interviews with the patrons were done by Scotty. Collectively, the diners inform us that Mrs Caine and her son were dining peacefully until he got up. Next thing, they hear screaming and Mrs Caine is on fire.'

'And Berrigan was closest to her when she screamed?'

'Correct.'

'And when he was a kid, Berrigan set a school on fire?'

'Correct.'

'And Elvis thinks he set Miriam Caine on fire. Let's say he's right. Why would Berrigan do something like that?' said Jill.

'He's an arsonist. Disillusioned with life and wants attention. So he gets close to Miriam, squirts her with fuel, lights her up, then puts her out. And he becomes the hero again, can play cop again, be part of the investigation. You know he was a whistle blower over at Redfern LAC? Copped so much shit after it that he had to get out. It must have hurt to have gone from hero to zero in a few months.'

'It sounds like a reason,' said Jill. 'But you said that you don't think he did it.'

'That's because he didn't.'

'What makes you so sure?'

'Berrigan is all wrong. Completely wrong personality profile for this type of killer. Berrigan is hot-tempered, he's compassionate, he drinks too much because he feels guilty about not being able to save his partner. Our perp is devoid of empathy, he's narcissistic, over-controlled, he doesn't abuse alcohol.'

'I don't know where you get that from,' said Jill, 'but let's back up a bit first. You interviewed Berrigan. You think he's not the one – but if Berrigan didn't do it, who else was close enough to have started the fire?'

'No one.'

'And she didn't do it herself?'

'Nope. No ignition device found on her.'

'Could she have tossed it after lighting up?'

'No matches, lighter or candles within throwing distance of Mrs Caine.'

'And no one saw anything?'

'Oh, people saw something,' said Gabriel. 'Miriam Caine was not on fire, and then she was.'

'A remote device?' said Jill.

'Yep.'

'The son – David Caine.'

'He looks good to me.'

'What's he got to say for himself?'

'I'm playing this carefully, Jill. We talked to him at first, of course, but the guy's as cool as a carrot.'

'I think that's cucumber,' said Jill with a small smile.

'What is?' asked Gabriel, his brow furrowed.

'Never mind, keep going. You interviewed him. What did his body language tell you?'

'Actually, Jill, I haven't gone near him.'

'What? Why?'

'He thinks all cops are stupid. So I sent in Elvis.'

'You want him to think he's right, that he has the upper hand.'

'Exactly. But I've been right up his arse on paper. I know everything that can be known about his past. And I also had Elvis and Emma record their interview with him.'

'Great,' said Jill. She'd often been stunned at the information Gabe could glean from watching recorded interviews. 'So, what'd you get?'

'Well, the interview is the main reason I looked into him so hard. He just did not look like a man who'd lost his mother that way. I watched it with and without sound, and I'm convinced I have his personality type right. He's a logic-dominant, inactive extrovert.'

'What the hell is that?'

'Well, you would see him as extremely controlled, cold and unapproachable, unless he has a reason to get close to you. He'll have no true friends and contributes virtually nothing to any relationship. But it's actually an extremely efficient personality type. He uses no more energy than is necessary to express any emotion in order to get the job done. It's all about the logic, and he sees himself as more logical, rational and clever than anyone else.'

'What told you all this?'

'Well, Caine would view any interview with police as an interrogation, but rather than displaying stress cues, there's almost a complete absence of them on the tape. The more intense the questioning, the calmer he became. Sometimes he was even amused, almost giving the impression that what Elvis was discussing – his mother burning to death – was of no consequence. That's what gave him away to me. Not what he did or said, but what he didn't do and didn't say. This type of personality has the fewest kinesic and verbal cues of all subtypes.'

'Like a psychopath?'

'Well, some of them are. But Caine isn't devoid of emotion, and he's extremely skilled at detecting it in others. He manipulated Elvis throughout the whole interview. Whenever Calabrese displayed heightened interest in one of his responses, he used it, almost absorbed it, to throw Elvis off track. He was a hunch-detector, and he ran the whole show like a puppet-master. But Emma Gibson, clever girl, got a rise out of him.'

'What was it?'

'It was when she suggested that there could be a link between his mother's and Scotty's murders.'

'How did he react?'

'He was furious.'

'Maybe he's angry we're onto him. He didn't think we were smart enough to make the link.'

Gabriel took his cap off and tossed it onto the lounge. He stretched his neck from side to side. 'Maybe,' he said. 'Maybe.'

'But he is our main suspect, so have we searched his house?'

'We have no grounds without using the remote-device theory.'

'Well, why haven't you?'

'I want to leave Elvis on Troy Berrigan for a while. I want to keep Caine in the dark for a little longer. I think maybe he's done a lot more than commit matricide.'

'Yeah, he killed the man I love!' Jill stood. 'How can you let the fucker sleep in his own bed another night, Gabriel? We have to go and pick this prick up.'

'You have to listen to me, Jill,' said Gabriel. 'Please, just sit down and listen for a bit.'

Jill snorted and dropped into the chair, her arms folded.

Gabriel leaned forward and put his hands together on the table. 'If we go into this guy's house and don't find the remote, which we won't, because it will be tiny and he'll have destroyed or hidden it, then he's going to know we're onto him and change up. We won't be able to arrest him, and he'll run. We have to get him on Scotty's murder, but I think he's also been up to a lot of other shit. We can get him on the lot if we just do this properly.'

'What other shit?' asked Jill.

'Well, can I take you through my reasoning first?' said Gabriel. 'Believe me, Jill. We're not going to let him get away, and if I can get you up to speed, you can really help out here. I couldn't trust Elvis not to go blundering through this and clue Caine up. But I can trust you not to, can't I?'

'I'm listening,' said Jill.

'So, I was thinking about why Caine might have decided to kill his mother in Berrigan's restaurant. My first assumption was that it was all about the restaurant's name. For a narcissist like Caine, it's a perfect fuck-you to police to get away with burning someone to death in a place called Incendie. I thought that was it – just an ego thing, a smartarse nod to us. But then I realised it could be more than that. I think Caine deliberately targeted Berrigan. It can't be a coincidence that the manager of the restaurant just happens to have the perfect arsonist's profile. Well, the arson profile for dummies, anyway.'

'It's a pretty big coincidence,' said Jill.

'So it's probably not,' said Gabriel. 'I believe that Caine must have had some knowledge of Berrigan's background. It turns out that Caine was living and working in the same area of Sydney at the time of Berrigan's school fire – maybe he remembered the names of the kids involved. There were a rash of school fires at the time, and there was quite a lot of media comment as well. He could've heard Troy's name back then. Maybe he was a cleaner at the school. I don't know how yet, but I think Caine knew about Berrigan's history and I think that Caine targeted this restaurant because of Berrigan. And on the night, he waited for Berrigan to be physically close to his mother, then he detonated the device. Once Berrigan had put her out, Caine just had to reach under the sheet and take the trigger mechanism. It would have been a brooch or something small he'd pinned to his mother's clothing, chest area. So then we're all looking at Berrigan, and Caine's home and hosed.'

'Smart motherfucker,' said Jill.

'Which is what I thought,' said Gabriel. 'This is a smart motherfucker, and someone used to getting away with things. It just didn't seem like a first-offence crime of passion to me. He's also someone who wants to stay hidden – he's gone to all that trouble to find us our suspect and frame him. I think this means that he's someone practised in doing research in order to cover his tracks. Of course, I looked for any priors first up with this guy and got nothing. But he stinks, you know? I'm thinking there's more. So I start fishing.'

Jill knew that the databases in Gabriel's unit were better than in any copshop she'd worked.

He continued. 'I name-searched and data-matched through all the Medicare, credit-card numbers and tax records, and I found that David Caine has lived in four states in Australia over the past ten years.'

'No big deal,' said Jill. 'People move around a lot more than that.'

'And then I looked into unsolved deaths within a fifty-kay radius of where he was living.'

'Oh, come on, Gabe,' said Jill. 'Not every murderer is a serial killer.'

'You want to know what I found or not?'

'Go.'

'Well, there was only one murder in one of the areas he lived – the poisoning of a water dispenser in an office building in Perth. The top of the bottle was pierced with a syringe and a highly toxic pesticide was squirted into it. It killed William Curtis, forty-eight. Curtis had recently undergone chemotherapy and was physically weak. Eight of his colleagues were more lucky, but they all had to be hospitalised.'

'I don't get it. Why think Caine had anything to do with it?'

'People don't listen enough,' said Gabriel.

Jill groaned and rested her head on her hands on the table. She just wanted to go and arrest the bastard who killed Scotty. She did not care about William Curtis or even Miriam Caine. She felt guilty even as she thought it, and tilted her head to the side to peer up at Gabriel.

'Listening,' she said.

'I like your hair like that,' he said.

'Don't push it.'

'So,' Gabriel went on, 'then I'm thinking about people who might have been almost killed in the radius around Caine. People badly injured. Or maybe unexplained deaths. You know, other ways that this guy might have killed without causing any suspicion, like hits that appeared to be accidents.'

'Anything?'

'Everything.'

Gabriel smiled widely. Jill waited.

'In every state that Caine has lived, within a fifty-kilometre radius of his home, there has been at least one unexplained or accidental death, and there have been several serious injuries.'

'Are you for real?' said Jill. 'I mean, I'm trying here, Gabe, but you would probably get a pattern like that for hundreds of people.'

Gabriel smiled again. 'And in every one of these cases – unexplained deaths, fatal accidents or serious injuries, all within fifty kilometres of David Caine's place of residence – the victims were some type of government employee.'

'Huh?' said Jill.

'A connection,' said Gabe.

'Same MO?'

'Completely different,' said Gabriel.

'What are you talking about here, Gabe? You're saying that David Caine is a serial killer who targets government employees, and that he's killing using a different method each time?'

'Yep.'

'Why?'

'Well, why he's doing it, I don't know yet. He could be paranoid, a hard-right or hard-left extremist, even a hardcore technophobe or environmentalist. We'll get that out of him on interview. But he kills with different MOs because he's an opportunist.'

'So he kills these people whenever he gets an opportunity?' said Jill. 'You mean it's not just about the killing, it's about the ideology too? He's trying to get his message across by killing and maiming?'

Gabriel nodded.

'Which means you can sum up that possible list of yours with one word,' said Jill. 'Terrorist.'

Gabriel grinned.

'So why target Scotty then?' said Jill. 'Because he's a government employee? Or did Scotty have something on him, or at least Caine was worried he did?'

Gabriel frowned. 'I don't know. I don't know that yet.'

'Well, what do we do now?' said Jill.

'We've got to gather more evidence, quietly and very, very quickly. That's the other thing I learned from the tape, Jill. Although he's a master at hiding it, Caine is full of rage.'

48

Monday, 6 December, 2.04 pm
Jill sat in the passenger seat next to Gabriel, miserable in the dark pantsuit she'd worn to Scotty's funeral. Each time she moved she was aware of a black-clad arm or leg, which triggered the memory of watching Scotty's casket being lowered into the ground, away from her forever. There was no way she'd waste time going home to get changed, though. Food, clothes, sleeping, breathing – all were inconsequential until she put some fucker behind bars or in the ground.

She stared out at the road ahead, thinking through what she'd learned this afternoon. 'Gabe,' she said finally, 'why hasn't Elvis considered that a remote device could have been used to start the fire that killed Miriam Caine?'

'Occam's razor,' he replied. His trucker cap was low and she couldn't see his eyes.

'Huh?'

'You know, Occam. The fourteenth-century philosopher.' Gabriel made it sound like he was talking about someone they'd gone to school with. '*Entia non sunt multiplicanda praeter necessitatem* – things shouldn't be multiplied unnecessarily.'

'Okay,' Jill said tiredly, pushing her fringe away from her eyes and leaning back into the headrest. 'Your translation makes about as much sense as the Latin, or whatever the fuck you were speaking. Psych patient here, remember? Can you cut me some slack?'

He laughed. 'Sorry. The principle of Occam's razor states that in any puzzle or conundrum, usually the simplest explanation is the correct explanation.'

'You're saying that Elvis has gone for the simplest explanation?' she said. 'I understand that. Elvis has simple down pat. But wouldn't even he want to have a look at Caine? Setting someone on fire is just about as passionate a crime as you can get. You'd want to look at the family first.'

Gabe took his right hand off the wheel, held it up in front of the windscreen, checking off points with his fingers.

'One, Caine has no priors,' he said, dropping his pinkie finger. 'Two, Caine is more than ten metres from the vic when she goes up.' He lowered the next finger. 'Three, your boy, Elvis, has his little arson profile on Berrigan.' He dropped another finger. 'But more than all that,' Gabriel waggled his remaining index finger, flicked a glance in her direction, 'Elvis has a boner for Berrigan. You know Elvis is a cop's cop. He doesn't like whistle blowers. It also turns out he shared piss-ups and whores with one of the Redfern knuckleheads that Berrigan took down. When Elvis learned Berrigan was a suspect, he didn't want to look any further. He wants Troy trussed up, and he's even willing to work at it.'

Jill shifted. She became aware of her black suit again and lost focus. She saw Scotty being lowered into the ground. She closed her eyes. Worse. She leaned her forehead on the window and watched the road go by. Scotty's next agenda on the Incendie case was to come out here to speak to Miriam Caine's community group. She pictured him in the shower last Saturday morning, telling her his plans. The road blurred outside the window.

'Can you keep an eye out for four-four-five?' said Gabriel. 'It's on your side.'

'Four-oh-seven,' she said, watching the pet, sporting and fashion wholesalers slide by. 'Four-twenty-nine,' she said. 'Slow down. There. Pull up in the loading zone.'

She and Gabriel entered a two-storey brick building, its render so thick with paint that its walls were rounded at the corners. A grafittied sign at the front told them they could have their cards read, meet with a solicitor or a Mary Kay consultant, or attend a Weight Watchers meeting. Jill wondered whether anyone visiting the building had ever run the gamut – partaken of all the services on offer. She could see it happening.

'Who'd you say we're meeting again?' she asked Gabriel.

'Heather Smith organises the meeting,' he said. 'It's just a social group. Heather makes sure everyone knows what's happening and when. Up the stairs there, Jill.' He pulled out a notepad, flicked it open. 'She promised that some other group members would be there too – Hazel Wilson, Walter Gilmore and Rosa Gordano.'

Jill followed Gabriel into a room at the end of the dingy corridor. Who would want to come here to meet every week? Four people sat around a bare formica table.

A smaller table with a coffee urn and disposable cups was the only other furniture in the room, other than a noticeboard stuck with layers of curling memos and posters.

'It's okay, please don't stand up,' she said. 'I'm Jill and this is Gabriel. We're with the police.'

'Hello, I'm Heather,' said a trim woman in glasses, standing anyway.

Jill put her age at maybe sixty-five.

'I spoke with you on the phone,' Heather said to Gabriel. 'This is Walter.'

A stooped man in a cardigan used his hands to push himself up from the table. Gabriel stepped forward to shake hands. Walter nodded at Jill.

'This is Rosa,' continued Heather.

A hugely overweight woman aged between thirty and forty waved and smiled. Jill guessed that Rosa's mental age was probably pre-adolescent.

'And this is Hazel,' said Heather. Hazel had to be seventy.

'Would you like some cake and coffee?' asked Hazel, smiling.

'No, thanks,' said Jill.

'Great,' said Gabriel at the same moment.

'It's a cinnamon teacake,' said Hazel.

'Hazel baked it last night,' said Heather.

'Because she knew you were coming,' said Rosa.

'Well, maybe a small piece,' said Jill.

'She makes us a cake every week,' said Rosa.

Jill smiled.

'Or sometimes biscuits.' Rosa's plate was empty and pulled close. She stared at the cake.

While Heather made coffee for everyone, handing the cups to Walter, who shuffled them over to the table, and Hazel carefully cut a slice of cake for six plates, Jill sat on her hands. Literally. The process going on around her was clearly a ritual for the group, and she sensed that asking questions before it was completed would be rude. And pointless: Rosa's piece of cake was gone before Hazel had cut the next, and Rosa watched the rest of the slicing with complete devotion. Walter was pinpoint-focused on the brimming plastic cups as he hobbled from one table to the other. Heather and Hazel were busy playing perfect hosts.

Jill wondered how the group would feel about her doing some short interval sprint training across the room; she reckoned she could get six laps in for every one of Walter's crosses. She caught Gabriel's eye and gave him a please-kill-me-now look. He shovelled in cake, grinning. Finally, Heather and Walter sat down at the table and Jill flipped open her notebook.

'If it's all right with everyone, I'd like to get started asking a few questions,' said Jill. The group watched her, suddenly solemn. 'Firstly, Gabriel and I would like to say how sorry we are about the death of your friend Miriam.'

Heather nodded and Walter bowed his head.

Hazel, slowly shaking her head, said, 'It's just terrible. We can't believe it. She came here every week for years. It just won't be the same without her.'

Rosa began to cry, and Hazel stood and moved around the table to comfort her.

Jill ploughed on. 'I'm sure you all know now that we believe that Miriam was actually murdered.'

'Just terrible,' said Hazel again.

Rosa blew her nose. 'She always said it was going to happen,' she said through her tissue.

'She always said what?' asked Jill, sitting forward.

'Someone's going to kill me,' said Rosa.

'Miriam said that someone was going to kill you?' said Jill.

'No, *me*,' said Rosa. 'She said someone's going to kill me.'

Jill looked at Gabriel.

'Rosa's saying that Miriam was worried that someone was trying to kill her,' he said.

'That's what I said,' said Rosa.

'Sorry,' said Jill, writing. She looked up. 'When did she say this?'

'You've got to understand that Miriam was a very suspicious woman,' said Hazel. 'I've known her for a few years now, and she's always been worried about something.'

'Like what?' asked Jill.

'She had a list,' said Heather. 'She used to say there would be a war or a terrorist attack, or that Indonesia would invade Australia.'

'And she thought that the government were watching her,' said Hazel.

'Because she's a Jew,' said Rosa. 'That's what she said.'

'She survived the Holocaust, you know,' said Hazel. 'I think that made her a suspicious person. And who could blame her? But she wasn't always talking about these things. She liked playing cards with us.'

'And picnics,' said Rosa.

'And she would tell stories about the war,' said Heather. 'I could listen to her for hours.'

'But she also mentioned that she thought that someone was trying to kill her? Is that correct?' asked Jill.

'Yes, just recently,' said Hazel. 'Within the last six months, I would say – would you say that, Heather?'

'Yes,' said Heather. 'One week she'd come in here and tell us all that she didn't have long to live, that she was going to be killed.'

'And then the next week,' continued Hazel, 'she'd be right as rain. We'd ask her how she was feeling and she'd say she was fine. She'd talk about her granddaughter or about her childhood.'

'We were a little worried about her memory,' said Heather. 'She's been forgetting things a lot recently.'

'Like when we were going to meet at the bus stop in Mascot, remember?' said Rosa. 'To go to the beach? She forgot.'

'And she was getting mixed up with dates,' said Heather.

'And she'd repeat herself a lot,' said Hazel.

Gabriel pushed his chair away from the table. 'That's a great cake,' he said.

'Please, can I offer you another slice?' asked Hazel. 'Would anyone else like another piece?'

Gabriel and Rosa slid their plates towards the cake, both beaming. Jill glared at him.

'Did Miriam ever talk about any specific threats?' asked Gabriel, drawing his plate back towards him.

The room stilled.

'Yes,' said Walter – his first word for the meeting. 'She said that someone was going to set her on fire.'

49

Monday, 6 December, 4.35 pm
Erin decided to pass on the swimming after work idea for today. She had an evening community meeting at six pm and she couldn't be bothered doing her hair and make-up again. She ate an apple and browsed an online foodie forum, torturing herself with the recipes. Her email alert sounded and she clicked on the icon. A message from Shane. She wondered whether it would always feel like she'd been punched in the gut each time she saw his name.

'Hey, I'm going away for work this weekend,' he had written. 'I'm going to have to reschedule with Callie and Reece. I'll call them tonight. Sorry.'

She hit reply. 'Hey,' she wrote. 'Why are you sorry? Because you're taking your whore away for the weekend rather than keeping your promise to your kids? Because you promised me that we'd be together forever and you're a fucking liar? Because Christmas is coming up and I'm never going to get to spend it with your family again?' She took a deep breath, highlighted the text and typed over it. 'Right,' she wrote. 'Thanks for letting me know.' She hit the send/receive button, and instantly another email with an attachment came through.

The subject line shouted in capitals: 'DO YOU WANT THIS TO HAPPEN TO CALLIE?' There was nothing in the message body.

Erin became very still. Her computer fan kicked in, droning in her quiet office. She stared down at the screen. Moments ticked by. She moved the cursor towards the attachment symbol of the email. Holding her breath, she opened the attachment.

Erin's hand flew to her mouth. The acid attack on those kids in Pagewood – a scanned newspaper article. No one had ever threatened her kids. What kind of sicko had sent this? She reviewed the article quickly – the police hadn't caught anyone.

She picked up the phone. Stabbed in the number. 'Callie!'

'Mum, what's wrong?'

Erin forced herself to speak more calmly. 'Nothing, honey,' she said. 'I just called to check that you guys are okay.'

'We're fine,' said Callie.

'Reece in his room?'

'Of course. Online.'

'And no one else is over there?'

'Nope.'

Erin relaxed her grip on the phone, sighed. 'Your dad called you yet?' she asked.

'Why? Is he cancelling again?' asked Callie.

'I'll let him tell you.'

'I'm glad, anyway,' said Callie. 'I mean, it's not like when he was here we were all hanging around each other anyway. We've all got stuff to do.'

'What are you thinking about doing this weekend?'

'Danni's party? Remember? I've only told you, like, ten times.'

'Oh, right. And I said yes?'

'Mum! Don't muck around with things like this. You know me and Danni have been planning this for ages.'

'Tell me again,' said Erin. 'Tell me who's going, what you're wearing, where her mum will be, Danni's address, what time it starts, whether or not there'll be alcohol, who uses drugs at your school, whether you've ever been arrested, had sex or smoked a cigarette.'

'I have homework.'

Erin smiled. 'I am going to call Danni's mum, though, honey.'

'Fine. If you've got all this time to talk, why aren't you home?'

'Another CCTV town meeting. Remember? I've only told you, like, ten times.'

'Well, at least I've got an excuse for forgetting,' said Callie. 'The things you do at work are so boring.'

'My excuse for forgetting is called old age.'

'I'd call it Korsakoff's,' said Callie.

'I'll call you grounded this weekend if you're not nicer to your mum, smart aleck.'

Erin felt her daughter grinning on the other end of the phone.

'What time will you be home?' asked Callie.

'Around eight, I hope. I'll let you go. Don't let anyone come over and don't answer the door. And make sure your brother eats something. The fridge is chockers with stuff.'

This time some sensible questions were asked and there was a reasonable turnout for the meeting. Erin thanked her fellow committee member, Ron Kennedy, for attending and fielding questions with her. She told him to go home, that she'd be fine to pack up. Ron, a senior constable from Glebe Local Area Command, had been with her since the beginning. The local police were her biggest champions for the camera project.

'I'll wait for you,' Ron said, walking through the seats and collecting leftover information booklets. Erin noted that even though she put him at late twenties at best, his ginger hair was already thinning. Policing was a hard job.

'You want some of these quiche things?' she asked, throwing some paper plates into the large waste bin next to the food table. Sheesh, it would have been easier for these people to have dropped the used plates into the bin instead of onto the table. Some people just had that attitude – the government owes me, the free food's not enough, someone else can pick up the mess.

'Are you serious?' Ron said. 'Some squirrel out there might've left a little something there hoping the cop would eat the leftovers.'

Erin stopped what she was doing and screwed up her face. 'What are you talking about?' she said.

'You know – bodily fluids.'

'Ron, you're paranoid,' said Erin, shaking her head. 'Not everyone is out there to get you.'

'Yeah?' he said. 'Used to be, when my dad was on the job, citizens were always dropping stuff off. There was always a cake, biscuits; shit, sometimes some lady would bring in a roast chook around dinnertime with all the trimmings. No cop ever had to buy his own meals. Not like that now.'

'No one brings stuff to you guys anymore?'

'Oh, people still bring stuff,' said Ron. 'But it goes straight in the bin or we send it back home with them.'

'That's crazy,' said Erin. 'A little old lady bakes the boys in blue a chocolate slice, and, what, it's seen as a bribe or something?'

'You're not getting it,' he said, stacking chairs. 'That little old lady might have had her old man or son jammed up by one of us, and the chocolate in that slice might not be Cadbury, if you know what I'm saying.'

'That's disgusting.' Erin stood motionless with a stack of plates.

'That's life nowadays,' said Ron.

'It's sad, that's what it is.' Erin went back to the tidying.

'I'm not sure what would be worse,' said Ron, 'getting a mouthful of shit or a mouthful of needles. A few years ago, some poor prick out at Guildford bit into an orange from a big bag dropped off by some kind citizen and got two sewing needles rammed into his tongue and gums. Some loony motherfucker had spent his weekend studding every orange with at least ten needles. But hey, don't cry too hard for us. Every couple of weeks a bloke will come in and drop off a slab. Now, that gets put to good use, I can tell you.'

Erin moved about the hall, collecting discarded fliers. 'A few people had something to say tonight about that stabbing murder in the city on Thursday night,' she said.

'Well, of course they did,' said Ron. 'It was bound to come up – it happened right in front of the camera. And a few people made the same point; it was a valid point too. These cameras – even these new cameras – aren't going to be able to catch everyone. But I think you handled it really well. You just acknowledged that this project is not going to solve every crime in every place, but it will increase the success rate.'

'There's not a lot a camera can do when someone's wearing a mask like that,' she said. 'I swear that footage gave me nightmares.'

Ron snorted. 'Good thing you didn't see the whole thing, then.'

Erin stopped and turned. 'Did you?'

Ron paused as well, leaned on the stack of chairs in front of him. 'It was about as bad as anything I've seen in my life,' he said. 'Whoever did that is completely deranged. The perp went absolutely mad shanking that poor bloke. He stabbed him eight or nine times, and it wouldn't have been easy, Erin – a screwdriver through clothes?' Ron shook his head. 'We better get that one quick. He's a mad bastard.'

When the hall was reasonably tidy, Erin and Ron made their way out to the quiet council carpark. At her car, Erin's mobile sounded.

'Night, Ron,' she said before answering it. 'Thanks again for everything.'

Ron Kennedy was half-lowered into his driver's seat when he heard Erin's scream. He pulled a muscle in his calf springing back up again.

Erin Hart ran full pelt towards him, eyes wild, frantic.

50

Monday, 6 December, 8.25 pm
Jill used a face washer to remove the last of her make-up. Just as she did every night, she rinsed the cloth and used it to polish her sink before lobbing it into the laundry basket by the door. She turned back to the basin, automatically reaching for a hair band. She caught her reflection in the mirror and realised she didn't need one now. She pushed her new fringe to the side. Scotty had never seen her hair like this.

She smiled at herself in the mirror. He'd have given her hell. Would've told her it made her face look fat, or something. Jill turned away from the mirror when her eyes began to brim again. He'd had a thing about wrapping her long hair in his hand, trapping her and pulling her to him gently. When he'd first tried that she'd brought him to the ground with a kick behind his knee.

The second time, she'd pushed him flat on her bed and climbed aboard.

She went back into her bedroom and picked the black jacket up from the bed. She hung it in the wardrobe. When she'd bought the outfit, she'd thought she'd wear it a lot – to court, when visiting the lock-up – but it turned out she'd worn it just twice. Both times to funerals.

My Scotty. Jill grabbed his pillow and curled up with it on her bed.

The phone rang. Her mobile was in the kitchen. She dragged herself up and shuffled out there. It'd be her mum – she'd already left four messages – but Jill didn't feel like talking; she'd call her back tomorrow. She checked the display anyway. Frowned. Hit the green button.

'Gabriel?' she said, and cleared her throat.

'You want to come out?'

'No.' What's wrong with you?

'There's been another firebomb.'

'What? Who?'

'House in Glebe. The local member; name's Erin Hart. Her kids were in there.'

'Give me the address.'

Jill muted her GPS and followed the fireys' lights strobing through smoke in the night sky. She pulled up beside a patrol car that was blocking the street. Kids in pyjamas ran about while adults clustered together, gossiping. Two news vans were parked up on the sidewalk. Jill approached the uniformed female constable guarding the perimeter; another woman, standing with her, watched Jill approach.

'Detective Jill Jackson,' she said, showing her badge. 'Maroubra.'

'What are you doing out here, Detective?' asked the cop. 'Sorry to ask. It's just I've been told to keep everyone out until the techies get here.'

'That's okay,' said Jill, wondering about the best way to answer. No way was she going to let the listening civilian know she was linked to Scotty's case, and that they were thinking these acts could be related. Jill could tell by the woman's demeanour that she was a journalist. She looked over towards the house with the broken front window. Soot ringed the window like a black eye. Two suited-up fireys were standing by their truck, laughing. And then Gabriel walked out the front door of the terrace, stepping gingerly. He saw her, waved. Big smile.

'My partner,' said Jill.

'You're with the Fed?'

'On this I am,' said Jill. She moved past the patrol car and the civilian.

Gabriel waved her over towards the rear of his car.

'I've got some new stuff,' he said.

'Okay, first of all, Gabriel,' she said, 'was anyone hurt?'

'Nope. The living room light was on but the kids were in their rooms. It was another Molotov. Did some pretty good damage. I doubt it was petrol, though. First glance at the fire pattern makes me think it was something else. It burned out in the dining room. Erin Hart wasn't home.'

'Where is she now?'

'At the copshop with the kids. We'll interview her later.'

'Who's running things out here?'

'Glebe, but they're happy for me to take what I need.'

'Why?'

'Because Colby called them.'

'You're kidding?' said Jill. James Colby was the AFP Deputy Commissioner in charge of National Security. 'Why?'

'I told him we're dealing with a terrorist.'

Jill ran a hand through her hair, then looked back at the house. A trickle of dark water dribbled out the front door. 'But calling Colby over a Molotov cocktail? That's pretty big.'

'This is all pretty big. A firebomb at a politician's home equals domestic terrorism until we prove otherwise. But when you can possibly link it with the murder of a cop, you got two crimes against the Commonwealth and we get access all areas.'

'You think this is definitely linked to Scotty?'

He shrugged. 'Could be copycat – someone got all horny over the news his death got, wanted to recreate the thrill, see their work on TV. Or it could be all about Erin Hart – maybe she's doing something that someone from her electorate doesn't like.'

'Or it could be the person that killed Scotty. It could be David Caine.'

'That's why we're here,' said Gabriel. He popped the boot of his car.

Jill stared. 'What is all that?' she asked.

'Told you, I got some new stuff. This here –'

'Hang on a sec, Gabe. Maybe you and I should just leave this to the techies. They'll be here soon. I'm really worried that we're wasting time here – I think you and I should at least go and talk to Caine; bring him in for an interview. If he's done this firebomb too, he'll be hyped right now – we can have a crack at him while he's emotional.'

'Jill, you've got to trust me,' said Gabriel, leaning into the boot of his car. He looked back at her from under the rim of his cap. 'Caine won't interview. We'll get nothing. This is not the kind of guy you, me or anyone else is going to crack. You could torture this prick and he wouldn't crack. We'd bring him in and let him go because of lack of evidence, and he'd cut and run. The only reason he's still taking his arse to bed in Rosebery every night is because he thinks we're stupid. We can't disabuse him of that opinion.'

She sighed.

'We'll get him on evidence,' said Gabriel.

'Show me your new stuff,' said Jill.

'First, suit up.' He handed her paper overalls and booties.

In the entryway of the politician's house, Jill wondered if her life could ever have turned out like this. Spread out ahead of her was a home. Photographs of children growing, playing, Christmassing with cousins; schoolbooks on a coffee table; lamps, throw rugs and cushions. A busy calendar in the kitchen, a schoolbag in the hall. Intellectually, Jill knew that at thirty-four she still could have all this, but right then and there, she saw her future stretched ahead of her, and it was alone. Her sunny Maroubra unit seemed suddenly sterile, barren.

She covered her mouth to block some of the burning stench in the house and moved towards Gabriel in the dining room. He was videotaping the scene. Maybe her apartment figuratively had a blackened, blistered heart, but this house had the real thing. She stepped carefully through the crime scene. It was obvious that the firebomb had been hurled through the front window of the home, evidently smashing against the dining table and exploding. The fireball had deeply scorched most of the polished wood table, but it was still standing. A hairlike curl of smoke rose from the remains of a rug underneath the table, the mirror-shine of the floorboards around it now charred. The innards of two of the dining suite's leather upholstered chairs protruded white and exposed through split skin.

'It could have been worse, I guess,' she said. 'The whole house could have been set alight.'

Gabriel was squatting next to blackened, broken glass. 'That doesn't happen very often with a Molotov,' he said. 'Usually they're out within ten seconds or so, especially if it was ordinary petrol. But I'm pretty sure we're going to find that this device contained a napalm mixture.'

'Napalm! What? Isn't that used in war?'

'And by terrorists,' said Gabriel. 'I think the lab will find it was also in the bottle thrown at Scotty. It's easy to make,' he continued. 'You just mix your accelerant with styrofoam, soap flakes or paraffin wax. It keeps the burn going longer, and it's stringy and gluey so it'll stick to your target.'

Jill felt rage swell within her throat. She had to open her mouth to breathe.

'My guess is that the perp wanted this shit to hit a human. He threw it towards the light. It's rare to survive if a napalm bomb hits you. The thing is,' said Gabriel, seeming not to notice that Jill had reached out a hand to lean against a chair, 'when they explode, they deoxygenate the air and the vic usually passes out because they can't breathe.'

Jill leaned her head down to meet the hand on the chair.

'Shit, sorry, Jill,' he said. 'You shouldn't be here. It's too soon.'

'Tell you what, Gabriel,' said Jill, pale but now standing straight again. 'I won't tell you what to do if you keep your opinions about me being able to cope to yourself. You said we were going to get some evidence to nail this prick. What can I do?'

Gabriel squatted next to the huge toolbox he'd lugged in from the boot of his car. He unfolded another tier of shelving from inside the box and handed her a specimen jar. 'I need a soil sample from under the house, from right underneath where we're standing. I'll rest my torch against the floorboards so you can see what you're doing.'

Jill took the jar, cocking her head to the side. 'You don't just want to get me out of here?' she asked.

'Look,' said Gabriel. 'All the residue from the accelerant is gone from here. It combusted or was washed away, but accelerants will run quickly to the lowest level. So when the bottle smashed, some of the liquid could have run through the floorboards before the rest of it ignited. It's definitely a long shot – if this was a napalm cook, it would have been a thicker mixture and it probably all combusted, but you never know; soil has great retention properties for flammable liquids.'

'Okay,' she said. 'I'll go in a sec. I want to watch for a bit. What else you got?'

Still squatting, Gabriel scraped with a small spatula at a red blob on a blackened floorboard.

'What is it?' Jill asked.

'Not sure,' he said, holding it to his nose and sniffing. 'Some sort of rubber.' He smeared the mess onto a glass slide, topped it with another and dropped it into a plastic bag.

'Aren't the techies going to be mad that you're fucking around with this stuff?' she asked.

'Probably,' he said. 'But I videoed it all first, and I'm only taking small samples. I'll get all this to the lab when I'm done with it, but even with the hurry-up they've put on this, you know things can take time. Some of this stuff I can process myself.'

He then used a pair of rubber-tipped tongs to pick up a thick, circle-shaped piece of glass. He held it up to Jill and then dropped it into another plastic bag. 'Base of the bottle he used to make the bomb,' he said. He carefully picked through the rest of the glass and selected another rounded piece.

'You're not going to get any prints from that,' said Jill.

'You'd be surprised,' he said. 'We can lift latents that haven't been completely dissolved by fuel. They can even survive the flames.' He put the bag into his box. 'But if this was Caine, he won't have left prints. No way in the world. If I'm right – and I'm right – Caine has been committing acts of terror for maybe twenty years, and he hasn't even got a sheet.'

'So what's the glass for?'

'Well, two things. The techies said the bottle thrown into Scotty's car didn't have a wick.'

'But doesn't a Molotov cocktail need a wick to work?'

'Well, that's the way the pissants do it,' said Gabriel. 'But I think we're going to find evidence on this piece of glass –' he held up the bag and pointed to the flatter shard, 'of a chemical trigger.'

'What's that?' asked Jill.

'They add sulphuric acid to the accelerant inside the bottle and tape a package containing sugar and potassium chlorate to the outside. When the bottle breaks, the acid reacts with the sugar-chlorate, causing a super-high temperature flame which ignites the fuel.'

'Why not just do it the old way? Seems like a blowarse way to go about things.'

'Unless you want to avoid detection,' said Gabriel. 'There's no flame needed for this method. You don't have to stand outside, light a wick, make sure it catches and then throw. You're gonna attract a lot of attention doing it that way. You're gonna get eyewitnesses. With a chemical trigger, you can be jogging by, lob it in and keep running.'

'How do you know all this shit?' asked Jill.

'It's what I do.'

Jill's mouth twisted. 'Good,' she said. Knowing she had the Feds – well, Gabe in particular – hunting this arsehole gave her a vicious thrill. 'You said two things,' she continued, needing to know. 'You're collecting the glass for two reasons.'

'Oh yeah, cast-in production data.'

'What?'

'You know, the stamp they put on bottles – date, place of production, and production batch. We might be able to link it to other bottles at his house.'

'We're going to his house?'

'Probably. AFP is preparing a warrant for us now. We just need to process some of this shit. If we find any connection whatsoever to Incendie, or to what happened to Scotty, we can use it to get in. Then this evidence here can be checked against anything we find in his house, car, clothes, shoes, boat, arsehole and whatever else we want to stick our dicks into.'

'Oh, thank God,' she said. 'Does Elvis know about this yet?'

Gabriel gave her a now-what-do-you-think look. 'Elvis needs to keep his waddling arse away from Caine. When we get there, we're going in heavy. It'll be AFP all the way.'

51

Monday, 6 December, 8.25 pm
Seating a party of five, Troy tried to stay smiling when one of the garrulous men in suits stumbled into another diner. Before the group had arrived, he'd had a call from the hotel's clubroom to warn him that the group was on its way up. They were already hammered, and the loudest of them – an executive from Perth – stayed at the hotel five times a year, tipped well, and always paid the full fee for a suite. Important customer. The important customer asked for the wine menu before he even sat down. Troy signalled to Dominique and then caught James's eye.

Troy took himself away from the party; he had an image of himself headbutting the clown. He'd hated leaving Lucy this afternoon. She was still so upset. He simmered, thinking about her alone in the flat when they'd barged in last night with a warrant. She'd tried to keep it together when he finally got home from the copshop, but when she saw that he didn't have Chris with him she'd sat down on the floor and sobbed. All the way home, he'd rehearsed a story he could give Lucy about what Chris had done – another act of vandalism, maybe shoplifting. He'd crouched next to her on the floor and she'd looked up at him with her opal-green eyes. Her face wet with tears and snot, she'd asked him what Chris had done. And he'd told her. It was always that way with Lucy.

'But a *gun*?' she'd said.

'I know.'

'What's going to happen to him?'

'It would help if he'd tell them where he got it,' said Troy.

'That's why the cops were over here, huh?' she'd asked. 'They wouldn't tell me anything. I thought maybe he must have stolen something and they were looking for it.'

Troy couldn't imagine how Lucy would feel if she'd known they'd really been tossing the house to find something to pin on her other brother.

'Well, they got nothing,' he said.

It wasn't until Elvis had walked into the room at the copshop last night that he'd realised that he was in more trouble than Chris. Of course, when they found nothing in his flat, they couldn't hold him. He knew there was no evidence anywhere linking him to any of this shit.

'When can Chris come home?' asked Lucy.

'I'm not sure yet, Luce,' he'd told her. 'I'm going to find a lawyer when I wake up. You have to get to bed now, though. It's two o'clock in the morning.'

Now, Troy entered the Incendie kitchen. He was so tired. He'd finally fallen asleep at five and was up again at eight with a nightmare and the knowledge that he had to find a lawyer for his little brother. The Aboriginal Legal Service had referred him to a criminal lawyer in Surry Hills whose services wouldn't require him to get a second job. She'd sounded all right on the phone and had promised to make some enquiries about Chris. Troy hadn't been allowed to speak to him last night; he had an appointment tomorrow at ten.

He walked over to the stove, ripped a chunk of bread from a hard Italian loaf left there for this purpose, and dunked it into a huge simmering pot. He shovelled the sauce-saturated bread into his mouth. 'Great drop,' he said to his chef, swallowing. 'The new group out there – they're a bunch of fuckwits.'

'You want me to piss in the soup?' asked Roberto, his sous-chef.

'Don't be a smartarse, Robbie,' said Troy. 'I'm taking my tea break.'

Troy cracked the cool-room door and walked in. Immediately he felt calmer. The icy fog and silence wrapped him up. He walked a familiar path – straight to the cases at the back. He twisted the top off a Heineken, took a seat on a tub of fetta cheese and drained half the beer. Who'd have thought, two weeks ago, that tomorrow night's function, which he'd been dreading for months, would be the least of his problems right now. Not that the new perspective made him feel any better about the party. To be honest, the function would be that much worse because of the events of the past two weeks.

Caesar had booked it himself – all eighty seats. 'I'm on the guest list myself,' he'd said, beaming. 'So you'd better make it a bloody good job, Troy, my boy.'

Pressure enough, but then Caesar had added, 'You'll probably know half of the bastards there too. It's Chief

Superintendent Norris's retirement party – he's an old mate. This place is going to be wall-to-wall bacon.'

Oh, great, Troy had thought at the time. Just what I want to do – serve a bunch of fuckers who hate my guts. Now he felt like pissing blood every time he imagined it. He knew the way news spread amongst them. Someone had something good happen to them and you'd find out a year or maybe ten later. Someone had a pile of shit drop on their head and you'd smell it before it stopped steaming.

Troy knew he'd be on the menu tomorrow night for sure. He cracked the seal on a jumbo tin of mammoth olives and shovelled a couple in. There, dinner done, with another Heineken to wash it down. Maybe he could get pissed enough to trip and fall into the deep-fryer; it'd get him out of tomorrow night.

52

Monday, 6 December, 10.02 pm
The people of Glebe had gone back to the late-night news, checking emails before bed, maybe a last glass of something. The younger kids were sleeping, the older ones online. Back to normal for a Monday night, their train in no danger of derailing, just a brief detour past a scenic route. Something to talk about in the office tomorrow. Jill leaned against Gabriel's car. There'd never been a 'back to normal' for her.

A fallen leaf from a branch above the car startled her briefly, landing in the canoe of her collarbone. She picked it up and held it to her face, taking a deep breath and closing her eyes. The night air was warmer here, but with that scent she could have been back on the veranda at Lyrebird. They'd be wrapping up there, too, getting ready for bed. Layla would probably be settling a new roommate in tonight.

Jill opened her eyes to a snapping noise. Gabriel had locked down his evidence kit. After he'd collected the small samples from the scene, he'd spent half an hour taking photographs. He lifted the toolbox into the boot of his car.

'I don't want to go home,' she said.

He took his cap off, looked at her, then turned back to the house. Crime scene were still processing, but the fireys were long gone.

'I'm going to be working pretty late,' he said. 'Processing some of this shit.'

'I could help.'

Gabriel rubbed at the stubble on his chin. 'It's not gonna work, you know,' he said.

'What?' she said.

'Trying to distract yourself. Haven't you learned that you have to face it?'

'I don't want to go home,' she said again.

He beeped the doors open. 'Get in,' he said. 'We'll pick up your car tomorrow.'

The first thing Jill did was to slide open Gabriel's balcony doors. The summer night blew in. The tree whispered to her; she closed her eyes and listened, but she couldn't understand the words.

'You should get some rest, Jill,' said Gabriel. 'We've got a lot to do tomorrow.'

'You got anything to drink?' she asked.

He cocked his head. 'Help yourself,' he said.

Jill found a bottle of port in a cupboard above the sink. She filled a coffee mug and put the bottle on the bench. She went to find Gabriel. He sat in his computer room, the glow from his machines the only source of light in the room.

'What are you doing?' she asked.

'Accessing the glass evidence database.'

'There's a glass evidence database?'

'Yep. The techies will put samples of the bottle through spectrographic analysis; that'll tell us its elemental make-up, but we won't get access to the results until tomorrow. I did get the results of the bottle thrown into Scotty's car, though. I'm going to check the database for that now. It holds more than seven hundred glass samples from manufacturers and distributors. It's not going to give us the source of the glass, but I might be able to assess the chance that two glass samples from different sources would have the same elemental profile.'

'But you won't be able to compare them until tomorrow.'

'And I'll be ready.'

Jill took another sip.

'You hungry?' he said to the computer.

'Nah,' she said.

She moved about the room, tapped the keyboard of a sleeping screen. The machine droned into life. 'What are you going to do after that?' she asked.

'Start trying to identify the exact type of accelerant. We know from the prelim analysis that the general type is the same at each scene, but if we can get an exact chemical match, we're laughing.' He stretched his arms over his head. His biceps bulged under his black T-shirt. 'I'm still confused about the results at Incendie, though.'

'Which results?'

'The accelerants. Why would he use two – one on the face and one on the clothes?'

'More bang for his buck?' she said.

'Yeah, but more risk. It doesn't make sense to me.'

'I'm so tired,' she said.

'Your bed is ready. You just have to unfold the sofa. No one's slept in it since you were here last; I left the sheets on. You want a hand?'

'No, I'm good.'

Jill kneeled on a computer chair. She swivelled around, catching the desk when it slowed and then spinning it around again. She laughed.

'Why don't you have a shower?' he said, still to the computer. 'You can sleep in one of my T-shirts. Just get one from the drawer.'

'You trying to get rid of me?'

'I'm busy.'

Jill drained her mug and left the room. From the benchtop in the kitchen, Ten watched her, blinking slowly. She moved towards the little cat, and the purrs began before she even stretched out her hand. She gave Ten's cheeks a massage and poured another drink.

She took her coffee into the bathroom and rested it on the sink. She closed the door. A shower would be good. She hadn't had a chance to have one when Gabe called tonight, and now her hair stank of smoke. Oh fuck, she suddenly thought. What am I going to wear tomorrow? Should've thought of that earlier, Jackson, you idiot, she told herself. She took her cargos off and stripped her singlet over her head. She folded her clothes and stepped out of her underwear, steadying herself on the sink. She threw her knickers into the shower cubicle and joined them.

The water felt great until the walls started spinning. She turned the heat down. The last shower she'd had was at Lyrebird. She couldn't believe everything that had happened since then. She couldn't believe they'd buried Scotty just that morning.

Jill lost the sound of the shower under all that sobbing, and when the walls would not stop rotating she sat down. Five minutes later, the stall door opened and Gabriel stepped in. She saw his boots first. He squatted and put his hand under her chin, lifted. She met his eyes. He smiled through the water streaming over his face; his black T-shirt slick against his chest. He reached his hands under her armpits and pulled her to her feet.

She clung to him. Desolate.

Gabriel turned the taps off and stepped out of the shower. He unfurled a huge chocolate bath sheet and held it out in front of him. Jill couldn't move. Gabriel stepped back into the shower and wrapped Jill in the towel and his arms. She stood there, her head bowed into his chest. Gabriel moved his hands over the towel, over her shoulders and the small of her back. With one hand he lifted the edge of the bath sheet, and with the other hand he lifted her face and dried it. He wiped the towel around each ear. Jill watched his eyes, her own still running. He dried her cheeks again, gently. And then he lifted the towel over her face and rubbed at her hair. Not so gently.

'Ow,' she said.

Gabriel led Jill out of the stall and into the lounge, where he'd unfolded the sofa into a bed; the sheets and a light blanket had been folded back. A T-shirt waited on a pillow. 'You put that on and I'll be back,' he said.

'Don't go,' Jill said. She sat on the edge of the bed wrapped in the towel, half her blonde hair spiked at ninety degrees, the other half flopping in her eyes.

Gabriel moved to the pillow and unfolded the T-shirt. He sat next to her on the bed and pulled the shirt over her head, manoeuvring her arms through the holes. The shirt swum on her.

'Lie down,' he said.

She reclined back onto the bed and Gabriel pulled the sheets up over her. She didn't take her eyes from his. Gabriel moved to stand. Jill reached up and wrapped her arms around his neck, pulling his face to hers. Gabriel kissed her once, the briefest touch, and pulled away.

'You've got to try to sleep, Jill,' he said.

'Don't go,' she said.

Gabriel straightened. 'Close your eyes, or I'm leaving.'

Jill closed her eyes, reached for his hand. He held it until she fell asleep.

53

Tuesday, 7 December, 8.38 am
'I thought you could do with something more than fruit for morning tea today, Mrs Hart,' said Hamish, standing in her office doorway. He made a knocking gesture and she waved him in. He placed a white cardboard box on her table and dragged a chair for himself closer to her desk. 'I've put the kettle on,' he said. 'Instant okay for you?'

'I'm not sure I need any more stimulation,' said Erin. 'Maybe I should just have water.'

'Open the box,' said Hamish, 'while they're still warm. Then you can decide.'

'God bless you, Hamish,' she said. Six churros, dusted with cinnamon sugar. She peeled the lid off the container inside the box. Yep, melted chocolate. 'You are going to love your Christmas present this year.'

Over coffee and the fluffy Spanish donuts, Erin gave Hamish the details about the firebomb thrown into her dining room. Hamish kept a hand to his throat through the whole tale.

'Thank God Callie and Reece are okay,' he said.

Erin's lip trembled. She nodded, not trusting herself to speak.

'Where are they now?' he asked.

'School,' she said. 'After I called you last night, I contacted a therapist friend and she told me to send them to school this morning. She said that it was best to try to stick to routine after a traumatic event.'

'I think that's good advice,' said Hamish. 'My friend Toby Darnell quit his job and moved to Canada when his husband left him. He'd never even *been* to Canada. He was back within a month and had to start all over again, trying to get his life back together. I really think it's best to just get on with things, if you can.'

Erin smiled. 'Reece was okay to go,' she said. 'But Callie was teary. She kept asking if I was going to be okay.'

'Poor little buttons,' said Hamish.

'Neither of them wants to stay at their dad's this week, either, but I don't want them home until we fix the place up a bit.'

Hamish nodded. 'Do the police have any idea who might have done it?' he asked.

'They couldn't really tell me anything last night,' she said. 'I just gave my statement to Ron Kennedy. But first thing this morning I got a call from someone. He's coming around this morning with his partner to go through things.'

'A cop from Glebe?' asked Hamish, dunking a churro.

Erin smiled. She knew Hamish was always willing to

stay late or come in early when she had a meeting with the local police.

'Nope. Get this – he's a federal agent.'

'Shut – up!'

'I know.'

They grinned at each other.

'Well, you are an elected representative, Mrs Hart,' said Hamish. 'They should be taking this seriously.'

She made a face.

'You haven't changed your mind about tonight, have you?' he asked.

'Hamish, I don't want to go out tonight. After all this –' It's the perfect excuse to get out of it, she thought.

'Oh, come on,' he said. 'What are you going to do – sit in a smelly house by yourself all night?'

'I thought I might go and stay with my parents tonight.'

'But you promised! I spent all the money I don't have on my outfit.'

Erin sighed. Not a day had gone by that Hamish hadn't mentioned the dinner tonight. She'd asked him months ago, when she'd first received the invite, whether he'd like to come. He'd only just started working with her, and she'd imagined it would be a big imposition to ask him to come to a work function after hours, but she just couldn't imagine showing up at that swanky do alone. It turned out, though, that Hamish couldn't wait. He'd circulated the menu to all his friends and had begun shopping that afternoon for something to wear.

'Well –' she began.

'Oh, can't you see that it's destiny? Your house was firebombed and we're going to a restaurant named Incendie where a woman just got burned to death!' He grinned.

'Oh. Now that you put it that way, I'm ever so much more tempted.' The doorbell sounded at the front of the office. 'I'll think about it,' she said. 'I'll let you know after lunch. See how I feel.'

'I'll get the door,' said Hamish, pouting. 'I locked it again after I came in. It seemed like the right thing to do.'

'Yep. Thanks, Hamish,' said Erin.

As soon as Erin heard his voice, she madly considered scraping the rest of the morning tea into the garbage bin or her desk drawer, but he was at her door too quickly. Great. Shane. Her estranged husband was the only person on earth she worried about seeing her eating donuts dipped in chocolate.

She stood and moved to the front of her desk. Maybe she could block the donuts with her arse? They'd probably already contributed to its donut-blocking abilities.

'Erin, are you okay?' Shane reached his arms out and she stepped into an awkward hug. She stepped away as quickly as he dropped his hands.

'Yeah,' she said. 'I guess so.'

'It's just terrible,' he said. 'Was there a lot of damage?'

'Well, it could have been a lot worse. I was just about to call the insurers. Get them to come over so I can start looking around for repairers.'

'Should I come and take a look?' he asked.

'If you want to,' she said.

'I mean, I trust you to handle things. I just thought, because it's our house . . .' He trailed off.

'All that work we put into that room,' she said. 'It made me cry.'

'I'm sure the insurance will pay for a tradie to fix it up.'

'Yep. I'm sure they will.'

After a moment of silence, Erin said, 'Oh, thanks again for taking the kids this week.'

'No. Oh, of course. That's okay.'

'It's not putting you out, is it?' she asked.

'Well, I was planning to go away Friday. I don't suppose things would be back in order by then?'

'Oh, yeah. Right. I forgot,' she said. 'No. That will be fine, I'm sure. Callie wanted to go to a party, anyway. I'd rather she came home after it – I just want to make sure she's okay.'

'Well, I mean, if I wasn't going away, I would have made sure she came back to my place all right,' he said and smiled. Then frowned.

'Oh, I know that,' said Erin. I hate these fucking careful conversations. 'I mean, I wasn't meaning to –'

'That looks like quite a breakfast you've had there,' said Shane, craning his neck to look around her at the desk.

'Yeah, Hamish just thought, what with the shock and all –'

'Turn to chocolate. Makes sense.'

'You hate chocolate.'

'I don't hate it,' he said. 'I just hate that I have to work extra hard in the gym to get it off me.'

Erin flicked her shirt sleeve back, took a long look at her watch. 'Look at that,' she said. 'The morning's marching on.'

'Yes, I should get back to work too,' he said. 'I just wanted to make sure you're okay.'

She smiled sweetly.

'Do you have any idea who did it?' he asked.

'Not really,' she said.

'Not really?'

'Well, I've been getting the usual threats,' she said. 'This is the first time anything's come of it, though.'

'Well, there was that paint thrown at the car that day,' he said. 'And the egging of our front door. And all those phone calls that went for months at home.'

'I remember,' said Erin. 'I was there. What's your point?'

'Well, I just wondered how long you were going to keep doing this.'

'What? Working?'

'No. The politics stuff. You're a teacher, Erin. I always thought you'd go back to teaching when you'd got this out of your system.'

'Yes, you always were *so* supportive.'

Shane sighed. 'I did my best, Erin.'

'Maybe we should shut the door, or catch up about my political career on another date,' she said.

'Well, I should have some sort of say,' he said. 'They're my kids too, and all this –' he swept a hand around the room, 'could have got them killed last night.'

Erin folded her arms across her chest. 'Oh, yes, you're so concerned about your children's welfare,' she said. 'That's why you left them to be with a slut half your age.'

'And here we go again,' he said. 'I'll be going, then. But I don't know when you're going to get it, though, Erin. I didn't leave Callie and Reece. I left you.'

54

Tuesday, 7 December, 8.38 am
Jill cradled the little cat carefully, holding her close, as she had all night – sleeping, but always just aware of the warm body nestled against her stomach. She could feel Gabriel's apartment bright around her, but she kept her eyes closed, unwilling yet to face the day. She listened to him moving carefully around the kitchen. Did he really believe she could sleep through that? She was pretty sure she shouldn't be trying to sleep at all. It seemed pretty late; she wondered what time it was.

'It's after eight-thirty.' Gabriel's voice above her. 'Did Ten help?'

'Huh?' Jill blinked her eyes open.

'She's good that way. When she feels I'm sad, she snuggles into my solar plexus.'

'Your solar plexus?' Holding onto the blanket, Jill

sat up cross-legged on the couch.

'Yep, she always makes things right.'

'Sorry about last night,' Jill said, wincing.

'Sorry for what? It was just a bad day. But you probably should follow up with someone about what you learned down at the hospital.'

'I guess.'

'It's pretty good there, huh?'

'Yeah. It was.'

'You wanna get dressed?' Gabriel said. 'Breakfast is nearly ready.'

In the bathroom, Jill found her knickers dry and folded on top of yesterday's clothes. She glowered at the shower. I'm not getting in you again. She pictured Gabriel helping her last night. She supposed that she should feel mortified; embarrassed, at least. She searched around for the feelings, but found nothing particularly strong. She didn't think she was especially numb, either, her usual defence. Mainly, she just felt tired, sad.

And hungry. Gabriel was a great cook.

Fifteen minutes later, Jill finally spoke. 'What kind of crumpets are these?' she asked. 'I've never had anything like them.'

'They're from the bakery. Great, huh?'

'You can buy crumpets at the bakery?'

Gabriel lifted his eyebrows and took another bite of the crumpet in his hand. His fingers pressed into a thick fold of smoked salmon, which was blanketing a blob of his gorgeous scrambled eggs. Jill could see the whole concoction falling apart at any moment. She stuck with her knife and fork.

'I love your eggs,' she said.

'It's the cream,' he said.

'So, we're going to see this Erin Hart first up?' she asked.

'Yep. And I've advised everyone that we're to get the evidence updates as soon as they come through from the labs. I got a hit from the glass database for the bottle thrown into Scotty's car.'

Jill snapped her head up from the plate, no longer hungry. 'What?'

'The perp drinks juice. It's a Spring Valley juice bottle.'

'What do we do with that?'

'Wait to find out what kind of bottle was thrown into Erin Hart's house.'

'They'll call you as soon as they know?'

He nodded, taking another bite of his crumpet.

'How are they fitting me into this?' Jill asked.

'They're not,' Gabriel replied. 'You're not up with the Maroubra squad, and God knows the AFP wouldn't run you with them.'

'So I'm –'

'Not really here. No one's said to put you in, and no one's said to leave you out. You're still on study leave.'

Jill shrugged. Whatever. She didn't really care; she'd be involved one way or another.

55

Tuesday, 7 December, 9.58 am
As Troy climbed the stairs of the dilapidated terrace house in Surry Hills, he understood why Gail Cole's legal services weren't going to cost him much more than a couple of thousand dollars. He hoped that she could do something; Chris was in a shitload of trouble. When he reached the two-roomed office on the second floor, he realised that Gail's office suite was a former bedroom in this rundown house – and a small one at that; he began to wonder whether he should be shelling out a bit more for a better lawyer.

The secretary offered him one of three mismatched chairs. All of the furniture in here, even the boxy computer on the desk, looked to be government-issue. Troy was pretty sure Ms Cole had gone to an auction clearing-house and bought a used job lot, probably from a school. Even the carpet was primary-school blue. But two thousand would already empty his bank account. He could ask Caesar for a loan, but who knew whether there were going to be more costs after the first court appearance? Troy tried to assuage his feelings of guilt for penny-pinching with Chris's future; at least he wasn't just throwing him to the duty solicitor when his case came up in court. He wanted the judge to see that someone cared about Christopher Berrigan. Hell, maybe this Gail Cole was just being practical – she'd know her clientele. Even a local hopper who found himself in here wouldn't be back to steal any of this shit.

'Hello, Troy? Gail Cole.'

Troy stood and shook hands, and immediately forgot his money concerns. Gail Cole smiled warmly, wore a suit and looked him right in the eye. She seemed confident. Better still, he couldn't smell any alcohol or learned helplessness on her. He put her at around his own age, maybe thirty. He followed her into her micro-office.

'Lovely place you got here,' he said before he could help it.

'Well, I don't want to be shopping for new furniture every week,' Gail said, using a finger to restrain a lock of auburn hair behind her ear. 'It gets the job done.'

'Sorry. I mean, of course. Smart. I was a cop around here, so I get it.' *Why did I just tell her that?*

'Yeah?' said Gail. 'Surry Hills?'

'Redfern,' said Troy. 'But I've been out four years or more now.'

'And you work in a restaurant now?'

'Yeah. I'm managing a restaurant called Incendie.'

'That's a bit of a switch.'

'Yep. I'm the one committing all the robberies now.'

Gail laughed, her teeth flashing white against red

lipstick. 'I've heard Incendie's expensive. And very good. I've never been.'

'Well, you'll have to come up. I'll make sure we look after you. It's pretty romantic, I'm told. A lot of people come for anniversaries. You could do that.'

'Hmm, maybe I will. It's my second anniversary in January.'

'Great,' said Troy, smiling. 'I'm sure you'll both like it.'

'Oh, I won't be bringing him,' she said. 'It's the anniversary of my divorce.'

'Oh.' Troy smiled again – for real this time.

'So, your little brother, Christopher,' said Gail.

'Do you know where they sent him? Is he okay?'

'He's okay,' she said. 'He's at Cobham, out west. I enquired again about bail but they're having none of it.'

'Doesn't that seem a bit harsh to you?' he asked.

'Well, it's a serious charge,' she said. 'I mean, I know Christopher wasn't pointing the weapon at anyone, or using it to commit another offence, but a lot of shots were fired. The bullets could have gone straight through the sheds and killed somebody.'

'You don't think I've thought of that?' said Troy. 'It's killing me. I don't know what the hell he was thinking, mucking around with a gun. He's been staring at my hand every day now for more than four years. He knows what they can do.' He held his hand up, watched her face.

She winced. 'What happened?' she asked.

'Shotgun, on the job.'

'Uh huh. Sorry. Well, it would help if he gave a full statement about where he got the weapon. He keeps saying they found it, and apparently his mate, Jayden, said the same thing.'

'Well, they probably did, then.'

'Which would wash, except they each gave a completely different location as to where it was found.'

'Little fuckers,' he said.

'Quite,' said Gail.

'And the arresting officers don't seem to have a lot of time for you, Troy,' she said. 'They said they worry you haven't been supervising Christopher well enough. He hasn't been going to school much lately.'

'I've been on it,' he said. 'He went every day last week.'

'I'll check it out,' she said, making a note on a pad in front of her. 'They worry that with you working nights, if he's released he'll just run wild again.'

'Christ.' Troy groaned, raking a hand through his hair. He stood and paced. 'I've got to work,' he said. 'People have to work. Okay, so if Chris has to do remand, when will his court case be?'

'Monday.'

'Monday? He has to stay there the whole week?'

'Well, we've just got to hope it isn't longer than that,' she said.

'Really, a committal? You don't think he'll have to go inside?'

'It's a gun, Troy. And he's still got the vandalism charge from the week before.'

'Can't you do something?'

'Well, I've asked them to roll the two cases together, so basically I'll try to make it look like a first offence – a bad week spent with bad company.'

'That's good,' said Troy. 'That's what it is.'

'He's an angry boy, Troy,' said Gail.

'Did you talk to him? They wouldn't let me.'

'Just by phone,' she said. 'I'll go out there this week. I tried to encourage him to cooperate, to make a statement about where he got the gun, but he has a hard-arse attitude. That's not going to play well in court.'

Troy sat down again. 'Let me talk to him.' He leaned forwards in his chair. 'Can you get me a visit?'

'Not until the weekend,' she said. 'Sorry.' Gail paused, then readied her pen. 'How long has he been living with you?'

'Since he was five. His sister was four.'

'What was wrong at home?'

Troy stared at his hands for a beat, then met her eyes. 'What wasn't?'

'Drugs, alcohol, domestic violence?'

'Check, check, check. I got out and left them there.' He put his eyes back on his hands.

'You came back.'

He snorted. 'Yeah. Three years later. They were just babies when I left them in there.'

'How old were you?'

'Eighteen when I came back.'

'Just a kid yourself.'

'I shouldn't have left them.'

'Does Chris remember what happened back then?'

'He doesn't talk about it.'

'What did happen to him?' Gail asked.

'I don't talk about it,' he said.

'It could help.'

'Who?'

'Well, it could help Chris's case if I can show that he's done it tough. The judges are usually more understanding.'

'He has a DoCS file. I'll bring it in.'

'Great. And when I said that it could help to talk about it, I also meant that it might help you too,' she said.

'Oh, I'm beyond help,' said Troy. He forced a grin.

'Well, there's a challenge,' she said. 'I'm the champion of lost causes.'

'Yeah, I can tell by your office.'

'I can always raise my fee,' she said. 'Spruce things up a bit on your dollar.'

'You know, I actually find it quite charming in here.'

Gail laughed and stood. 'Well, Mr Charming, I've got work to do, so –'

'I'll bring the file by tomorrow?' he said.

'That'd be great.'

'Around lunchtime? We could grab something.'

'That would also be great.'

Troy didn't stop smiling until it was time to go to work and he remembered that tonight he'd be entertaining half the brass in the force.

56

Tuesday, 7 December, 10.06 am
Erin splashed her face in the small office bathroom. How Shane could still make her cry, she had no idea. How he could say things to her that he knew would cut her so deeply, she also had no idea. He used to become teary when he saw her cry.

When she'd sensed him falling out of love with her it had been the most terrifying experience of her life. She'd told her counsellor that sensing what was between them dying felt as bad to her as being told she had a terminal illness. Not that I've ever had to go through that, she'd acknowledged, but at least I could try to fight an illness. But how do you fight against something that's slowly slipping through your fingers? Grabbing on tighter made Shane withdraw faster. Backing off and pretending not to worry just made it easier for him.

The anger always followed the grief. How fucking dare he come here and try to make me feel guilty for what happened last night? He had no real concern for her. Why had she imagined he would? Hamish cared more about how she felt than the man she'd built her life around.

How she felt about the fire, she still hadn't quite determined. Before last night, the threats had always been unnerving but they'd also seemed remote. God, there are really some fruitcakes out there, she usually thought to herself. They were always Out There. But last night, one of them had hurtled a piece of himself into her world, into her dining room, exploding in the heart of her home. She'd had the emergency glass repairers on the phone before she'd even left the police station last night, but now she knew there was nothing more between her and them than a sheet of glass. Nothing between them and Reece, between them and Callie. She thought about the threatening email and her stomach heaved. She leant forwards and splashed her face again.

Maybe Shane's right? Erin thought. Maybe I don't need this anymore. Running for office and being elected by her community had made her more proud than almost anything she'd ever done, but none of it was worth having a target on her back, on Callie's and Reece's backs.

The front buzzer sounded. Erin straightened her jacket and did up a button. She hadn't been able to do that in this suit for a couple of years; the action cheered her, and she left the bathroom. From the hall, she saw that the couple waiting with Hamish were not what she'd expected. She'd met a few federal cops before, two of whom were older than her – they were shrewd, suited, sensible. The others were part of what she always thought of as the super-race, the elite of the human food chain. Last year she'd been invited to a touch footy match – federal cops versus special forces. It had been like watching the gods hurling lightning at one another. But the two in her foyer didn't fit either type.

Hamish was preening himself by the water-cooler. She caught his eye and he mouthed, '*Oh my God!*'

Erin understood. The male – that would be Delahunt – looked like a cross between a drug-dealer and Jason Bourne. Unlike his superhero compadres, he stood just a head taller than his partner, and although he didn't have their gridiron neck, his chest and biceps looked like they could keep up. With a gun-belt sitting low on his hips and a baseball cap shading his eyes, she was pretty sure the majority of her constituents would have given him a pretty good perimeter. The female looked like nothing more than a surfie chick, cargo pants and a singlet, tousled blonde hair, flicked around her face; snubbed nose, freckles. She seemed too sweet to be a cop. The woman then turned sightly, surveying the room, and Erin saw the tattoo on her chiselled deltoid: the scales of justice. She felt suddenly glad that they were here.

'Erin Hart,' she said, walking into the foyer, hand outstretched.

'Federal Agent Gabriel Delahunt, Detective Sergeant Jillian Jackson,' said Delahunt. Everyone shook hands. 'Gabriel and Jill,' he added.

'Erin,' she said and smiled. 'Did Hamish offer you coffee, tea?'

She heard her PA cough behind her. *Of course I did!*

'Yep. We're good with water,' said Gabriel.

'Shall we go into my office?' asked Erin. She led the way and closed the door behind them.

'We're sorry about what happened to your house last night, Erin,' said Gabriel.

'You've got a lovely home,' said Jill.

'You two were out there, then?' asked Erin.

'Yes,' said Gabriel. 'We photographed the scene, took some small samples of evidence.'

'Do you know who might have done this?' asked Erin.

'That's why we're here,' said Gabriel. 'We don't know yet, but you can help us piece things together.'

'Okay – ready when you are,' said Erin. She noticed that Jill Jackson sat intently, poised over her notebook.

'Right, we'll start with the obvious,' said Gabriel. 'Have you had any recent threats?'

Erin began by telling them about the email of the acid attack on the kids in the mall.

'You got that email handy?' asked Gabriel.

'I deleted it,' said Erin. 'Sorry. It seems stupid of me now, but it just upset me so much when it mentioned Callie.'

'That's okay,' said Gabriel. 'We can get it back. Just keep stuff like that from now on. Anything else like that?'

Erin told them about the string of phone hang-ups over the previous year, the egging and paint on the car. She told them about the phone calls and emails from people who thought the CCTV project was designed to read people's minds. She watched Jill write it all down.

'We'll look into those crazy emails, but I don't think they're significant,' said Gabriel. 'The person who threw the incendiary device into your dining room is not psychotic. The bottle had a carefully designed, self-igniting trigger. Nobody thought-disordered could have created it.'

Erin saw Jackson turn towards Delahunt, her eyebrows raised.

'You get that last night?' asked Jill of her partner.

'Yep. Found traces of the tape used to secure the sugar-chlorate package, just like I thought.'

'What if the tape was there for another reason?' asked Jill.

Gabriel shrugged. 'What else is this squirrel gonna tape to the outside of a bottle full of accelerant?'

Erin saw Jill shake her head and resume writing; she could hear the pen scratching furiously.

Gabriel continued. 'So, this CCTV project you mentioned. Tell us more about that. Is it a big part of your work at the moment?'

Erin told them about the committee formed to implement and evaluate the effectiveness of a major increase in high-quality surveillance. When she paused, unsure whether to go into it further, Gabriel nodded.

'We're pretty happy about the project over at AFP,' he said. 'We've been hoping it gets spread city-wide – hell, cities-wide.'

'I can understand people's concerns about privacy,' said Erin. 'We knew there'd be a bit of a backlash, but we believe the way we've addressed those concerns has allayed a lot of people's fears.'

'But not the loonies?' said Jill.

'Not the loonies,' agreed Erin.

'Has anyone else on the committee had similar threats?' asked Gabriel.

'Well, most of us have had some weird calls or emails, but I guess I've had the most because I'm the chair.'

'Anyone on the committee had anything sinister happen to them?' asked Gabriel.

'Like what happened to me last night? No. We spoke about these calls at the last meeting, and there was nothing really to worry about.'

'What about things *not* like what happened to you last night?' said Gabriel.

'Sorry?' said Erin.

'What?' asked Jill, simultaneously.

'You said, "Nothing like what had happened to me".'

'Ah, yeah?' said Erin.

'What about other nasty things? Anything at all.'

Erin paused. 'Well, there was only Sheila,' she said, her heart suddenly heavy. 'But that was just a horrible accident.'

'What kind of accident?'

Erin felt Jill's eyes on her, and she shifted in her chair with the sudden intensity of their attention. She'd hate to be one of their suspects. 'Well, it was just a terrible tragedy,' she said. 'One of those things you could never foresee. You probably heard about it – Sheila McIntyre. She fell off a platform into the path of an oncoming train. There were a lot of commuters jostling, it was wet. It was out at Riverstone – a couple of weeks ago now.'

'I remember,' said Gabriel. 'She was on the CCTV committee?'

'Yes,' said Erin. 'I talked her into joining us. She was such a determined person, and a really good friend.'

'I'm sorry,' said Gabriel. 'What was she doing out at Riverstone?'

'Distributing fliers about the project, actually,' said Erin.

'But I thought it was only around the Glebe area?' said Gabriel.

'Well, it is,' said Erin. 'But one of our terms of reference is to educate the wider community about the benefits of the cameras, and one of the ways we are doing that is to talk to people who don't currently have any cameras, or who might benefit from an increase.'

'So they'll pressure their local members?' asked Gabriel.

'Something like that, yes,' said Erin. 'It's no secret that the government would like this project to work and then be implemented state-wide as quickly as possible.'

'And Riverstone Station doesn't have a camera,' said Gabriel.

'Just the one,' said Erin.

'Convenient,' said Jill.

'What – what are you saying?' asked Erin, her eyes wide.

'Nothing,' said Jill.

'You're saying Sheila was *pushed*? No one saw anything like that.'

'No one ever does,' said Gabriel.

'What's going on?' asked Erin, standing. 'Do you think there's some psycho out there killing people? Is that why the Feds are involved? Because there's no evidence of that here. I saw the footage myself. There was just one idiot captured that morning flipping a bird to the camera, and we get that all the time. All the witnesses just said that it was wet and she slipped.'

'Look, Erin. We're really not sure yet,' said Gabriel. 'But we have our analysts working on this as their top priority. Today. It could be that this isn't connected in any way. What happened to you could just be a random attack. But right now you're helping us a lot. Our job is to look for patterns, connect the dots. We brainstorm sometimes – you know about that, Erin. You throw ideas out there, bark up a lot of trees. Most of them don't work out. Don't get too worried about minor comments that we make here and there.'

'What about your personal life?' asked Jill. 'Is there anyone out there who really doesn't like you?'

'Enough to firebomb my home with my children in it?' asked Erin, feeling heat at her throat. 'Who do I look like, Tony Soprano?'

Jill smiled. Despite herself, Erin gave a short laugh.

'Does your house have a mortgage?' asked Gabriel.

'No,' said Erin. 'Why?'

'It's a standard question in a fire investigation,' said Gabriel. 'Don't be offended. It's just that most domestic arson attacks are committed by the homeowner when they're in financial straits.'

'Wrong tree,' said Erin.

'We know,' said Jill. 'Gotta check these questions off, though.'

'Your children's father?' asked Jill.

'Is an arsehole,' said Erin. 'But he loves his kids.'

'Again, wrong bush,' said Gabriel.

'Tree,' said Jill.

'What?' said Gabriel.

'It's okay, just keep going, Gabe,' said Jill.

Erin smiled.

'I'd rather go back to your professional life,' said Gabriel. 'How is the CCTV project going generally? Are you convincing the punters?'

'Yes. We've had a lot of support, even from sectors we were worried about. People want to see it in action, of course, look at the outcomes, but the message of lowering crime without reducing the privacy of law-abiding citizens has been getting through.'

The questions paused. Erin waited.

'Of course, there was that terrible incident the other night,' she said.

'What incident?' said Gabriel.

'That poor man in the city. Father of four children. Stabbed to death right in front of a carpark CCTV camera.'

'That's right,' said Gabriel. 'The man in the mask. Shanked to death by a Ninja Turtle.' He shook his head. 'Harsh.'

'It was just horrible,' said Erin. 'That's why we've got to keep doing what we're doing. But that incident didn't help the project at all. The lunatic looked straight at the camera, as if to ask what good these things are anyway. "They can't catch me", or something like that.'

'Something exactly like that,' said Gabriel.

Erin saw the look that passed between Jackson and Delahunt, and for the second time that morning she felt her stomach heave. What the hell is going on here?

57

Tuesday, 7 December, 11.28 am
'What's wrong?' asked Gabriel, leaning into the open window of the passenger seat of his car.

Jill sat with her hand on the doorhandle. 'Nothing,' she said. 'It's just that I feel a bit underdressed.' They'd parked in a cop bay out the front of Central Police Station.

Expressionless, Gabriel appraised her bare arms and singlet. He opened the rear door and reached inside.

'Hoodie,' he said, throwing a sweatshirt through her window. 'But you'll get hot.'

'Thanks, Gabe,' she said, stepping out of the car and shrugging into the jumper.

A uniformed constable buzzed the security door open for them. Jill had seen her around plenty of times, but they'd never really met. 'How can I help you guys?' she said when they walked through.

'We wanted to talk to whoever caught the stabbing death on Elizabeth Street, Thursday night,' said Gabriel.

'The vic was Frank Vella?' she said typing. 'Here it is. Yep, thought so, that's Campbell and McCann. McCann pulled a night shift last night, but John's in. I'll let him know you're coming. You know where the detectives' rooms are, right?'

'Yep, thanks,' said Gabriel. 'What's Campbell like?' he whispered to Jill as they walked past offices.

'He's an okay bloke,' she said. 'We'll be right.'

John Campbell stepped out of an office to their left. With three pens protruding from his shirt pocket, he resembled an accountant more than a homicide detective. He wore business pants, spectacles and shiny shoes.

'Hi, Jill,' he said. 'You shouldn't have dressed up on my account.'

'Sorry,' she said. 'I just got back from a ball.' They shook hands. 'John, this is –'

'Delahunt, isn't it?' said Campbell, reaching out a hand. 'We met during the Delfranchi thing.'

'Yep, yep. That's right. Delfranchi. Sick paedophile,' said Gabriel.

'How's he going, anyway?' asked Campbell, ushering them into his room.

'He applied for forensic status to keep him out of the main,' said Gabriel.

'Bullshit! You fuckers didn't let him get away with that, did you?'

'It took us six months to process his application,' said Gabriel. 'During which time, a processing error occurred and he was sent over to Silverwater. Stomped to death his first night there.'

Campbell gave a short laugh. 'Well, that'll happen,' he said.

313

'We've reviewed our procedures,' said Gabriel.

'So, what are you doing with the Feds, Jill?' asked Campbell. 'And what do you guys want with my Ninja Turtle?'

'Probably nothing,' said Jill. 'We're working Scotty's case.'

Campbell leaned back in his chair, exhaled hard. 'Sorry, Jill. I saw you at the funeral but I didn't come over. Everyone had swamped you, and you looked like you wanted to be out of there.'

'Thanks, John,' she said. 'It's fucked up.'

'Where are you at with it?' asked Campbell.

'Scotty was investigating that restaurant fatality,' said Gabriel.

'Ah, the restaurant at the top of that hotel over at Hyde Park. I know the one,' said Campbell.

'They seem to be connected,' continued Gabriel, 'and we've got someone in mind. But he's a slippery motherfucker. We're working this political motive – it's possible the prick has a thing for government workers.'

'Well, sorry to break it to you – Vella was just a drug rep.'

'This could be nothing,' said Gabriel, 'but would you mind giving us a run-down on what you've got so far?'

'Of course,' said Campbell. He banged a few times on his keyboard to bring the screen to life. 'Here it is. Married, three children, same job for the past four years. Vella trained as a chemist, but his wife told me they didn't have the money for him to open his own pharmacy. Apparently, the drug company paid better. She can think of no reason he might have been attacked. The neighbours put him as a great bloke; his employers loved him.' Campbell scrolled down. 'He'd just finished dinner with eight local doctors when he got jumped by this lunatic.

We interviewed all eight of them. Same story – great bloke, wouldn't hurt a fly, yada, yada. No priors, doesn't look like he had a gambling problem. Seems Vella was just in the wrong place at the wrong time.'

'And he wasn't robbed, is that right?' asked Gabriel.

'The fucker took nothing. Just stabbed the fuck out of him, did a jig for the camera and pissed off.'

'You get the murder weapon?'

'Nothing,' said Campbell. 'You wanna see the vid?'

'Yeah, why not,' said Gabriel.

Campbell opened another folder and a black-and-white horror movie filled his screen. The ferocity of the attack jarred grotesquely with the smiling cartoon face of the perpetrator. The victim curled into himself like a puppy being beaten; he'd had absolutely no chance. Jill suddenly felt glad she was wearing a jumper. She shivered.

The three sat silent for a few beats.

'Thanks, John,' said Gabriel. 'That was really helpful.'

'You get anything out of all that?' asked Campbell.

'Well, there was nothing much to get, was there?' said Gabriel, standing.

Campbell frowned. He and Jill also stood. 'Listen,' he said, 'you get anything on this case, you put me in the loop first, okay?'

'Of course,' said Gabriel.

Sydney's summer beat down and the air shimmered in Gabriel's car. Jill peeled off the hoodie before she got in.

'Why did you say that was helpful, Gabe, if you got nothing?'

'Because nothing is everything with this cunt.'

'What do you mean?'

'You gotta look for the absence of information for an explanation with Caine,' he said. 'He loves to hide in plain sight. He's an expert at hiding his emotions and he also hides his crimes. Let's think about this poor drug rep. There seems to be no reason for what happened there. And yet it happened. Was it just a random attack by a crazy – was Vella just unlucky? Of course, that's possible. But why's the perp in a mask? That shows some degree of planning, at least. And how did this fucker know the camera was even there? Why did he do his little dance for the camera? And if he knew it was there, why didn't he just stab some random prick in the park in privacy? I think it's all about the camera.'

'You think that was Caine?' she said, staring at him.

Gabriel raised his eyebrows.

'And that Caine has a problem with CCTV cameras?'

He pursed his lips.

'And government workers? And his mother? And Scotty?' she said.

He made a clicking sound with his tongue.

'It all seems a fucking tangle, Gabe. And even if that was him behind that mask, Vella's death puts us no closer to him. I hope we're not wasting our time with this guy.'

'What did you think of him flipping the bird?' Gabriel asked, just as his mobile sounded. 'Yep,' he said. Paused. 'Yep. Draw it up. I'm coming in.'

He ended the call and met Jill's eyes.

'What?' she said.

'The bottle thrown into Erin Hart's house was a one-litre Spring Valley juice bottle.'

58

Tuesday, 7 December, 3.14 pm
Jill stood beside her car with arms folded, squinting in the Glebe sunshine. 'I think I'd prefer to come with you to Caine's house,' she said. 'I really think that's where we're going to get him.'

Gabriel leaned against his own car, which was double-parked beside hers. 'Look, Jill,' he said. 'The warrant on Caine is thin. This guy's a cleanskin. And all we've got on him is that he was at Incendie. Scotty's linked to Incendie. And now we've got physical evidence that probably links Scotty's death to another fire-related incident. I had to lean real hard yesterday to get my boss to promise that if we got a link he'd let me at him. And all I can say is that we'd better find something at his house connecting him to one of these crime scenes. I'm pretty sure we will, though. We've got five crime scenes now that possibly link to him.'

'I want to come,' Jill said. 'No one will even notice I'm there.'

Gabriel laughed. 'You're funny.'

She scowled. 'Do you really think his workplace is going to be helpful?'

He paused. 'Who knows? Maybe. But in an hour he's going to know we're onto him. So, if you wait until four you can go there and be pretty sure he won't show up. But, Jill, you have to promise me you'll back right off if he's there. He shouldn't be, though. It's a contract cleaning company – the cleaners phone in for their assignments. Just poke around. See what his colleagues think of him. I haven't done any of that stuff yet – didn't want to scare him off.' From the side pocket of his cargos Gabriel pulled out a notepad and pen. He scribbled, tore out the page and gave it to her.

An address in Alexandria. 'It's something, I guess,' she said, kicking at gravel on the road.

Helen Herrmann tssked, straightened at her desk and waited for the approaching blonde woman. For goodness sake, not another one. When are they going to fix those signs?

'It's next door,' said Helen, before the woman could speak.

'Pardon?' said Jill.

'Party Hearty, the party supply shop,' said Helen.

The young woman turned her head to look around the factory unit and Helen spotted the tattoo on her arm. Why do girls do that to themselves? Her two daughters would never have dared, and if any of her four grandchildren even thought about it, she'd come down on them *and* their mothers like a tonne of bricks.

'You're K&Z Industrial Cleaning, right?' asked Jill.

'Oh, yes,' she said. 'I'm sorry. We don't have many customers come in off the street.' Helen paused. 'You're not here for a job, are you? We don't take cold-call applicants.'

The young woman reached into a back pocket and Helen tensed. Oh my God – this could be like that robbery over at Hung's Fabrics. Well, if this little miss thinks she can come in here and –

'Detective Sergeant Jillian Jackson,' said the woman.

'Are you sure?' asked Helen.

'I think I know who I am,' said Jill.

Well, if this is how the police dress themselves nowadays, no wonder this society is in so much trouble, thought Helen, rising from her chair. 'My apologies again,' she said, holding out her hand. 'My name is Helen Herrmann. I'm the office manager and dispatcher. How can I help you? Is this about the robbery at Hung's? Because I don't know anything about it.'

'Actually, Mrs Herrmann, I'd like to ask you a few questions about one of your employees.'

'Ahmed Riaz?' I knew it, thought Helen. Those Lebanese are always stealing things.

'Maybe we should have a seat?' said Jill.

'Of course, of course. May I get you a tea or coffee, Miss –'

'Detective Sergeant Jackson,' said Jill. 'I'm right, thanks.'

The woman took a notepad from a big pocket situated halfway down the leg of her wrinkled, baggy pants. I suppose those pants are good for something, Helen thought. But why doesn't she just carry a handbag?

'I'm here about David Caine,' said Jill.

'David?' asked Helen. 'Is he all right? I just spoke to him. He has a job over at Milsons Point tonight.'

'May I have the address?' asked Jill, her pen poised.

'Well, I suppose so,' said Helen. 'I can't see that there could be a problem with that.' She sat down, swivelled in her high-backed office chair and tapped her gel-tipped nails against the keyboard. After a moment she read out the address from the screen.

'A moment, please,' said Jill, flipping open her mobile. 'Gabe? Is he there? Okay, send someone around to the corner of Cliff and Glen Streets, Milsons Point. Gleanoaks. They're an engineering firm. Yep.' She snapped the phone closed.

'May I ask what this is about?' asked Helen.

'We're trying to find Mr Caine, that's all,' said Jill. 'We need to speak to him.'

'Has he done something wrong?'

'Why do you ask that?' said Jill.

'Well, he just doesn't seem the type, that's all,' said Helen. 'He's been with us for five years now. He worked for three years, I think, at our Adelaide branch. When he asked for a transfer to Sydney, we were happy to take him. We've never had a single complaint about him. Not a one.' Helen slightly adjusted a framed photograph of her granddaughter, then moved it back to its original position.

'What shifts does he work?' asked Jill.

'He favours the early pms,' said Helen. 'That's four until twelve. But he's very obliging and doesn't turn down anything we have available.'

'Uh huh,' said Jill, jotting. 'And what kind of a person is he?'

'What kind of a person? What do you mean?'

'Does he have a temper? Does he drink? Does he talk about his family? Does he get on well with people? Is he a flirt? Does he talk about religion or politics?'

'Well, aren't these interesting questions,' said Helen. She laid her palms flat on her blotting pad, smoothing it. The detective waited, reclining back in her chair with an ankle crossed over her knee in a most unladylike pose. 'To be honest with you,' said Helen, 'we don't have that kind of working relationship. I'm not social with the staff. And I don't actually see them very often at all. We phone or email the job details through to them, and the cleaners are given enough supplies to last four to six months. They might come in two or three times a year. But David, especially, is a private person. He doesn't even come to any staff get-togethers, like the Christmas party, and we do a thing for the Melbourne Cup.'

The detective sighed noisily. Suddenly, she dropped her foot to the floor and moved to the edge of her seat.

'What about Saturdays?' she asked. 'Does he ever work Saturdays?'

'As a matter of fact, yes,' Helen said. 'He's worked the last three. Sanje Singh had to fly back to his country for a death in the family, and David kindly took over his Saturday shifts.'

'Pms?' asked Jill.

'No, it's a day shift, actually. Serviced offices in North Sydney. Seven am to twelve pm.'

'Hang on a sec,' said Jill. 'Let me get this right. On Saturday the twenty-seventh of November, David Caine was cleaning offices for you?'

'That's correct,' said Helen.

'But how do you know he showed up?' asked Jill. 'And he could have left early, isn't that correct?'

'Well, as to that, Detective Jackson, I can assure you that David showed up.' Who does this woman think she is? Now she's questioning my integrity? 'And I can promise you that he did *not* leave early.'

'How can you know that?' asked the detective. 'This is very important, Mrs Herrmann. I'd really prefer that you do not make statements that you can't be sure of.'

Helen arched her brows, swivelled in her chair and clicked at her keyboard again. 'You might need to stand to see this, Detective Jackson,' she said. 'My screen won't rotate enough.' She picked up a biro for extra emphasis – pointing power. 'Whenever we can, Detective Jackson, we make use of a company's security system to keep track of our staff. When a cleaner is assigned to a building that has internal security, he is usually given a keycard, an access card, which he has to swipe to enter the building. Most major office buildings systems like that for after-hours access. I'm sure you're aware of that?'

'Yes.'

'Well, Detective Jackson, here is a log from the building indicating that David Caine did indeed use the access card when he arrived. And you can see here that he also used it to exit – at twelve-ten pm.' Helen tapped the screen twice with the pen tip. 'Moreover, I can assure you that the offices were thoroughly cleaned. Almost every week, this particular company complains about at least one nit-picky issue they feel wasn't done properly by Sanje Singh. But for the last three weeks, since David Caine has been cleaning the offices, I've heard not a peep from them.'

Back in her car, Jill ground the heels of her palms into her eyes. She didn't want to cry anymore. The tears that threatened to break right now were more of frustration than anything. They had the wrong man. Caine was working the morning Scotty was killed. Nothing had seemed quite right about this investigation from the beginning. Gabriel kept trying to shove everything that came up into a box marked 'Caine', but the lid just wouldn't stay down. Well, he needed to know that this particular piece of information sent the whole box to the shredder. She dialled his number.

'Jill,' he answered. 'We've got a shed full of accelerants.'

'You're kidding!' she said. What?

'Yep,' said Gabriel. 'Methyl alcohol, nitric acid.'

'Wow,' said Jill. 'You find anything else to link him?'

'Not yet,' said Gabriel. 'He's a slippery bastard.'

'You send someone over to Milsons Point?' she asked.

'Yep. Haven't heard back yet. They should be there soon. I told them to bring him in.'

'Is the daughter home?'

'No one here,' he said. 'We've got the place to ourselves.'

'Gabriel,' said Jill.

'Yep?'

'The chemicals in the shed – could they be cleaning supplies?'

'No. There's a shitload here.'

'Like, six months' worth? Gabe, K&Z send their contractors home with about six months' supply of cleaning chemicals.'

'Yeah, well there's a lot of cleaning gear in there too. The cleaning job is a perfect cover for this squirrel.'

'He's pretty good at his job, they reckon,' said Jill.

'He's pretty good at a lot of things, Jackson. Look, I've got to get some more shit on this fucker. I'm going to go and search the bins. I'd better go.'

'He has an alibi,' said Jill.

'What did you say?'

'He was working at the time Scotty was murdered.'

'Says who? That's bullshit,' said Gabriel.

'He swiped in electronically at an office building in North Sydney on the Saturday morning and swiped out at ten past twelve. I got the call from Andreessen about Scotty at ten past twelve.'

'So what?' said Gabriel. 'It's another game. He's swung it somehow – got someone else to cover the shift. You'll see. Fucking clever cunt, though. I'm going, Jill. I really have to get this fucker.' He disconnected.

Jill didn't know what to think. She knew she was hungry, though; it was now five pm and she'd had no lunch. She drove back to the main street of Mascot but couldn't see a cafe with tables, and she didn't feel like eating in a hot car, waiting for Gabe to call. She drove over to the Eastlakes shopping centre, parked in the street and walked inside. The aircon blasted noisily and the plaza stunk of the stale oil used to fry donuts. Her appetite evaporated. Regardless, she ordered a roast chicken and salad roll from a takeaway shop and took a seat at a small plastic table in a dining area nearby. A young couple sat at the table next to her, each eating a plate of chicken and chips. They were using knives and forks, smiling across the table at one another, as though they dined at Bennelong.

Jill sipped an apple juice while she waited for her food, watching a man opposite closing up his electronics store for the night. Tired shoppers wheeled grocery carts past the shop. On their way home to their families and a proper dinner. Jill felt completely lost. She should be getting ready for a night class right now, but she knew she wouldn't be going back this semester. Not while she didn't know what happened to Scotty. Same deal for heading back to real work. She didn't even have a place to sign in. She hadn't been posted back to Maroubra –

and anyway, she couldn't imagine working there right now, with Andreessen, Emma Gibson, Elvis. And with no Scotty. She just had to see this through before she could even begin to think about what she would do next with her life.

And yet she was no closer to knowing what had happened. She had let Scotty down big-time. She felt that she'd just been wasting time since he was killed. All that time at Lyrebird – just sitting around talking, for fuck's sake. Jill pulled the straw out of her drink and twisted it. At least then she'd had hopes that Gabe was on it. Now, she wasn't sure of anything.

Jill usually trusted Gabriel's instincts, but now she was worried that he'd spent so much time formulating his serial-killer theory that he was blind to other possibilities. She hated to even imagine it, but maybe Elvis was right and Troy Berrigan *had* killed the woman at Incendie? Maybe he was bored shitless working in a restaurant, wanted to make himself a triple-zero hero again. Maybe Scotty's death was completely unrelated? Every cop had enemies. It might just have been some sick fuck who decided to throw a Molotov into a car – and a police car was the perfect score. And the petrol bomb at the politician's house could also have been anyone. It was not that uncommon to see a local member's office firebombed; maybe someone had just expressed their dissatisfaction a little closer to home this time? And this bloody woman pushed in front of a train, the man stabbed in a carpark – was Gabriel going to blame every death in the city on some fucking cleaner from Rosebery?

A girl in a too-tight uniform that was smeared by the day's trade brought Jill's chicken and salad roll to her table. She tore off a big bite savagely. Her mobile rang.

'What?' she said, mouth full.

Gabriel. 'Guess what I found in the bin?'

'What did you find in the bin?' Jill asked flatly.

'Spring Valley juice bottles. Could match the bottles we got from Scotty's car and Erin Hart's house.'

'A lot of people drink juice.'

'Okay, and maybe what we found in the false floor in Caine's bedroom is really nothing as well.'

Jill held her breath. He waited.

'Gabe! What?' she said.

'Defence-issue assault rifle, with five loaded magazines and thirty charger clips; a Browning semi-auto nine-millimetre, with twenty boxes of fifty rounds of ammo; and four M-67 hand grenades.'

'Get fucked!'

'I'm busy.'

'Have you got him?'

'He's in the wind, Jackson. He didn't show up at work. Meet me at AFP. He's escalating. We gotta get him fast.'

59

Tuesday, 7 December, 6.12 pm
Jill had been inside the Australian Federal Police building on a couple of occasions, but never in Gabriel's office.

'I didn't even know you have an office,' she said, sticking her head through his open door.

'Yeah, well,' he said, not turning from his computer screen.

Files and paperwork occupied all the surfaces that Gabriel's computer terminals and keyboards did not. Jill moved a stack of books from the only other chair in the room and wheeled it over next to him. The view from his window was the hallway outside the office.

'You had anything to eat?' she asked.

He looked at her for the first time and shook his head.

'Chicken and chips,' she said, plonking a plastic bag on a file.

He dipped into the bag and removed the foil package, then ripped it open. 'Anything to drink?' he asked.

She pulled a bottle from her pocket. 'Spring Valley,' she said, balancing the bottle of orange juice next to the chicken. 'Good job, Gabe.'

He stuffed chips into his mouth. Jill reached for the bag and took out some serviettes.

'Where are we up to?' she asked.

'Caine's now a Level One priority,' he said. 'Everyone's out there looking. The weapons were stolen from an ADF site. We recovered a similar assault rifle in a bikie raid last month.'

'How many firearms were stolen?'

'Dozens.'

'You're shitting me!'

Gabriel tore half the meat off a drumstick in one bite.

'So, he could have more?' asked Jill.

'He could have an RPG as well. The missing military weapons included assault rifles, munitions, grenades and disposable rocket-launchers.'

'How the hell did someone get all that off a defence force site?'

'Insider,' said Gabriel. 'A lot of the weapons and ammo were past their use-by date. They were going to be destroyed. We got the fucker who took the shit, but not before he'd offloaded pretty much everything.'

'I remember now,' said Jill. 'Wasn't that a couple of years ago? Are these some of the same weapons that were captured during that Lebanese street war?'

'The same. Over the past two years, thousands of casings have been recovered in several shootings across Sydney, and eleven live grenades were recovered in four drug raids in the south-west. We got back a live M72 rocket-launcher after a plea-bargain in a drug conviction, and we think another six of them are with that particular offender's associates.'

'Is Caine connected to them?'

'Not as far as we can tell. And no bikie connections that we can find, either. I told you, he's a loner,' said Gabriel. 'He could have bought them from the original squirrel, he could have bought them from an on-seller – he could even have stolen them from someone else. He's a resourceful bastard.'

'What do you think he's going to do with them?' asked Jill.

'Well, he was probably saving them for something big,' said Gabriel. 'But now he knows we're onto him, anything could happen.'

'How do you know he knows we're onto him?'

'Why didn't he show up at work?' said Gabriel. 'You told me about his employment pattern – he's the perfect employee.'

'Shit,' she said. 'I wonder how he found out.'

'We're tearing his house apart. He could have rigged up some kind of warning system, like an alarm. Or a neighbour could have called him. Hell, maybe he just forgot something after leaving for work, spotted us and kept driving. Either way,' he said, 'the clock is ticking.'

'What if he just takes off, goes into hiding again?' asked Jill.

'That's another possible scenario. He could do that. He's evaded detection for a long time.'

'But what about his daughter?'

'The school told us she's there, hanging with her new bestie.'

'Lucy Berrigan?'

'Yep. Troy Berrigan's little sister.'

'This whole thing's getting pretty incestuous, isn't it?'

He raised an eyebrow. 'Anyway, I've arranged for someone to pick her up because, one way or another, her father's not coming back.'

'What are you working on in here?' asked Jill.

'Just trying to put the whole thing together. I got some more info back from the lab. You want the run-down?'

'Go,' she said.

'Exactly the same accelerant mix was used in the firebombs thrown at Erin Hart's house and into Scotty's car – a bastardised napalm, just like I thought. The fire techs at the Incendie scene still don't know for sure what was used on Miriam Caine's face – there wasn't enough skin left. But whatever it was, it was one of the two accelerants Caine used. Methyl alcohol had been squirted onto her blouse, and this shit was there by the box-full in Caine's shed. We also found sulphuric acid. Remember I said he would have added that to the mix to ignite the sugar-chlorate package taped to the bottle?'

'Yep,' she said.

'And that red substance we found in Erin Hart's home,' said Gabriel. 'Remember?'

'Uh huh. Some kind of rubber.'

'A balloon,' he said. 'What I figure is that instead of putting the lid back on the juice bottle, he'd fitted a balloon over the top, like a condom. One of the problems with Molotovs is that sometimes they don't connect with something hard enough to break the bottle. That's not going to be a problem if you're using a wick, but we know our boy didn't play that way. So, using his condom, even if the bottle didn't break, the shit inside would corrode through the balloon and react with the sugar-chlorate.'

'How scary is this guy?' Jill asked.

'Scary,' said Gabriel. 'Know what else I found in the shed today?'

'I don't know if I want to know.'

'Nitric acid.'

'What does that do?'

'It's an extremely potent solvent.'

'Meaning it could be used for cleaning?' Jill said, hoping but not really believing that some of these chemicals could just be for Caine's legitimate employment.

'Yes. And for making bombs,' he said. 'Nitroglycerine.'

Jill rubbed her forehead.

'But you remember that email, Jill, the one that Erin Hart told us about this morning?'

'The acid attack on those kids? Someone threatening her daughter. Are you saying the attacker used –'

'Yep. Nitric acid.'

60

Tuesday, 7 December, 6.14 pm
Erin threw the mid-length sensible skirt and black ruffled blouse onto her bed. Yuck, she thought. Maybe the only thing that could make her feel worse about going to this thing tonight was going dressed in that. It screamed 'mother of the bride' or maybe even 'nanna out for the night'. It would render her immediately invisible. Not that she especially wanted to stand out, but she still felt a pang in her heart every time a man's glance slid over her as though she weren't there. Their eyes used to pause, question, flirt. Would she never get to flirt again? How much did it suck to get older?

And fat. She turned back to her wardrobe and flipped through the hangers. Stopped at the red dress. The red dress. She'd worn it only once. She'd paid more than she ever had or ever would again for the most amazing shoes to match it. She slid the fabric through her fingers. It'll never fit.

Why had she asked Hamish to come to this party? She had the perfect excuse to get out of the excruciating embarrassment of explaining, to those who didn't know, why she wasn't accompanied by Shane; of thanking those who did know for their kind words of support; and of pretending she couldn't hear the whispers about the affair he'd been carrying on behind her back. It had been the same at every function since he'd walked out on her.

Having one's home firebombed the night before definitely counted as an excuse not to attend a dinner. But Hamish had looked up at her so hopefully this afternoon when she'd started to tell him she wouldn't be going. Instead, she'd smiled at him and thought, What the hell!

Erin spun at a sudden sound downstairs, her breath catching. She exhaled when she realised it was just the fridge kicking in again. She definitely didn't want to spend the night here alone, jumping at every noise. Gabriel Delahunt had told her that people who threw firebombs generally didn't attempt more personal assaults, but Erin could tell that he and Detective Jackson had told her a lot less than they suspected about what had happened here last night. And despite Ron Kennedy's assurances that the local cops would patrol every hour, it was just too quiet without the kids.

Erin gave the red dress one last caress, and it slipped from its hanger into a blood puddle on the floor. She picked it up and held it to her chest. The skirt flicked out full and swirly under the fitted bodice. Maybe she could get away with it with the super-sucker-inerer underwear she'd bought when she was in the US last year. Damn it, she thought. I can at least try it on.

Twenty minutes later, Erin waved at the waiting taxi driver and locked her front door. Vaguely, she realised that she never could have walked out of the house in this dress if she hadn't had the shot of whisky. Maybe she was going to regret it tomorrow. In the mirror, her cleavage had been so . . . well, so *there*; the streamlining underwear had squeezed and hugged very effectively, and all those lumps had to go somewhere. But when she'd twirled, the skirt had done its thing and she'd fallen for the dress all over again. She'd told herself she needed a drink, and then she'd have one last look. By the time she'd gone back upstairs, slipped into her shoes and spritzed her neck with her favourite scent, Erin had decided that not only would she wear this fabulous dress, but that she was going to enjoy herself tonight too.

61

Tuesday, 7 December, 6.40 pm
'Maybe you should go home now, Jill,' said Gabriel. 'I'm going to be here a while.' He scrunched the remains of his chicken into the plastic carry bag, wiped his hands, then swivelled back to his computer.

'What are you going to do?' she asked.

'I want to go back over the crime-scene footage from last night. Something is snagged in my brain and it's driving me crazy.'

'What is it?'

He gave her a look. 'Well, I don't know what it is. That's why it's driving me crazy.'

'Okay,' she said. 'Can I help?'

'You don't know what you're looking for,' he said.

'You just said that you don't either.'

'Well, there's that,' he said. 'Okay. I'll load up the

video I took before we began investigating the scene. I've already dumped it into this terminal – hold on, I'll send it over to yours.'

'What am I looking for?' asked Jill, when Erin Hart's ruined dining room appeared on the screen in front of her.

'Do we have to do that whole conversation again?'

'So, just anything that strikes me,' she said.

'Bingo,' he said, lowering his ball cap.

Gabriel had loaded the crime-scene footage into a program that allowed the user three-hundred-and-sixty-degree rotation by manoeuvring the mouse. Jill was experienced with the application. She moved carefully through the dining room, panning, slowing and zooming over every inch. Next to her, she saw that Gabriel was doing the same.

Jill studied the black scar across the beautiful polished table, the ruined rug and floorboards, which at that stage were still slightly smouldering. But the decor the fire hadn't blemished was truly lovely. In the past, Jill would never have imagined that she could live in a home with so many colours. With so much to try to still in her mind, she did not want a riot around her when she was trying to relax at home.

But Erin Hart had combined the colours so skilfully. Deep emerald, ruby and sapphire harmonised in the heavy drapes; the jewels held back with a golden rope. Thank God they hadn't been burned – that would have been such a shame. A mirror-polished redwood side cabinet sat against the front wall of the dining room, and atop it were happy photographs in mismatched frames. But the mismatching seemed perfect. Whenever Jill bought an ornament, she always bought an exact match to create a balanced pair. She zoomed in close on the photos.

A raven-haired, serious little boy, each of his eyes a universe. And that must be Callie, here captured chubby-kneed and enchanted by an Easter egg, her immaculate toddler skin smeared in chocolate. Wow. Jill took a deep breath and let it go slowly.

The video had somehow managed to capture the glitter of the lighting reflected off each facet of a cut-crystal vase, the centrepiece of the mantle. Bruised purple lilacs and crushed crimson crepe myrtle spilled from the vase. Jill wished she'd noticed the flowers last night and had stopped to smell the lilacs. Then the acrid stench of the fire came back to her, and she realised that even if she'd tried, she'd have smelt nothing but the destruction.

The scent memory focused Jill's attention. She didn't think this was what Gabriel wanted her to look for. She zoomed down to the floorboards, noting the depth of char where the accelerant must have hit, and a clear line of burn demarcation where the accelerant had failed to catch. Thank heavens, she thought. Had the fire caught fabric, the whole house would probably have burned. She zoomed in tighter, then tighter again, noting the large rolling blisters in the centre of the burn, indicating the most rapid and intense heat.

She continued to focus on the damaged area but saw nothing that would add to what they already knew. She widened again, then decided to use a strip pattern to search, as she would if she were there, searching for evidence. She scanned imaginary horizontal lanes, reaching the bottom of the scene and moving back up. She focused on every surface, wall, ceiling, object, floor. She got nothing new.

Jill looked up and stretched her neck. Gabe's eyes were completely shadowed by his hat. He was scrolling intently.

'Anything?' she asked.

'Fucking nothing,' he said. 'I mean, everything in the scene is there, but it doesn't scratch the itch that I've got in my head. I feel as though I registered something last night but I didn't file it properly, and now I can't find it.'

'File it?'

'You know, in my brain.'

'Maybe we should take a break,' she said. 'Or start again tomorrow, with fresh eyes. It's been a long day.'

'Yeah. Nah. You go.'

'There are a lot of people out there looking for him, Gabe. It's not just you now. You made the case.'

Gabriel tightened in on something and sat forward, his shoulders bunched. Suddenly he flopped back into the chair. He flicked the mouse and the room on the screen span. He groaned. 'Something, something, something,' he muttered.

'What about the stills of the scene that you took after you collected the evidence?' said Jill. 'I doubt we'll find anything else though. You've got every part of the scene here.'

'Worth a shot,' he said. 'You up for it?'

After Gabriel sent the pictures to her computer, Jill went through the first few carefully, trying to find the minute changes caused by Gabriel's investigation of the crime scene. She felt as though she were completing one of those magazine puzzles – spotting the difference between one picture and another, where each, at first glance, appears identical. Again, other than a tiny scrape here and a scuff mark there, she found nothing to remark upon.

Suddenly tired and impatient, Jill began flipping through the still shots more quickly. *I don't even know* what I'm looking for, she thought. How am I supposed to know if I see something that would scratch Gabriel's itch?

The images in the photographs began to extend beyond the immediate crime scene, and again Jill became captivated by Erin Hart's decorating style. At first glance, the kitchen seemed much too country for her tastes. In her home, Jill loved the cold efficiency of German stainless-steel appliances, granite, lots of clean, cold surfaces. But she had to admit that Erin's kitchen looked like the kind of place you could hang out.

A heavy wooden table in the centre invited you to pull up a chair, shuck some peas, drink some wine while you chatted to the cook. Suspended from the ceiling above the table was a wrought-iron rectangle, with cooking utensils, colourful enamel pots, bunches of herbs, a string of garlic and a strand of fairy lights all hanging from it. Jill couldn't imagine having a jumble of food and utensils on display like that. But it actually fitted perfectly here, and was probably very useful too. She was surprised that she hadn't registered the rack last night. She flipped to another photo. She also hadn't noticed that the refrigerator was a bright cherry-red. A red fridge. Huh.

There was the calendar on the wall that she'd noticed last night. She zoomed in: birthday and Christmas parties, sporting matches, a concert, exam dates. She panned across to the fridge.

'Wow,' she said. 'That's weird. Gabriel, take a look at this.'

She honed in on a card, which had been opened out and stuck to the fridge with a magnet in the shape of a cauliflower. Gabriel wheeled his chair closer to hers.

'It's an invitation,' she said. 'To Erin Hart, for a black-tie dinner at Incendie.'

'That's it,' said Gabriel, his chair rammed up against hers. 'When is it for?'

She moved the mouse.

'Tonight,' she said. 'Um, now.'

62

Tuesday, 7 December, 7.10 pm
Troy walked the line of his troops – down the row in front of them, back around and behind them, taking in everything from the shine on their shoes to any errant hairs around their faces.

'You all look good,' he said. 'The restaurant also looks great. Well done. Are you ready for tonight? If you haven't had a chance to sneak a look at the guest list these past few months, I'm here to tell you that we'll be entertaining the Premier of New South Wales, the Lord Mayor of Sydney and all the highest-ranking police in this state. Far more important than that, though, we'll be feeding Caesar, and if anything goes wrong in his restaurant, in front of these people, you won't find a job in another restaurant in this city. James, take us through the run-sheet.'

The reflection of a down-light glowed on James's mirror-shined bald head; the circle of light seemed to beam directly from his scalp. Troy knew that when he dimmed the lights in a few minutes, the effect would be less disconcerting.

'Champagne and cocktails at seven-thirty,' said James. 'We've three hot and three cold canapés. Make sure they're moved around quickly – get some food into these people to soak up the piss. Wait until you see the grog we're pumping out tonight. Entrée is at eight, so please begin moving them to their seats at five to. Mains are at eight-thirty. They'll start the speeches then, and they'll be sloshed, so expect the usual. We're rolling desserts out at nine-fifteen. Liqueurs at ten. The function officially runs until eleven, but you know what Caesar's like once he gets going. Don't count on getting much sleep tonight.'

Troy frowned down some of the grumbles. 'Come on, how long have you known about this thing?' he said. 'There'll be overtime. Don't you lazy bastards need spending money for Christmas?'

Troy dismissed them and spent the next twenty minutes rushing through an hour's worth of work. When the first of his beautifully dressed guests began to arrive, he greeted them graciously, steeling himself for the first round of whispers.

63

Tuesday, 7 December, 7.20 pm
'It might be nothing,' said Jill, staring at the photo of the invitation on the refrigerator in Erin Hart's home. 'Still, it is weird.'

'Think about what you just said,' said Gabriel.

'That it's weird. But there's no real reason that Erin shouldn't be attending a function at a restaurant like Incendie. I mean, it's one of the best restaurants in the city. People are going to have parties there.'

'Not that bit,' said Gabriel. 'Not the weird bit.'

'Huh?' she said.

'You said that this might be nothing. Remember what I said about nothing and David Caine?'

'Yeah,' said Jill, her forehead creasing. 'You said that nothing is everything with this guy.'

'Exactly. Look, Jill, over the past two weeks there

have been six attacks around Sydney that look to have been committed by this squirrel. You might as well call that a spree. I know that, technically, spree-killers don't stop in the middle of their attacks to go to work and get on with life, but six in two weeks indicates this guy's in some kind of frenzy. And don't forget that, as far as we know, the whole thing started with the murder of his mother. I think that's unhinged him.'

'You're probably right,' said Jill, 'but I don't see how we can connect Caine to this dinner tonight. Why would he go back there?'

'Symmetry,' said Gabriel.

'Symmetry?'

'Uh huh. It's poetic, it's planned, it's meticulous. It's very David Caine.'

'So, you think he might go there tonight and, what – try to attack Erin Hart? I don't know, Gabe. It doesn't make a lot of sense, you know? I mean, why firebomb her house last night if you wanted her to be at a dinner tonight? Not many people would just skip off for cocktails and canapés after something like that.'

Gabriel took over the mouse, started scrolling. 'Yeah, I hear you,' he said. 'You're right. It would have been smarter to not do that.' He tried focusing even tighter on the invitation. 'Shit,' he said. 'I can't see what the event tonight is for.'

'It'd be printed on the front of the card. Why don't we just call her and ask?'

'We could,' said Gabriel, 'but we might panic her.'

'It's better if she's panicked than if she walks into a trap.'

Gabriel fiddled again with the mouse.

'Gabe?'

Nothing.

'I get it,' she said. 'You don't want to call her because you don't want her alerting anyone that something might happen tonight,' said Jill. 'In case it spooks Caine. You want to use Erin as bait.'

'She might not even attend, like you said. It might be nothing, like you said.'

'Nothing,' said Jill.

'Nothing,' said Gabe.

'Let's go. I'll drive,' said Jill.

64

Tuesday, 7 December, 7.41 pm
Erin couldn't believe it. She tried again to catch Hamish's eye, and this time he saw her. He winked. She beckoned. How the hell was he going to drag her arse to this thing and then dump her? Halfway through the welcoming cocktail, he'd squealed and rushed over to talk to a short man with a ginger beard. Erin recognised him immediately. God. He wasn't even Hamish's type.

'He's not even your type,' she said when he reached her side.

Hamish threw his head back and laughed. His dark fringe was slicked back, his skin perfect. She'd never have known he was wearing make-up if he hadn't once told her, 'I never go anywhere without my concealer.'

Now, he said, 'Silly. That's just Brian. I've met him a

couple of times out dancing. Well, he tries to dance, poor love. Does his best.'

'I know that's Brian. *Inspector* Brian Featherstone. Are you saying he's on the scene?'

'Well, I wouldn't say on the scene, exactly. I've just seen him out a few times.'

'Well, we're going in to dinner soon,' she said. 'Can't you just hang out with me until we're seated? I don't know what I was thinking wearing this dress. I feel like a giant pimple.'

'Would you stop it?' said Hamish. 'You are spectacular. I shouldn't leave you alone, though – you'll be harassed to within an inch of your life.'

'You are a sweetie, Hamish. A liar, but a sweetie.'

Hamish stayed by Erin's side as she was greeted by one or two people she was pleased to see, and five or more who just wanted to be seen speaking to a local member.

'The premier,' Hamish hissed. 'Don't look – he's on his way over here.'

Erin accepted the premier's concern and good wishes about the firebomb in her home; she talked global warming with the deputy commissioner, and about the Glebe CCTV project with the retiring Chief Superintendent Norris, the man of the moment. He was her ticket to this event, having championed CCTV for public safety over the past decade. Finally, Erin saw people beginning to move towards the lavishly set dining tables.

'Isn't this all just gorgeous?' Hamish said, smiling at a dark-haired waiter who must have walked past them three times within the past five minutes.

'Just gorgeous,' she said, lifting another glass of champagne from the waiter's tray.

65

Tuesday, 7 December, 8.15 pm
Jill waited at the intersection of Elizabeth and Hay Street. Gabriel sat silently beside her, his lips moving. He did that. It was like he was having some kind of dialogue with someone. When he was really into it, sometimes he'd make the facial expressions that would go with a proper conversation. He'd nod, frown and smile. The first time Jill had seen it, she'd kind of freaked.

By now, though, she'd learned that it was pointless to speak to him when he was like this. She turned the scanner up a little and listened to the dispatcher sending out jobs, other cops checking in. Sometimes she found the chimes and quiet mumbles soothing – especially in the evening, for some reason. The civilians in the cars around her were unaware that this ceaseless verbal grid weaved through the night, wrapping them all in a protective web of signals and code.

Jill switched off the aircon and dialled the vent to pump in air from the street. While it was probably about twenty-eight degrees out there, in here the aircon on her bare arms made her conscious that she was still in the same singlet she'd put on twenty-four hours ago. She wished for the twentieth time that she'd had a change of clothes over at Gabe's last night. Maybe she should leave some stuff there, in case something like this happened again. She shook her head. What is it about this guy? She'd never even stayed the night once at Scotty's place, and yet here she was thinking about moving clothes in to Gabriel's apartment?

'You're very quiet,' Gabriel said. 'You looked like you were talking to yourself.'

Oh, for God's sake. 'You reckon we should call the restaurant, Gabe? Ask them what the function's for?'

'I don't know. Not really,' he said. 'I mean, to get that kind of info we're going to have to identify ourselves. I'm assuming Troy Berrigan is still running the show over there, so he's going to hear about it. Berrigan's probably stretched to the wire on this thing now. I told him a week ago today that he's a suspect in two murders. And then Elvis organised a house-call with a warrant a couple of nights ago. If I call up asking about a do at his workplace, he's not gonna let that go. He's going to flip out.'

'I could call,' said Jill.

'Still a cop call.'

'And he might overreact and that could spook Caine.'

'If he's there at all,' said Gabriel.

'If you think it's possible Caine's going to go to Incendie, Gabe, we should probably send in the troops.'

'What do you think you and I are?' he said. 'Besides, we're nearly there. We'll just check things out quietly. No need for the whole catastrophe just yet.'

Jill motored up Elizabeth Street. As they approached Hyde Park, she scanned for a parking spot. Ordinarily, parking a cop car was no biggie. Loading zone, bus stop, taxi rank – they were all the same to her. The meter cops would never tag her car. But on this part of Elizabeth Street, there were enough people with enough money to vie for the same spots. An eighty-dollar fine for illegal parking out the front of a restaurant was considered just part of the cost of the evening. She continued past the hotel and turned left on Market Street to circle the block.

'Fuck!' said Gabriel. 'Did you hear that? Turn the radio up, Jill, I think we're too late.'

66

Tuesday, 7 December, 8.33 pm
From the corner of his eye, Troy saw the huddles go down every time he left a group. One hour and a thousand dollars' worth of booze into the festivities, the buzz of the comments now reached his ears clearly.

Bullshit! That's not him. You're pissed.

Of course I'm pissed, you dickhead. Jonesey, get your arse over here. Isn't that Troy Berrigan?

That Abo cop from Redfern? Yep. Shot the prick that killed Jonno.

No, it can't be. That fucker lost his arm, didn't he?

Next time he comes past, check out his right hand. If he has five fingers, I'll wrap my five fingers around your stumpy prick.

You couldn't fit your little hobbit hand around my king cobra, you poofter.

The next group would be into the next story.

You know he's the coon that ratted out Herd and Singo, don't you?

Yeah, Jonesey was telling us. He dogged them for giving some of his cousins a hiding.

That's him. They've got his little brother locked up now, too.

Well, things are back to normal, at least. We're locking them up instead of one of them having the keys.

Racist prick.

Yeah? Come over here and suck my racist prick.

It was always the same and always would be, Troy knew. It didn't matter how high up they got in the chain of command. He hurried into the kitchen to stop himself putting his foot up someone's arse.

The fire alarm suddenly blatted into life.

'Oh, not now!' said Robbie. 'We've got the mains ready to go out. They'll be fucked.'

'I'll check it out,' said Troy. 'Hopefully it's nothing.'

'It's never nothing,' said Robbie. 'The chicken will be cardboard by the time we get everyone back in here.'

The volume of the alarm increased steadily and Troy held a finger up to Caesar, who was glaring at him from across the room. He picked up the phone, stabbed a button.

'Evacuate? Oh, shit,' he said. He hung up.

Troy's staff watched him from various points around the restaurant. He held his hand above his head and made a lassoing motion. The waiters efficiently began moving the patrons towards the exit. He flattened the doors back against the walls to allow everyone out. In the foyer he smelled smoke, and a thin wire of adrenaline shot through his stomach. He'd actually never smelled smoke during a fire alarm before. Usually, the alarm had been something small triggered by a drunken guest in a hotel room, put out before it even really got started.

He re-entered the restaurant, moving quickly, flattening himself against the wall to give the diners room to leave. Most of them were still clutching glasses, their dinner conversations ongoing as they exited the room. He snatched the fire-extinguisher off the kitchen wall and carefully pushed back through his guests and out the door. Just a minute had lapsed since he'd last stood here, but now the smoke had greyed the air and the diners moved determinedly towards the stairwell. They had a long climb down to the ground.

Troy followed the acrid stench around the corner from the elevators, and within moments he had spotted the smoke, which was rolling like baby breakers from under a conference room door. He tried the handle. Locked, but not hot, thank God.

He dug into his pockets for his master key and opened the door. What the fuck? A metre from him a small bonfire burned merrily: some conference notepads, stacked in an orderly pile in the middle of the floor, had been set alight. The flames crackled and reared as more pages were consumed, black smoke curling from their tips. He pulled the extinguisher pin and jetted foam onto the fire.

Who could have done this? There was no question this had been deliberately lit, then the door locked. With the flames now extinguished, Troy took his mobile from his pocket.

A sound behind him. He spun.

'What the hell is this?' Caesar O'Brien stood in the doorway; Lester Conway, the hotel's duty manager, stood beside him.

'Someone doesn't like us,' said Troy.

'You found these on fire?' asked Lester.

'Door was locked, too,' said Troy.

'Motherfucker,' said Caesar, swaying a little.

'I'll call the police,' said Lester.

'They're all fucking here already,' said Caesar. 'Well, they're on their way down the fire stairs, anyway. I'll get everybody back up again.'

'Not yet,' said Troy.

Caesar glared at him.

'Lester, grab a couple of staff and do a quick search of the function areas. Just make sure this isn't the only pile of dogshit left for us.'

Lester nodded and jogged off.

'I'm going down to our guests,' said Troy. 'We'll give Lester ten minutes and bring everyone back up. Coming, Caesar?'

'Nah, you go, Troy, my boy. I'll keep an eye on our restaurant.'

'Yeah? Have one for me too.'

Caesar barked out a laugh and clapped Troy across the shoulder. 'Good job here tonight, son,' he said. 'Now go and get me my drinking buddies.'

Troy made his way back to the elevators, trying to figure out who could have done this. The function rooms were always locked when they weren't being used. It had to have been a staff member with a hell of a fucking grudge. He or she could have killed people.

Watching the numbers above the lift climb to his floor, Troy decided that Caesar really should think about renaming the restaurant. Two fires in two weeks? Was the name Incendie attracting these psychos? Wait until the media got hold of this shit. And it had to happen tonight, too. The elevator doors shooshed open and Troy stepped in. He'd probably beat the slowest guests to the evac point; there were a lot of stairs. But there was no point trying to intercept them now; once you went through those fire doors there was no getting out again until you hit the street.

Troy reached the lobby and made his way through a squadron of air stewards all trying to check out. The smoke-detectors had done their job; it looked like they'd only had to evacuate his floor. Another ten minutes, though, and it would have been a different story. He made straight for the street. To the left, twenty metres down, there they all were, dressed to the nines. His second restaurant-load of customers not exactly getting what they paid for. And he was right – there were still some stragglers stumbling from the fire doors. Troy took a deep breath, staring across the road into the park and trying to calm himself.

What the fuck?

Preconsciously, Troy registered that death waited across the road. The events of the past fifteen minutes, and the last two weeks, somehow dropped into place in his brain. He couldn't access the files, but he didn't need to. He exploded into movement, and sprinted across the road towards David Caine.

67

Tuesday, 7 December, 8.42 pm
'Two minutes,' said Jill. 'I can't believe they won't move. Oh, get out of the way!' Even with a siren right up their arse, some motorists just didn't get it. 'There's a fire up there, Gabe! It's got to be Caine.'

'It doesn't make any sense,' said Gabriel. 'It can't be him. There's no way Caine would start a fire tonight and not cause complete mayhem. A pissy little fire? You heard the radio – they've got the fire contained, no casualties. It's out already. It's not Caine. He'd have to have someone in a coffin to risk coming out to play tonight.'

'Well, we're almost there now. Let's check it out.'

Gabriel suddenly shot forward in his seat.

'Oh, fuck,' he said.

'What?'

Gabriel had his radio out. 'It's not about the fire, Jill. Please, just do whatever you have to do to get us there!'

68

Tuesday, 7 December, 8.43 pm
Well, she couldn't really blame herself. Every single decision she'd made tonight had been a mistake. Giving in to Hamish, the red dress, these frigging shoes. Erin Hart scowled at the stilettos dangling in her left hand and held on to the filthy stair rail with her right. Still, having a bomb go off in your dining room would probably whack your common sense out of shape a bit, she figured.

She kept moving, trying to watch where she stepped. Just what she was stepping on in her bare feet, she shuddered to imagine. She knew that stairwells, even stairwells in five-star hotels, also doubled as spittoons, romantic rendezvous locations and piss troughs. Erin would bet her feet were a biohazard right now.

At least Hamish had walked down with her – the last of the restaurant guests, the wooden-spooner, the absolute loser. She'd seen the smile the gorgeous waiter had flicked over his shoulder at them when they'd first started out. Hamish could have caught him up in a heartbeat; he'd have had his phone number by now.

'Last flight, Mrs Hart,' said Hamish. 'We're nearly there.'

'Hamish,' she said.

'Yes?'

'If you don't start calling me Erin right now, I am going to perform upon you an emergency tracheotomy, using the heel of this shoe.'

Hamish grinned. 'But Mrs Hart sounds so important, like I work for a member of parliament.'

Erin lifted a shoe in the air.

'All right, all right, *Erin*,' he said. 'We're here!'

Hamish pushed open the heavy fire door and leaned against it, holding it open for her.

Erin stepped barefoot into the street, the world exploded, and then there was nothing.

69

Tuesday, 7 December, 8.44 pm
Hurdling across the bonnet of a slow-moving taxi, Troy Berrigan watched Caine register his movement, then pivot towards him. Caine met his eyes and smiled.

Just fifteen metres from him now, and clear of moving cars, Troy ratcheted up the pace. Ten strides would do it.

Nine.

Caine held something dark and round in his hand. He raised it to his mouth.

Ohgodohgodohgod. He threw it.

Elizabeth Street exploded. The car alarms barely preceded the screaming, and each competed for decibels. Troy pulled himself into a sitting position on the street and tried to get to his feet. Everything bled – or it seemed that way through the veil of blood in his eyes. He used a parked car for cover and got himself into a crouch.

He reached up to where the blood began, touching gingerly. He felt a thrill of horror when his fingertips contacted goo. Panicked, he pressed harder and felt the resistance of his scalp. He breathed out and let his hand pad around. A lot of blood, but at least his fingers didn't slip inside his skull. He'd once attended a suicide where the vic had blown off the top of his head, but the prick hadn't realised he was dead. He'd stayed conscious until they were three minutes away from the hospital, when the fact had caught up with him.

A fucking grenade. Where's Caine?

When Troy spotted him again, the rush in his ears silenced the screams and the sirens. Just his blood surging and the sound of his breathing accompanied him as he crouched his way along the row of parked cars. Troy could see that Caine held another bomb, and this time, from the cover of a white people-mover, it looked as though he was positioning himself for better aim.

As Troy sprang from his squat near the wheel well of the white van, Caine put both hands on the grenade and hooked his finger through the pin.

70

Tuesday, 7 December, 8.45 pm

'At the scene of a bombing on Elizabeth Street, opposite Hyde Park, David Jones end. Multiple casualties. Suspect was sighted involved in a struggle with civilian. Suspect is no longer in sight. Special Agent Delahunt is in situ.' Jill crouched next to the car, watching him run while she called it in. She felt naked without her firearm. 'Suspect's name is David Caine, current AFP terror target. He's in possession of light military weapons and looks to have detonated a fragment grenade.'

The sirens closed in from everywhere. Jill heard the dispatcher calmly requesting further details. She clipped the radio to her waistband and moved. They had what they needed for now.

Fucked if she was going to sit there while Caine still had his liberty.

She sprinted across the road, ignoring the two bodies twenty metres away and her urge to assist the hysterical group beyond them. She spotted Gabriel cautiously making his way around the white van, behind which, a minute earlier, they'd witnessed Caine being crash-tackled by Troy Berrigan.

She reached the van just as Gabe disappeared beyond it. She followed.

71

Tuesday, 7 December, 8.45 pm
Everything had become super-slow, as it always did. Frame by frame. Mid-spring, Troy had watched Caine's hands come apart. Troy connected, body-charging Caine to the ground. He brought himself to his knees, rammed one of them into Caine's spine.

Now he could see the grenade. Caine's throwing arm was outstretched, flat against the pavement. Troy reached down, restraining Caine's left hand with his own, and then, with his mangled right hand, he reached forward and grabbed the fist holding the grenade.

Caine coughed once beneath him. They lay together quietly for a bit, breathing in synch.

'I've released the pin, Troy,' said Caine.

Troy squeezed his thumb and forefinger tighter around Caine's fist. Although his good hand easily restrained

Caine's left, his right had no real power anymore. He could feel his grip weakening. He let himself moan quietly with the exertion.

Right then a pair of black combat boots filled his vision. Oh God, there's another one. I'm sorry Lucy, Chris. He angled his face upward.

Delahunt, above him.

'He's pulled the pin,' said Troy.

'I heard,' said Delahunt.

'I can't hold it,' said Troy.

'I can see,' said Delahunt, squatting beside them. Delahunt wrapped his hand around both of their own. Troy's arm began to shake.

'Hi, David,' said Delahunt, pressing the barrel of his Glock into Caine's temple.

Another pair of boots appeared in Troy's line of sight.

'Jackson, just there,' said Delahunt. 'To your left. Would you retrieve that pin?'

Troy felt Delahunt shift his weight just a little.

'Thank you,' said Delahunt. 'Now, Jill, you need to just thread the pin back in through the top of the safety lever.'

Jackson kneeled in front of them.

'Caine's finger's blocking it,' she said.

'David, you're going to have to move your index finger,' said Delahunt. 'Just your index finger, or I'm going to put this bullet right here through your head. After I've done that, we'll still have four seconds to get the pin in, and Jackson here will accomplish that while your brain is still smoking.'

Troy felt a slight shift beneath his fingers. He watched Jackson slide the pin into the grenade. He shuddered and unclawed his hand. Jackson retrieved the grenade.

Delahunt wrenched Caine's hands behind his back and Troy rolled off, sat up, then rubbed at his missing fingers. While Delahunt cuffed Caine and searched his pockets, he watched Jackson take a step closer. She stopped at Caine's face.

'Are there any more surprises for us out here?' she yelled down at Caine.

Nothing.

Troy winced as Jackson pulled back and kicked Caine full in the face. He only faintly heard Caine's moan. The lights now accompanied the sirens, and he could feel a chopper thumping in.

'Stop,' said Delahunt. 'We've got company, Jill. Can you give me the radio? We have to get this whole area closed off and searched. Right now.'

72

Wednesday, 8 December, 10 am
For the first time in two weeks, Jill slept right through the night. She woke at eight, pulled a T-shirt and shorts over her bikini and jogged across the road to the beach. She kept to the dry sand; with no resistance under her feet, the shifting ground sucked at her ankles, sapping her momentum. She ran harder, wrenching her feet free with each step. Her thighs were already burning by the time she got to the surf club. When she reached the tidal pools at the end of the beach, every breath shredded and her lungs sucked for air. She turned at the rocks and, with her feet finding better purchase on the wetter sand, ramped up the pace, sprinting to maintain the effort until she reached the shifting sand again.

Two laps later, she could not run anymore, but she imagined Scotty, beside her, laughing down at her while she busted a gut to try to beat him, just once. Her face wet, Jill pushed through it. Every waking moment of every day brought the realisation of one more thing she'd never do with him again. When she dropped, in the middle of her fourth lap, she stayed there, her head between her knees, trying not to vomit.

After a swim, Jill headed back to her unit, then showered and washed her hair. She'd been so exhausted last night that she'd fallen into bed in the same singlet she'd been wearing for thirty hours.

She decided right now that she would burn it. She grabbed an apple for breakfast and rang Gabriel.

'You had breakfast?' he asked by way of hello.

'Yep,' she said, crunching.

'Want some more?' he asked.

'Yep,' she said.

Jill arranged to meet Gabriel at the coffee shop underneath the AFP offices. She ordered raisin toast and was served a piece of bread the size of a textbook. Gabriel bought a yoghurt. They took their food to an outside table, steering clear of the smokers.

'You're not hungry,' said Jill.

'Something's not right,' he said.

She waited.

'We got nothing from the first round of interrogation,' he said. 'I knew we wouldn't. Caine won't talk. Not for a long time, anyway. So we put him in a safe cell around two, to make sure he doesn't off himself.'

'You could have at least overlooked his belt,' she said.

He gave her a look.

'Joking,' she said. 'Keep going.'

'Anyway, I'm watching his non-verbals as we're going at him. He's a calm motherfucker. But I got some stress signals when I went in on the anomalies, the actions that just don't make sense to me.'

'Like what?'

'Well, this guy . . . You've gotta understand that this squirrel has been out there committing murder undetected for at least a decade. No priors for anything. This is an extremely contained, obsessive individual. He's acutely paranoid, but not psychotic. He's at once profoundly disturbed and completely, coldly sane.'

Jill shook her head, pushed most of the toast away. 'Why do you think he does it?'

'Oh, he'll have some obsessive dogma about the government trying to control people's lives, some manifesto to bring them down or at least disrupt them as much as he can. And this latest spree is obviously all connected with the cameras. He doesn't want more surveillance. Of course, CCTV cameras are the ultimate symbol of Big Brother, but at a practical level, he wants to continue going about his work undetected. The more cameras there are around, the less likely that he can do that.'

'Well, he's not going to be doing any more work in this country,' Jill said. 'Except maybe in the kitchens at supermax, if he's lucky. That double-fatal last night is enough to see him never released, but now there'll be plenty of time to tie him to everything else.'

Gabriel stirred his yoghurt. He hadn't eaten any.

'So, the cameras,' Jill said. 'That explains last night, the bombing at Erin Hart's house, and maybe the stabbing of the drug rep and pushing Sheila McIntyre in front of a train.'

'Oh, I think we'll find he did the last two,' said Gabriel. 'He tried, but he just couldn't keep the superiority out of his eyes last night when I took him through the Ninja Turtle stabbing. I told him that with the stabbing, he was trying to tell us that he's the invisible man and he'll kill when he wants to – cameras or no cameras.'

'And he looked proud of himself when you said that?'

'Oh, he fucken loved that I got it. He's so proud of himself. But when I mentioned the bombing at the politician's house, I got the stress signals. He was not happy.'

'You don't think he did that, then? But everything puts him there. And Hart is the head of this CCTV committee.'

'I know. I told him that I thought it was sloppy work – he didn't even get a kill and he risked Hart not attending his big show at Incendie the next night. You should have seen him when I said that! He had to move, Jill, he started shifting in the chair, and I got a full cluster of deception and blocking signals.'

'Maybe he's just mad at himself,' she said. 'I don't know.' She thought for a moment. 'It's not like he's totally single-minded. I mean, hating surveillance cameras doesn't explain why he killed his mother.'

'These fuckers always have a mummy thing. And everyone's dispensable to them. But killing his mother *was* connected to the cameras, don't you see? He needed to know where the evac point at Incendie was. He knew about the retirement party for Norris. Of course, he knew that Norris had been the driving force behind the cameras for years, so he wanted to send him off with a real bang. Him and as many of his cronies as he could manage.'

Jill was silent a moment. Finally, she said, 'You think he killed his mother to shape his *tactical* plan?'

'She would have copped it eventually, anyway. Doing it there was just convenient.'

'That just leaves Scotty,' she said quietly, her eyes on the table.

Gabriel sighed. 'Well, yes, Scotty. That and the acid attack on those kids.'

'Really, Gabe, that acid attack could have been anyone.'

'And yet the chemical used is in his shed. And Erin Hart receives an email about it. It's all tied up together somehow, but it doesn't seem his usual style.'

'What's bugging you about it? Why doesn't it fit?'

Gabriel suddenly scraped back his chair, snapped his head up. His eyes bored into hers. 'I'll tell you why, Jill. The acid attack on the kids, the firebomb into Erin Hart's home – they're adolescent acts. Ill-conceived, impulsive. The very opposite of David Caine.'

Jill took a deep breath. 'Oh my God. An adolescent. An adolescent who had access to the shed.'

Gabriel grinned, the smile was bitter, his eyes dead.

'Mona,' Jill said.

'You're not going to believe this,' said Troy Berrigan, after Jill had identified herself when the call connected. 'I was just trying to find the card Delahunt gave me last night. I need to talk to you.'

'Shut up a minute, Troy,' said Jill. 'Do you know where Caine's kid is?' She jogged down the steep stairs to the street, a hand on the railing. Gabriel was waiting by an AFP vehicle.

'So, you know already?' said Troy.

'Know what?'

'About the gun.'

'Fuck,' said Jill. 'What gun?'

'My little brother's locked up,' said Troy. 'Discharging a firearm. He wouldn't tell anyone where he got it, until today.'

'Mona?' asked Jill.

'Mona,' said Troy.

Jill opened the passenger door, stepped in. 'Where is she?' she said into the phone. 'Do you know?'

'She was here last night,' said Troy. 'Lucy told me that some social workers showed up at school and wanted to put her in a shelter or some shit. Lucy made them call me. It was before all last night's bullshit happened, and I convinced them she could stay here. She slept in my sister's room. I didn't know what the hell I could say to her about her father this morning, so I just stayed in bed when I heard them get up. I figured DoCS would know how to break it to her when she got to school this morning. She's only sixteen.'

'She's gone to school?' asked Jill. 'Which school?'

'Randwick Girls High,' he said.

'Randwick Girls,' said Jill to Gabriel.

He rocketed the car from the curb.

Troy spoke again. 'If that's not why you called me, what do you want her for? Are you going to tell her about her father?'

'Something like that,' said Jill.

'Well, I just want her away from my sister,' said Troy. 'There's something not right about that whole fucking family.'

73

Wednesday, 8 December, 11.27 am
'And you don't think we should bring some uniformeds in with us?' asked Jill as they raced along Anzac Parade.

'We don't want to corner her,' said Gabriel. 'Looking at what we think she's done, she's going to be impulsive, and who knows what the fuck she's carrying. We just want to play this calmly. Let's just try it this way at first.'

Jill glowered. 'I'm not fucking armed,' she said. 'Again.'

'I noticed. We'll be fine,' he said. 'She's just a kid.'

They found the school office and the deputy principal pulled Mona's schedule. She directed them towards the library. Jill left the woman with the impression that Mona had some family problems and they'd be taking her off the school grounds with them. Jill and Gabriel crossed the deserted quadrangle and slipped into the cool, quiet library.

Mona was the first kid in eyesight. Sitting in the first row of desks, next to Lucy Berrigan. Jill noticed that the pair appeared as mismatched as they had at the hospital: Lucy, warm skin, sunshine hair. Mona, pale, pierced, midnight fringe framing jet-black eyes.

These eyes now met Jill's across the entryway. Widened.

'Hey, you're the girlfriend,' said Mona, smiling as they approached.

Lucy Berrigan smiled up at them inquisitively.

'What did you say?' Jill stared at Mona. How does she know that? 'What did you just fucking say?'

Gabriel spoke calmly. 'Are you Lucy Berrigan?' he said, ignoring Mona.

The blonde girl nodded, her eyes very wide. 'Yes . . . Is something wrong?'

'Your brother needs you, Lucy.' Gabriel held out a hand.

'Stay with me, Luce,' said Mona. 'There's nothing wrong with your brother. They're here for me.'

'Mona, let go! What's wrong with you?' The Berrigan girl tugged to move away from Mona, whose hand clutched the sleeve of Lucy's uniform.

Jill saw Mona reach her other hand down under her desk. Gabriel took a step forward. Lucy suddenly pulled away, thrown off balance when released, and Gabriel shook his head once at Mona, his hand on the Glock at his hip.

Mona grinned, but Lucy had missed the gesture. Jill stepped forward quickly to guide Lucy behind them.

'Call your brother from the front office, Lucy,' said Gabriel. 'Now.'

Lucy gave them all a last startled look and set off at a jog.

'What did you say just then?' said Jill slowly, moving forward. 'About me being the girlfriend?'

'Yeah, the girlfriend,' said Mona, her voice carrying, 'of that big, goofy cop I set on fire.'

A moment to register – play it back.

And then every cell in her body screaming for her to act, Jill crouched to spring. Gabriel moved first. He swung his arm sideways, slamming a fist into Jill's diaphragm. Her vision darkened and she dropped, completely winded, to one knee.

'Stay there or get out, Jackson,' he said.

Across the table, Mona barked out a laugh. 'Hey, good shot,' she said. 'My turn?'

Jill sucked in air. Through watering eyes, she watched Mona wave a syringe in front of her. If she had lunged for this sick-fuck bitch, she would have run straight into it.

Gabriel had his weapon drawn.

Right then, a single scream from a balcony above them triggered a chain reaction, and the library erupted. Someone had seen Gabe's gun.

'Call the police,' yelled Gabriel above the noise.

Jill tried to breathe through the pain in her chest. She sucked in air, still on one knee, as the library emptied around them. Gabe and that creature stared at one another across the desk, the girl's dark eyes glossy, animated. She had not stopped grinning once since they'd walked in.

'*You* killed the cop in the police car?' said Gabriel, when the din had died down. 'I don't think so.'

'Well, I wasn't actually planning for it to be him,' said the evil vampire bitch. Jill listened in horror. 'It could've been anyone that day,' Mona continued. 'I had the bottle with me and I wanted to get it into a car window. I waited at the bus stop for someone to get caught at the red light. And that cop recognised me – can you believe it? He actually wound his window down to say something to me. It was just wrong place, wrong time for him.' She smiled.

Jill rose to her feet. Gabriel shot her a look: *Stand down.*

'You used one of your father's Molotovs?' he said.

'Shit. You don't get it. *I* made that one. With love.'

'What was in it?' asked Gabriel, speaking to this devil as he might to a cashier.

'Petrol, with styrofoam to gel the mix. Really, it's napalm,' said Mona. 'It sucks all the air out if you can get it into an enclosed space. You shoulda seen that bitch burn. Course, I wasn't expecting the bus crash as well. Honestly. It was fucking spectacular, man.'

Jill thought a vein would burst in her brain if she couldn't shut this bitch up soon.

'Your father teach you how to make that?' asked Gabriel.

'Nan, actually,' said the girl.

'Your grandmother taught you to make napalm?'

'She taught me a lot of things. Dad too. I've been schooled. You got my father?'

'He's in custody,' said Gabriel.

'And Nan's dead,' she said.

Mona dropped the smile with her bright bird-eyes to the table.

'I'm sorry,' said Gabriel.

Mona's eyes snapped back up. She grinned again. 'What are *you* sorry for? Nan took herself out. It was her idea. She died a soldier.'

'What are you saying, Mona? That your grandmother killed herself?' asked Gabriel.

How does he do that? wondered Jill, still on the floor, her vision still blurred. How can he just keep speaking to this demon this way?

'Well, Dad helped, of course,' continued Mona. 'The problem was that Nan had dementia. She kept it together as long as she could, but she'd find herself rambling shit to people. She knew she was a risk to everything we've worked for. She was the one who thought of doing it at the restaurant so that Dad could learn where everyone would run during a fire.'

'Because your father had already targeted the party last night at Incendie. Right,' said Gabriel. 'But if your Nan was part of it all, it explains a lot more. Mona, did your nan apply an accelerant to her face before she entered the restaurant?'

Mona laughed. 'Yep. I told you she's a soldier. And then, before they left, Dad hooked up a small charge under her blouse, remote-detonated it, and . . . toast.'

'I guess then he just had to remove the charge. And he could do that while pretending to try to help her.'

'They worked through it for weeks,' said Mona. 'Pretty perfect, huh? I decided not to go. Nan said it would have been good for me, but I guess I catted out.'

Had anyone told Jill right then that the girl sitting in front of her was an actor or an alien, she'd have believed either explanation immediately.

'Why were your family doing these things?' asked Gabriel.

'You'd never get it,' said Mona. 'You're all brainwashed to go about your business like fucking sheep. If my own mother couldn't understand, I'm not about to try to explain it to you.'

'I'm sorry about your mother,' said Gabriel. 'I know she was electrocuted.'

'In the bath,' said Mona. 'I still see it.'

'You were there?' asked Gabriel.

'Dad sent me in. He and Mum didn't get on. But he knew she'd let *me* go over to her.'

'Oh, Mona,' said Gabriel. 'How old were you?'

'Four,' she said.

'You threw the hairdryer into your mother's bath?'

'Sometimes, at night, I hear her screaming.'

Jill cried quietly now, still seated on the floor.

'I can't do that anymore,' said Mona, gazing at Jill, her head on an angle. 'I can't cry like that. I've tried everything to make myself, you know. But I think the wiring's snapped.'

'We can get you help, Mona,' said Gabe.

Mona met Gabe's eyes.

'There is no cure for someone like me,' she said. 'I've read up – it's in my blood.'

Jill watched Mona register the first of the sirens.

The girl raised the syringe.

'Don't. Please don't, Mona,' said Gabriel, his voice thick.

'Nitric,' she said. 'It's my favourite acid. I used it on those kids at Pagewood. But don't worry. It's not for you.'

Something in Mona's voice made Jill reach for the deepest breath she could. She scrambled up at the same moment that Gabriel hurled himself across the table.

By the time Jill was on her feet, Gabriel had frozen. He stood there, shoulders stooped, blocking her view of the girl.

Jill raced around the desk. Mona, in her school uniform, sat motionless in her chair. The syringe quivered, the lever fully depressed, protruding like a dart from her luminous white neck.

At first Mona just watched them both, her black eyes surprised, questioning.

And then her screams of agony split the air.

74

Saturday, 11 December, 6.54 pm
Jill arrived half an hour early, to ensure that she'd be the first of the group at the pub. She waited in the corner of the beer garden set aside for the gathering, facing the entrance. The hostess who'd directed her to the reserved space had seemed surprised when she mentioned she was with Captain Andreessen's party.

'The farewell drinks for Scotty?' said the girl, her eyes filling. 'Oh, shit,' she said, pulling a tissue from beneath her black apron. 'Sorry.' She wiped her nose carefully around a silver piercing. 'I told the boss that I wanted to take care of you guys, but she'll be pissed if she catches me bawling already.'

'Did you know Scotty?' asked Jill.

'Well, we're his local.'

'I know. It's just, I never came here with him.'

'I didn't think I'd seen you before. My name's Kadee,' said the girl. 'Just follow me and I'll show you where you guys will be.'

Jill followed the petite, dark-haired girl. An intricate butterfly tattoo was in full flight on the back of her neck; as she had a number-one buzz-cut, the tattoo was especially striking. Jill's heart swelled with pain as she remembered the butterfly pendant Scotty had given her. Delicately perched atop a magnifying glass, he'd told her it meant that he thought she was smart and beautiful. She'd told him to shut up. With no curtain of hair now to hide any tears, Jill swallowed them, her throat aching.

The waitress stopped in front of an area of several reserved tables. Jill manoeuvred around the last table and took the seat in the corner.

'What can I get you?' said Kadee, her notepad in hand, determinedly efficient again. 'Everything's on the house for you guys tonight.'

'Really?'

'We loved Scotty here too.'

It took Jill a moment to form the words. The waitress dropped her eyes while waiting. 'Just some water, please,' Jill said.

'I'll bring you sparkling.'

'Thanks, Kadee.'

Jill watched a group of people playing pool back inside the spacious hotel. Their laughter carried over the music. Above her, the twilit Maroubra sky peeked in through the open-air trellis enclosing the beer garden. A warm breeze blew in through the wisteria plant swinging with swollen bunches of honey-scented purple flowers. Jill thought she could smell the ocean too. She took a deep, shuddering breath. Scotty had loved it here.

Where are you now, my Scotty?

Kadee arrived with her water with Gabriel behind her. Jill lifted her wet face. Nobody spoke for a moment. Finally, Kadee said, 'What'll you have, mate?' and Gabriel ordered a beer. He moved around the other chairs and took the seat next to Jill.

'You don't like beer,' she said.

'I like it with chips.'

She smiled. 'How'd you go talking to Caine today?'

'Same as yesterday,' he said. 'Nothing. Like I told you, no one's going to get anything more out of him. We're going to have to accept that we'll never really understand why he did what he did. We just have to go on what we know and what Mona told us.'

'Poor kid,' she said, shaking her head, hearing the screams again.

'I think he was probably once a poor kid too. What Mona said about her grandmother indicates that the woman was paranoid as hell. I'd say she raised Caine from birth to fear all governments, all systems. She made her family unit her very own terrorist cell.'

Jill again shook her head. 'It's all so pointless,' she said. 'It's such a waste. Look what they've done to all these people, to themselves. To Scotty.'

'How're you going with that?' he said.

'I miss him a lot.'

'You always will.'

'It's like that with Abi? You still miss her as much?'

'Exactly as much. The amount of pain is always the same – it's just that you get so used to it being there that it just becomes like one of your arms or legs. You forget it's there sometimes.'

Jill covered Gabriel's hand with her own. A tear splashed onto her finger. She couldn't be sure it was hers.

'Anyway,' she said, pulling back her hand. 'The week away helped, Gabe. Thanks for looking after me like that.'

'Do you think they'll automatically bring chips with the beer?' he said.

'I wouldn't think so.' She smiled. Then her eyes became hooded again. 'Hey, I keep wondering whether Caine would have known that Mona killed Scotty. What do you think?'

'I think he figured it out pretty quickly, Jill. And he was pissed. That's why he was so upset during the interview when Emma Gibson linked the crimes together. But he wasn't angry because she killed someone, just that she'd drawn attention to them – that she hadn't yet learned how to kill quietly.'

Jill was silent a moment.

'Speaking of Gibson . . .' said Gabriel.

Jill stood when she saw Emma Gibson crossing the courtyard towards them. Emma wore a black sheath dress, her jet-black hair curled in a side ponytail around the white skin of her neck. She looked pale and daunted when she saw them waiting.

'Excuse me a sec, Gabe,' said Jill. She manoeuvred out from around the table to the other side just as Emma reached them.

'Hi, Jill,' said Emma.

For weeks later, Jill would startle herself with the memory of her next action. She breached the space between them and threw her arms around Emma's neck, hugging her close. They stood quietly for a moment, then each broke away, wiping at their eyes. Jill didn't speak. She just grabbed Emma by the hand and led her around the table to sit with her and Gabriel.

Superintendent Last was next to arrive, followed by a glut of uniformeds from Maroubra and Central.

Captain Andreessen showed up later, when the courtyard was noisy and glasses already covered the tables. Jill spotted Elvis in a huddle near the front of the courtyard and he caught her eye at the same time. He began to walk towards her.

Gabriel ate chips as he watched Elvis approach. Jill took another sip of water.

'Jackson, you got a minute?' said Elvis when he reached them.

Jill again weaved her way behind the chairs around the table, and met Elvis in a small pocket between people sitting and standing. Ordinarily, this scene was Jill's image of hell, but she'd felt strangely calm since Emma and Lawrence Last had arrived. She'd even coped with the speeches and toasts for Scotty.

'Hello, Eddie,' said Jill.

'Ah, Jill. I just wanted to say that I'm sorry for what happened to Scotty,' said Elvis. He carried his half-full beer glass like it was an extension of his hand.

'I know,' said Jill. 'Everyone is. It's fucked.'

'And I wanted to say that I know you, me and Hutchinson had our moments, but I really respected Scotty as a cop.' He took a long sip, came up with the glass empty. 'And you, Jackson. You're a good detective.'

'Thanks, Eddie,' said Jill. 'I feel the same about you.'

Elvis belched and let out a laugh. ''Scuse me,' he said. 'Look at us, bonding like two old women.' He dropped the smile. 'I don't know how good a bloody detective I am when I fingered the wrong perp. I was sure it was Berrigan.'

'Caine has been getting away with shit like this for years, Eddie,' said Jill. 'At least we got him.'

'And that cunt daughter of his is dead.'

Jill looked back towards her seat.

'I'm gonna get another beer, Jackson,' said Elvis. 'What are you drinking?'

'I'm right, thanks, Eddie. I'm still going on mine.'

As Elvis made his way through the throng, Jill stood in the pocket surrounded by people. Lawrence Last was bent over a Scotch, speaking quietly to Emma. Andreessen shouted out a laugh. Jill met Gabriel's eyes over their heads.

It was time for her to go home.

Epilogue

One year later. Tuesday, 20 December, 9.25 pm
'Reece, you can't be serious! There are five days to go until Christmas. You can't open anything yet.' Erin Hart sat in a corner of her lounge, her feet tucked up, sipping a Scotch.

'Mum, don't you know that because of months of marketing propaganda, us children are being whipped into a Christmas frenzy by greedy corporations?' said Reece, cross-legged under the Christmas tree, picking through the wrapped presents. 'I'm in a frenzy.'

'I really must stop sending you children to school,' said Erin.

Callie, in shortie pyjamas, her skin spotted with coloured lights from the tree, was stretched out on the other lounge. She put her book down. 'Yeah, Mum. Let's do one,' she said.

'Do one? Open a present? Come on kids, where will it stop?' said Erin. 'If we open one tonight, you'll want another tomorrow.'

'No, we won't,' said Reece. 'We promise.'

'And anyway,' said Callie, 'who writes these rules? It's our family. We can make it a tradition. You don't have to do everything the government tells you.'

'And you're the local member anyway, so you're the boss,' said Reece.

'We can just do one of Dad's,' said Callie.

'Oh, yeah, put me right in it. I would never hear the end of that,' said Erin. 'Okay. Just one, and it has to be one we've given each other, so no one else gets offended.'

She and Callie joined Reece at the tree. There really are too many presents here, Erin thought. Next year I'll buy fewer. Which is just what I said last year. Still, not all these were for her children. Erin spotted one she'd wrapped yesterday. She'd take it in for Hamish on their last day at work tomorrow.

'Mum, you go first. We bought you one together,' said Callie. 'I chose it.'

'And I thought it was dumb,' said Reece. 'But Callie wouldn't let me get you a chemistry kit.'

'Oh, thanks, Callie,' said Erin. 'How am I supposed to make rubber now in my spare time?'

'Which is what I said,' said Reece.

Erin grinned and accepted the soft package from Callie. Oh oh. Clothing. Her children had bought her something to wear. She kept the smile fully fastened and opened her present. Huh. A black one-piece swimming costume. She turned it over. A gorgeous red ruffle delineated the bodice. Cute. It would never fit.

'What size is this?' she asked.

'Twelve,' said Callie. 'Your size.'

Erin's smile widened. How thoughtful. Since the bombing, she'd swum every day, determined to make the most of her life. After all, she'd been three metres away from losing it. Two people in the five-metre kill-zone had not been as lucky.

She turned the pretty suit over and over in her hands, checked the label. Size twelve. Wow. A year ago that would have read sixteen.

'All right, children,' she said. 'I guess I shall feed and clothe you for another year at least.'

Callie and Reece grinned and dived for a present.

Troy sat at the back of the school gymnasium, as far as he could manage from the huge speakers he'd paid for. He wanted to like the music – he gave it ten minutes of concentrated focus, trying to get it – but in the end he contented himself with the fact that almost everyone else in here seemed to be into it. A few beers could have made it sound all right, he supposed, but that would bust his twelve-month drought, his promise to Lucy, and ruin his plans for Christmas night. No, he'd wait to quench his thirst with the two-hundred-dollar bottle of champagne that had been chilling for a year in his fridge.

He passed time trying to spot her through the strobe lights and the fifty or so writhing kids. There. Now, over there. Gail Cole. Troy tried to order the list of reasons he was grateful that Christmas night would mark their one-year anniversary. Pretty close to the top was the fact that, for the past ten years, Gail had been organising a Christmas party like this for underprivileged kids in Redfern. Did that beat the fact that she'd hired

Christopher to play tonight, his first gig since finishing his sound technician course? It definitely didn't beat her getting Chris out of a custodial sentence last year. Troy figured he could safely put that at the top of the list; she'd helped Chris to have a chance.

Troy took his eyes off Gail for a moment and watched Christopher, on stage, behind his black glasses, turntables and the wall of girls. He hadn't been in trouble once since he'd been given the suspended sentence.

He turned his attention back to Gail and his list. Maybe he should start using fractions for ranking? Gail's philosophical debates with Lucy were right up there – they went for hours sometimes. Troy would join in when he could, but he loved to just sit back and watch his little sister flex that brain of hers, sparring with someone who could go the distance. Just last week, Troy had noticed that Lucy had listed 'lawyer' as her first preference on a career-planning chart she'd done for school.

As a cop, Troy had often had to work Christmas night. And since beginning at the restaurant, he'd worked every single one. It would be the same this year. But this time, at a table for four, Lucy, Chris and Gail would be waiting – waiting for everyone else to leave, and for Troy to join them for a midnight drink at Incendie.

Dr Leah Giarratano has had a long career as a clinical psychologist. An expert in psychological trauma, sex offences and psychopathology, she has had many years' experience working with victims and psychopaths. She has worked in psychiatric hospitals, with the Australian Defence Force, and in corrective services with offenders who suffer severe personality disorders. She has assessed and treated survivors of just about every imaginable psychological trauma, including hostages; war veterans; rape, assault and accident victims; and has worked with police, fire and ambulance officers.

Leah was also the host of the prime-time television documentary series entitled *Beyond the Darklands*, in which she delved into the minds of some of Australia's most infamous criminals.

You've finished the book but there's much more waiting for you at

www.randomhouse.com.au

- ▶ Author interviews
- ▶ Videos
- ▶ Competitions
- ▶ Free chapters
- ▶ Games

▶ Newsletters with exclusive previews, breaking news and inside author information.

▶ Reading group notes and tips.

▶ VIP event updates and much more.

ENHANCE YOUR READING EXPERIENCE

www.randomhouse.com.au